C000090537

About the author

I was born in Enfield, North London in 1988 and I have lived there ever since, although I dream of a future in a more rural setting, in the countryside or by the sea – I'll take crashing waves and rolling hills over busy streets and crowded trains any day! I'm a huge fan of comedy; I appreciate anyone who is kind enough to try and make people laugh. I like music that was made before I was born. I love great storytelling, the kind that puts you in another world. I am slightly obsessed with miniature things, and I adore cats.

SAMANTHA DRURY'S SECRET DIARY:

OUT OF THE WORMHOLE, INTO

THE SNAKEPIT

To Thalia love from Emma

Emma Everitt-Story

SAMANTHA DRURY'S SECRET DIARY:

OUT OF THE WORMHOLE, INTO

THE SNAKEPIT

Vanguard Press

VANGUARD PAPERBACK

© Copyright 2019
Emma Everitt-Story

The right of Emma Everitt-Story
to be identified as author of
this work has been asserted by her in accordance with the
Copyright, Designs and Patents Act 1988.

All Rights Reserved

No reproduction, copy or transmission of this publication
may be made without written permission.
No paragraph of this publication may be reproduced,
copied or transmitted save with the written permission of the publisher, or in
accordance with the provisions
of the Copyright Act 1956 (as amended).

Any person who commits any unauthorised act in relation to
this publication may be liable to criminal
prosecution and civil claims for damages.

A CIP catalogue record for this title is
available from the British Library.

ISBN 978 1 784654 58 0

*Vanguard Press is an imprint of
Pegasus Elliot MacKenzie Publishers Ltd.*
www.pegasuspublishers.com

First Published in 2019

**Vanguard Press
Sheraton House Castle Park
Cambridge England**

Printed & Bound in Great Britain

Dedication

To Neil, who never doubted me.

Friday 13th September 2019

BREAKING NEWS: JUNIOR JOURNALIST, DRURY, JOINS DUKE JOHN JAMESON!

Eleven-year-old Samantha Drury, a young and one hundred percent unpublished journalist, has made the hugely unsurprising move to join a secondary school this September. Duke John Jameson School, established 1720, have yet to comment on this greatly anticipated revelation.

This is my escape. I am surrounded by people who know nothing, trying to get me to change who I am and how I think, so I need this journal to keep all my rational thoughts safe before they get driven out of me by the madness and the falseness of the outside world. I need this journal to keep me sane; to compartmentalise my thoughts in their organic state before they are all tainted by the mad people. I know they are mad and yet they still make me doubt myself, still make me wonder if they are right and I am wrong; if they are sane and *I* am the one who is mad.

They want me to socialise. Today marks the end of my first week in year seven. The preceding summer holidays were a time of simple bliss – I realise now, I may never see that same freedom again. Everyone I went to primary school with went to the local secondary, but I got sent to Duke John Jameson because it's 'better' and I passed the exam to get in. I don't care that it's meant to be better, but I was happy to be coming here to sever all ties with friendships I'd outgrown years ago. Fresh school, fresh start.

I was worried though. I spend a lot of time reading (to avoid talking to people, mostly) but I wouldn't have called myself an academic. I'm good with words but terrible with maths and I don't know any facts or statistics, or any other languages and I don't even seem to have much common sense, but here I am, and I'm up against the best and brightest. I'm an imposter. My entrance exam was a fluke. So, instead of enjoying the holidays I spent them in fear of the inevitable unknown, the abyss I was being sucked towards by the inescapable tunnel of time. The whole six weeks were a terrifying wormhole slowly transporting me to this brave new world of separate sciences, organised sport in P.E. and homework which takes more than ten minutes a week.

That was the wormhole, this is the snakepit. My predictions were not wrong but academic competition and daily homework have turned out to be the least of my concerns. I thought in a smart school everyone would be like the stereotypical smart kid in class, bookish, shy, nervous, obedient, plain to look at and basically uncool. Wrong! Wrong! Wrong! Most of them are exceptionally confident and well-adjusted, they give attitude to the teachers and, for reasons I cannot explain, many of them are far more perfectly beautiful than anyone I see walking down the street or at the local shopping centre. Some of them are even TV beautiful! Obviously, it's intimidating but it gets worse…

I'm supposed to talk to these people. I'm practically being forced, and it's not just small talk either, we're supposed to 'get to know each other' ugh! I don't know what's worse – me, trying to relate to these super-humans or them, trying to pretend to take an interest in my pathetic little life – of course, we have nothing in common! But apparently, they do this to all the year sevens when they start, to give them the opportunity to 'bond' – ugh!

Classes are all mixed up, so you never get the same lot of people in different subjects. They still expect us to learn everyone's name though and the first lesson of each subject has been a variety of 'getting to know you' exercises – some of which have involved working as a pair (literally the worst thing ever). Everyone I've been paired up with has been the total opposite of me – they love the sound of their own voice and want all the attention for themselves. That suits me just fine but when the teacher gets to us and we're meant to do a joint presentation it gets awkward. So far, what I've learnt from these 'bonding' sessions is that everyone I end up working with would prefer it if I wasn't even there.

Not that I mind. The last thing I want is to make friends and have people clinging onto me, seeking me out and cornering me into social activities. I wound up like that in my last school and trust me, once you're in a situation like that it's almost impossible to get out of. I became best friends with this girl called Summer when we were in year two. The whole 'best friend' thing was her idea right from the start. We played together a few times in the playground and suddenly, she was like 'let's sit together; let's eat lunch together; come over for tea; let's have a sleepover' ugh! I mean, it was all right at first, but I just kind of grew up and she didn't. I was reading Orwell and she was still practising flying because she truly believed she was a fairy. But that didn't stop her wanting to be my friend.

Truth be told, I'm still trying to distance myself from her. It's easier now we're back at school but over the summer holidays she kept calling me.

"What are you doing tomorrow?" she'd ask.

"Tomorrow's my day with my dad," I'd lie.

"OK, well what are you doing the next day?"

Dammit.

"The next day I have to go to my cousin's party," I'd lie again.

"Oh OK, well how about the next day?"

You see where this is going. I carried on making up excuses for about half an hour until Mum called me down for dinner (phew!) and I swear Summer didn't have the faintest idea that I didn't want to see her. In fact, I know she didn't because she tried calling again the next day! I stopped answering the phone but occasionally Mum would pick up and I'd be forced to go through that whole excruciating conversation all over again. *Take the hint, Summer, jeez!*

Monday 16th September 2019

NEWSFLASH: SECONDARY SCHOOL IS A SINISTER SNAKEPIT!

A ground-breaking, new study reveals that at least one UK secondary school is forcing its youngest pupils into awkward social situations. The victims cannot be named for legal reasons.

Today was the worst one yet. We didn't have to do P.E. last week because we had to watch an hour-long, patronising as hell, 'educational' video about bullying, which was aimed at six-year-olds but today I'd have given my right arm to watch that video again (not literally – that's my writing hand). So, as it was our 'getting to know you' session for Physical Education, they made us do physical trust exercises. So, cliché. We had to pair up with different people and one person would deliberately fall backwards and the other person would stand behind and catch them. They had safety mats on the floor as well so even if we did somehow fall, we wouldn't get hurt.

I hesitantly paired up with Fiona Rutter, who seemed sensible enough not to pull any tricks. She was a bit giggly – presumably her way of dealing with the awkwardness of it all – but she pulled herself together, she fell backwards, landed in my arms and seemed rather elated at this very minor achievement of hers, even though almost anyone could do it. I say almost...

We switched places. She was ready to catch me. I knew she'd catch me. Even if she didn't, I knew the safety mats would cushion my fall, but I just couldn't bring myself to do it. I kept trying to just fall, *just fall, dammit!* But you can't just let your body go crashing to the floor like that – it goes against every human instinct! And the more I kept telling myself to 'just fall' the more anxious and frustrated I became that I couldn't do it and everybody else could.

"It's OK, Samantha," the teacher said. "Fiona's going to catch you, aren't you, Fiona?"

I know Fiona's going to catch me, that's not the problem!

"Yes, I'm right here, I'll catch you, I promise," Fiona said helpfully. Everybody else had finished their trust fall and they were all watching me and Fiona.

How the hell do they expect me to do it now?

"OK, perhaps you'd feel more comfortable if *I* caught you," said Miss Milne. She shooed Fiona to the side to join the silent, gawping audience. I felt a surge of irritation as I thought about what a stupid woman she was to believe that her taking Fiona's place would make any difference whatsoever. But, I tried. I tried to forget that I was going to be caught by a stupid person who didn't understand me and who I didn't trust at all; I tried to forget that twenty-eight other girls – who I also didn't trust – were all watching, probably willing me to fail or do something even worse, like fall forward flat on my face. I tried to

14

forget my basic human survival instinct to not cause myself any harm, and in that one, serene moment I almost did it. I say almost…

I couldn't do it. Miss Milne kept egging me on, but I knew the moment had passed and it was never going to come back around.

"It's OK, you can do it, I know you can do it!" said Miss Milne. "Come on girls, cheer her on!"

Gradually, excruciatingly, the rest of the girls sang out their disingenuous words of support, "Come on! You can do it! It's easy!"

Now I'm feeling angry and upset, both at Miss Milne for putting me in this situation, and at myself, for not being able to do this thing that was so easy. I felt the heat clouding behind my eyes and I knew I was close to tears. This could not happen. I opened my eyes, stood up straight and said, "No. I can't do it, I just can't."

I walked away and sat on the bench. Miss Milne, probably feeling guilty for putting all that pressure on me, didn't push the issue further and changed the subject, telling us all about what sports we'd be doing over the next term, but I was still so focussed on not crying that I didn't catch any of it.

Later, in the afternoon, a teacher I'd never seen before interrupted our maths lesson. He whispered something to our maths teacher and then she told me to go with the mystery teacher.

Me? What have I done now?

He led me to the school office, and that's when I knew it was something serious. Either I'd somehow got the blame for some atrocity performed by an older kid, or

Mum had been in a car crash, but we didn't go into the office, we went in a small room just next to it that always has its door shut.

"Samantha," he said slowly, and patronisingly. "Please take a seat," he said, holding eye contact with me the entire time. I sat down, wondering what the hell was going on.

"I've been speaking with your form tutor, who had a message from Miss Milne today. I'm Mr Donahue, the school counsellor, and I want you to know that I'm always available to talk to if ever you want to."

Oh God.

"Miss Milne is concerned that you may have some trust issues. I've looked at your file and it says that your parents recently divorced, is that right?"

"Well, it was two years ago..." I replied, but he carried on talking.

"Your father had an affair, didn't he?"

"Does it say that on my file?" I asked, astonished.

"No... just an inkling I had."

Ugh, what an arrogant, presumptuous, smug, little man! The worst part is he's right.

"Well, yeah," I said. "But what does that have to do with falling into the arms of a stranger? Call me mad, but I think it's quite sensible not to trust strangers!"

"Nobody's calling you mad, Samantha."

I know that – it's a figure of speech you idiot!

"We just want to look out for you, and to offer you a bit of extra help and support, that's all."

"Well I'm fine, seriously," I said, but this Mr Donahue just stared at me, like that would somehow make me want to pour out all my innermost thoughts – as if I was really holding something back. It started to get weird, all the silence, so I got up to leave and he didn't stop me.

Just as I reached the exit, he spoke in a tone which was no doubt meant to be soothing, but came out downright creepy, "My door is always open, Samantha." And then he shut the door behind me.

I'm surrounded by idiots.

"Did I tell you who I bumped into today?" Mum said the minute she got home from work.

No, you literally just got home.

"No."

"Trudy Palmer! You remember, she ran the Weight Watchers back when we lived in the old house."

"Oh yeah," I said, feigning interest. "How is she?"

"Really fat! Honestly, she must have gained at least three stone. Anyway, she's started up her own business selling beauty products and make-up. She does it with her daughter – isn't that lovely? You remember Jessica Palmer? She's around your age, I think."

"No. We never met," I replied, with a creeping suspicion about where this conversation was heading.

"Oh, I think you and her would really get on. Apparently, she's good at tennis – that's what Trudy was telling me. Anyway, what they do is, they go around to people's houses and demonstrate their products to a group of that person's friends. It's good stuff, apparently, and great value. I said they'd have to come over here and I'll invite all the ladies from work and she said yes! They're coming next Thursday!"

Oh God. A house swarming with middle-aged women fussing over make-up AND I'm going to have to try and be friendly with Jessica. I can usually avoid social interaction but it's hard to avoid a person when they're in your house and your mum wants you to be friends.

SAMANTHA'S TOP TEN TIPS FOR AVOIDING PEOPLE AND NOT MAKING FRIENDS

ONE – Do your research! Before I started secondary school, I assumed eating lunch in the canteen was mandatory, as it was in primary, so I asked for school dinners. Imagine how annoyed with myself I was when I saw people going outside with their packed lunches! In the canteen, you have to pick a table and you never get one all to yourself. Out in the playground, and on the field, you get your pick of dozens of well-hidden spots. Obviously, I switched to packed lunches immediately, despite Mum's inability to spread the butter right to the crust.

TWO – Go where the quiet people go. Even though it seems like everyone else in the world loves to natter on about sod all at any given opportunity, there are others of our kind out there. Find them; appreciate them; and never, ever, talk to them. They go to the library at break and lunch when the weather's no good. You're not meant to eat in there but if you pick at your lunch surreptitiously (and it's not too smelly) you won't get caught. The best part is you can do all your homework in the library before you even get home! Yeah, yeah, I know what you're thinking, *she's a bit keen!* Well I'm not, OK? But when I get home I say,

"I'm going to my room to do my homework!" and then Mum and my moronic brother Frog who thinks he's a professional wrestler and is rather more ape-like than his amphibian name suggests don't bother me until dinner.

THREE – Walk fast. Always. That way if you unexpectedly bump into someone you know you can say, "Sorry, I'd love to chat, but I'm in a hurry. Bye!"

FOUR – Headphones. Obvious reasons. They work well during weekends and family gatherings, but you're not allowed them at school. Also, some heartless individuals will still deem it acceptable to interrupt your music because they know you can pause and play at the click of a button. Hence…

FIVE – Books. No decent human being would ever interfere with someone who is engrossed in a book. Anyone who has ever enjoyed reading knows better than that.

SIX – No limelight. Ever. Distance yourself from all potential gossip or talking points. Even if people are saying something *stupid* about a topical issue that you have an opinion on, don't get involved. You will get caught up and then you will get noticed. And in that same vein…

SEVEN – No fashion statements. Don't get caught up in the current trends in school shoes, tights or hairstyles. Don't wear badges with band names on them – people will comment on things that stand out.

EIGHT – Don't join any clubs. Obviously, clubs encourage people to bond over a shared interest. In fact, don't show any interests. People who like things love nothing more than meeting other people who like the same things as them. It's like they need validation that their obsession is healthy or something. They're like vultures, I swear.

NINE – Scheduling. Knowing when certain places will be busy means knowing where and when not to be present.

TEN – No one-on-one. Never. With no-one. If you *must* hang out with people, do it in a casual group, not an intense duo, otherwise you might end up *bonding*. Summer and I mostly 'bonded' over stuff she liked and wouldn't stop talking about, so I just ended up agreeing with her (verbally – not in spirit) to save me from having to point out how ridiculous some of her obsessions were (boy bands, fictional TV characters, etc.) and in doing so risk upsetting her. God, people are complicated!

Wednesday 18th September 2019

REVIEW: 'ORANGE RIDING HOOD' – A DRAMATIC, MODERNISED INTERPRETATION OF THE CLASSIC FAIRY TALE; A 'CHILLING EXPERIENCE' FOR ANY AUDIENCE.

Remember how I said reading a book was a good way to deflect unwanted attention? Yeah… just wait. So, I was sitting right at the front of the top deck of the school bus reading my book when three boys from my year got on and went to the back. At first, they chatted amongst themselves, laughing at nothing, they must have known each other from primary otherwise they'd never have acted so stupid in front of each other. But then it died down and they noticed me. They started whispering and sniggering inaudibly and that's when I grew suspicious.

"Hey! Hey, what's your name?"

I didn't move. I just carried right on reading, but I knew they were talking to me.

"Hey, you! Girl! What's your name?"

They had well and truly intruded on my reading now; after that point I could not have absorbed a single word even if I'd put my headphones in.

"What are you reading?"

They continued to harass me. I thought this was a smart school? I thought reading was OK here? They were whispering and sniggering again. Then I heard them moving to the front of the bus, so I glanced to the side, trying not to turn my head because I didn't want them to see me looking – to see that they were bothering me. I looked in the mirror at the front of the bus – you know, the dome-shaped one the driver uses to see what's going on upstairs? And I saw them coming closer to me carrying a bag of oranges. My heart began to pound. My throat went dry. I once heard that people use bags of oranges to beat people with because it doesn't show bruises, so they can't get caught. Panic-stricken, I began rummaging through my bag looking for my water bottle, desperate for some small relief of at least these physical effects of fear. But I couldn't find it and my throat grew drier. They sat two seats behind me, all three of them crammed in… a united trio; a gang.

"Tell us your name!"

Intimidated and desperate, I replied, "Samantha Drury."

"Cheer up, Samantha!" the ringleader said. "Give us a smile!"

I scowled venomously and turned to face the front of the bus once more.

"What a miserable girl!" he said, "You're no fun, Samantha *Dreary*!"

Then each of them peeled an orange. Then all of them threw the orange peel at me, aiming for the hood of my jacket. Almost every shot was successful, and my hood was filling with orange peel, but I knew turning around would only make it worse. So I pretended to read, even though focussing on the words was impossible, while they peeled the entire bag of oranges and landed all the peel, along with a few segments, into the hood of my stupid jacket, which I'd had since the winter of year six and which I'd long suspected was making me look like a loser. They waited for me to get off the bus first, so they could watch me empty out my hood into the bin by the front gates. They all laughed hysterically and made irritatingly clever jests. Of course, they did. They are smart kids from a smart school and I am 'Orange Riding Hood'. I am Samantha Dreary.

Thursday 19th September 2019

CRISIS ALERT: FORTY-SOMETHING FEMALES FOUND FLOCKING IN FRONT ROOM TO FRUSTRATION OF FAMILY!

Catastrophe strikes as local mother, Cassie Drury, invites strangers into her home. The domestic intruders, who have been described as garrulous and imposing women in their mid-forties, posed a serious threat to the two children of the household, who were robbed of all access to the living room TV and were subject to brutal harassment in the form of questions about school and general interests.

So, mum had her make-up and skincare party today. It would have been fine if I'd been allowed to hide in my room like Frog but *noooo* – just because I'm a girl, it means I have to get involved! – It's not the make-up I have a problem with, it's the need to *discuss* the products incessantly. Either you like it, or you don't – now shut up! But they did not shut up, neither did Jessica bloody Palmer. Jessica, I discovered, is not 'about my age' as Mum said, she's in year nine, only a year younger than Frog. I think Mum forgets what a big difference that makes when you're still in school.

I knew if I went up to my room Mum would have told Jessica to go with me, so to avoid that one-on-one situation I stayed downstairs with all the women Mum had invited.

"So, let's get started, shall we ladies?" Trudy began. "First up we have our cosmetics line, which includes a huge range of the latest colours…"

The latest colours? I thought, "You mean this small-time make-up company has actually discovered *new colours*? Surely a scientific miracle like that would have drawn a bit more attention?"

They're already talking rubbish and it's barely even started. Ugh. She got out six different tester palettes and the other women, Jessica included, cooed over them like they were new-born babies in fluffy onesies.

Alana, Mum's assistant, who's probably in her early twenties, was sitting on my left, and I guess she thought that she could relate to me because she was younger than the rest. Or maybe she was trying to get close to me as a way of sucking up to Mum. Mum's the manager – basically their boss – and not one of those women seemed like they were really her friend.

"What do you think of this shade?" Alana asked me.

It's purple, that's what I thought of it.

"Um, it's lovely," I said, trying to appear normal.

"Ooh, is that frosted plum?" said Jessica, who was sitting on my right. "It's gorgeous, isn't it? But just seeing it on the palette doesn't do it justice, it's high pigmented… really makes your face pop! You have to try it on!" Jessica got up, palette in hand, and went over to Alana. "Oh, you're already wearing a shadow, aren't you? That won't

work. Ooh! Samantha, you're not wearing any make-up…
You could be our model for the night!"

And at that point, I swear, all the other women turned
to face me. All the other women. All of them caked in
make-up, suddenly looked at me and my plain, blank
canvas of a face like they were starving on a desert island
and I was a giant meatball sub. It was to be a long evening.

Jessica was my make-up artist, doing her mum proud
by demonstrating every bloody product in their catalogue
on my face, gradually transforming it from boring, to
bright, to clown. Sometimes the group watched to see the
ever-changing results, but most of the time they chatted
amongst themselves, leaving just me and Jessica. Having
someone literally two centimetres from your face for an
hour straight is surely intense, even for a normal person,
let alone someone like me! Jessica tried talking to me
about boys, boy bands, boyfriends, boy crushes, boy
actors, and of course, make-up and tennis. And just when
I thought it couldn't get any worse my older brother, Frog
came down for his second dinner (he eats like a horse) and
nearly wet himself laughing when he saw the state of my
face.

"You look amazing, Sam!" he said, only disguising
his sniggers so that the other women wouldn't realise he
was being sarcastic. "Such an improvement on your
normal look!" and then he took a photo on his phone,
laughing as he walked out of the room.

"Oh. My, God… Your brother is gorgeous!" Jessica
said.

Ugh!

Frog is in year ten and he's nearly fifteen. He's also nothing like me. I guess we're both tall for our age, but he has dark hair and skin that tans easily, whereas I'm super pale and mousy. He has long hair like a footballer – and that's where the real difference comes in – he loves sport and interacting with people. He's sociable, loves being part of a team, always has friends round and is always full of energy. He plays on the school's football and rugby teams, but his favourite sport (if you can call it that) is wrestling. Not the proper skilled sort of wrestling, the kind they have in the USA which is all staged and full of trash talk and nonsense.

His real name is Fred, but everyone calls him Frogsplash or Frog for short because the Frogsplash is his favourite wrestling move, probably because he's so big so he can just throw himself on top of his opponent and floor them. I often come home from school to find all the furniture out of place and him and his mates brawling on the living-room floor like idiots, trash talk and all. Ugh. Frogsplash goes to the local secondary school for the exact reason I didn't want to go there – he wanted to stay in the same school as all his friends, Billy, Joshua and Hayden – they're all exactly like him.

We never had much in common, Frogsplash and I, but we used to watch cartoons together when we were younger and sometimes, we'd be a team, me and Frog against Mum and Dad. Mum worries because she thinks we've 'drifted apart' since Dad left and it's because 'the dynamic has shifted' and 'Fred feels outnumbered' but I just think we're growing up, and we never really had much in common to begin with. It's amazing to think I share more of my genetic makeup with him than I do with anyone else in the word!

Make-up… don't remind me! By the end of the night, I looked like a crash test dummy in a pantomime. The worst part was the mascara, Jessica had applied eight or nine layers of it to my eyelashes and they were all stuck together and gritty, and so, so heavy! It was uncomfortable! I'm still in the process of removing it all now and I'm pretty sure I won't get it all off before school tomorrow. I'm going to look ridiculous.

Saturday 21st September 2019

DUNCAN DRURY: FATHER, EX-HUSBAND, TOILET HUMOUR ENTHUSIAST

It's our weekend with Dad. How do you describe Duncan Drury? Well, for a start, he's the type of guy who feels awkward around his own kids. Not kids, not Frogsplash, just me. Maybe it's because I'm a girl but I think it's more to do with the fact that he just doesn't get me. I'm the quiet type (in case you hadn't already picked up on that) and I don't enjoy things that he would consider 'fun' like theme parks or pool parties. I think he's just a big kid, and I think he thought that parenthood would just be an extension of childhood and maybe it was when we were younger (and it probably still is with Frogsplash!) but I'm growing up and he can't deal with it.

The only time I've ever seen Dad act mature is around work people. I think he's quite successful at work and people take him seriously there – he's the regional manager now, I think. – I guess he found marriage boring after a while too. I'm sure he loved Mum and they seemed to get on better than most parents do but with his job being so demanding and with the whole domestic routine thing,

I suppose he started to crave a bit of excitement. It's understandable when you think about it, but he shouldn't have done what he did.

It all started with these budget cuts at his work. You might be wondering how I know all this as it's not like parents are *ever* open with their kids about any problems; like they expect us to see them as invincible super-humans like we did when we were three! Well, parents talk at night, I think all of them do and I suspect a lot of them assume we're oblivious. Maybe mine didn't realise how late I stay up reading or how thin the walls were or maybe it was just 'out of sight, out of mind' but I could tell they didn't know I was listening. I get the feeling Frogsplash heard a lot of it too but even if he had, I knew he wouldn't admit to it. He likes to bury his head in the sand when it comes to serious stuff, he and Dad have that in common.

Anyway, there were these budget cuts and it was clearly stressing Dad out. I don't know if they cut his pay or if he was worried he'd lose his job but he started being really cautious with money – whereas before he was always the first one you'd go to if you ran out of pocket money ('don't tell Mum' he'd say, and slip you a tenner with a matey wink) – and for a while he wasn't the fun one anymore. It wasn't the money that made him fun but, in the face of all that adult responsibility, Dad just sort of retreated into himself; faded away into a grey-faced nobody on autopilot. He had to switch himself off to cope.

Then his company introduced a graduate scheme and all these young people, fresh from university, came in all enthusiastic and willing to work for a fraction of what Dad was earning. A lot of the old staff did lose their jobs and I can't imagine what would have happened to Dad if he'd been one of them. He might have stayed married to Mum but I'm still not sure it would have been good for us.

And just like that, the old dad was fully revived! It was his job to introduce the new interns to the company and show them the ropes, so he spent a lot of time with them. Not only was his job safe but he had all these fun, young people who looked up to him – no longer did he have to pretend to be serious in front of work people – he could be himself! I heard him telling Mum all about it one evening and he sounded more excited than I've ever heard him and that's saying something. I think for the first time ever he enjoyed his job. Mum didn't sound quite so excited to hear it – she works hard too and as the manager, she needs to be strict and authoritative – basically the one everybody hates. She didn't get to have fun at work then and I don't think she does now.

Maybe Dad sensed Mum's resentment, because he started spending less time at home. The new guys at work must have loved this old dad who was always up for a laugh and made the working day fly by. Or maybe he just bought them all drinks but, either way, they started going to the pub after work.

That was when Frog started to withdraw too. He'd never have admitted it, but he always looked forward to when Dad got home from work, and suddenly, he was getting back an hour late every day – even more on Fridays. Mum noticed too and that's when the arguing began. He was 'shying away from his responsibilities' and leaving her to deal with things alone. Mum being mad at him all the time just pushed him further away though, and then he started going out on Saturday nights too. I'm not saying it was Mum's fault; she had every right to be mad at him. He was being selfish.

Then comes the shady bit – the bit they somehow managed to hide from me and Frogsplash – one way or another, Mum found out that one of the female graduates was more than just a friend of Dad's... they were having an affair. I don't know if Mum figured it out or if Dad confessed, but one day he left, and all Mum's friends came around to console her. That night I couldn't sleep at all and I heard her telling them about the other woman, about how young and beautiful and carefree she must have been. Her name was Sophie. I felt really sad for Mum. Somehow, all the hard work and sacrifices she'd made picking up the slack for my useless, fun-loving, responsibility-avoiding dad, had made her seem boring to him instead of making him feel like the luckiest man in the world.

I thought it was unfair, too, that a few weeks before that she was upset and angry because he wasn't spending enough time at home and then suddenly, he's done this bad, selfish betrayal and the only right thing for Mum to do is to chuck him out of the home for good. Now he's never here to help her with the housework or look after us when she wants to go out or when she's too sick or too tired to cook for us. It's like even though he was the one in the wrong, she still ends up worse and there's not one thing she can do to change that.

That was all two years ago. Dad broke up with the other woman after only a month. Or she broke up with him, I don't know. Anyway, he lives on his own now in a flat, half an hour away. It's a nice, modern flat with a bedroom each for me and Frog to stay over but that's the problem with this weekend, Frog couldn't come. He's at a sleepover thing at Hayden's house for some horror movie marathon or something so it's just me and Dad. Ugh.

Usually, when we visit, I can go to my room and do my own thing while Dad and Frog watch sport on TV and make fart jokes until dinner but today was different. Dad picked me up at twelve p.m. and immediately informed me that he was excited to spend some time just the two of us and was 'really going to make the most of it'. Oh God. No escape. He suggested we go out somewhere, 'anywhere you like – your choice!' See, that's the problem with Dad, he doesn't really know me that well, or at least he *feels* like he doesn't, because I can tell he *wants* me to enjoy our weekends together, but he has no idea what I want, and it makes him kind of nervous. He was always the fun one when we were little, and we just wanted water fights and silly pranks because all that stuff came naturally to him; but now, at least with me, he has to *try* to be fun, and I think he's feeling the pressure.

I don't like making decisions – especially decisions about where to go out – I don't really want to go out. Then again, I didn't want to stay amidst the awkwardness in Dad's flat, all empty just with me and him in it.

What to do… what to do… Mum never puts me on the spot like this. It's just different when you live in the same house, you don't have to force the time spent together. It was warm outside so Dad suggested a picnic and a walk in the park. Bless him, he thinks because I'm a quiet person I want to do quiet things as a family activity. *That's not how it works, Duncan!* Quiet activities mean small talk, awkward silences, social batteries getting drained and not ever being left to get lost in my own thoughts, which are far more amusing than conversing with a dad who's trying too hard.

Cinema was an obvious choice for me. I couldn't think of any films I particularly wanted to see but you're not allowed to talk in the cinema so that's at least two hours of awkwardness avoided. Plus, even afterwards, the uncomfortable silences can potentially be filled with banal observations about the movie which might spark conversation to pad out the rest of the seemingly endless day. Well that was my thinking, anyway.

We arrived at the cinema after a lunch of supermarket-bought sandwiches and bruised fruit from the glove compartment of Dad's car (still better than a picnic). The main foyer was full of kids, some my age but most of them a year or two older. I had a brief panic that I might see someone from my school there, before remembering that Duke John Jameson is nowhere near Dad's house.

The cinema was absolutely heaving though, the floor was sticky with popcorn and spilled drinks and everywhere there were clusters of teenagers just hanging about, not queuing or waiting for anyone – just standing there talking and laughing – where's the fun in that?

Turns out this new comedy film, *American High School,* had just been released yesterday and that was what most of them were watching.

"We should watch that," Dad said, gesturing towards the poster. "It's meant to be hilarious!"

"Err… maybe," I said, looking around at the hordes of thirteen and fourteen-year-olds laughing between mouthfuls of hot dogs and nachos. "But look – it's a certificate twelve."

"You're nearly twelve! It's fine as long as I'm with you, trust me, I used to do it with Frogsplash all the time."

Dad always calls him Frogsplash, not Frog, like that's the name on his birth certificate or something! *American High School* looked like the exact sort of immature boy humour that Frog would love. And Dad, for that matter.

"OK," I said, because the poster did say it was 'the most hilarious film of the year' and 'side-splittingly funny' and those quotes come from film critics, don't they? Besides, these weekends are a lot easier when Dad's kept entertained.

WARNING: THIS FILM CONTAINS ADULT LANGUAGE AND SCENES OF A SEXUAL NATURE

Oh. God. No. I did not think this through, I did not think this through, I did not think this through. *Hey Samantha – didn't you wonder why none of these other kids came to see this with their parents? No, you didn't. You didn't think this through! Hey Samantha, do you know what American high school movies tend to be about? Well, you will soon enough!*

And now I do.

It was the most excruciating two hours of my life. Apparently, nothing is off-limits for joking about, provided it's something to do with the human body… and especially if it's to do with the pubescent (or post-pubescent) human body. Ugh.

The only (small) saving grace was that Dad seemed oblivious to the awkwardness of some of the scenes. The downside to this was that he was laughing at them louder than anyone else in the bloody cinema. I was frozen rigid throughout the whole experience, my body petrified in pure, molten embarrassment but my eyes and my mind were active enough— too active… they witnessed things no eleven-year-old girl should ever see. It wasn't even funny. I could've forgiven it if it had just been a bit funny.

Those scenes in the film – the ones that were so unsubtle you could practically choke on them – I just want to go back and scrub them all out with steel wool until they're raw and bloody. Not the scenes but the experience of having *shared them* with *Dad.* I want to scour them into oblivion.

So, it's Saturday evening and I'm in my room at Dad's. I never thought I'd say this, but I wish Frog was here. Not just because he'd fill the role of participating offspring for the weekend, but because things are so much less awkward when he's here, he's the thing that draws all other things together. Frogsplash is so outgoing he makes awkward *impossible!*

But he's at Hayden's house and I'm here and it'll be dinner time soon. A dinner date with Dad. Just the two of us.

"So, what did you think of the film?" he asked when we sat down with our pizza and chicken wings.

"It was OK," I said. "There were some funny bits."

"What about that bit where that guy brought his girlfriend over for some private time while he was meant to be babysitting his little brother, but the little brat put a secret webcam in his bedroom and sent the live stream to his parents – that was hilarious! Oh, and then it accidentally got shared to all his contacts and spread around the whole school! Classic!"

"Well, yeah but, I mean, that wasn't very fair was it, especially on the poor girlfriend."

"Oh… Yeah, I suppose… So, anyway, Sam, do *you* have a boyfriend?"

Ugh.

"Ugh, Dad, I'm eleven!"

"I didn't mean like in the film! But there must be a boy you like at school, surely or maybe someone from a boy band? I hear a lot of girls like that group The Dreamers… Especially that one, Dillon James – is it? He's a good-looking lad!"

Oh God, what is he doing! He's trying to talk to me about boys! What the hell is he doing! Make it stop, make it stop, please let me spontaneously combust! Oh God give me the power to teleport, oh ground swallow me up! Anything, please, please, oh please, this is the worst thing ever! I will never get over this, this will haunt me for the rest of my life, I will remember this on my death bed and it will be the thing that finally kills me and my God that will be a sweet relief from the lifelong embarrassment that this conversation is going to cause me, oh God let it end!

"You mean Dillon James Scott?" I said casually. "Yes, a lot of girls like him – a lot of *six-year-old* girls!"

"All right, all right, so I'm a bit out of touch… I bet most dads have never even heard of him!"

That's exactly the sort of thing most dads would say.

"So, how are things at your new school – apart from the boys, of course – have you made any friends?"

"Not really, no. It's OK, but the teachers try too hard to get us to talk about ourselves."

A bit like you right now actually, Dad. Adults – ugh. They don't understand how much communication has changed since their day.

"In my day, teachers usually told us off for talking – 'children should be seen and not heard!' was a common saying, back in my day."

Did you go to school in the fifteenth century, Dad?

"Well, they're encouraging it now when nobody wants to talk but as soon as people actually start getting to know each other and making friends they'll tell us we're not allowed to. That's always the way it works, as soon as we start enjoying something it gets taken away from us."

"That's very negative!"

"Just because it's negative doesn't mean it's not true."

You don't know what to say, do you, Dad? But I know what you're thinking. You're thinking, 'This is much harder than talking to Frogsplash!'

"I suppose not," Dad conceded at last and that's when I knew I'd won.

My prize was the cessation of that ridiculous, forced conversation, and when Dad flicked through the TV guide trying, and failing, to find something that I'd like, I told him he could watch Match of the Day. So, he's watching that and I'm here in my room writing and it feels like I can breathe for the first time since Dad picked me up! Bless him, he tries – it's just that he tries way, way, too hard.

Sunday 22nd September 2019

BROTHER DRAMA BOTHERS MAMA –
SISTER THINKS IT'S PERFECT KARMA!

"OK, so I've never called her Mama in my entire life," *said the younger sister after further questioning. "But* *without it the headline isn't catchy."*

After an eggy breakfast, Dad dropped me off home just before noon and the atmosphere when I arrived was palpably tense. I'd expected Frogsplash to still be at Hayden's house, but it didn't take me long to realise he was already home.

Normally when we get back from Dad's, Mum asks what we got up to, what we ate, if we went out anywhere, if any of Dad's mates were there, but today she was far too distracted.

When I walked in, Mum was in the living room texting furiously. She did, eventually, become aware of my presence, "Where's Dad?" she asked vacantly.

"He's driving home," I replied. Dad never comes in when he drops me off. That's just how it goes.

"Oh," Mum said. "I wanted to talk to him. Never mind." She carried on texting, so I retreated to the partial safety and semi silence of my room. I tried to ignore the weird vibe that I felt pulsating through the house like a tell-tale heart, but it's not easy when it feels like something huge and ugly is about to erupt and you're right there amid it. Even though it was obvious that something had happened with Froggo, I still had all these creeping doubts and self-analyses regarding my own potential guilt and possible ways in which I might be the one in the wrong here. I knew I wasn't, but the thing – whatever it was – was looming so heavily I couldn't shrug it off even with logic and reason. That's just how powerful feelings, especially unspoken ones, can really be.

I'm all for the power of unspeaking.

Eventually, instead of trying to ignore the vibe, I succumbed to listening intently. Whatever Frogsplash had done it must have been juicy! I'm not normally one for gossip or *Schadenfreude* but Frog really left me in the lurch leaving me alone with Dad this weekend, so I kind of felt like it served him right getting in big trouble like this. He gets away with enough stuff.

I heard Mum going into the utility room, which usually means she's checking on her home-brewed 'wine' (I don't think you can really call it wine, officially speaking). Then I heard her go to the living room. Then I heard her on the stairs because I heard the creak of the third step up, but it seemed like the sound of it freaked her out a bit because I didn't hear her come up any further.

She's obviously restless. Maybe that's normal for mums of teens, but who knows? I wouldn't call my mum *normal,* no matter what the circumstances. Don't get me wrong – she's not doolally; she's just, well… basically, she has no shame. Nothing embarrasses her. I mean, there's more to it than that – she's kind of an adventurer, she likes to try things, to challenge herself but unlike most people, she doesn't care what she looks like trying it or even if she's any good. She doesn't do it to get good; she does it for the *experience*. She says she wants to experience as many things as she can. That sounds kind of cool, right? But when I give you a few more details you might not think so, and you might just start to wonder how broadly one can stretch the term 'expeeeeeeeerience'!

There was the time last year where she conducted an 'experiment' to see how people reacted to her depending on what colour she wore that day. She started with black: black trousers, black shoes, black shirt and black jacket. That was fine, in fact, no one really noticed her at all that day, possibly because she was dressed like a ninja. The second day she wore all white. She stood out a little bit at first. She stood out a lot more when she spilled orange juice in her own lap while sitting at her desk and came to pick me up from school with a massive yellow stain on her white jeans (people *reacted* differently to her that day!)

But that was just the beginning. Neither Frog nor I had expected that Mum would carry on like this with quite such an extensive *range* of colours. I guess I thought this experiment would last for another week, as in the seven colours of the rainbow. When it came to luminous yellow day, three weeks later, Mum really had to dig at the back of the wardrobe. She found these highlighter yellow leggings that she'd worn to some themed party when she was at university, only they were so tight that when she put them on they stretched so thinly you could see her knickers straight through the fabric. The only shoes she had of that colour were some summer wedges, and this was in November! To top it all off she wore a high visibility jacket with *nothing underneath* because, funnily enough, she couldn't find a neon yellow shirt anywhere!

Now imagine me queuing up at the school's exit at the end of the day looking for my mum and seeing this *beacon* with her knickers on show waving shamelessly at me, occasionally pausing to say hello to the other parents, who were trying not to stare. They must have thought she'd gone nuts! The stupidest part was that she seemed oblivious to the second glances and chuckles of the people around her – not much of an experiment, unless her hypothesis was, '*how much can I embarrass my children without them realising what I'm up to.*' In that case, she nailed it.

She didn't just lose it when dad left – she's always been that way. I don't remember it, but when I was a toddler, she was a stay-at-home mum. Frog had just started school and she was so bored she ended up going grocery shopping every day just because it was something to do. That's when she got the idea that she wouldn't spend any money on breakfast or lunch for a whole week and would try to fill herself up on free samples from all the supermarkets in the area. Apparently, she lost half a stone that week, but she swears she didn't do it for that.

She's done some other more normal things – fun runs and the like, but she always has to make it cringe-worthy by dressing up as a dinosaur or doing the whole thing backwards or something.

Eventually Mum stopped pacing the house aimlessly and started cooking. We always eat dinner together on a

Sunday, but it's not often we have a full roast. Mum does a roast whenever she's stressed. I suppose it keeps her busy; distracts her from whatever's on her mind. When Dad left, we must have got through at least five chickens a week. We had chicken and stuffing sandwiches in our lunchboxes every day. The worst part is that it was summertime, and who wants a roast when it's twenty-eight degrees outside? On sports day, my sweat smelled of gravy; you could've mopped my brow with a Yorkshire pudding. It really is the children who suffer most during a divorce.

Anyway, whatever it was that Frog had done, it must've been bad to prompt a roast.

At six p.m. we all sat round the table, the domestic tension even heavier now that we were all near.

Mum had really outdone herself with the roast though. Real gravy with caramelised onions, a whole roast chicken with sausage meat stuffing, crispy roast potatoes with light, fluffy insides, steamed veg AND roast butternut squash with crushed garlic. And a whole MOUNTAIN of homemade Yorkshire puddings! Yum! I'd skipped lunch earlier because I hadn't wanted to leave the safety of my room in case Mum decided to offload all her worries on me, so I was *starving.*

I dived straight in, starting with the Yorkshires, but I felt a bit greedy because Frog was just pushing his food around the plate with his fork, cutting it up but not really eating any, just playing with it sulkily and Mum didn't seem to have time to eat in between gulps of wine. What on Earth had he done?

"Have some potatoes, Frog, carbs are a good cure for a hangover!" Mum said.

Ah.

"I'm not hungover, Mum! It was only a few beers!"

"AND some of my home-made wine... you didn't think I knew about that, did you? Hayden's mum found the remnants of it in a Lucozade bottle behind the toilet... What must the other mums think of me, leaving a huge vat of wine up for grabs in a house with a teenager? I'm so irresponsible! I bet they think I can't cope since your dad left. I don't want their pity and I don't want them thinking you're going off the rails!"

This stuffing is delicious. Really top notch.

"Oh, come off it, Mum, I'm not going off the rails – it was Joshua's idea!"

And the chicken! So moist!

"And that's another thing!" Mum continued. "That beer belonged to Joshua's dad – and the wine belonged to me – you STOLE from us."

Did she butter the broccoli? Nice touch, Mum.

"Well, how else were we supposed to get it?"

And what's this with the butternut squash? There's something new here – is it sage?

"You weren't *supposed* to get it, Frog, that's the whole point!"

No, not sage, rosemary – it goes so well! How did we ever eat a roast without it?

"OK, I'm sorry I stole it. Do you want some money? How much for a bottle of home-made wine? Do you give a family discount?"

Wow, angry roast is awesome. WAY better than sad roast!

But maybe Mum was a bit sad because that empty, sarcastic offer Frog made to reimburse her seemed to take all the wind out of her sails, because after that she said no more on the subject. She asked how my weekend with Dad went and just like that, we were back to normal.

Or so I thought.

Frog went back up to his room as soon as he'd finished his dinner, and like a fool, I stayed expecting dessert (even though I was stuffed). Mum got up, and so did my hopes. She went over to the fridge but all she came back with was a re-filled glass of wine.

"Never grow up, Sam," she said philosophically.

Oh God. Here we go…

"Except you are… You *are* growing up – both of you. You're my baby and you're in secondary school already! I know everyone says this, but it really does feel like only yesterday that you were a tiny toddler who could barely speak. Well, maybe not yesterday… more like a week ago… I just – I thought I had more time with Frogsplash…"

There is literally no escape.

"… I mean; his name is *Frogsplash* for heaven's sake! That's not a grown-up name. And he's so much like your father, so… young at heart; so… immature."

"But Dad's still like that, Mum – and *he* drinks beer all the time!" I said. Was that a good thing to say? Probably not for Dad.

"I don't even know him anymore," Mum continued, like she couldn't even hear me. "It's like we used to be

47

friends and now he's doing things behind my back and just *pretending* we're still on the same team. He was my baby too, not so long ago!"

And then she started to cry. And I realised this was about something much bigger than a few idiotic cans of beer.

"I always wanted to have more children."

Oh God. What do I say to that? Please someone fill this gap…

"There was just never enough money and I guess I always thought there'd be more time. But now I'm alone and I'm too old…"

Should I be dealing with this? I'm eleven…

"You're not alone, Mum, you have us," I said reassuringly (I hoped).

"Yes, but for how long?"

She appears to be inconsolable. What's the matter with her? The home brew must have gone sour.

"I know!" she said, saving me from having to come up with some input, "I'll text your father! This should be his job, the first beer; peer pressure; all that teenage boy stuff – he'll know what to do about Frog."

Dad IS a teenage boy! Knowing him he'll PROVIDE the beers and probably watch **'AMERICAN HIGH SCHOOL: UNCUT!'** *with Froggo and call it educational!*

But I didn't stop her. Partly because I wanted OUT of that conversation; and partly because I knew she shouldn't be dealing with this alone. And while Dad might not have the whole responsibility thing sorted out, he's *surely* better equipped than me to give parenting advice on my older brother! And anyway, Dad understands Frog a lot better than me and Mum do; and Frog listens to *him* (for some reason).

So that was that. Another relaxing weekend for Samantha Drury. Ugh.

Monday 23rd September 2019

BREAKING NEWS: ENTIRE COMMUNITY DEVASTATED WHEN A SCHOOL'S DECISION TO TAKE PUPILS ON A TRIP TAKES A DISASTROUS TURN FOR THE WORSE

"I for one am horrified," said one of the pupils affected by the news. "This is the last thing anybody wanted to happen, assuming they all feel the same way I do." The young girl was in too much shock to make any further comment at that time.

Great News! Year seven trip to Isle of Wight is back on!

This is what was written in large font on the whiteboard when I entered our form room this morning. There had been 'concerns' that there wasn't enough interest in the Isle of Wight trip, and someone in 7JC had heard that they were already arranging refunds to the parents who'd paid for it. Whenever that happened in primary school, it meant that the trip was **definitely** cancelled, and you can bet I was relieved about that, because Mum already paid for me to go.

"It'll be a great experience," she'd said. "It'll give you a chance to really get to know people," she'd added. "These are the things that create memories for life!" and "Anyway, I've already booked that week off work – I'm having a five-day crash course in synchronised swimming and I can't do that with you moping about."

It turns out that no one had wanted to go because they wouldn't know anybody, but now that they'd all made *such* good friends (when did that happen?) most of them had changed their minds and suddenly they were all really upset that it was going to get cancelled and before you know it, they'd got what they wanted despite being fickle, unreasonable and immature about the whole business. So now I have to go too. Six whole days and five whole nights. Ugh.

I was so sure it wasn't going to happen, it had almost entirely escaped my consciousness, so when I walked in this morning, I couldn't believe it. I wondered if it was all a mistake, or if some kid was pulling a prank and it was *them* who'd written it on the board. Then the teachers confirmed that it was true, and *everyone* started talking about it and getting all excited, and that's when I got really annoyed. I mean, there was a deadline on the application form and that was September 1st! Deadlines are deadlines! When we don't hand our homework in on time, we get in trouble, right? But apparently, when people don't consent to a school trip on time and then change their mind last minute, they just get it their way, no argument. How is that fair?

Then I started to wonder if perhaps there's a way out of it. I bet there aren't enough spaces for everyone who wants to go, and I bet there's someone who'd be *desperate* to take my spot. Mum wouldn't have to worry about me while she's at synchronised swimming (why is she doing that again?), I wouldn't bother her. Or what if she never found out? I could just tell her that the trip is still cancelled... that is quite a massive lie though...

"Just got a text from school!" she messaged me at break. "The trip's back on – fantastic! Xx"

Oh God. There is literally no escape.

The moment I realised there was no getting out of it was when I started to truly picture just how dreadful it was going to be. I'll be sharing a room with people from school. There will be nowhere to hide and it's in two weeks' time!

I suppose the activities won't be so bad. If I *must* talk to people, I'd rather it was while we're in the middle of doing something, so we can talk about the thing we're doing rather than filling awkward silences with the dreaded 'small talk'. It's just like weekends with Dad: quiet picnic = bad; distracting film = good.

The thing I'm most nervous about is co-habiting. We'll all be in a cabin, six to eight girls in each, which means I won't have any alone time to recharge my social batteries. People who aren't like me don't understand it, but it's like I'll go mad, just mad, mad, and it's not down to any one thing; it's not something you can put your finger on. It's like an accumulation of quite general, probably ordinary pieces of human existence, but without some interlude, they are entirely relentless. Am I making sense?

I think some people get *energised* by being around other people, like it fuels them and keeps them going, keeps them up, up, up! Whereas others (like me) get the energy syphoned out of us like petrol from an old car that's just trying to keep on carrying on. No one's doing it on purpose, it's just that some people need other people and other people need to be alone. When I'm alone, I can get that petrol back all by myself, I'm self-sufficient, if I get a bit of solitude.

But if that's true, then it's so much more than self-sufficiency. All those people who need to bounce off other people like me – what would they do without us? *Some people need other people and other people need to be alone.* Does that mean they need me more than I need them?

It certainly doesn't feel that way. It feels like the world was built for people like them. I feel like I'm surrounded by people like them and I'm the only person like me.

Wednesday 25th September 2019

"Guess what?" Mum said when she got home from work, "Trudy called me today!"

Fascinating.

"And she said she's done it – she finally quit her day job. She's going full time make-up saleswoman! And she wants me to be her business partner! Isn't that fantastic?"

"Um, yeah," I said. "Would you have to quit your job though?"

"Oh no, it'll only be in the evenings, a few times a week and from the comfort of my own home!"

Oh God. They're coming here. All the women will be coming here.

"I don't have to help, do I?"

"No, no, don't worry… I mean you *could* pop your head in from time to time, ask around, see if anyone needs any refreshments, that sort of thing… We start tomorrow!"

Ugh.

Friday 27th September 2019

We need to talk about Thursday.

Brace yourself.

OK.

Here goes.

Ugh.

"Mum! I need to get ready for school!" I shouted through the locked bathroom door.

"I won't be long, Sammy! I'm just doing my hair – I want to look my best for tonight!"

Ah yes, the meeting of the maniac make-up mums. What a waste of money. Make-up is stupid.

I went downstairs to make myself some toast while I waited, and that's when I noticed my unwashed lunch box in the kitchen sink. Mum's so distracted thinking about tonight, she forgot to make my lunch! I'd have made it myself if I'd known, but I only had fifteen minutes until my bus was due and I hadn't even washed and dressed yet.

Mum swept through the kitchen like a hurricane on her way out the door.

"Does my hair look OK?" she asked as she threw on her coat.

"It looks great, Mum. But didn't you forget something?"

"Oh God – your lunch! I'm sorry, I haven't had time. Here – take this, you'll have to have school dinner today," she said, flustered, and handed me a fiver.

"No, not that, Mum," I said as she opened the door to leave. "Your hair looks great, Mum, and your make-up, but… you're still in your pyjamas."

I've never seen her move so quickly.

I had to run for the school bus thanks to Mum hogging the bathroom. My face always turns bright red and shiny and puffy when I run, especially outside with the wind blowing straight at me.

The boys from my year were all sitting in a flock at the back of the bus.

"Hey look, Orange Riding Hood's turned red!" one of them shouted, and they all sniggered cruelly.

"Look at her face – it looks like a tomato!"

And just like that, make-up doesn't seem so stupid.

I know their names now, Jake Atkinson, Demetri Michael, Rob Battley and Hassan Ahmed. They all went to the same primary school and Jake and Hassan have brothers in year ten. How do I know this? I may not talk much but I listen, and sadly what I'm hearing (mostly in the girls' toilets) is that they're the coolest boys in our year and every girl has got a crush on at least one of them. It's so annoying; they're so arrogant and rude and somehow that's attractive! They don't even seem the least bit interested in girls; they still act like they're eight years old.

I ignored them and fortunately, they weren't armed with oranges on this occasion, so they soon lost interest. I managed to keep my head down until lunchtime but without a packed lunch, I had to eat in the canteen.

When I arrived, it seemed to be roaring with voices: an indistinguishable chorus of jokes, laughter, gossip, complaints about teachers and classes and, I was soon to discover, plenty of fabrications and bragging.

I joined the queue for hot food, standing behind some year nine's who were talking about their Biology teacher, who apparently always has sweat patches under her arms and lipstick on her teeth. Mrs Barratt, she's called, I don't know her – we don't do separate sciences yet – but I feel sorry for her being laughed at like that. I guess it reminded me of mum in her pyjamas that morning; I wouldn't want anybody laughing at my mum (apart from me, obviously). It's like even when they're just trying to do some normal job, women are always being judged on what they look like. That's why the make-up thing annoys me so much.

I decided to treat myself for having to endure the densely populated dinner hall, so I got pizza and chips with jelly for dessert. That was the easy bit, but then I had to find a seat and there were no empty tables, so I'd have to sit with some other people. The unwritten rule is, as it was in primary school, that you cannot sit at a table with anyone from other years *unless,* somehow, you're already friends with them.

So that narrowed it down a lot and from what I could see, there were no obviously 'quiet' people like me because, of course, they were all in the library or elsewhere concealed in shadowy silences. In these situations, you don't have much time for hesitation. You can't just stand there looking at everybody, trying to assess every one of them and somehow, just by looking at them, decide which one is the best of a bad situation. The longer you hover, the longer you give people to plan their defence against you. I think.

I was wary of boys after the morning's proceedings – they have a real knack for ganging up, so I looked for year seven girls, and the only ones I could see that had space on their table was a group of three who seemed far too consumed in their own conversation to be bothered about me. This was the best I was going to get. It was going to be OK. It would be character-building!

I pretended to eat my pizza absent-mindedly, but surely by now you've figured out that my mind is never, *ever* absent. The one they called Beth was clearly running the show, with the other two hanging on to her every word, only occasionally interjecting when Beth allowed them to – purely to egg her on to tell more of the story, never to offer their own opinion or anything else that might pull focus from Queen B.

The way they were talking – especially Beth – it was like they were fourteen, at least! She must have a big sister or something because I *know* that kind of maturity doesn't come from brothers like Frogsplash.

No wonder I can't make friends with people in my year – they're eleven going on sixteen!

Yes, Samantha, because you tried so hard to bond with them…

"My sister just got a scholarship to fashion school. All she did was copy designs from magazines from other countries – it's so unfair!" said one of the hangers-on.

57

"You think *that's* unfair? Let me tell you what happened to *me* last year," said Beth. *ElizaBETH. Queen Elizabeth the Third...*

"In my primary school we had a special visit from – wait for it – the *actual, real* Victoria Beckham!" Here she paused to allow her audience to gasp and 'ooh' and 'ah' in approval, but then she shot them all a cold stare, like they were all wrong to react that way, even though she'd totally built them up to do exactly that.

"In preparation for the visit, we all designed an outfit which were displayed in the main hall. *I* designed the most stunning party dress, I'm telling you, you've never seen anything like it. Ever."

By now, they were all hooked on her every word and there was an uncomfortable tone to the whole thing, like she was still mad at them for getting excited about Victoria Beckham, and like they were all desperate to get back in her good books.

"So, when she finally came (fashionably late, of course) she did this speech in the hall about working hard, following your dreams, believing in yourself, all of that, then there was a quick 'Q and A' and we had to go back to normal classes. It was a big fuss over nothing, all that hype. Like she's such a big deal? She's just a person, you know?"

They all nodded and murmured in enthusiastic agreement while Her Royal Highness caught her breath.

"Anyway, fast-forward a few months, and what do I discover blowing up all over the fashion mags? *THE* party dress of the season. *MY* dress. *MY* design. And guess whose name was on the label: Victoria Beckham. She must have had a look at all our designs on display in the hall. But did I get any money for it? Did I get any credit? No. Not a penny."

The three worshippers were all gasps and tut-tuts and 'oh my God'. Surely, they didn't *believe* her; it was such a blatant lie! If I was one of them, I'd have asked a few more questions, like what did the dress look like? If it was only last year, surely you can look it up! But no, they just accepted it as an irrefutable truth from Their Glorious Leader.

"I don't even care though," Her Majesty continued. "She's the loser, stealing ideas from little schoolgirls. I'm going to get into fashion *my* way. I just need to lose ten more pounds and then the modelling agency says they'll sign me. God this diet is killing me, though!"

"Oh, my God, me too, it's so hard!" the others bleated in agreement. And then, for a moment, there was sweet silence as they all took a moment's rest from desperately trying to impress each other. I took a huge, satisfying bite out of my slice of cheesy, greasy pizza, and then I felt eyes on me. They were watching me eat and I'm pretty sure I heard one of their stomachs rumbling.

They were staring at my chips and pizza, practically salivating with desire, but Beth managed to snap them out of it with one simple comment.

"Well *she's* clearly not on a diet!"

And that's when they all laughed at me.

It felt awful. Suddenly, I felt like this massive, greedy pig with no self-control. I could see the grease pumping sluggishly through my veins, feel the cheese suffocating my heart until it tightened in my chest, feel the calories expanding my stomach, thickening my thighs and puffing up my face into a big, beige dough ball. I couldn't bear to eat another bite, so I got up and emptied my plate into the bin, not even touching my jelly. I *am* the jelly, red and wobbling all over. I am Red Riding Hood. I am Samantha Dreary.

They all laughed again when they saw me chuck my food away. They knew they'd got to me and they were enjoying it.

This is why I don't like people.

The rest of the school day went by without incident but I was distracted, replaying the horrors of lunchtime over and over in my head, over-analysing every detail, remembering the image of their wide eyes all staring at me and my food like a parliament of owls, remembering that moment when I became conscious of myself as this visible thing that these people could just look at whenever they wanted and I couldn't do a single thing to stop them, and imagining what I must have looked like to those big, staring eyes, all bemused and nervous: a big, fat, greasy rabbit in the headlights.

It was only one sentence 'She's clearly not on a diet', and it wasn't even an insult, just a statement of fact, but it was the implication. Did she mean that there is something *generally* wrong with not dieting? Or that I, personally, should be on a diet. The really insulting part of this non-insult was the way she spoke about me directly, right in front of me, but not *to* me. If she'd said, "Well you're clearly not on a diet, are you?" I would have had an opportunity to defend myself and not look stupid by saying something like, "No, I'm not on a diet, I like my food and judging by the hungry look on each of your faces, so do you!"

But those responses never come to me in the moment, anyway. I'm always in my bubble, forgetting that people can burst it in an instant and get straight at me, right through my skin and right inside my head. So, when they get through, I always panic and I'm completely speechless for far too long to think of a comeback.

"Sammy! Sammy, over here!"

Oh God. Is that Mum? What's she doing at my school?

"Surprise! I took the afternoon off because I was far too distracted thinking about this evening, what with Trudy and the girls all coming over. Anyway, I'm just twiddling my thumbs at home, getting all nervous in case I've forgotten something, so I thought I'd come pick you up to take my mind off it, saves you getting the school bus, eh?"

"Yeah! Thanks Mum!"

What are you doing in my bubble, Mum? Go back to your own bubble.

I looked down at the ground for the entire duration of the walk to the car, so as not to make eye contact with anyone and draw attention to the fact that my mum was right there with me. At least she wasn't wearing the neon yellow see-through leggings this time.

She talked about her make-up club the whole car ride home.

"I like to try new things, you know that about me I'm sure, but this thing with Trudy seems like *more* than just a 'thing'... you two are growing up and I need something

61

for myself, something fresh and empowering. Trudy quit her job for goodness sake! Self-employed! How empowering is that?"

She'd pre-made a tuna pasta bake so that Froggo and I could 'help ourselves' whenever we wanted dinner, but it was covered in cheese and it reminded me of that shiny, stringy, inch-thick pizza I'd shamefully eaten at lunch, so I stayed in my room until the action began.

It was nice to see how excited Mum was about all this, I can always tell when she's in a good mood because she starts calling me 'Sammy' like she did when I was little. And after that thing with Frogsplash last weekend, I thought she deserved a bit of fun, so I made a vow (in my head) to be on hand to help, even if I hated every minute of it. Also, it would distract me from my own gut-wrenching hunger pangs.

Eat, Samantha, eat, eat, eat...

No!

Trudy and Jessica arrived at six twenty p.m., ten minutes early to get all their wares on display. Mum called me down and, truth be told, I was kind of in the spirit of things (weird, right!) I don't know, I was just happy for Mum because this was the first time I'd seen her like her old self since the divorce, and, well, as uncomfortable as I was last time we did the make-up group, everyone was so nice to me and told me I looked pretty when they tested a new product on me. Usually, I'm resistant to things like that but after the day's events, I guess I needed some friendly reassurance.

Mum's assistant Alana came and obviously Trudy and Jessica were there, but everyone else was new – mostly

Trudy's friends, I think – I don't remember too clearly. Anyway, rather uncharacteristically, I was determined to try.

The first part was easy enough, on paper. While they all got to know each other, and Mum and Trudy explained about their business, I was on drinks and snacks duty. Only, whenever I went to the kitchen to top up the bowls of crisps and olives my stomach lurched and clenched, and it felt like it was folding in on itself. I had some tropical juice to keep me going and stop the rumbling from within and after a while, the sugar kicked in and I felt better.

When they were all settled in and were testing out the make-up, I sat with them and Jessica, lovely, friendly Jessica, immediately made the effort to involve me.

"So, how are you getting on with secondary school? It's a big change, isn't it?" she asked me.

"It's tough," I said. "Not the work, but all the new people! How about you?"

"Well, I guess I've just about settled in, but I have been there over two years!" she replied.

"Sorry, I keep forgetting you're in year nine!" I said. "My mum told me we were the same age."

"Typical. She was probably just trying to get us to 'make friends'! My mum is *always* doing stuff like that… It's like, why can't you just let us make our own decisions? Get out of my space! You know?"

"Totally!" I replied, feeling giddy with excitement – Jessica totally gets it! This is totally brilliant!

Why do I keep saying 'totally'?

I must admit I was excited, the way Jessica always went with her mum to these groups, I thought she and

Trudy were best mates! But it's the make-up that Jessica likes. She gets annoyed with her mum just like I do with mine! Still, I didn't want to come off too keen – she's a year NINE! So, I casually went to the kitchen to top up the snack bowls and get myself some more juice.

I will not eat crisps. I will not consume calories. Juice is good. A juice fast.

"I look so cool!" I said when I saw my reflection after Alana and Trudy's friend, Denise, did my eyeshadow. They'd done it in this gradient from dark blue to light pink, they called it 'blending' and it was awesome.

"You look beautiful!" they all said, and then they tried some other, more boring (beiger) products on me before they started talking sales and I went to get more drinks. I brought more juice for everybody, and it was lucky mum had made a whole big bowlful of it because Alana was chugging it down! She must have been craving vitamin C. So was I, come to think of it.

"Ugh, this is the boring part." Jessica said to me quietly, rolling her eyes. "It always starts out so friendly and personal, but all they're really getting at is the sale. Sell, sell, sell! It's so fake. But it's my mum's living now so keep it quiet, yeah?" she giggled and winked at me. At me! Samantha not-so-Dreary! Not that hot, sweaty, red-faced disaster child, just Samantha. Sammy. Sam.

I guess I was getting into the spirit of things because after getting to know Jessica a bit I asked her to give me a makeover – totally out of character! If you can't beat them, join them, I suppose... although that kind of thought process doesn't seem much like me either. Jessica was happy to have something to do that made her look like she was working without having to do any unsubtly veiled sales pitches, so she gratefully obliged.

Having her right there in front of me, her face so close to mine, I had little choice but to really get to know her face, to study her features and her flawless brown skin. I really started to notice how beautiful she was, and for some reason I felt utterly compelled to tell her... repeatedly!

"You're so beautiful, Jessica! You're just... so beautiful!" I said, taking a break to finish my juice. Then I don't remember so much but Frog was more than happy to fill in the gaps for me this morning.

"It was *hilarious!* First you started telling everybody you loved them and that you wanted to be best friends with all of them – *best friends* with forty-year-old women, Sam, it was classic! Then you went a bit quiet and went over to the TV. Everyone thought you'd just got a bit embarrassed because you'd accidentally let yourself get caught up in the whole thing and made a fool out of yourself.

"But *then* – and this is the best part – then you put a music channel on and turned it right up loud and started *dancing!* You, dancing! And you wanted them all to dance with you, but they were all just watching you make a fool out of yourself, so you went back over to the table to try and encourage them to get up and dance, but when you opened your mouth the only thing that came out of it was loads and loads of puke – all over Trudy Palmer and all over her make-up samples!"

Frog was laughing hysterically, enjoying every minute of it. I felt hollow and emptied out. And not just because I'd emptied my guts all over Trudy Palmer. Something he'd said jogged my memory, and I suddenly remembered spilling the rum punch all down myself, especially my school tie. Drunk as I was at the time, I took it off and shoved it in my school bag, and I truly believed that I would remember to take it out and wash it later. I couldn't face it this morning, though; not even the thought of it. I ate some buttery toast and I felt a lot better, but mum still insisted on giving me a lift to school.

"Are you sure you feel up to going in today?" she asked before she started up the car. "I really don't mind taking the day off to look after you."

Ugh. What could be worse than that?

"No really, Mum, I'm fine."

"Oh, Sammy, I'm so sorry, it's all my fault. I thought you were just drinking normal juice! This is worse than Frog with the home brew. God, I'm the worst mother in the world!"

Here we go, Guilt City.

"It was just an accident, Mum, you didn't know I was drinking from the punch bowl and I didn't know there was alcohol in it. And that thing with Frog – he went behind your back, that was *his* fault."

"Oh, that's sweet of you to say, Sammy, but you don't understand."

Ugh. Even when they're apologising to you, they find a way to be super patronising.

"You see, I'm supposed to be a responsible parent. I'm supposed to be able to see these things coming and prevent them before they even happen. Maybe I shouldn't go into business with Trudy. Working full time and trying to be an evening saleswoman on top of that is too preoccupying. I've been so distracted I've allowed *both* of

66

my children to get drunk in the past week! I just feel terrible."

"*You* feel terrible?" I said. My turn to vent some guilt. "I threw up all over Trudy's merchandise!"

"Oh, don't worry about that, Sammy, they were only testers. And to tell you the truth, it was Trudy's idea to put the rum in the punch in the first place. It's a sales tactic, you see, people buy more stuff when they're drunk."

I'm not sure that's what a sales tactic is, but I'm in no mood to discuss it with mum.

Friday 27th September 2019 (again)

I survived school and, it would seem, my first ever hangover. I got called Samantha Dreary several times, presumably because I looked and felt like a zombie all day. But it wasn't all bad. One of the boys on the bus asked me why I looked so moody and I told him it was because I drank too much last night. Obviously, they didn't believe me; *I* wouldn't have believed me. So, I plunged into the cluttered depths of my school bag, fished out the rum-soaked school tie that I inevitably forgot to put in the wash and threw it in his face. He was flabbergasted, and apparently quite repulsed by the smell. It was the most satisfying moment of my life.

I will not, however, survive the humiliation of my first drunken experience in front of Mum and all her mates. Oh, and Frogsplash. I didn't even notice he was watching. He must have been standing in the doorway out of view so that no one caught him filming me. Yes, he filmed me. He tried to make me watch it this morning when I still felt like retching. I don't usually 'tell on him' but this was one of those times when I just had to.

"Frogsplash, delete that right now!" Mum said sternly. "I know this is all some big joke to you but for me this is very serious. First, trying to humiliate your little sister is cruel; you should be asking if she's all right! And secondly, I could get in big trouble for this – she's severely underage and if anyone saw that video, they might think I'd knowingly let her get drunk right under my nose!"

In the end, he had no choice but to delete it from his phone, but I'm pretty sure he backed it up on his computer, because when I got back from school, I could already hear him and his mates laughing at something in his room.

"I wish I could delete it from my memory," I said to Mum afterwards. "I wish I could delete it from history so that *no one* remembers it!"

"Oh, don't worry," Mum said. "There'll be plenty more times you'll feel that way in your adolescent years!"

Yeah thanks, Mum; I don't doubt it for a second.

I'm going to lay low for a while. Dwelling on things is too much to handle right now.

Saturday 5th October 2019

BREAKING NEWS: THE END OF THE WORLD IS NIGH! SO PANIC BUY! BUY! BUY! BUY!

The year seven school trip, otherwise known as the end of the world, is just a week away, and people are panic-buying supplies which they believe will help them survive the upcoming apocalypse. "Yes, I do believe it is going to be the end of the world" said sceptic, Samantha Drury. "What I'm sceptical about is that buying raincoats and disposable cameras will help me ride out the storm."

Monday the 14th of October, the day the world ends. Today I had to go shopping with Mum for school trip supplies. I wish I could say that this was the worst part of the whole experience but, in all honesty, I know that the worst is yet to come. You should see some of the things on the list of 'essential items' to bring:

- Absolutely no electrical items.
- No open-toed shoes, sandals or flip-flops.
- Waterproof jacket with hood and zip pockets.
- Fully waterproof trousers to go **over** regular trousers.

- Knee-high wellington boots – **NOT** calf or ankle length.
- Thick washing-up rubber gloves.

And that's just a few. Are we going on a school trip or are we going to decontaminate alien life forms before introducing them into human society?

The alien thing sounds better. At the very least, it'd be something to write about.

FAKING NEWS: INTELLIGENT ALIEN LIFE FORMS HAVE LANDED ON THE ISLE OF WIGHT. WE SEND OUR YOUNGEST, LEAST EXPERIENCED, MOST VULNERABLE JOURNALISTS TO MEET THE POTENTIALLY DANGEROUS MARTIANS FIRST-HAND.

The UK Space Agency has confirmed speculations from local UFO enthusiasts that aliens have indeed made attempts to invade our planet via the Isle of Wight. Top scientists reveal that the small British Island has been plagued by unwanted Martians for several months and, after trying to control the problem internally, has sought the help of over one hundred secondary school students, who, they have assured us, will be fully competent and prepared for the situation. They are so well-prepared, in fact, that they are even bringing their own rubber gloves.

There was a lot of speculation on the coach about what they would look like: would they be the cute, green ones with buggy eyes and antennae like in kids' movies? Or would they be more like the giant, horrifying, cockroach-looking thing from adult alien films? After much debate it was concluded that they probably looked nothing like either of those. They would probably look like nothing we'd ever seen before.

I was far too anxious to join in with their playful guessing games; this is a serious business – don't they know the risks? Maybe making light of it is their coping mechanism; personally, I'd rather try and take my mind off it, take stock and remember why I'm doing this.

We've arrived at base camp now, just outside the quarantine zone. It's like a little village, only more clinical. We share our dorms, of course, but they're all out to dinner. I couldn't eat a thing, so I'm here alone sitting on my bed, trying to appreciate the solitude – who knows when I'll next get a peaceful moment to myself.

I can hear them out in the dining tent they set up for us, laughing. One of them keeps doing a dumb alien impression like it's all some big joke, 'take me to your leader'. We already know they can't speak English. How are we going to assimilate them into our society? But they can learn, we know that, because they have already learnt to communicate with us.

And *that's* why I'm doing this. Because of what they said. They said their planet is undeveloped and bleak and they don't want to live there anymore. They said they *will* live here and if we don't let them, they will take our planet by force. We either live with them in peace, or we get taken over by them. They have powers that we can't compete against, strengths that we can't defend against, and knowledge beyond our comprehension.

It's our job to prepare them for entry so that they can thrive and flourish living amongst us. We *must* make it better for them to live amongst us, otherwise they will destroy us. We must also find out as much as we can about them to report back to the rest of the world, to prepare them for adapting to their new lives with these new life forms. We don't get to sleep tonight; there's no time. It's dinner and then that's it, we enter the quarantine zone and our lives are changed forever. We don't talk about what will happen if things don't go according to plan. There's no sense talking about it since we can't do anything to prepare for it. Like I said, we have no defence.

All we have are our rubber gloves.

Saturday 5th October 2019 (still)

Sorry, I got carried away. Shopping with mum is just so *boring!* She was totally panicking about how unprepared I am for the trip, and shopping on a busy Saturday is stressful enough as it is. I was meant to see Dad today, and Mum considered sending me to him with the Isle of Wight shopping list, but in the end, she decided he couldn't be trusted to get it right and we'd just have to come back and exchange it all tomorrow. This was a fair assumption. He once bought a girl's jumper for Frogsplash because it had a dinosaur on it, so it *must* have been for boys! Ugh!

So, the trip is happening, there is no escape. Try to think of the positives, away from mum, away from Frog, and I'll miss a week of make-up and beauty group with Trudy, Jessica and the gang. That still leaves this Thursday, but I can hide in my room, I'll say I'm packing my suitcase. Apart from that – well, it's the great unknown, I suppose. It will be a break from routine.

Will it, though? I suspect there will be a lot of 'team-building' exercises like there have been throughout the first few weeks of secondary school. On top of that, I'm picturing those super enthusiastic camp guides you see in the movies, all full of positivity and insistent that everyone joins in. I hate those people. I think those people *are* the aliens.

People at school have been enthusiastic too, though. There will be a lot of buzz around the imminent trip this week. Well *this* journalist doesn't do 'buzz' articles. Goodbye.

Monday 14th October 2019

Well, I'm here. I survived the journey but that was never the problem. I'm here in the dorm but they've put the lights on dim for 'bedtime reading' eight thirty p.m. to nine thirty p.m. That's nice of them. If they *are* aliens, they're doing well to make us feel at home. It's not so bad, but then we haven't had to *do* anything yet. The doing of things could be catastrophic. And do you know who they've bunked me with?

No, seriously, do you know? Because I don't have a clue who any of these people are. There are four bunk beds per dorm, so that's seven other girls besides me. They seem OK, some of them are dreading the day activities as much as I am! The sixth formers seem cool, too. They came with us from Duke John Jameson, they're in year twelve and thirteen and they're just here to help at meal times and things. I thought they wouldn't want to talk to us because we're so young, like how Frogsplash never talks to me seriously, he just winds me up. But I guess being that bit older makes the sixth form more mature because they talk to us like equals and I appreciate that.

Tuesday 15th October 2019

This morning was OK, I guess. Breakfast wasn't nice, though. Usually, I have toast for breakfast every day; sometimes with eggs, beans or jam, but usually just butter. I wouldn't say I'm a fussy eater, but there really is no excuse for bad toast. It should be toasted just enough to get a bit of colour on it and, of course, it should be toasted evenly, up and down and on both sides. But the most important thing is that it's hot when you spread the butter on it so that the butter melts into the bread and makes it soft and moist. Otherwise, what you have is dry bread with fat smeared on the top. It needs to *absorb* the butter, like a crumpet.

Personally, I like to spread the butter right to the edge, even on the crusts, because there's nothing worse than dry toast, even if it's just one part of the slice. I think this is a girl thing though, because when Frog or Dad make toast, they just slap one blob of butter in the middle and barely spread it at all. It was the same when Dad used to make my packed lunches: there'd be filling right in the centre of the sandwich and then nothing at all anywhere else. Maybe it's because they always eat everything in one great big mouthful, so they don't care where the butter is as long as it's somewhere on the bread.

Anyway, at breakfast today, all the toast was on these metal toast racks, stone cold and stale-looking. They had those little pots of butter you get in some restaurants (at least it wasn't margarine) but it was straight out of the fridge and you couldn't spread it at all on the horrible cold toast, which was a bit over-done if you ask me. On the upside, this did give me something to talk about when one of the girls from my dorm called me over to sit with her and the others. Don't worry, I didn't go on about toast in *too* much detail, even I'm not that socially inept! But complaining about things is always a safe conversation starter.

"This toast is completely cold and rock solid – how am I meant to spread the butter?" I said.

"I know!" said the girl in a croaky, raspy sort of voice. "I heard that whatever food doesn't get eaten gets put out again the next day, so it might not even be fresh!"

"Ew! I hope that's just a rumour!"

"Probably – there's always old tales people make up about these places. I overheard some boy on the coach yesterday saying that a few years ago a kid from another school got attacked by a bear while she was here – can you believe that? Bears in the Isle of Wight!"

"Ridiculous!" I laughed. "My name's Samantha, by the way, but you can call me, Sam."

"I'm Danielle," she said. "But everyone calls me Danny." Danny had paper-white skin and light blonde hair in a French braid, as well as a mouth full of metal braces like Frogsplash. "Ha – Sam and Danny, we sound like we should be in the boys' dorm!"

"Ha, no thanks; if they're anything like my brother, they won't shower all week and then try to cover up the smell with body spray."

"Gross! How old is he?"

"He'll be fifteen in a few weeks."

"Oh God – a teenager! I have younger brothers, Jim and Finn – they're twins and they're a *nightmare*. What's your brother's name?"

"Well, officially it's Fred, but, don't laugh…"

And so, despite the distressing toast situation, the day got off to a good start. The rest of the morning was spent 'getting to know' the grounds. It's mostly muddy fields, if you really want to know. There's one adventure playground that we'll probably never get to go on, there's an empty hall, and apparently, we'll be travelling a few miles down the road to do archery on Thursday, and that's about it.

Somehow, during this tour of the campsite, they missed the go-kart course. I was not aware of the go-kart course. I suppose they'd planned it as a 'fun' surprise for this afternoon, because presumably normal kids enjoy go-karting. Am I the only eleven-year-old who has no idea how to control or steer a motorised vehicle single-handedly! It was terrifying! The track was rocky, and they hardly taught me anything before they shoved me in the seat, on my own, with literally *everybody* watching me crash and burn in a mad panic which probably had them all pointing and laughing, though I was far too busy trying not to *die* to register their reactions.

I didn't even want to do it in the first place, but they gave me no choice. Who are these people anyway, who come and work at these resorts in the middle of nowhere, all sodden with mud, torturing school children, living in huts – do they even have families? No. Their families are still back on their home planet; they are yet to arrive. But they will come, once they've worn down the human children. The children are the future, they are thinking, wear us down and leave the rest to die out. Make us suffer with these pointless challenges until we succumb to their bizarre customs and rituals. Go-karts: the mode of transportation favoured by the modern life-form.

Wednesday 16th October 2019

Well, today was another mixed bag. You know something's wrong when they make you all wear your waterproof trousers, wellies and raincoat when it's not even raining. Then they gave us all blindfolds and told us to put them on. Then they had this long rope and we all had to hold onto it and walk, following instructions from the leader, who passed it on to the person behind and then they did the same and so on and so on. Never in my life have I felt more like I was walking to my own execution.

This is it. This is how I die. I always knew I'd die from a team-building exercise.

The reason for the weatherproof outfit was that there were tunnels to crawl through and nets to wriggle under, with plenty of mud underfoot (and under hand, knee and belly. Ugh.) It was basically a military boot camp exercise. The instructions that came from the girl in front of me were, understandably, stilted and nervous, because she was blindfolded too, and she was feeling her way and at the same time having to listen to the person in front of her. And then *I* had to try and pass on *those* instructions. And then, to top it all off, they started chucking cold water all over us! It was an incredibly stressful situation, which I imagine is a useful thing to get used to if you're preparing to enter a warzone. As far as I know, the Isle of Wight is not war-torn right now, and even if it was, I'd like to think they wouldn't send a bunch of eleven-year-olds to defend it.

So that was an awful experience from which I learned nothing. We showered, had an underwhelming lunch and then it was time for the afternoon's 'surprise'. I've never much liked surprises; I think the idea of a surprise party has to be one of my biggest nightmares, what could be worse than finally getting home to some peace and solitude after a long day, only to discover your house is full of people, you can't hide and you have to be 'on' socially for the rest of the day when you were all prepared to withdraw happily in your room where you can *breathe?* That's got to be the worst thing ever – even worse than whatever the hell that thing was we did this morning.

The biggest surprise of the afternoon's surprise was that it was fun. It wasn't messy, it wasn't awkward, it was something I've never tried before, and I *enjoyed* it. It was trampoline basketball and it was awesome! I think I was pretty good at it too; my team won, but the rules weren't exactly clear! It's typical though: I finally find a sport I enjoy, and I'll probably never get to play it again! Still, it was good fun and I even liked playing as a team. Now I must wonder, why do they make most team-building exercises so horrible, like this morning when we were basically treated like hostages, or the one at school where we had to fall backwards into the arms of someone we'd just met?

The best part of the day was still to come, though. At dinner I sat with the girls from my dorm again. There's Danny, who I chatted with yesterday morning, and then there's Alexa, Nefa, Caroline, Vicky, Anne and Jan (Anne = dark, curly hair; Jan = blonde – need to remember that). Over our dinner of unidentified brown substance, we began to build *our* team.

"So, you know how we were talking about stupid rumours and old stories about this place?" Danny said to me.

"Yeah?"

"Well, there are certain ones that are true, so I'm told."

"Who told you?" I asked, intrigued. "And which ones? Not the bear!"

"No, not the bear!" she laughed. "The sixth formers told me at lunch that when they were here in year seven, they performed some of the greatest pranks of all time."

And that's when we got the attention of all the other girls.

"It's true!" said Alexa. "My sister's in year ten and she did the same – it's tradition: the girls prank the boys and vice versa. I didn't want to say anything in case I was the only one who was into it, but I actually brought some supplies with me."

And so, as soon as bedtime reading hour struck and the teachers and site workers finally went off duty, we all sneaked into the boys' toilets as quietly as we could to set up our pranks.

"OK," said Alexa. "These little red pellets are full of concentrated dye. All you have to do is unscrew the shower head, put the pellet in, and tomorrow morning all the boys will be showering in blood!"

"Amazing!" we all said gleefully.

"And if we're lucky, the blonde ones might come out with pink hair too!"

"Awesome!"

Between the eight of us, we made light work of it. It was so much fun! My heart was racing, in fact, it still *is* – the thought of getting caught had the adrenaline pumping through my body, and the mental image of the boys showering tomorrow morning is just glorious!

Wait, that came out wrong. I am *not* picturing the boys showering.

Anyway, that wasn't the only thing Alexa had planned.

"We don't want to push our luck," she said. "So, we'll just pour some of this olive oil on the floor and then go, yeah?"

"Wait, what?" I said. "Olive oil on the floor?"

"Yeah, so they'll slip over!" she said.

"That seems kind of dangerous," said Jan.

"Yeah, they could really hurt themselves, the floor is ceramic or something," Nefa said.

"Oh yeah," said Alexa. "Fair point."

"That is a shame though," said Danny. "I was having so much fun; I want to do more!"

"I have an idea," I said. "How about we empty all the soap dispensers and refill them with the olive oil – that way when they wash their hands they'll get all greasy!"

"That's genius!" said Danny, and so we got to work. It was a messy job, and surprisingly tiring, because we had to pump all the soap out one squeeze at a time. But we took it in turns and eventually we emptied them all. Alexa filled them all up with olive oil while the rest of us washed away all the soap.

"Brilliant!" said Anne. "But there's just one problem."

"What?" we asked.

"How many boys do you know who actually wash their hands *with soap*?"

"Oh, my God, you're right!" said Danny. "My brothers *never* do!"

"Neither does mine," I said. "Unless…"

"Unless what?" they all whispered eagerly.

"The only time he washes his hands properly is after he's put on his hair gel. And look – they've left loads of tubes of the stuff here! Why don't we cover all the tubes of toothpaste and all the toothbrush handles with hair gel, then when they go to brush their teeth their hands will get greasy, then they'll go to wash them with the 'soap' and they'll get even greasier!"

"Sam, you're a pranking genius!" said Danny, and once more we all got to work.

It was amazing working with the girls like that – all day long doing 'team-building' exercises and I didn't bond with a single person, but in less than an hour of setting up pranks, I felt like I was really part of something. I feel *wonderful*. Incredibly, after all that activity and far too much talking, we managed to slip back into our dorm before nine thirty p.m. They'll be here any minute now to turn the lights off. Can't wait for morning to come!

It was EPIC! They *screamed* when they saw the red water coming out of the showers! Then, once they realised they'd been pranked, they all had a good laugh with it, splashing each other and so on. But then, would you believe it, one of them claimed that *he* had set up the prank! How dare he? All our hard work! But then of course it backfired, as one of the others had brought water balloons with him and so they all started filling them up with the red water and throwing them at him! We're all a little worried that they might have some water balloons saved for us though.

I don't know if it was just because it was my idea, but I think the greasy hands bit was the best part. Once they realised that they'd been pranked *again* they kept squirting out the olive oil and trying to get each other with it, rubbing it on their clothes or in their hair. It must have got *everywhere*! I felt a little bad for the cleaners, and for the one boy that slipped over, but it was the boys' fault for getting carried away with it like that!

It was amazing to see them all turn up at breakfast, some of them sporting pink highlights and all of them with greasy hair and covered in greasy handprints. We tried not to pay too much attention or to giggle too much so as not to raise suspicion, but it was so hard not to smirk at the sight of them – they looked ridiculous! They seemed to have taken it in good spirits, too, because they were still joking around and acting silly when they walked in, and I guess because of that the teachers thought that they were the ones responsible. They didn't get in too much trouble though, Mr Achilles, our History teacher, told them off for 'getting carried away with the hair gel' and told them to calm down and act sensible as he'd be keeping a close eye on them for the rest of the trip.

There were no team-building exercises today (the stupid grown-ups probably thought that by the last day, we'd all be one big happy family. Ugh.) We did archery this morning (I wasn't very good) then went on a long country walk, and my group was led by Mr Achilles himself, as well as Sherry and Morgan, the sixth formers. I like walking; obviously I prefer to do it alone, but I enjoyed it today, Mr Achilles is a funny guy. He kept making up fake historical facts about the landmarks we walked past.

"And if you look to your left, you'll see the dog poo bin commemorating the spot where Prince William proposed to the Duchess of Cambridge…"

I probably laughed a bit too hard at that, because everyone seemed to turn and look at me, apart from Mr Achilles, who carried on being our faithful guide. The other girls weren't listening to him; they were too busy swooning over Morgan, who was wearing a very tight shirt and is apparently the best football player the school's ever seen. He was acting as though he was the best football player in the world! He kept talking about himself and they were all lapping it up, apart from Sherry, the other sixth former, who kept rolling her eyes and trying to remind him that this was a *year seven* school trip and it was meant to be about us!

I ended up walking at the front with Mr Achilles on the way back, which is probably a weird thing to do but I enjoyed it. He doesn't seem much like a teacher, really. He has scruffy hair that sticks up in no style, and he's never clean-shaven, always with a bit of stubble. At school, he wears funky ties – my favourite is the green one with the melon slices on it. But here on the trip he's been wearing t-shirts with old album covers or retro cartoon characters on them. We had dinner at five p.m., then we all rushed back to get changed and ready for the last night disco at six p.m. I didn't really know what to expect from the disco; I wasn't really looking forward to it before, it was obviously going to be the usual awkward dancing and hovering around the refreshments table like it was at my year six leavers' party, but I thought I might as well get into the spirit of it, what choice did I have?

Some of the girls brought make-up with them, but you could tell they weren't really used to using it because they kept messing it up.

"Oh my God, I look like I've got two black eyes!" said Vicky.

"Here, let me help," I said. "You don't want to cover the whole eyelid with a dark colour like that, especially not on young faces like ours. You just do the lash line, see? And then you find a lighter shade in the same palette and you brush that over the rest of the lid. Then you find the lightest shade and that goes above the lid up to the brow, then you use the brush to blend where the different colours meet."

"Woah, that's amazing!" the others stood around in awe, watching and learning. It turns out I didn't forget everything from that night I got drunk – Jessica taught me well! It was nice to take part in that way, with everyone around me encouraging and appreciating my efforts. If only all human interaction could be that positive! Perhaps I have been unlucky in the past, or maybe I've been lucky on this trip. Don't get me wrong, it hasn't changed me. It might have changed the way I feel about other people though – just a bit.

There must be something about putting on make-up that makes young girls think about boys, because Jessica always talks about all her crushes on make-up Thursdays and before long, this lot started to do the same. Apparently, Vicky fancies Rob Battley, one of the boys who like to torment me on the school bus. There was no way I was going to tell them all about my public transport humiliation, so I withdrew from the conversation and faded back into the background where I belong, eventually leaving alone to go to the dance.

People seemed a lot more comfortable with themselves and with the whole disco arrangement than they had been at the last one I went to. Everyone seems to have lost that awkwardness, everyone apart from me, that is. I didn't want to be the only loser sitting down, but there was no snack table to hover around, so I just stood near the wall like a spare part, watching the others and trying to figure out a way to infiltrate the group seamlessly so that no one would notice my sudden involvement. It occurred to me that I was drawing more attention to myself by *not* dancing – and something had to be done about that.

I thought back to that film I watched with Dad, *American High School,* and how the kids in that film were always partying and dancing, completely uninhibited, and I thought, how can I be like that? Well, in the film they're always drunk. *Yes, Samantha, because that worked out so well for you last time.* And then I realised something, they weren't *drunk*, were they? They were *acting*. It was just a film. So that's what I need to do; I need to *act*.

So, I got myself a cup of water (for some reason having something in my hand made me feel more comfortable) and I did my best to glide into the groups of dancing kids and blend in, waving my arms about stupidly, trying to remind my body of this thing we call *dance*. I pretended I was someone else, someone who wouldn't care if anyone was watching or what they were thinking. I tried to shut out the voice in my head that tells me I should be hiding, and I think it worked, because some of the girls from my dorm came over and started dancing with me, and then it didn't feel anywhere near as bad.

We danced for a while and I started to get really into character, I really didn't care what people thought of me because I *wasn't* me; I was Brooke Adams, the American teen girl living life to the full! I was cheery, energetic, Brooke Adams, social butterfly; and I was letting loose! No one seemed to notice; we were all just enjoying ourselves right up until eight p.m., when the lights went dim and a slow and soppy song came on that none of us knew how to dance to and so we all started to disperse.

Well, almost all.

Right in the middle of the dance floor two people remained. Apparently over the course of the school trip, a romance had been blossoming, and apparently, I was the last to know. Not that I cared. The only thing that bothered me was the way other people watched them, like they were the cutest couple ever, like they were *angels* or something.

But I know the truth. Jake Atkinson and Beth Amory are no angels.

<u>Thursday 24th October 2019</u>

Well, it's been almost a full week of school and things have almost returned to normal, except for everybody's favourite power couple flaunting their puppy love everywhere, and everyone else lapping it up like the dopey dogs that they are. I have been saying hi to the girls from my dorm whenever I walk past them, and I got to work with Alexa and Nefa in Biology on Tuesday, but I'm still going solo when I have any choice in the matter. I am still me, after all.

Friday 25th October 2019

SCHOOL TRIP HAS YEAR SEVEN IN HIGH SPIRITS!

This year's Isle of Wight trip was a huge success, with many new friendships being made as well as one very happy couple! The first years went out with a bang with some wild celebrations at the last night disco.

And there I am, right on the front page, the one celebrating wildly in that huge photo. Oh, dear God, no. I did not write this article, and I'm not the only one who can see it.

I've checked the online version of the school newspaper and I'm there too, along with some photos of Jake and Beth and some of the activities we did earlier on in the week. I try to see if there are any better ones of me, just to try and make up for it, but all I can find is a photograph of our group from the long country walk with Mr Achilles, but they cut me out of the picture so that they could get all of Morgan in the frame.

It could not be worse. There I was, being uninhibited, carefree Brooke Adams, but on the outside, I was sweaty, uncoordinated, arm-flailing, mouth-gaping, Samantha Drury, and she's the one who's paying for it now. Behind me in the photo Jake and Beth are dancing together, not the slow dance at the end but a fun, happy dance. They're both smiling, laughing maybe, but they don't look defective or red-faced at all; they look beautiful. Underneath the photo was the brief caption: 'Year sevens were in high spirits at the Last Night Disco last week'.

There's no doubt about it, though, I was the intended subject. My whole body is in the photo, right in the foreground, you can see every bead of sweat on my giant tomato, dough-ball face. I scrolled down to the bottom of the page to see who did this to me. Charlotte Henderson, year seven editor for the school paper. I didn't even know year sevens *could* be editors – the school paper is just about the only club I'd want to join! I flick to the back page, where there are headshots of all the editors, and there she is, Charlotte Henderson, and I recognise her too. She's one of Beth's cronies. *Of course she is.*

Well, I don't want to be on the school paper now; not with Charlotte.

It's the first time year seven have made the front page of the school paper since we all joined the school; usually it's about year ten concerts or year eleven exams, so of course this was a big deal to everyone in my year. Of course, it wouldn't go under the radar – nothing bad ever does. And that photo is *bad.* I have heard sniggering as I walk down the corridor and people are saying hi to me who never used to, but they're smirking so I know they're just mocking me. Beth and Rob and their entire entourage didn't even try to hide it when they were pointing and laughing at me by the lockers after lunch, and to top it all off in History this afternoon Mr Achilles said, 'Hey Samantha, still in high spirits?" and everyone laughed.

If only I had been born in the middle ages, I'd probably have died as an infant. They had it so easy back then.

I know what they say about today's news being tomorrow's chip paper, but people don't use old newspapers for fish and chips anymore, and anyway, we have the internet now. The good news is it's Friday today and half term next week; let's hope today's school news is next week's school library scrap paper, at least.

Thursday 31st October 2019

It's Frogsplash's birthday party today. I'm not sure how normal it is for a fifteen-year-old to have a full-blown party at home, unless they happen to be a Latin-American girl, but Frogsplash was born on Halloween, and in this house, we *love* Halloween. It started when Frog was seven and he wanted to go trick-or-treating for the first time. Mum hates the idea of trick-or-treating because it's basically going around to people's houses demanding food you don't need.

She told us about her aunt Ruby who lived around the corner from us before I was born. Her husband had been dead for several years and she was living on a basic pension. She couldn't afford to buy sweets for all the kids in the neighbourhood, and by the sounds of it, they were all horrible brats anyway. So, these teenagers came trick-or-treating and she had to tell them sorry, but she didn't have anything to give them. So, they egged her house and I'm talking *a lot* of eggs.

Aunt Ruby was only a little old lady, and she was frail and all on her own; she couldn't reach all the dried egg that they'd splattered all over her house, so she called Mum and Dad the next day and asked them to help clean the front doors and windows with her. When they arrived, she was still shaking; she was an absolute wreck, so Mum says. So, Mum made them all some tea and tried to calm her nerves while Dad got to work on the egg-stained windows. Ruby was really, really distressed, and after that she wouldn't come to the door when you knocked unless you called in through the letterbox to say it was you.

After hearing that story, I can understand why Mum hates trick-or-treating – at best it's greedy, but it can be so much worse. If kids turn nasty, when they don't get what they want, that's when it's gone too far. Everyone should have the right to say no.

And that's exactly what Mum said to Frogsplash (who was just Fred back then) when he asked to go trick-or-treating. The only reason he even wanted to go was so that he could wear his Batman costume, so Mum decided to throw a huge party for him instead and invited his friends as well as most of the kids from the neighbourhood – that way, they'd be off the streets and not harassing innocent old ladies.

And so, it became tradition. Dad used to get really into it too, trying to scare us kids by eating boiled eggs that looked like eyeballs and telling us this story called 'Jonny, I want my liver back' which always massively creeped us out! But, of course, he won't be coming this year. We're too old for all that stuff now anyway.

This week also happens to be half term, so we can have the party on his actual birthday, which is today, Thursday. This is perfect, because we get to do a special Halloween edition of Thursday make-up club with gruesome monster make-up – even Frog says he wants to get involved! It'll be my first time back at the club since the incident with the rum. Mum says she's told them not to bring it up.

"Don't worry about that," said Frog. "Sam already brought it up... all over Trudy's make-up samples!"

Ha. Ha. Ugh.

But maybe I should try and make a joke out of it. That's how I cope with things in my head, right? *Try not to stress, Sam, go and enjoy the party.*

<u>Thursday 31st October 2019 (later)</u>

"How does it look?" Mum asked as she was finishing up with the spooky decorations in the living room.

"Great!" I said. "Aunt Ruby would be proud!"

"Who?" she asked.

"You know, your old Aunt Ruby!"

"Oh, I'd forgotten all about that!" she laughed. "I never had an Aunt Ruby. I made the whole thing up!"

My entire childhood is based on lies. Does Frogsplash know about this?

Apart from that shocking revelation, the evening went well. I went as a pirate, and that was the perfect excuse to make loads of rum jokes, and the make-up group loved it! Mum invited a few new people this week because she's thinking about branching out to face painting. Like I said before, we always go big on Halloween, so we're pretty good at face painting. I painted on my own beard first and then I got to do Frog's zombie make-up. First, I painted his whole face a pallid sort of yellow, then I gave him dark shadows to make it look like his cheeks were sunken.

"Woah, that's amazing!" Jessica said. "His face looks so gaunt!"

"Cool," Frog said when he looked in the mirror.

"Hang on, I haven't finished yet; let me give you some scars."

"That's so realistic!" Jessica continued. "If you can do that, I bet you could do contouring."

"What's contouring?" I asked.

"Sounds cont-*boring*!" said Frogsplash. Jessica ignored him. I don't think she fancies him anymore – I think she's realised that even though he's older, he is in no way mature.

"It's for older girls and women really," she went on. "My mum does it. It's where you use darker and lighter shades of skin tone make-up to change the way the shape of your face looks. So, like how you've used dark shadow under your brother's cheekbone to make his face look thinner."

"Oh, I see," I said. "I really could've used some of that before they took pictures of me on my school trip!"

"Oh no!" she said. "There's nothing worse than when people take photos of you when you're not ready."

"Oh really?" I said. "Try having those photos being published in the *school paper*!"

"No way! You poor thing!"

And just like that, I was back in the comfort zone with Jessica and the rum incident was forgotten.

As the evening progressed, she and I settled in to a game of people-watching. At first, we watched Frogsplash and his friends showing off to each other. Mum had bought them two cans of beer each to keep them away from the wine and other alcohols, but we saw them sneaking a few cups of punch.

"Should we tell your mum?" Jessica asked.

"No. Frog and I have a sort of unspoken sibling code: I only tell on him if he's doing something that's going to be bad for me, and he does the same."

"Makes sense," she said. "I don't have any brothers or sisters; it's nice the way you look out for each other."

"Also," I went on. "If he gets drunk, I can get him back for filming that video of me throwing up!"

At one stage, they all started wrestling on the living room floor, and Jessica thought it was hilarious. Billy, Joshua and Hayden were in a tangled mess on the carpet and Frogsplash was standing on the sofa looking over them like a king surveying his subjects.

"You're going to see it any second now," I said to Jessica.

"See what?"

"Where Frogsplash got his nickname from."

And right on cue he leapt off the sofa, arms and legs spread like a frog in mid-air, and landed on top of the pile of half-drunk teenagers on the floor, who all moaned in pain when he fell on them. I was sure Mum was going to intervene any minute, but when I looked over to the other side of the room, I saw she was far too busy chatting away and giggling with a man I'd never seen before. My attention turned quickly to the adults, who were far drunker than Frog and his mates, and starting to show it too.

"Have you seen the state of your carpet?" Jessica said. "Your brother and his friends have smeared face paint all over it!"

"Never mind that; look at the state of my mum!" I replied.

"What do you mean?" she said.

"Just look at her giggling away like a school girl; she must be really drunk!"

"Well... it could be that..."

"What? What do you mean?"

"I hope you don't mind me saying this, but I'm not sure she *is* drunk. I think maybe she's giggling like a school girl because she likes that man she's talking to."

"Oh my God!"

"Are you OK?" she asked, worried she'd said the wrong thing.

"Yeah, I'm fine. It's just... this is so weird! But it's good. She deserves to be happy."

"Take it from me; it's *definitely* a good thing. My mum and dad split up when I was a baby and my mum dated quite a few men since then. When she's got a boyfriend, she's way happier and she's usually too wrapped up in it to notice what I get up to! It's basically a free pass to do what you want."

"Nice!"

"But if they do start going out, be prepared for the fact that he might not stick around. My mum usually gets bored after a few months and dumps them!"

"OK, well let's not get too carried away; we don't even know if he likes her back yet!"

"Do you know who he is?" asked Jessica.

"No; I've never seen him before. He must be a work friend or something."

"That's good. He *must* like her. You don't go to a work friend's son's birthday party if you don't like them!"

"I don't know if I want him to like her yet! I don't know if I like *him* yet!"

"Oh, I'm sure he's nice! Look at the way he's looking into your mum's eyes!"

"Yuck, too lovey-dovey – I'd rather watch Frogsplash picking eyeballs out of his braces!" I showed Jessica where I was looking, and there was Frogsplash showing off to his friends by trying to fit as many boiled egg eyeballs into his mouth at once. It was beyond gross; it was *grotesque*. He managed about four and then spluttered most of them out onto the carpet, which the others found hilarious. He swallowed what was left in his mouth then let out a huge, eggy, beery burp. *Disgusting.*

The party started to die down around nine thirty p.m. when most of Frogsplash's friends got picked up, but Jessica stayed later because her mum was having far too much fun on the dance floor to go home. Billy, Joshua and Hayden are staying over so they're still here, I can hear them messing about in Frog's room.

But here's the interesting thing, just before I went up to bed, mum's mystery man came into the living room from the kitchen, and this is what he said, "I'm off home now, Billy, don't stay up too late, and don't make too much noise. I'll be back in the morning to pick you up, but we're going to stay and help Frogsplash's mum clean up, OK? You lot have made a right mess in here."

"Oh, all right! Goodnight, Dad," Said Billy. *Dad!*

"Goodnight, son!" he replied. *Son!* He's Billy's dad! If he and Mum start going out, Frogsplash is going to *freak out! Brilliant!*

Monday 4th November 2019

Back at school and things seem to have blown over re. the terrible photo in the school paper, *thank God.* Today was a typical Monday; the most exciting thing that happened was me getting a hole in the toe of my tights and my big toe poking through the hole and the fabric pulling tightly every time I took a step, so it felt like it was going to cut my toe off. Tights are the worst. I can never find the right size – they're either too small and the crotch comes right down to my knees or they're too big and they keep sliding down. I think I might be wearing a pair of mum's tights today; if I pull them up, they can easily stretch to the bottom of my training bra. *Training bra, because my tweeny boobs need to be 'trained' like a dog that disobeys its owner. Naughty wayward mammaries – how dare you protrude from the torso in that recalcitrant manner! You must be trained to stay in place so as not to distract boys!*

I'm looking forward to tomorrow, at least. Tomorrow we have History with Mr Achilles. We didn't do a lot of History in primary school, and when we did, it was just facts and dates, and I'm so bad at memorising stuff I find boring that I always thought I was just rubbish at History. But Mr Achilles teaches us about the *people* from history, the ones involved in whatever we're learning; he tells us about their lives and experiences and helps us to imagine what it would have been like back then; he explains to us the impact these people have had on the world, and that's amazing stuff to think about.

It helps that he's a funny guy, too. He's just so *engaging,* I find myself hanging on his every word. I'm always disappointed when the lesson's over. I can't wait to see what he's written in my workbook about my essay on the Battle of Hastings; I worked hard on it. I really want him to like me. I mean *it…* I want him to like *IT.* I mean… Oh God… oh no.

SHOCK HORROR! PATHETIC PRE-TEEN DEVELOPS INFATUATION WITH SCHOOL TEACHER!

In a move which has shocked the nation, an eleven-year-old girl has decided to fancy an attractive, older gentleman with an easy confidence and good sense of humour. Reports suggest that this is a world first for all of humanity, citing evidence from the past two hundred thousand years which shows that this incident is completely unparalleled, and we may not see its like again in several dozen millennia. The girl in question, who cannot be named for legal reasons, is thought to be of stable mind and in good health despite the dramatic revelation that she is, in fact, a complete idiot...

This is the most embarrassing thing ever. I have a crush on my History teacher. If this gets out, it'll be worse than the Isle of Wight photo! What's happening to me? I don't get crushes! I've been spending too much time with Jessica Palmer, she's rubbing off on me! And it just *had* to be a teacher, didn't it? So, cliché. This is the first time I've ever felt worried that someone might read my diary. If Frog ever gets his hands on it, my life is OVER. When I was younger, I loved the idea of having a secret diary. I had one of those ones with the little padlock on it. The only problem was I didn't have any secrets to write in it. I was *desperate* for a secret. Little did I know how burdensome they truly are!

Tuesday 5th November 2019

Well, I saw Mr Achilles today and let me tell you, the sparks were flying.

But that was because he gave us a special lesson on the gunpowder plot and he ended it all with some indoor fireworks that were probably in violation of health and safety codes, because he told us not to tell anyone – what a rebel! It was awkward though. Now that *I'm* aware of the fact that I fancy him, I feel like everyone else will be able to see it, too, *especially* Mr Achilles. When he's talking to me, I look him straight in the eye and suddenly I'm conscious of that. Do I always look a teacher in the eye when they're talking to me? It feels weird with Mr Achilles; I feel like he can sense the intensity of it.

I suppose there's not much point worrying about that anyway – even if he can tell that I fancy him he'd never, *ever* bring it up. What I should be worrying about is if one of the other kids notices, because they *will* bring it up, and they will torment me with it. It's lucky it was a special lesson really, because if I were to be tested on it later, I'd fail. With all these thoughts swimming round my head, I couldn't focus on anything! Apart from the fireworks – they were a welcome distraction. But now, every time I hear a firework go off outside, I think of him and it makes my heart flutter. Why do we even celebrate bonfire night?

A failed act of treason resulting in a torturous execution, it's not exactly Christmas!

Wednesday 6th November 2019

It's freezing outside now, proper winter weather, but Mum's refusing to buy me a thicker coat.

"Wear your school blazer under your jacket," she said. "Wearing layers is a much more effective way of keeping warm."

"But girls don't wear the school blazer in my school; they just *don't*! It's just not cool!"

"That blazer was the most expensive item on your school uniform list. You will wear it!"

Ugh. I will NOT wear it. I would rather freeze.

Later, waiting for the school bus.

Ugh. I will wear it. I would not rather freeze. Brrrrrrrr…

Thursday 7th November 2019

I don't know what I was so worried about; it's not like I had much to lose. I deliberately avoid social interaction so I'm hardly Miss Popular. I am *taciturn.* I am *misanthropic.* And as much as people might have stopped talking about the photo of me at the disco, it pretty much determined my social status for the rest of my entire life (thanks, Charlotte Henderson). I quite like the blazer, it has loads of pockets for my phone, my headphones, my lip balm, my keys, my bus pass… And I guess it does keep me warm. The thing I don't like is standing out.

I was in the girls' toilets at the end of lunch and Danny, the girl from my dorm on the trip, said to me, "Hey, you look cool!"

I was so taken aback I just blurted out, "So do you!"

Even though she was clearly referring to my blazer, and she clearly wasn't wearing one. This is why I prefer to be a wallflower.

In other news, I'm finally over my crush on Mr Achilles. I guess it was just one of those fleeting infatuations. Just kidding; I'm going to love him forever! But that's a good thing, because one day I'll be twenty and he'll be forty and the age gap won't be such a big deal. For now, though, I just want to impress him in any and every way I can. It still haunts me knowing that he's seen *that* photo. I will never forget his words, "Hey Samantha, still in high spirits?"

Ugh. Worse than ugh. *Shudder.*

Monday 11th November 2019

I can never wear my blazer again. I usually go to the library at lunchtime but today it was reserved for kids working on the school paper, so I had to go elsewhere. I ate my lunch quickly in the dining hall and then I decided to go for a walk by the lake, seeing as I'd be warm enough in my many layers. I was just thinking how nice it was that we have a bit of nature on our school grounds that we can enjoy whenever we want, when I heard someone shouting at me.

"Hey!" it was a girl's voice, but I couldn't see where it was coming from. "HEY!" she yelled again.

And then, in a big cloud of smoke, four girls emerged from the wooded area behind the lake. They all wore school blazers with the sleeves rolled up, despite the cold, and they'd covered them in badges and sewn-on patches. None of them was wearing the school tie. The one in front had half of her hair shaved off; the other half was jet black. She chucked her cigarette on the floor and came right up to me.

"What do you think you're doing?" she said to me.

"Nothing! I'm just walking…"

"No. What do you think you're doing wearing that blazer? *No one* wears a blazer apart from us."

"But it's cold," I said, like a wimp.

"Oh no! She's *cold*!" she said, mockingly. "I don't care if you're cold. If I ever see you wearing it again, it's going in the lake."

She was making me angry now; she had no right to talk to me that way, to pick on a younger girl. She was a year ten, at least.

"I don't care," I said, more defiant now, less wimpy. "I don't even like it; if you throw it in the lake, my mum can't make me wear it anymore and then I won't look so stupid in my uniform."

"WHAT? Are you saying blazers look stupid? Are you saying *we* look stupid? How dare you! You don't get to talk to me like that, little girl! Take it off!"

And so, even though it terrified me, I locked my gaze on her, held her stare, my eyes focussing on her piercing blue ones surrounded in black eyeliner, and I took my blazer off and threw it on the ground. True to her word, the half-shaved girl picked up my blazer and threw it in the lake. Her retinue laughed like hyenas, but she wasn't satisfied. How could she be, all she'd done is exactly what I'd told her I wanted her to do. And I'd said she and her mates looked stupid in the process! I was winning!

"And your shoes," she said.

"What?" I replied.

"Take off your shoes."

"No way," I said.

"Either you take them off or we take them from you. Either way, they're going in the lake."

It was fight or flight time, and I couldn't take on four-year tens, so I ran. I ran back towards the school, knowing that there'd be teachers on patrol or at least some other witnesses to back me up. I'm not exactly fast, but I knew almost straight away that I'd made the right decision, because I could hear them coughing and wheezing behind me after less than a minute – they were smokers, after all.

"Oh my God, are you OK?" came a different, friendlier voice. "I was on the other side of the lake, I saw everything!"

"Yeah, I'm fine," I said, catching my breath. I turned to look at her. She was a little shorter than me with olive skin and long, black hair with thick, black eyelashes to match, standing in striking contrast to her bright, blue eyes. I don't know how I've never noticed her before.

"Come, let's get you inside, you must be freezing! I'll get you a hot chocolate in the canteen," she said with a smile.

"No, it's OK, that run warmed me up! Anyway, there's too many people in the canteen; I don't want them to see me all red-faced and out of breath!"

"You look fine!" she said. "But fair enough, I don't much like it in there either. Let's just go sit down somewhere."

She was being so nice, I could hardly say no.

"I'm sorry I didn't do anything to help," she said when we found an empty bench. "I was on the other side of the lake and I didn't know what to do."

"Don't be silly – there was nothing you could have done. Anyway, you're helping now."

"You were really brave standing up to them; they were terrifying! They're just a bunch of losers; all they do is stand around in the woods, smoking cigarettes and looking miserable."

"Do you go there a lot, then?"

"Most days, yeah. I haven't really made any friends here yet. My parents couldn't afford the Isle of Wight trip, so I missed out on all that bonding and stuff."

"So, you're in my year, then?"

"Yeah, my name's Carla."

"I'm Sam and don't worry, I *did* go on the Isle of Wight trip and I still didn't manage to make any friends!"

"Ha! It's not as easy as the teachers think, is it? Like when we were four and we first started school, we could just say, 'Hey, do you want to play with me?' and that's how you made a friend. I don't think that'll be quite as effective nowadays!"

"Ha, can you imagine if I'd said that to those girls by the lake? I think they'd have pushed me in!"

"Ha-ha!"

Just like I told that mean girl, I really don't care that I can never wear my blazer again. I may have lost a blazer, but I've gained a friend.

Tuesday 12th November 2019

Mum hasn't noticed my missing blazer yet, but it's only a matter of time. I can't tell her what really happened because she'll *definitely* contact the school about it and I know that'll come back around to haunt me. But if I tell her I just lost it, she won't believe me. It's times like these when Dad comes in handy. Dad, being the big kid that he is, understands the code of the playground, and when I tell him what happened, he won't get all worried and overprotective and have a breakdown about the woes of parenting and what the 'right thing to do' is. He'll probably laugh, knowing him. Dad is the perfect antidote to Mum, and Mum is the perfect antidote to Dad; it's a wonder they were ever married!

Back to today, though. I was sat in the library, where I like to believe I am anonymous, invisible even, but somehow my identity sneaked in with me this lunchtime.

"Sam!" said Carla. "I figured you'd be in here." She completely took me by surprise; I never told her I'd be in there, and I'd never seen her in there before. I felt exposed and a little imposed upon. I was safe in my bubble – the zone I get in when I'm deep inside my own head and forget that anybody else exists. But there she was, existing right in front of me. *Oh God, is she going to turn out to be a weirdo stalker?*

"Oh, hey!" I said, trying to conceal the fact that she'd just violently popped my bubble.

"It's OK, I'll leave you to it if you're busy," she said. So, she noticed, then. But I didn't mind. She said it like she meant it, like her feelings wouldn't have been hurt if I had said yes, I was too busy. *I don't think this one is a weirdo stalker. I think you're safe, Sam.*

"No, it's OK, I just wasn't expecting to see you. Before yesterday, I'd never even met you – now I see you twice in two days!"

"Well that's not by accident. I came looking for you. I remembered you said you didn't like the canteen, and I guessed you wouldn't be going back to the lake anytime soon, so I thought, where else could she possibly go? Somewhere quiet, I thought, and warm, too. And here you are!"

"Excellent detective work," I said. "I come here most days. It's not ideal, I usually sit on the floor because there aren't enough seats, but it's better than the canteen, and like you said, it's warm. I need all the warmth I can get now my blazer's sleeping with the fishes!"

She laughed at that, and that made me feel more at ease as I was talking to her.

"You're right, it's not ideal," she said. "But I think I know somewhere better – do you want to see?"

I was intrigued, and a good place to sit at lunchtime is a truly precious thing, in many ways invaluable, so I agreed. She led me in the direction of the music block, talking all the way.

"My sister told me about this place," she said, half-excited, half-anxious. "My oldest sister. She's in sixth form now so she's allowed to go out for lunch to the café or even the pub, but she and her friends used to come here every day to get away from all the other people in their year."

"I'd love to have a sister!" I said. "I got stuck with a moronic brother instead."

"Louisa's all right – we're more alike, anyway. My other sister, Rosie, is in year nine and she's an obnoxious brat. She spends every lunchtime in the canteen surrounded by her fan club. For some reason, she's incredibly popular. I guess she's not horrible, really, she's just so full of herself. I asked her about those girls from yesterday. I told her what they did to you – I hope you don't mind. She said you were brave, too. And she laughed at the part where you ran away and they couldn't catch you! She said she likes the sound of you – she admires a girl with confidence."

"Me? I'm not confident!"

"Well maybe not in the same arrogant way she is… in a *better* way. You know yourself. You stand up for yourself. Anyway, she told me all about those nasty girls. They're year elevens – that's *four years* older than us! The main one is Megan, and *everyone* fears her – even some of the teachers! She's been excluded from school at least five times but for some reason, they won't expel her. The other three are Ali, Fiona and Yasmin, and they're just her cronies. Those three are idiots, whereas Megan is apparently very smart. Maybe that's why they won't expel her. All in all, though, they're just a typical gang who get kicks out of intimidating other people. Stay away from them, Rosie says."

"I intend to!" I said, quite terrified reflecting on my close encounter from yesterday.

"Ah, here we are," she said triumphantly when at last we reached our destination. "Welcome to my place of respite!"

I was right about the music block. We were in a music room full of instruments, speakers, microphones and nice, comfy chairs, nothing like the ones we have in classrooms. It had no windows and pleasant lighting. It had a good *feel* to it.

"What is this place?" I asked.

"It's the soundproof room for when people want to record music or practise something loud like drums or opera singing. It's basically a recording studio minus all the flashy equipment. I come here to practise guitar sometimes, but it can get lonely. I like the idea of coming here with all my friends like Louisa used to."

"And it's soundproof so no one can hear you in here when you're not supposed to be – genius!"

"Exactly! They hardly ever use it anyway; it's just for random little music projects and the occasional audition."

"Nice, I love it!"

"Me too, it's so peaceful. And look, there's speakers so we can listen to music. You like music?"

"Of course I do! I don't go anywhere without my headphones."

"What kind of stuff do you like?"

"Punk rock, I guess. My favourite band is Free Parking."

"I *love* Free Parking! I have their latest album on my phone, I'll put it on."

111

"You buy *albums*?"

"Of course! I know it's old-fashioned and I suppose you take a risk not knowing what you're paying for, but it's totally worth it for the hidden gems. My dad is into music *big time* and when he was our age, you *had* to buy the album. He plays me a lot of his old stuff. It's a whole different experience just sitting back and playing a whole album back-to-back."

"I'll have to try it. So, do you like the old stuff your dad plays? The stuff my mum listens to is *dreadful*."

"Oh yeah, it's way better than what we have now. If you like Free Parking, I think you'll like The Clash. They're *unreal!* You want to listen?"

"I'd rather hear *you* play guitar."

"No! I've been talking non-stop as it is."

"Please? I love guitar!"

"Another time for sure," she said as she plugged her phone in to the speakers and put on something which must have been The Clash. "First tell me about this moronic brother of yours."

"Well for starters, his name is Frogsplash. I think he gave himself the nickname after his favourite wrestling move. I mean, who gives *themselves* a nickname? He's a wrestling fanatic; I keep telling him it's all staged and totally meaningless, but he doesn't care about anything of substance anyway…"

Friday 15th November 2019

BREAKING NEWS: MISANTHROPIC MINOR MAKES MIRACULOUSLY MAJOR MOVE!

The minor, who wishes to remain anonymous, both in the context of this article and in life in general, has opted to acknowledge the existence of another human being after she persisted to exist and could not be missed despite efforts to insist that she was not in her midst. What an unexpected twist!

Carla's easy to talk to. She doesn't just go on about herself the whole time, but she doesn't expect you to fill the silences either. There's something so natural about the way you have a conversation with her, she doesn't force it out of you and yet you find yourself nattering away, it's like she's a talk show host or something!

When you talk to other people in this school it's like a mind game. They never say what they mean; they're always guarded, like they're trying to figure out what angle you're really coming from and what it is you want from them. And they're waiting for you to slip up, too. I think they even try to trip you up sometimes, try to make you say something you'll regret so they can use it against you in some way later. It's exhausting always trying to second guess people. With Carla, though, you never have to read between the lines. She's genuine. She's rare.

I still go to the library on my own at lunchtime some days, but Carla doesn't mind, she's just happy when I do show up at the music room. Today I wanted to see her to tell her what happened in P.E. yesterday.

"It was excruciating," I began. "I got paired with Ruby Driscoll – do you know her?"

"Kind of," said Carla. "She's in my art class but I don't *know* her. I don't know anything about her except that she treats me like I'm from another planet. No... it's not another planet... it's more like we're in parallel universes. Yeah, it's like we both exist in the same world and yet it's impossible that we could ever occupy the same space. Does that make sense?"

"Yes!" I replied. "It's like she thinks she's on a higher plane than the rest of us; like there's something wrong with us and she's worried she might catch it if she associates with us in any way. Of course, the problem was she *had* to acknowledge my existence yesterday because we had to play tennis against each other."

"Ohhhh *shudder* that must have been awful! What was it like?"

"OK, well, here's the thing, I've never played tennis before. My mum's not sporty and my dad only likes football, so it's hardly surprising. I've never even *watched* tennis before, so I was learning everything for the first time. And you know what I learned?"

"What?"

"That Ruby Driscoll has her own tennis court *at home.* She has a tennis coach and she plays tennis competitively *all the time.*"

"NOOOOOOOO!"

"I almost felt bad for her having to play against me, but she didn't seem too worried about it when she was celebrating her victory before the match was even over. She kept rolling her eyes when I couldn't serve the ball and I got so flustered because I kept missing it and she was watching me the whole time with such a look of contempt on her face that I found myself actually *apologising* to her!"

"Oh, you didn't!"

"Oh, but I did. It was awful."

"I hate P.E., but I hate Ruby Driscoll more. I'm going to confront her in Art this afternoon."

"You what? You can't do that!"

"Of course I can. I've been meaning to do it for ages, but because she's never actually *said* anything to me, I was wondering if the whole thing was all in my head! But now I know she's exactly who I thought she was."

"Yeah – she's a horrible person who revels in the failure of others – so I bet she's *waiting* for someone to call her up on it just so she can cut them down to size in front of an audience."

"Then I'll do the same to her! She doesn't scare me. She can treat me like I'm invisible if she wants but I won't let her treat my friend like that."

"Carla, you're amazing, but you're crazy!"

"I know. I just can't stand injustice. She has all this privilege, she has the advantage of an *actual* tennis court and a coach and she's acting like she's a better person; like she's got something in her core that's better than what you have in yours. I can't stand it, Sam!"

"OK, it sucks, I know, just please don't say anything. She's not worth it."

"OK, if that's what you want. But if you ever change your mind, just let me know. I can handle it, Sam, I have two older sisters and we were born in America, where people always speak their mind."

"You were born in *America*?"

"Yeah… I don't really remember it, but Louisa and Rosie do, or at least that's what they say. My dad is English, but he was working over there when he met my mum."

"Cool! So, your mum's American?"

"She's Puerto Rican, actually, but she was working in Miami and she has American citizenship so yeah, to put it simply!"

"That is *so cool*. My family is so boring. We come from nowhere and travel nowhere."

"It has its downsides. We hardly ever get to see Mum's side of the family, but when we do, it means a *huge* holiday. We're constantly saving up for plane tickets, but when we get there, it's totally worth it!"

"That sounds awesome! Whenever I visit family, it's never further than Sheffield, and most of the time, it's just thirty minutes down the road to see my dad."

"So, your parents are split up then?"

"Yeah they divorced about two years ago. Of course, it was a shock at the time, but now when I look at things, it seems mad to think they were ever together. They're so *different*."

"There must have been something they liked about each other once."

"Well, yeah. I guess the reason they're so different to each other now is that Mum's changed since they were together. She was always the responsible one of the two, but she was quirky with it. She used to do all these horribly embarrassing spontaneous things that Dad found hilarious. She's more serious now, always worrying about something. Meanwhile Dad has become even more immature now that he hasn't got the responsibility of full-time fatherhood."

"Parents are never perfect. My mum and dad argue about money all the time. Now, they're worrying about Louisa's university fees, plus she wants driving lessons but they're *so expensive*. I feel sorry for them having me *and* Rosie left to worry about as well!"

"It's weird, isn't it, how our parents are worrying about us from the day we're born, and then at some point somewhere along the way, we grow up and start worrying about *them* worrying about *us*."

"You're a great thinker, Sam!" she said laughing. "If only we could all stop worrying!"

Sunday 17th November 2019

Frog and I both stayed at Dad's this weekend and he took us on a shopping spree, so Frog could pick out his belated birthday presents. Everything is belated with Dad. Mum gets annoyed about it but it's nice having a second birthday and a second Christmas to look forward to after the main event is over. We're too old for the *magic* anyway.

In the car on the way to the shopping precinct, Dad asked me how school is going. Usually I just say 'fine' but this was the perfect opportunity to tell him about blazer-gate. As suspected, he found it amusing and offered to buy me a winter coat. *Result!* Even Frogsplash liked my story, his one-word review was 'impressive', which I like to think means that he's proud of me. As per our unwritten sibling agreement, he's not going to tell Mum what happened to the blazer.

Friday 22th November 2019

There's been a flu epidemic going around the school all week so there's hardly been anyone in. It's been pleasantly peaceful for a change. The only downside came this afternoon in German when I got paired with my now arch-nemesis, Charlotte Henderson. Remember her? One of Beth Amory's clan, the girl who deliberately put that awful photo of me on the front page of *The Daily Duke* (it's a weekly newspaper, it should obviously be called *The Jameson Journal,* but whatever).

Usually, Charlotte would have some other friend from her posse to work with, or at least someone higher up the social ladder than me, but they're all sick so she had to settle for me. *Poor Charlotte.* It wasn't a whole ordeal like with Ruby Driscoll and the tennis.

It was just two sentences that she said to me as I was walking over to sit at her desk, "Your hair's a bit greasy, isn't it? And you probably shouldn't wear your skirt that short."

She didn't say anything more than that, but for the rest of the lesson, I was fighting back tears. So many thoughts sped through my head. First, there was the shock of it, the sheer brazenness and callousness with which those words came flying out of her mouth, right in front of me, in the flesh, in real time, not through a friend or via the internet but directly and without shame, she said those things which she *knew* – she must have known – would hurt my feelings.

Then of course, I had to work with her, saying *'Guten Tag, wie heißt du?'* like nothing was bothering me; I just had to swallow it all down. And I wondered – what did she expect me to say to those comments? Did she *want* me to cry? Surely, she didn't think she was being *kind?* She knew I'd have to swallow it all down, and that was the bit she was enjoying the most.

Then, after the initial shock and bewilderment it reduced to the core of it. I'm disgusting because I don't wash my hair often enough and because I have fat, wobbly thighs at the age of eleven. Am I fat? I don't know. But my thighs are. If I were the type to read beauty magazines – which I'm not – I'd say my thighs were my problem area. But there's no problem with them, they work just fine. They can walk and run and swim and dance. They've never caused me any problems. Until now.

What bothered me the most, though, is that it bothered me. Why was it so easy for her to break me, just with a few curt words about my appearance? I've never strived to be the prettiest: beauty is not my interest, nor my currency.

My value is in my mind and in my nature. *She* may care about people's looks, and that makes her shallow. Her values are not my values. So why do I feel so devalued?

Thursday 29th November 2019

DRAMA FOR SAMANTHA AND CARLA, BUT THE LEVEL-HEADED DUO COULD NOT BE CALMER!

I had it in my head today that I was going to tell Carla about my crush on Mr Achilles. We don't normally talk about crushes, but I know she wouldn't laugh at me. That was my plan – but when do things ever go according to plan for Samantha Drury?

The lunch bell rang, but my art teacher Mack doesn't agree with the whole 'structure' of the school system and particularly struggles with the notion that lessons must start and stop according to a timer. He believes it interferes with the 'creative process' to have to suddenly stop what you're doing just because of the social construct of time.

"Art is a process, not a discipline," he often says as he arrives twenty minutes late to his own lesson smelling of cigarettes. I like Mack. I don't even know if that's his first name or his surname; he is simply *Mack*.

He never dismisses us from class, but he never stops us from leaving either, so we've learnt to just wander off once we've packed our things away. He probably wouldn't even stop us if we left the classroom before the end of the lesson, but none of us have been brave enough to try it yet. I washed my brushes and washed the paint off my hands then headed off to the music room. Carla was already there listening to music, and for the first twenty minutes it was just the two of us eating our lunches and chatting away like usual. I asked her who her favourite teacher was, and she said probably Miss Simmonds, her English teacher. I was just about to tell her about Mr Achilles when in burst Mrs Willis, head of lower school drama.

"Oh, hello girls!" she said gleefully, like we were two little sprites she'd found at the end of the garden. "What a pleasant surprise to see you here so early – I hope you didn't skip lunch just so you could get here before the others. Still, I appreciate your enthusiasm!"

Of course, we didn't have a clue what she was going on about, but Mrs Willis was so distracted and excitable, there was no chance she'd notice the looks of shock and confusion on our faces.

"Please be patient with me, ladies. I have to set up the recording device and have a quick flick through the script – there are a lot of characters to be cast this year!"

The year seven Christmas play. Carla said they sometimes held auditions in this room.

It was all falling into place in heavy, heart-pounding pieces. Like a puzzle through quicksand, slowly sinking in.

While Mrs Willis shuffled and scanned through the script, I locked eyes with Carla and at once I knew that she'd realised what I'd realised: we were about to audition for the school play, completely by accident. Can you imagine anything more terrifying for anxious, socially inept, living-in-a-bubble Samantha Dreary? But Carla was smiling, and so was I. We were in this together, not just as equals but as partners in crime, and whatever happened, it was going to be OK. Even when the other audition hopefuls started flocking in and it became apparent that we were going to have to perform *in front* of them, it was all just fine, because I'm not Samantha Dreary, I'm Samantha Drury, and my best friend is Carla Figueroa.

Mrs Willis said we could go first since we'd been the first to arrive, but Carla said we were auditioning together and we weren't ready because in all the fog of nerves and excitement, she'd forgotten to get her guitar.

"It's not really meant to be a musical audition," said Mrs Willis. "But I admire your spirit and I must admit I'm intrigued!"

I went with Carla, filled in earnest with that fog of nerves and excitement that she had used as our excuse.

"We're not *actually* doing this, are we?" I asked when the door shut behind us. "We're running away now, right?"

"What, and disappoint that lovely lady? Did you see how excited she was? Anyway, we left our bags in there – we have to go back!"

"But we have nothing prepared!"

"So, what? She loves us! We have *chemistry*. And if we don't get the part, what have we lost?"

"Nothing," I said. "You're crazy, Carla!"

"Thank you. Now, I'm going to play you in with my guitar and you're going to read the first character in whatever script she gives you. Read to the rhythm I'm playing, OK? Then I'll read the second character and so on. Just make it dramatic – she'll go bonkers!"

"Oh God… this is crazy! OK… this will be fun, right?"

"Mega fun. Don't be nervous, OK, remember we have nothing to lose."

I still couldn't believe we were walking back into the belly of the beast when we'd just had an opportunity to escape, but Carla was right – what could possibly go wrong? We watched the closing end of a rather nervous audition from a small girl who I've seen floating around the library like a ghost most lunchtimes, then we were up. Carla played me in. it was the first time I'd heard her play and it was astonishingly beautiful. I knew she'd be good. I was so in awe of her talent it threw me off slightly, but it was too late to back out, and all I had to do was read to the beat.

It was an excerpt from A Christmas Carol I think, but it had been modernised in a kind of bizarre way. Still, it had that dreary Dickensian vibe which was so easy for me to tap into, me being Samantha Dreary and all, so I read it slow and dramatic, rhythmically brooding. It was ridiculous, of course, but Mrs Willis loved it. Carla joined in, as planned. Her part was small, so she managed to keep playing as she read it. The effect was incredible, thanks to her perfect timing, she was just strumming and talking softly to the music like a songbird with a story to tell. No wonder she was so confident in her performance.

"Oh bravo! Bra*vo!* Wonderful! I *loved* your interpretation of the piece – very original. Thank you, ladies, that was a marvellous performance – I'm going to find some very special parts for the two of you!"

And so, my acting career begins. Maybe I'll land myself a role in American High School 2: The Trip to Europe.

"Don't forget it's make-up club later," Mum said as she poked her head round my bedroom door when she got home from work.

"Do you need me this week?" I asked, feeling a bit socially drained after the events of this lunchtime. *I still can't believe I did that!*

"I think we might," she said. "It's the new range for the party season and Alana's invited some of her younger friends along – could be some big sales. Do you mind?"

"I don't know… I've got some homework to catch up on. What would I have to do exactly?"

"The usual, Trudy and I will do the whole sales pitch, showing around the products and the pricing lists, and then Jessica will demonstrate some on you. You can skip all the introductions and chit-chat; I'll just call you when you're needed."

"Oh… OK then. What's my fee for all this modelling work, by the way? I hear they earn a lot!"

"Hmmm…" Mum feigned thoughtful contemplation. "Let's see… OK, next time an old family friend comes to visit, I'll allow you to hide in your room and I'll tell them you're out. Think about it, Christmas is just around the corner – there'll be plenty of drop-ins, people 'popping in' to give us a card, but of course they'll stay for a mince pie and a catch-up… could be a Great Aunt who can talk for hours, or an ex-colleague of your dad's who didn't hear about the divorce – *that* would be awkward… could be an old school friend…"

"Deal!" I said, a little too excitedly. Mum knows me so well.

There wasn't enough room for me and Jessica at the table, so we sat on the sofa away from all the ladies while she did my make-up. Jessica's a lot easier to talk to now we know each other a bit better, but she'll never get me like Carla does.

"So, what's the latest on your mum and that guy?" she asked.

"I don't know! She wouldn't talk to me about that sort of stuff."

"Oh, she will, when the time comes, trust me. And it'll be the most cringe moment of your life."

I really hope she's wrong about that.

"What about you?" she continued. "Any boys on the scene?"

Like I said, Carla and I don't normally talk about crushes. Maybe this can be my thing with Jessica. Look at me blooming socially! I'm like a butterfly! Except I still need my cocoon. I'm more like a snail – I'll pop out of my shell occasionally, I suppose.

"Not exactly," I replied a little sheepishly.

"Ooh – sounds like you've got something to tell me! Come on, don't be shy."

Ugh. Maybe this wasn't such a good idea. I'm engaging in girly gossip. How embarrassing.

"It's kind of embarrassing," I said.

"I won't tell anyone, I swear! Come on, it's only me."

"OK, well… it's my History teacher. I really, *really* like him."

"Oh, I see… that's OK, that happens. I bet he's charming and funny and *totally* different from the type of teacher you had in primary school. Am I right?"

Oh God, I'm the ultimate schoolgirl cliché. Give me pigtails and a lollipop and put me on the cheerleading team. Ugh.

Friday 30th November 2019

Carla and I were still buzzing from the spontaneity of yesterday's impromptu audition. It was all Carla's doing really, but I still feel proud of my bravery and ability to act out of character. Yes, I am a wallflower, but going against the norm is a thrill for anyone, isn't it? They announce the casting for the play on Monday and I honestly don't know what I'm hoping for. I suppose I will be disappointed if I don't get a part because that means I gave a bad audition, and I hate to be bad at anything. But if I do? I'll have to perform on stage. *Shudder.*

Carla and I decided we'd better find out a little bit about the play in case we do get in. It's called 'A Festive Carol' and it's a Duke John Jameson original, written by none other than Mrs Willis. We haven't been able to get our hands on the script, but we found a bit about it on the drama section of the school website. Mrs Willis describes it as 'a non-denominational production celebrating the festive season.' Should be interesting.

Monday 2nd December 2019

We made the play! And we're in it together! Carla and I make up two of the Three Wise Women. We got the scripts today and it seems there's no lead role, it's just a lot of stories all bundled together, but we sort of knit them together. We're the Three Wise Women but it also looks like we're the three ghosts from A Christmas Carol. It's a mess of a play really, a total mishmash, but our parts are important. But you haven't heard the best part yet... rehearsals are during P.E. We get to skip P.E!

Now there is only one question on both of our minds, who is our third Wise Woman? Who is the ghost of Christmas future?

Wednesday 4th December 2019

ELECTION RESULTS SPECIAL: THE PEOPLE HAVE CHOSEN, BUT WAS IT A WISE DECISION?

The third Wise Woman has been elected and we've been given exclusive access to their inner circle of wisdom. But will it be a case of the Three Musketeers or three's a crowd? Will your Christmas entertainment be led by the Three Stooges or the Three Scrooges? Read on to find out…

Today was our first rehearsal and Carla and I were chatting nervously on the way.

"What if it's Ruby Driscoll? I can't work with her!" I said.

"You mean Miss Tennis Prodigy? She'd never skip P.E.!"

"Thank God. But it could be Charlotte Henderson – she's even worse!"

"No chance! That girl is obsessed with what other people think of her. She'd never risk getting up on stage and exposing herself to criticism."

"Good point. What about Beth Amory?"

"I doubt it; she never leaves Jake Atkinson's side. The only way she'd audition is if he does, and he would never live it down if he volunteered to do something in the arts instead of sports."

"You speak the truth, oh wise one!"

"Ha, getting into character early! I wonder who it is though…"

"We're about to find out," I said as we stood outside the door to the assembly hall. "Here goes…"

The door swung open and there were around twelve other kids there already, with more arriving after us. It was impossible to tell who would be playing which part, and I couldn't see anyone I knew by name anyway. And that's when I freaked out. There I was, a shard of rusty metal poking through this soft tapestry of beautiful, creative people, people who knew what they were doing, people who hadn't auditioned *by mistake,* and I realised I was a fraud. I'd got there because I was in the wrong place at the wrong time and because Carla persuaded me to do it. It was part fluke, part free-riding off the back of someone else's idea. None of it was me.

"Oh, my goodness, girls!" Mrs Willis said dramatically. "I forgot all about your third Wise Woman! Totally forgot! I was so blown away by your audition I suppose I'd ticked the Wise Women off the list! But it won't work with just two, there *must* be three, there *has to*!"

It's a sign, it's all falling apart, the way things always do in the end. Ever since I met Carla it was all some great pretence, it was never going to last. I've always been alone, and I always will be. I can never be a social person or have a real friend. I was never like that. I'm not like that. Of course, I'd like to be, but people can't just change. Samantha Drury is a ghost set in stone.

Mrs Willis hadn't found us a third Wise Woman and I was having second thoughts. She was struggling to keep the whole thing together and I was struggling to keep myself together. I wanted to escape. *I am leaving; I am leaving.* And so, I did.

I ran out the door, not looking at the faces of the people I was running past, all the while just focussing on the exit. Once I was out there, I wasn't sure what to do; everyone else was in lessons. I thought I should probably go and hide in the toilets so that I wouldn't get in trouble, but before I could, Carla came looking for me.

"Hey, you OK?" she asked.

"I'm sorry, I freaked out."

"Don't be sorry! I'm the one who got you into all this. I'm sorry I pushed you into it It's just… I know how strong you are; I've seen you stand up to *Megan Brown* for goodness sake! But if you don't want to do it, just say."

"I don't know. I think I want to, I'm just scared. I've never acted before. In my old school I was shy, but I was good at reading, so they made me the narrator *every year*. I always thought it was because I was so boring, I couldn't possibly bring any character to the stage. And now I'm looking at the script for *A Festive Carol* and I realise what a big role this is; I'm supposed to be funny, to captivate an audience… I just don't know if I can do it."

"OK, first of all you are *not* boring, Sam! And secondly, do you realise why she gave you such a big role? Because you're good. Your audition was brilliant. I know

130

we did it as a bit of a joke, but you tapped into that character so seamlessly, it was incredible. Mrs Willis chose you for the part because she knows you can do it."

"Oh well, *that's* reassuring!" I laughed. "Mrs Willis is as mad as a box of frogs! Have you seen the play she wrote?"

"Ha! Yeah, it's crazy, but it'll be funny and entertaining – especially with you in it."

"Oh God… OK… you've talked me round. How can I walk back in there though? What do I say? I just walked out on a lesson; do you think I'll be in trouble?"

"Rehearsal, not lesson. And *please!* Mrs Willis is a *drama* teacher and you just created all the drama – if anything, she's going to love you even more!"

"You're right. I know she's not going to punish me. You know, that's the one thing I never knew I'd enjoy so much about secondary school, some of the teachers care more about the learning than the rules."

"And some of them just care about the drama – come on!"

She grabbed my arm and led me back in, where we found Mrs Willis in dramatic turmoil regarding her oversight in not casting our third Wise Woman/Ghost of Christmas Future. Some of the other kids were stifling giggles as they watched her flailing her arms as she approached us.

"Oh girls, it's all my fault, I'm so sorry!" she thought my little freak-out was about her and not about me. A good thing too – if she knew I was having second thoughts, she'd explode!

"We must find you another Wise Woman. I will hold more auditions, starting tomorrow!"

"Actually," came a raspy voice from the back of the room. "I want to be the third Wise Woman, if that's OK."

"But you're Eliza Scrooge – the cold-hearted businesswoman who kicks down snowmen with her stiletto heels!"

"Well I was just talking to Joanna – you cast her as my understudy – and she *really* wants to play Eliza, and I want to play the Wise Woman."

"Marvellous!" said Mrs Willis. "We have so much passion in this room! Very well, um… sorry, what was your name dear?"

"Danny."

"Girls, meet your new Wise Woman, Danny!"

No need; we've already met!

"Danny!" I said when she came over to join us. "You remember me from the Isle of Wight?"

"Of course! How could I forget Samantha, Queen of Pranks?"

"Sounds interesting," said Carla.

"Danny, this is Carla."

"I know," said Danny. "We have Geography and Maths together."

"Awesome!" I said. "I'm so glad it's you, Danny, I couldn't stand it if it had been someone horrible!"

Thursday 12th December 2019

Rehearsals have been *amazing*. Danny is the perfect addition to our little group – we hang out together every lunchtime now as well, even when we don't have rehearsals. The play is next Friday so we're rehearsing most of the time. Mrs Willis is in a constant state of anguish because she didn't really allow much time between casting and show time, but we're all confident. The best part of it all is just us three laughing at the ridiculousness of the play – it makes no sense!

It starts with us, as the three witches from Macbeth, predicting a dark and dreadful future for the hard-nosed businesswoman, Eliza Scrooge, who hates children and loves money. Then there are some scenes with Eliza being horrible to her employees, not allowing them to take time off to see their kids' Christmas plays, banning them from doing Secret Santa – that sort of thing. Then she goes home to her big, empty house and looks morosely over some paperwork and reads the financial papers dully. She spends Christmas day alone, briefly switching on the TV only to be sickened by the festive broadcasts she sees.

For some reason, us three visit her as the ghosts of Christmas past, present and future in January, February and March. By March, she has completely reformed, found a man (named Joseph, because the classic nativity story of the love between Scrooge and Joseph never gets old) and has already got herself knocked up. So, then us three Wise Women turn up in the form of the three best friends she never knew she needed, and we give her relationship advice as well as guiding her through her pregnancy and showing her the joy of children and of non-material pleasures in life. We do this in fancy bars and restaurants and on shopping sprees, sort of like on the female-based sitcoms mum watches. But, you know, material things aren't important.

And then, when the next Christmas comes around, she showers her employees with loads of material possessions and a lavish party, which kind of contradicts what she learnt from the Wise Women, but whatever. Then, naturally, she gives birth at the Christmas party, with the Wise Women as her midwives. There's also a sub-plot about Joseph reuniting with his estranged parents at the birth of their first grandchild, just to confuse matters even further. It is funny though – we three get a lot of the best lines – but who knows if anyone will be able to follow the plot!

Sunday 15th December 2019

Things have been going well at school, but don't go thinking my entire life has been magically altered. I still get sneers from Charlotte Henderson and eye-rolls from Ruby Driscoll, and I don't have any lessons with Carla or Danny this term (I'm hoping that will change) so every lesson is everlasting dullness apart from History, Art and occasionally English. My English teacher likes my writing – she says she can tell that I get a lot of practice!

But I'm still me. Danny was going out with some of her old primary school friends and she invited me and Carla along. Carla couldn't go because it's her dad's birthday, so it would have been just me and a bunch of strangers, basically. I thought about making up some excuse like I used to do with Summer, but Danny said,

"It's OK, you don't have to come. I know it'll probably be weird for you; I understand."

And because I knew she meant it, I didn't feel bad saying that I just didn't feel like it. I think that's how proper friends should be. If someone says they don't want to do something, you shouldn't be mad at them or try to make them feel guilty about it. It's OK to say no. Sometimes it's hard to say no but it's not wrong to say no. It's very easy for me to draw the comparison now, because we got an unexpected visitor at the house yesterday.

I have come to count it as a blessing that we have a gravel driveway at the front of our house, because the sound of footsteps crunching on the stones always provides a clear and distinct warning of approaching guests, and today was just one of those occasions in which the gravel proved it was worth its salt. Mum was in the living room. She heard the crunching. She looked out the window. I was in my bedroom. I heard the crunching. I looked out the window. Both of us saw Summer and her mum, Angie walking towards our front door.

"It's Summer and her mum! Do you want to use your free pass?" Mum asked me in a text.

She is a good mum. With no time at all for a lengthy response I simply texted her back *"YES!"* and she sent me the 'thumbs up' symbol as confirmation. But I could hardly rest at ease. I wish my bedroom was soundproof like the music room at school, but it's not. I heard Mum greeting them.

"Oh, hello… err… Summer; it's so good to see you!"

Oh no – that pause. She doesn't remember Angie's name. The least I can do is text her.

135

"Angie!" I sent.

"And you as well, Angie, how have you been?" I heard her say.

Mum has nothing in common with Angie. Angie is a clean-living fitness freak who divorced Summer's dad and married a twenty-three-year-old. Mum tells me these things on Saturday nights when she's drinking her home-brewed wine. Anyway, much like Summer persisted with me, Angie does the same with my mum. Now I feel bad that I left them to it like that, but by the time I'd processed all this old information which I'd resigned to old, recyclable material, it was too late.

"I'm afraid Samantha's not here," I heard Mum say. "She's at the cinema with a few of her school friends."

Good, Mum. A feasible excuse – and it lets Summer know that I've moved on...

"Oh, that's a shame!" Angie said. "Well we just came to drop off this card and a half dozen of my home-made sugar-free mince pies."

"Oh, how lovely!" Mum wasn't very convincing.

What even is a mince pie without sugar?

"Well thank you very much," Mum said conclusively, and then there was this long, horrible pause which I knew was Mum waiting to hear Angie say, *'you're welcome, have a lovely Christmas, bye then!'* I was waiting to hear Angie say it too, but the words never came. The tension was unbearable.

Come on Mum. Hold on. They'll break. Stay strong. Don't. Give. In...

"Would you like a cup of tea, then?" I heard Mum's voice breaking the silence. I can't blame her. It was deafening.

"Oh yes, we'd love one!" Angie said, and Mum ushered them into the living room where the sound was more muffled and yet more ominous.

I could hardly breathe through all the tension it was causing me, let alone do anything else, but that was still better than having to reunite with Summer. Anyway, if she knew I was home, they might have stayed for hours, but without me there, Summer would soon get bored and urge her mum to leave. That's what Mum and I were banking on, anyway. I could hear idle conversation between two people who were just going through the motions, then I heard Mum go into the kitchen to make the tea. A few short words were uttered between Summer and her mum, and that was the first time I'd heard her voice since the summer holidays. It made me shudder knowing that she was in my house, so near to me and my happy solitude.

If I'm not mistaken, I also heard Mum go into the utility room while the kettle was boiling. Mum keeps her home brew in the utility room; perhaps she was just checking on it, more likely she was filling her mug with it. Again, I don't blame her, you do whatever you can to endure a visit from Summer and Angie. They chatted for a while and I began to relax as the conversation started to wane and it appeared they were ready to make tracks.

They were back in the hallway where I could hear their voices more clearly, they were putting their coats on and thanking Mum for the tea when Summer asked Mum if she could go to the loo before they left.

"Of course, you can," I heard Mum say, with just the slightest edge of nerves in her voice. "You remember where the bathroom is, don't you?"

Oh no. The bathroom. Right opposite my bedroom. Stay quiet, Samantha. Stay very, very quiet.

I heard her climb the stairs. I tried not to listen to her using the bathroom, but I heard it anyway.

Go away Summer! How dare you pee in my house! Take your urine elsewhere!

I heard her flush and wash her hands. I heard her open the bathroom door. I held my breath. I heard her footsteps on the landing. But when I heard her turn my doorknob, I knew it was all over. Damn.

"Sammy!" she said when she saw me. "I just wanted to see if your room was still the same... your Mum said you were out!"

"Oh, did she?" I said, feigning surprise. "Stupid woman; she must have got confused – it's *tomorrow* I'm going out with my school friends."

"Mum! She's here! Sammy's here!" she shouted down the stairs to Angie. My poor mum had to act the total idiot and say she'd made a mistake, which was fine for Summer but I'm not sure Angie bought it.

"Oh well, we can't leave now then, can we?" Angie said, taking off her coat.

"I'll get us another brew," Mum said, though whether she meant tea or wine I'm not entirely sure.

"Your room hasn't changed much," said Summer, filling the silence while I was still getting over the shock of this full-on invasion.

"Well, it's only been four months..."

"*I've* got a *completely* new room – none of that babyish princess stuff; I'm all about ponies now. Do you collect the Prettiest Pony stickers? I've got the sticker album and I've got *loads* of sparesies – we could do swapsies!"

"No, I don't collect them."

"Oh, you *should!* It's super addictive. So, do you like your new school?"

"Yeah it's OK; a lot better than primary school!"

"But don't you miss primary school? Don't you miss *me?* We had such a good time together!"

"Um, yeah…"

"It's a shame we haven't had a chance to catch up sooner than this. It's been *too long,* hasn't it?"

"Err…"

"Ooh you have a computer in your room!"

"I always have had…"

"Have you heard of Eric Derek? I *love* him – he's so funny!"

"Yeah; wasn't that the thing the boys in primary school were always talking about?"

"Yeah but it's OK, girls like him too now – let me show you some of his videos…"

She was like a hurricane, whizzing round my room, disturbing everything, picking things up, putting them back down somewhere else, constantly talking, constantly changing the subject and never letting a single thought sink in long enough to take hold. I suppose that's why she never noticed that I outgrew this friendship a long time ago, she just never thinks about anything in enough depth. She couldn't possibly overthink things. I wonder what that's like.

Eric Derek is a grown man who goes around pranking members of the public and posting the videos online. He's made a lot of money out of it, and even some of his victims have become 'internet famous', but he's lost almost as much in law suits because, funnily enough, some of these unsuspecting people don't like getting tricked and then humiliated in front of an audience of millions. If he ever caught me, I'd rip his head off. I don't like people intruding in my life even if it's just to make small talk, so I can't help but sympathise with the people Eric Derek preys upon.

Even Frogsplash is too mature for Eric Derek. His pranks aren't even clever. But here was Summer guffawing at them and spitting out sugar-free mince pie all over my carpet (I tried one bite of one, they tasted… *different*). I couldn't help but feel this summed up our differences perfectly, we have very *different* taste. I also couldn't help but wonder what a better time I'd have been having with Danny and her old school friends – assuming, of course, that they're nothing like *my* old school friends. Sometimes when you think you're making the right choice for yourself, the world turns around and throws it back in your face. Yesterday, the world threw Summer back in my face.

She's not a bad person. I suppose I'd still choose her over the truly mean girls in my year at Duke John Jameson, but she's not for me, and I know now that that's OK. Eventually, Mum got rid of Angie by saying that she needed to go grocery shopping before dinner, so Angie called Summer down. I went down to see her off politely, but while she was putting her coat back on, she said, "It's been so fun seeing you again! We mustn't leave it so long – *promise me* we'll make more time for each other! I think we should meet up *at least* twice a month…"

"I'm not sure," I said cautiously. "I have a lot of school work now and you know I see my dad every other weekend so…"

"Come on, Summer," Angie said, sensing my tone. "Say goodbye now, Sam and her mum have got things to do."

It felt bad ending it that way, but I knew that it was the end, and I felt relieved.

"Was that as bad for you as it was for me?" I said to Mum once they were gone for good.

"Too right it was! I had to pretend that I had no idea you were in the house! My one and only daughter! I must have looked like an awful mother!" she laughed, so I knew she was taking it in good humour. "And don't forget – I had to entertain Angie twice, just when I thought they were leaving they did a U-turn! And how about those mince pies – yuck!"

"Oh, I know; they were *awful*," I said. "And the mince pies were pretty bad too!"

Mum laughed, "At least you did the right thing. It's a difficult thing to learn to say no to people but it's a very valuable life lesson."

"You don't think she'll be too upset, do you?"

"Her? She'll soon get distracted by some other, much deeper thought, like, *why don't fish dissolve in the water?*"

"Oh Mum, don't be silly! She's never even heard of dissolution!"

Mum has her own special way of making me feel better.

Tuesday 17th December 2019

"Have you noticed," said Danny this lunchtime at dress rehearsal, "The lengths Mrs Willis has gone to portray strong women in this play: Eliza Scrooge, the Wise Women, and yet the conclusion of it all is that the female lead finds fulfilment by finding a man and having a baby with him?"

"God. you're so right," I said.

"Totally," Carla agreed. "Of all the contradictions in this play, that has got to be the worst."

"I know she means well," said Danny, "But it's just ridiculous."

"Is that why you didn't want to play Eliza?" I asked.

"Well that, and I wanted to work with you guys."

"Aw, so sweet!" Carla joked.

"Yeah, right," I said. "You just didn't want to have to pretend to give birth in front of an audience!"

"Well duh! I think even Joanna's freaking out about it and she was *desperate* to get the main part. Come on – you don't want to do that in front of the whole school *and* your parents!"

"No way!" I said.

"So, are all your parents coming?" asked Carla.

"Just my mum," said Danny. "My dad has to stay home with the twins – there's no way they'd sit through it quietly!"

"Mine are *both* coming, *and* my oldest sister, Louisa. What about you, Sam?"

"Yep, both my parents, which is going to be weird because they usually go out of their way to avoid being in the same room together. It seems to be a stand-off between them in which they're both trying to prove that *they're* the most supportive parent."

"Oh no – awkward!" said Danny.

"Totally," I agreed. "But at least they didn't force Frogsplash to come."

Friday 20th December 2019

Today was possibly the weirdest, most wonderful end of term day ever. As usual it was a half-day, but as we were due to perform *A Festive Carol* to the whole lower school at midday, all cast members were excused from lessons. We spent the morning rehearsing, practising quick costume changes and mentally preparing for the task ahead. I couldn't have done it without Carla and Danny, my nerves were in pieces, but I liked it. I felt like I was someone else because of how surreal everything was. The whole school looked different; it was the same, but it *felt* different. Like I was through the Looking Glass; it felt magical.

As you know, we opened the play as a trio, but did I tell you I had the first line? It was nerve-wracking, but it was a good way to start, the costume and the props put me right there in the scene instead of on the stage. We were the three witches standing over a cauldron smoking with dry ice and hissing with pre-recorded sound effects. I did what I've done for many years of my life whenever I've been faced with a situation which makes me feel ill-at-ease: I pretended I was someone else.

I began, "Double, double, Eliza's in trouble;
Cigarette burn and champagne bubble"

I felt it. I felt I *was* the witch. It felt wonderful; powerful. As soon as it started, I didn't want it to end.

"Fillet of a sirloin steak;
In the cauldron, boil and bake…"

It was Carla's turn to speak, but I was still there, in character, with her and Danny as my fellow witches.

"Harvest richest roe of fish,
And chef will make you a caviar dish.
Wool of alpaca and sometimes goat
Will get you a fine, fair cashmere coat."

Danny's turn, "But what more luxuries can we provide
For Eliza Scrooge when she has died?
For what's in her wardrobe and what's on her plate
Will do nothing to help her escape her fate."

We had set the scene brilliantly and left to change into our ghost costumes while Joanna, a.k.a. Eliza, took the stage along with her poor, underappreciated employees. The whole thing ran smoothly – beautifully, in fact, and when we took our final bows, we were applauded heartily. It was reassuring, but it was hard to feel triumphant just yet, knowing that the real challenge was still to come. Six p.m. was show-time for real, not a bunch of kids in the audience staring at their phones, not paying us any attention. This was parents with video recorders and great expectations.

We arrived at five and Mrs Willis, bless her, had laid out a table of drinks and snacks for the cast. I was too nervous to eat, but I must admit that that tiny little taste of the star treatment felt good, even if it *was* just value lemonade and cheesy puffs. Rehearsing any more would have been pointless; it was a matter of taking our minds off the play so as not to overthink it. So, to fill the time, I went to chat to Mum and Dad, and luckily, they provided the distraction I'd been searching for.

To my dismay I found them sitting *next to* each other in the *front row.*

"You can sit wherever you like, you know," I said to them, hinting heavily.

"I wanted to sit in the front row; I want the best possible view!" Mum said.

"So, did I," said Dad. "I'm so proud of you, Sam!"

"So am I," said Mum, "So, so proud."

Obviously, they were still competing for the *Supportive Parent of the Year* award.

"But you didn't have to sit next to each other!" I said, realising quickly that even my heavy hints were too subtle for the two children sat in front of me.

"Oh, don't be silly – we're very comfortable in each other's company!" Dad said.

"Absolutely," said Mum. "We're both adults, after all. We can be mature about this."

What, like the time Dad came to surprise me for my birthday and you turned the sprinklers on him?

"We're here to support you, Sam, just like we always are," said Dad.

"We? *Always?*" Mum said, clearly affronted. "Where were you when Sam was sitting her entrance exam, Ibiza wasn't it? Drinking on the beach all day while your daughter was taking the toughest test she's ever had!"

Some of the other parents were now giving them the side-eye – some disapproving, others probably eavesdropping. Adults live for gossip.

"You really want to go *there*, Cassie?" Dad said. "The only reason I thought you *might* be friendly this evening is because I can tell you've already been drinking."

"*Been* drinking? I haven't 'been' drinking – I bought a white wine spritzer at the refreshments table… all of the profits go to FRED."

"Fred? You mean our son? You're not making any sense! You really are drunk!"

"I am not drunk, and you clearly know nothing about the school your daughter is attending. FRED is the 'Friends and Educators of Duke' association. They do fundraisers for the school."

"Ohhhh, FRED!" Dad said sarcastically. "Well, of course I know FRED!"

They're getting childish now; time to step in.

"Uh-hm," I cleared my throat to remind them that I was standing right there listening to every word. "This isn't very mature, is it?"

"Oh, I'm sorry, Sammy," said Mum. "It's your father – he brings out the worst in me."

"Oh really? THIS is your worst? HA!" Dad fake-laughed.

"Stop it, both of you! Do I have to split you up?"

"No, no, we'll behave," said Mum.

"Yeah, sorry Sam, we're being very selfish. This is your night."

"Exactly," said Mum. "This is about you, not us."

"I don't care who it's about! I just don't want you two causing a scene in the middle of the show!"

"We won't; we promise."

"OK. Don't make me regret not splitting you up."

I love that feeling when you're more mature than your parents. That'll keep them in their place for a bit.

I began the show as before.

"Double, double, Eliza's in trouble;

Cigarette burn and champagne bubble…"

It was easy to forget about Mum and Dad when I was up there, just as it had been easy to forget Ruby Driscoll and Charlotte Henderson in the audience earlier in the day. It was easy to forget them all because they didn't exist. All that existed was the world of Eliza Scrooge and us three witches.

It was when Danny was visiting Eliza as the Ghost of Christmas Future that I happened to peek through a slit in the curtain at the side of the stage and saw Mum and Dad exchanging irritated whispers. As they had insisted on sitting in the front row, I could make out what the problem was from their gestures, and I think I was able to read their lips.

"I can't believe you're *texting* during your daughter's school play. Is *that* what you call showing your support?" Mum said bitterly.

"I *was* filming the play, actually, but a very important work email came through and I thought, seeing as my daughter isn't currently on stage, it wouldn't be too much of a problem. Apparently, I was wrong."

"So, you stopped filming to open an email? That's going to look *great* when you play it back. Those are Sammy's friends up there – you're not following the storyline!"

"As it happens, Sam has told me all about this play and she said that the storyline makes no sense and that I shouldn't pay attention to it too closely. Now if you'll excuse me, I'd like to respond to this email before she comes back on stage."

"Honestly, I'll never understand how someone so childish can take his work so seriously!"

Those were the last words they said to each other, as far as I know, and I started to wonder how well I'd read their lips – was I capable of getting all of that, word for word? Or was part of me filling in the gaps because that's what *I* thought? I must admit, it threw me off my game when I went back onstage, especially seeing them sitting there smiling encouragingly as though no crossed words had been uttered between them. It took me a moment to get back into character.

Thanks Mum and Dad, that argument you just had about showing support sure was supportive!

I was a bit wobbly during my brief role as Gabriella, the washroom assistant in an uptown bar who candidly tells Eliza that she is surely with child, but that scene was mostly about Eliza anyway. The rest of the show went without a hitch, we received a standing ovation, I celebrated backstage with Danny and Carla and Mum and Dad greeted me with proud smiles and absurdly excessive praise.

Now, though, sat here in my room, my thoughts have circled back round to Mum and Dad's row. Did Mum really say what I thought she said?

I'll never understand how someone so childish can take his work so seriously.

I think that's what I wanted her to say, because it really hit the nail on the head. Dad is fun, and he gets what it's like being a kid, but he's irresponsible and unreliable when it comes to *looking after* a kid. I don't think it would bother me so much if he was just generally a bit useless, but he's a successful businessman. He's the area manager for a big catering company and he never misses an appointment or turns up late for a meeting. He never lets his clients down, nor his employees, just us.

Mum let me down tonight, too. She promised not to make a scene, but if anything, it was her who was being immature. Both times I saw them arguing it was her who threw in the first snarky comment which set things off. Well at least *I* can be mature. If they try and guilt trip me into anything now, I can throw it all back in their stupid faces!

Saturday 21st December 2019

SPECIAL REPORT: PARENTAL GUILT MAKES ASTONISHING COMEBACK IN RECORD TIME!

Spectators everywhere feared the worst for the long-running parental guilt, which appeared to be on its last legs yesterday afternoon after a disastrous display which brought it crashing down to its knees. However, the guilt has returned after a record-fast recovery time of less than twenty-four hours and is set to remain strong and undefeated for the coming season.

Well that didn't last long. After their disastrous attempts to co-parent me from the front row of the audience yesterday, they've decided it's best to do things separately, as they always did before, but with a newly added safety feature. From now on Frog and I get to decide which parent goes to which event. They say 'gets to' like this is some sort of treat rather than a massive burden of responsibility. And guess what they've given us as our first dilemma? Which parent reads the school reports? Nope. Which parent helps with a school project? Nope. Which parent gets to have their kids for Christmas Day? Bingo.

Whichever one we choose, the other one is not only going to be hurt, they're also going to have to spend Christmas alone and possibly sad. The last two Christmases we had no choice in the matter as Dad's catering company had some big clients throwing huge parties, so he was far too busy to have us round. But this year, he's delegated all the work to his assistant and other employees. I really wish he hadn't. It would be so much easier if the decision was out of my hands. My hands feel very, very full.

On the one hand, it seems like it should be Dad's turn to have us for Christmas, but on the other hand, it's unfair to punish Mum just because every year since they split up, Dad's been too busy with work (as usual) whereas Mum's always made the time for us.

Then there's the fact that Christmas with Dad will be *just* Christmas with Dad: me, him, Frogsplash and no one else. It won't feel special and it'll be kind of dull; it will feel exactly like any other Saturday at Dad's. Whereas, with Mum, we'll get to see our four cousins, our aunts, our uncles and our grandparents: now *that's* a proper Christmas. We play loads of games and open loads of presents and have a huge feast – it's so much fun! Then again, think of Dad sitting all alone on Christmas Day. At least if we choose him, we know that Mum won't be truly alone. She will miss us, but she'll have her sisters, her parents, she can still enjoy herself, maybe. But we want to enjoy ourselves too.

There's always the third option, I go to one parent and Frog goes to the other. But it would feel like whoever went to Dad's had pulled the short straw. Anyway, Christmas is one of those rare times Frogsplash and I really have fun together. We always get up early, talk about what we hope our presents will be, make breakfast together, sneak some chocolates off the tree and watch nostalgic kiddie Christmas cartoons. It's the one thing we share – other than the sibling code of honour. I suppose I need to discuss all this with him, really.

Ugh.

AMAZING ANTHROPOLOGY: EVOLUTIONARY ADVANCEMENT ENABLES SIBLING TO SPEAK MULTIPLE WORD SENTENCES!

Evolutionary scientists have spent years studying the phenomenon of monosyllabic teenage siblings and have been baffled by the strange, almost human-like behaviour of their subjects. Today they tell of a breakthrough as they have at last discovered that the siblings are, in fact, capable of speaking in full, understandable sentences.

I would never in a million years knock on Frog's bedroom door, so instead I sent him a text.

"Any ideas what we should do about Christmas? I'm totally stuck."

He replied almost instantly, which I suppose shouldn't surprise me, seeing as his phone is super-glued to his hand.

"Yeah same. Can't believe they're making US choose!"

"I know - it's like they're trying to ruin Christmas!"

"Exactly! And they actually believe they're doing us a favour!"

"They MUST know what a tricky situation they've put us in. It's not fair!"

"Well then, I guess we shouldn't feel too guilty about our decision. It was THEIR decision to do this to us!"

"True. We still have to decide though."

And then he knocked on my door and, for the first time since before Dad left, we sat in my room and talked. We discussed all the issues I've mentioned in here, and it seems they had all crossed Frogsplash's mind too. I like our usual sarcastic exchanges and our friendly-to-not-so-friendly mockery of each other, and I would always opt for a comfortable distance between me and *anybody*. I'm especially grateful that we're not one of those creepy families that still hold hands in public even though the kids are in their teens (come on, you know the sort, you've seen them and you thought they were creepy too), but it's nice to know that when a decision needs to be made, Frogsplash can talk intelligently and won't bury his head in the sand. I do him a disservice when I compare him to Dad. Frogsplash knows how to take responsibility. That's a weird sentence, isn't it? Maybe I should call him Fred when he's being mature…

Nah.

So, we weighed up the pros and cons and we reflected on years gone by ('the ghosts of our Christmas past' Frogsplash called them. I told him that was one of my roles in the school play. 'I know' he said. 'I heard you were really good!') But in the end, it was a matter of loyalty. Who had walked out on us? Dad. Who had always been there for us? Mum. Who had put work before us? Dad. Who had worked hard to provide for us? Mum. Who bought us thoughtless, last-minute presents? Dad. Who worked tirelessly to make every Christmas special, even when she was sad about her divorce? Mum.

We know Dad has been trying lately, but Mum has always tried. So, we've agreed we'll tell Dad that we chose Mum because we really want to see our cousins, not because of any of his personal defects. It's still going to be tough, but at least we know Dad will find a way to make light of it.

Saturday 28th December 2019

Dad took it well, on the surface at least. He said that whilst he'd have been happy to have us, he was relieved not to have to attempt Christmas dinner. Maybe he was just trying to make us feel better, but I'm sure there was an element of truth in it. Dad's signature dish (and I'm not complaining!) is takeaway food.

Christmas at home was fun and traditional. Aunt Lola and Uncle Rashid came over with our eight-year-old twin cousins, Sita and Satya (who Frogsplash still can't tell apart!) and Uncle Sean and Aunt Astrid came with six-year-old Anna and thirteen-year-old Roland. It was a full house, we sat on mismatched garden chairs and several drinks were knocked over while we were pulling crackers and passing the bread sauce (what even is that stuff? Where does it hide the other three hundred and sixty-four days of the year?) Then Frogsplash took Roland to his room to try out his new video games while I entertained the girls with some of the arts and crafts presents I got. They're a bit younger than me but I find that makes things easier. We can just talk and there are no hidden agendas; no social barriers.

We arrived at Dad's yesterday and we're still here now. Last night he made our favourite dinner, picky food platter, a.k.a. bits and bobs dinner. In case you don't have this at your house, it's a selection of party foods like sausage rolls, cucumber sticks, crisps, dips, mini pizzas, battered prawns, olives, garlic bread, mini peppers stuffed with cream cheese... it's *amazing!* If I could have that for every dinner and hotel breakfast buffet for every breakfast, I'd be living happy.

Sunday 5th January 2020

Wow, 2020, a new decade. Mum says that's nothing – the new *millennium* was incredible – apparently. She was a teenager when it happened, and she says there was a *huge* level of hype around 'Y2K' (that's what they called it – lame, I know!) She says all the grown-ups were scaremongering about computers crashing and planes falling out of the sky and all of technology failing and basically life as they knew it being destroyed, all because, somehow, they thought computers wouldn't understand that 2000 came after 1999. That's the most basic of basic maths, how would a computer not get that? She says they turned the River Thames into a river of fire, which sounds way scarier than not being able to order pizza online.

When it's our turn to host Christmas dinner, Mum buys LOADS of snacks and treats for our guests, and they bring LOADS more to thank her for hosting. We all get too full on Christmas dinner and the snacks remain untouched until after everyone's gone. So, I've been rewarding myself with mince pies, chocolates, crisps and nuts every time I complete a piece of homework or finish a section of my project. It's a good system, I think. Once all the yummy food has gone, it won't be there to tempt me anymore, and Frogsplash is certainly doing his fair share to help make it disappear, so it won't take too long. Mum is helping by drinking the excess of sparkling wine in the fridge – she says once it's all gone, she's not drinking alcohol for a whole month. One way or another, we're all desperately clinging onto our Christmas indulgences, but we know it can't last.

Mr Achilles asked us to do a project on 'life in the trenches' during WWI, and it was so grim I needed regular rewards. I've finished it now and I think (hope) he's going to love it. I'm handing it in tomorrow, so we'll soon find out. Ugh, back to school. At least I'll get to catch up with Danny and Carla.

<u>Monday 6th January 2020</u>

The day got off to a bad start. Getting dressed this morning I noticed that my school skirt, which mum bought for me to 'grow into' back in September would barely button up, and all day I felt it straining over the girth of my midriff. At first, I tried to convince myself that Mum shrunk it in the wash, but I knew deep down that wasn't the case. I'm trying to keep a level head about it; I over-indulged – this is the natural result; it's no big deal. Ugh. *Big.* I feel so big. I feel so thick and bulging. But I do not want a bigger skirt; I want a smaller waist. No more treats. I'm going on a diet.

Danny and Carla were kind enough not to say anything, and my day got better when I spent lunchtime with them. We all had copies of the videos our parents had recorded of the play, so we watched them back, cringing at our own performances and laughing at the play itself. I told them about Mum and Dad's argument, Danny told us about her spoilt, bratty little brothers and Carla told us how moody her middle sister had been because she wasn't allowed to spend Christmas with her boyfriend. I wonder if I'd have found some way to be annoyed by Frogsplash over the holidays if we hadn't joined forces to handle the parental situation. Maybe if Mum and Dad were still together, Frogsplash and I would hate each other.

When Mum got home from work, the sibling alliance came into play once again. Mum called us both down from our rooms to 'have a talk' with us. This only happens when there's something serious going on. When we came down to the living room, she was sat drinking a cup of tea and I knew then that the worst had happened. There could only be one reason she was drinking tea at that hour; the Christmas wine was all gone.

"January starts now!" she said abruptly, as though she was our sergeant and we'd just arrived for morning drill.

"It started five days ago, Mum," said Frog, being snarky. "Maybe if you put up that calendar I got you for Christmas…"

"I don't need a *Babes of Miami Beach* calendar to know what date it is, Frog, and by the way – I took it in good humour because it was Christmas, but I find prank presents very mean-spirited, and I did not enjoy opening that up in front of my parents and young nieces!"

159

"It wasn't a prank, Mum – I told you, they made a mistake when I ordered it online!"

"I'm not putting it up. But that doesn't mean you get to keep it either. Anyway, it may be a few days late, but I've made a few resolutions today. I want to be more independent – do things for myself and make my own money on top of my wages, so I'm going to get more involved in the business with Trudy."

"Oh no," I said. "More make-up evenings."

"Yes and no," said Mum. "We'll still have them here on Thursdays, but I'll also be spending Monday, Tuesday and Friday evenings with Trudy selling the products at a variety of locations. This means you two are going to have to look after yourselves and each other for those three evenings – including making your own dinner. Do you understand?"

"Yeah!" said Frog enthusiastically.

"That doesn't just mean sausage and chips every night. I will buy the ingredients every Sunday and I expect you to eat balanced meals, OK?"

"OK," we both chimed, wanting to get this thing over with. Mum on a Monday in winter without wine is just about the most serious version of Mum there is.

"I also want you two to become more independent," she went on. "And so, I have devised this chore timetable."

She presented us each with a photocopy of a fortnightly timetable, each of which showed the chores we were meant to do: clean the bathroom, tidy our rooms, hoover downstairs, do the laundry, that sort of thing. It didn't seem too bad, at a glance – there was less than one chore per day for each of us.

"So, hang on," I said. "*Your* New Year's resolution is to make *us* do chores? That's not how it works. What you've done here is assign several resolutions to *us*."

"My resolution is to teach you two to be independent and this is how I've chosen to do it. I could kick you both out of the house and leave you to fend for yourselves if you prefer…"

"No, you couldn't, that's illegal!" said Frog.

"There you go then, this is the only way," said Mum, and that was that.

Thursday 9th January 2020

P.E. GYM TURNS PRISON CAMP AS INMATES ARE FORCED TO TAKE EXERCISE IN BROAD DAYLIGHT WEARING HIDEOUS UNIFORMS AGAINST THEIR WILL!

See inside for a sneak peek of the cellulite cell mates!

My first P.E. lesson in over a month and OH what fresh HELL! First, Miss Milne, my P.E. teacher, is palpably bitter about me missing every December lesson so that I could rehearse for the school play. Apparently, she finds it 'outrageous' that P.E. is always the first thing on the chopping block when someone has a timetable clash.

"Physical fitness is an essential part of a healthy lifestyle – knowing how to ask where the library is in French is not!"

It seemed to put her in a right mood, especially with me. She probably noticed that I've gained a bit of weight and I bet she thought that was all down to me missing her lessons, the smug witch! Apparently, if you need to see Mr Donahue, the school counsellor, they always schedule that during P.E. too. The way things are going for me with Miss

Milne, I'm tempted to pay him another visit very soon and maybe play up the whole 'family issues' vibe I was giving off last time so that I have to go to regular sessions with him. I would, but I need to lose weight. Also, if I remember correctly, he was every bit as smug as Miss Milne.

Miss Milne is by no means the worst thing about P.E. lessons though. It's a new term which means a new subject, and for some insane reason, they've decided that right now, after Christmas, when it's freezing, we're to do gymnastics. And gymnastics mean gym shorts. The gym is a prison, those shorts are my cell, and my thick thighs are the guilty inmates. Yes, you can have cellulite when you're eleven. Remember when I said my thighs have always been my 'problem area'? And, if you'll recall, I have gained a noticeable amount of weight recently. Now, imagine me in tiny, just-barely-covering-the-bum, bright red, Lycra gym shorts. I MIGHT AS WELL BE WEARING KNICKERS! And to top it all off, we must walk past several classroom windows on the way from the changing rooms to the gym and back again. This has got to be in breach of human rights laws.

I'm too young to go to the gym or go out for a run, so the only exercise I can get is in P.E. or on Mum's exercise bike. She keeps it in her room in front of the TV, but as far as I can tell, the only thing she uses it for is a place to hang up her work clothes after she's ironed them. I used it yesterday while she was out on a sale with Trudy, but today was make-up club at our house so I had to leave it, not that I had much time for a workout anyway.

"Have you checked your chore chart?" Mum asked me the minute she got home.

"Yes, it's my turn to hoover, I know!" I replied. "I'm just finishing maths homework first."

But she wouldn't stop nagging me until I'd done it, so I had to put my homework on hold, which I hate. I like to get it out of the way, so I don't have to stress out about getting it finished on time, but having Mum breathing down my neck is far more stressful than dividing decimals.

Friday 10th January 2020

Remember Eric Derek, the online video prankster idolised by boys my age, as well as my former friend Summer? Well it seems he's expanding his brand by going into merchandising. The favourite Christmas present of at least half the boys in my year was the Eric Derek Epic Prank Kit, and today they all decided to unleash their weapons on the rest of the school. Most of it was harmless stuff: whoopee cushions, fake vomit, fake video cameras in the toilets, fake spiders hanging from doorframes... one teacher got done with the bucket of water on top of the classroom door trick, which is no joke when it's only about five degrees Celsius in the school. She was so furious she gave the whole class detention, went home to get changed and then called to say she wouldn't be coming back in as she'd 'caught a cold' after being soaked to the bone with freezing water. I think I'd have done the same.

The only other thing was the stink bombs. The stench was horrific. People kept setting them off in classrooms and honestly, the smell was so bad we *had* to evacuate and miss lesson time. It might have been funny if it hadn't been so revolting, but it got old very quickly and by the end of the day, all the teachers had a very short temper. Of course, all Eric Derek kits have been banned, but the stink bombs are these tiny little capsules that the boys can hide in any number of places without it being detected, until it's too late of course. Hopefully they'll use them all up and it won't become a trend, but they were all finding it utterly hilarious, even the twentieth time around, so that may be a bit too optimistic.

There was one good bit of news today. The school newspaper, *The Daily Duke*, comes out on Fridays, and in today's issue there was a review of *A Festive Carol*. I don't normally read it, but Danny brought a copy to the music room at lunch and read it out to us. It was a very positive review, but the best part was that I got a special mention for my 'entertaining performance'! The only other person who got a personal mention was Joanna, who played the main character. I must admit I was chuffed, even if it was written by Charlotte Henderson. It's nice to know that she's capable of saying something nice instead of just criticising everyone.

Monday 13th January 2020

I don't know why Mum bothered printing out the chore charts. It was a complete waste of time because she is *constantly* reminding me of the chores I need to do anyway. The chores themselves are fine – in fact, I'd say I probably did quite a lot of them before Mum started this new independence regime – but it is seriously driving me nuts getting ten text messages a day saying, 'don't forget to do this', 'have you done it yet?' 'Are you sure?' 'But did you remember this bit?', she's relentless! The thing that *really* annoys me is that I always do my chores on time, I've never given her any reason to doubt that I'm capable of doing them, and yet she persists with these incessant reminders – like I'm too stupid or too lazy to stick to a simple schedule! Ugh! I don't usually get so irritated by Mum but it's making me want to SCREAM! Yesterday she sent me a text while I was still at school – how am I supposed to clean the bathroom when I'm in Art, Mum? UGH!

The other thing that bothers me is that Frogsplash hasn't been doing all his chores, and while Mum nags him just as much as me, it doesn't seem to affect him in the same way. He seems utterly impervious to how truly, skin-crawlingly irksome it is! And because her aggressive prompting towards Froggo is largely ineffective, she tries to use me as her nagging mouthpiece.

"Has your brother done the laundry yet? Make sure he's put the load on a cotton cycle! COTTON!"

"Has he taken it out of the machine? It needs to go in the dryer ready for morning! But not my silk blouse! NO SILK IN THE DRYER!"

I don't know if it's better or worse having her out of the house so often. At least, if she was here in person, she could check the wash cycle herself. The one good thing about her evenings working with Trudy is the self-made dinners. I'm being strict with my diet now, and there's no way Mum would let me get away with eating so little if she was here. It's easy on school days, I have a bowl of mum's low-fat cereal for breakfast, I make my own salad for packed lunch and I eat half a portion of whatever's on the menu for dinner. It's harder on the weekends when I get bored and turn to the fridge for comfort, but this weekend Danny and I are going to Carla's house, so that will keep me occupied.

PERFECT PARENTS AND A HAPPY HOME: THE FIGUEROA FAMILY HAVE IT ALL FIGURED OUT!

This reporter goes undercover in a covert study of one of society's rarest and most bizarre households. The two parents, Maria and James, and their three daughters, Carla, Rosie and Louisa, appear to be living in a state of complete domestic bliss, being supportive and considerate towards each other and, most fascinating of all, apparently enjoying each other's company. We get up-close and personal in this in-depth exploration of the most unusual of modern tribes: the functional family.

"Danny, Sam, this is my mum, Maria," Carla introduced us to her mother, who was reading a book in the front room next to Carla's dad, who was flicking through music magazines. "And this is my Dad, James."

"Hello," we said sheepishly.

"Hello!" they both said cheerfully, and they got up to greet us.

"We haven't officially met," said James. "But we saw you in the Christmas play and you were both truly fantastic!"

"Absolute superstars!" said Maria genuinely. They seemed a very happy couple; I don't think I ever saw Mum and Dad like that. It didn't seem to be just for show either, there was a real warmth about them both.

"We're not watching the TV," James said. "We'll clear off if you want to sit in here…"

"That's all right, Dad, we're going to hang out in my room for a bit," Carla said.

"Your parents are so *lovely,*" I said once we were upstairs. "Do they always hang out together like that?"

"Literally always," said Carla. "They love each other's company. Even when they're arguing, you can tell they're happy."

"That's so sweet!" said Danny. "I'm pretty sure my parents love each other, but they love spending time apart too. So how come your mum kept her last name?"

"What?"

"Well you're Carla Figueroa but that's got to be your mum's surname, right?"

"Oh yeah – it is. They're not married. They spend all the extra money they get on plane tickets, so they could never afford it. I've asked them about it loads of times and they said they don't need to *prove* to anyone that they're in love, so the only reason they'd do it is for the massive party. Don't get me wrong, they love a big family gathering but it would cost a bomb – especially as it would probably be in Puerto Rico."

"Would you like to see them get married?" Danny asked.

"Of course!" said Carla. "They talk it down, but I know how much they'd love it – especially if all Mum's side of the family could be there; she always misses them."

"Aw, I hope it happens someday," said Danny, slightly dreamy-eyed.

"Ugh – you're so lovey-dovey!" I said to Danny, jokingly.

"No, I'm not!" she said.

"You are," Carla agreed. "You want everyone to live happily ever after in a big, sparkly castle!"

"It's OK, Dan, we all have our weaknesses. For me, it's Mr Achilles…"

"Ha! The History teacher?" Danny laughed. Then they both got into fits of giggles.

"What can I say? He's a very charming man," I said, but they were still laughing. "I don't know what's so funny, but I suggest you save the jokes for your bridesmaid speeches at the Achilles-Drury wedding in ten years' time!"

More fits of laughter erupted, and I joined in, not at all embarrassed about my confession.

After a delicious (but healthy) lunch that Carla's parents cooked together (they really are like a couple from a lifestyle magazine – in a good way!), we hung out in the front room because Carla wanted to play us some of her dad's records. Almost as soon as he heard her put on *London Calling* by The Clash, he came bounding in like a loyal dog answering the call of its owner.

"Excellent choice!" he said proudly. "Have you heard this album before?" he asked me and Danny.

"Yeah, Carla plays it at lunch sometimes," I said. "My favourite is *Jimmy Jazz*."

"Nice!" he said. "They were my favourite band when I was about fourteen. They still are, really, except that I have about thirty other ones now too."

"Did you ever see them live?" Danny asked.

"Not me, no," he said mournfully. "Even I'm too young for that but my mum went to see them when she was a teenager. You'd never have believed she was going to be a grandma if you'd met her back then!"

"Don't get the old photos out, Dad, *please!*" Carla said, looking alarmed.

"I won't; I won't!" he said. "Not today, anyway! You know, music really stood for something back then; and you can still hear it, even now, in the way they sing, and, in the lyrics they wrote. There was so much *energy* and *passion!*"

"Oh, here we go!" Carla said. "Dad's a frustrated music critic – it's all those magazines he reads!"

But despite a few comments like that, Carla didn't seem bothered at all about her dad hanging out with us, and she didn't even mind letting him take over the music selection and act as our resident DJ (only occasionally did she cringe at his song choices, and once because of his air guitar-playing). He played so many songs by so many different bands, I couldn't keep track of them all, but the ones I really liked were Led Zeppelin, David Bowie and Fleetwood Mac. It's no wonder really that Carla turned out so awesome, she has the coolest parents ever. Then again, so does her middle sister, Rosie, and she turned out rather different.

Rosie and Louisa, the two older Figueroa children, had been out shopping during the day, but they arrived home in time for dinner and we all ate together. Louisa asked us lots of questions about ourselves like our favourite subjects, what we thought of the school, which teachers we had, what our parents do for a living, and she seemed genuinely interested in our answers, as did James and Maria. Rosie, on the other hand, didn't pay us any attention whatsoever, and got repeatedly told off for texting during dinner. When she did talk, it was about herself, and I must admit I found her quite intimidating. She's one of those popular sorts of girls who would never in a million years hang out with the likes of me by choice.

After dinner, we sat in the living room watching reality TV and laughing at the ridiculous people on screen.

"These people are a joke!" said Danny. "They're happily trading in their privacy and their dignity for a bit of fame."

"And money," Carla added.

"Right," said Danny. "I can't stand it. People like that are earning God knows how much for doing what, exactly? How are they helping people? How does anyone benefit from what they're doing? And then there are doctors and nurses saving lives, police and fire-fighters protecting us, teachers educating us, bin men making sure we don't live in our own filth, and they don't even earn half as much!"

"That's the nature of the game," I said resignedly.

"Well it sucks," said Danny. "They shouldn't be rewarded for being shallow and self-obsessed. I hate them, especially that main one – what's her name? The one who's horrible to all the others and deliberately turns them against each other for her own amusement."

"Geraldine Tuck," said Carla.

"Oh, my God, Geraldine Tuck, I *love* her!" Rosie said, bursting into the room after changing into one of her new dresses. "I'm totally *obsessed* with her – she's amazing." She sat down, eyes glued to the screen as Geraldine talked directly to the camera about how she'd orchestrated a particularly nasty break-up between a once happy couple, cackling every time she recounted a particularly sneaky part of her plan.

During the ad breaks, we learned that Rosie was getting ready to go to a party. She straightened and styled her hair for what seemed like an hour, occasionally suffocating us with hairspray and swearing when a hair grip failed to stay in place. Then she began doing her make-up and the swearing escalated significantly.

"What's up?" Danny asked, trying to be friendly. Personally, I wanted to stay well out of it, and was secretly hoping that Rosie would finish getting ready in her room and out of our way. She makes me very nervous.

"I'm trying to do contouring without it *looking* like I've done contouring," Rosie said, not taking her eyes off her reflection. "I just want it to look like my face is naturally shaped that way."

"This party you're going to… it's someone in your year at school, right?" Carla asked.

"Yeah… so?" came the reply.

"So, they already know what your face looks like naturally!"

"It's not for *them;* it's for the photos, duh!"

"Samantha's good at make-up," Danny intervened. I could have slapped her.

"Is she now?" Carla said, surprised.

"Yeah, she showed everyone how to blend when we were getting ready for the Isle of Wight disco."

Oh Danny, no! Stop talking Danny, I'm begging you!

"You know anything about contouring?" Rosie asked. It was the first time she'd acknowledged my existence, and frankly, I liked it better when I was being ignored.

"Um, not really… I mean, I mostly just know face painting… it's not the same…"

Please, no! Somebody save me! If she asks me to do her make-up, I'll ruin it and then she'll scratch my eyes out or ruin my life like Geraldine Tuck does to everyone who crosses her! Agh!

"You know more than that – you have make-up club at your house every Thursday!" said Danny, once again being that friend who pushes you out of the plane when you've been saying all along that you never wanted to go skydiving.

I explained that I didn't *attend* make-up club and that it was my mum's thing really, but Rosie was already sold, and I couldn't say no to her. Doing somebody else's make-up is probably one of the strangest of all social interactions and I can just barely cope with the ordinary ones. Add to that the fact that Rosie scares me, and she cares *a lot* about the way she looks, especially at parties such as the one she was heading out to tonight and well, I'm surprised I didn't poke her eye out, my hands were shaking so much.

When Jessica does my make-up, I can look away and often she needs me to look down or close my eyes altogether, but it's different the other way around. You need to get close – *really* close and you can't look away. I was conscious of my breath near her face, conscious of my eyes examining her skin under her watchful gaze, even conscious of Danny and Carla watching me at work, but mostly I was conscious of my potential to make a mess of her face. I thought of Halloween and Froggo's sunken zombie face and how terrible it would be if Rosie turned out to look like that after I was done with her. So, I thought instead about Jessica and all she'd taught me.

Rosie was pleasantly surprised when I'd finished her contouring – she even thanked me. I'm not sure how genuine it was but who am I to complain?

She left shortly after and that's when Carla said, "I know what you're thinking, how the hell did *she* get into Duke John Jameson? Did she cheat the test?"

"I never said anything like that!" I said, grinning.

"Ah but you were thinking it – just look at that smirk on your face! Believe it or not Rosie is really, *really* good at maths."

Monday 27th January 2020

The diet's not working, or at least not fast enough. My school skirt still feels tight and I felt like a whale compared to Danny, Carla and her beautiful, tall sisters on Saturday. I don't want to be the fat friend. I don't want it to be like:

"Hey, do you see that girl over there?"

"Which one, the blonde one?"

"No, the fat one."

I'm already the average-looking one; Danny has her shocking bright white hair, Carla has those piercing blue eyes and jet-black hair, and I'm just here with my mousy, dark-blonde hair and hazel eyes looking like the very definition of a plain Jane. I don't have to be beautiful, though, I just don't want to stand out for being ugly. It cannot be my defining feature. I know fat doesn't equal ugly, but the way people talk, the way Charlotte Henderson looked at my thighs when she told me my skirt was too short, it feels like fat and ugly are the same thing.

So, I've been looking up fast diets on the internet. I can't do one where you hardly eat anything or one where you only drink liquids because I need food, or I'll go crazy – plus Mum might notice. So, I've found this one where you eat mainly vegetables and no sugar. I think it could work for me, I like vegetables – even the ones that most people hate, and I don't have that much of a sweet tooth. The only problem left is Mum. If she thinks I'm not eating properly, she'll worry – and neither of us need that. But I have a plan, and this evening when I heard Frogsplash making his dinner, I went down to have a chat with him in the kitchen.

"Hey," I said, leaning casually against the worktop.

Play it cool, Samantha, don't let him know that you want something...

"Hey," he said, not looking up from the back of the pizza box he was reading.

"So, I was thinking, now that we're making our own dinners and everything…"

"Yeah?"

"I've come up with a plan that could be... mutually beneficial."

I said play it cool, I did not say play it like an action movie villain.

At this stage he looked up; he wanted to know where I was going with this.

Good, good, the negotiations have begun. Now narrow your eyes and lace your fingers together in front of your mouth in a sinister fashion, that'll draw him in.

"Go on," he said, intrigued.

"So, I'm on this crash diet... nothing major, I just want to lose the Christmas weight, you know? But Mum won't like it if she thinks I'm just eating vegetables, and she won't like it if she thinks you're just eating pizza..."

I looked accusingly at the deep pan, stuffed crust, meat feast pizza on the oven tray.

It looks delicious. Don't get distracted. But look at all that cheese! Even in its frozen, pre-melted state I could eat the whole thing up. I won't even slice it, I'll just eat it like a giant piece of toast. I must have it, I must! No, no, stay strong, Samantha! Do not salivate!

"So, I was thinking we could make a deal," I continued. "I get all the vegetables, you get all the chips, pizza – anything greasy basically, and we split the fish and meat evenly, OK?"

"Can't argue with that," he said, looking pleased.

"Obviously, if Mum asks, we say we split everything equally, yeah?"

"Obviously," he said. "But what about desserts?"

"Hmm..." I said, trying to buy some time.

The negotiations continue! Think carefully now, Samantha, you do not want the desserts, he does want the desserts, you can use this in your favour. This could be a bargaining tool. You have something he wants – but what can he offer you?

"You can have my desserts if you do half of my chores," I said at last.

"No way!" he said. "Just because I don't go to your school for geeks doesn't make me an idiot, Sam. If you're on a diet, you can't eat desserts!"

Crisis alert! He's onto you and your tricks! Throw the contract in his face! Threaten to sue him! Make a false accusation to human resources!

"I could just chuck them in the bin," I said, but I knew I'd already lost.

"What, so we both lose out and you waste Mum's hard-earned money?"

"OK, OK, I'll be reasonable. You don't have to do any of my chores, but you do have to do all of your chores as soon as you possibly can – no procrastinating."

"Hmm," he said suspiciously.

Did he just 'hmm'? That's my trick! He's buying time – watch what he says next. Do not fall into his trap.

"What exactly are you getting out of this?" he asked.

"Peace," I said. "Every day that you have chores, Mum nags me to remind you because she doesn't believe you'll do them. She's already nagging me non-stop about my own chores and it's driving me up the wall! And that's another thing – if she texts you asking if you've done them, please TEXT HER BACK!"

"OK, OK, that's fair."

"So, we have a deal?"

"We do."

"Nice doing business with you," I said, and I shook his hand firmly.

"And for the record," he said, just as I was about to go back upstairs. "You don't need to go on a diet, but you can't back out of the deal now!" He laughed. I don't know if he thought he was winding me up, but it was a nice thing for a brother to say.

Thursday 30th January 2020

BREAKING WIND: TOXIC GAS LEAK CAUSES MAJOR DISRUPTION

Health warnings have been issued after lethal gases were accidentally emitted in several locations throughout a nearby secondary school. The incident is currently under investigation, but the person responsible for this atrocity is yet to be identified.

Today was the most embarrassing day of my life. And yet, in a way, it wasn't embarrassing at all – you'll see. It happened after lunch, but I'll give you a bit of background information first. Last night was Mum's day off from Trudy and the make-up business, but she looked absolutely shattered when she walked through the door.

"I hope you're not working too hard," I said when I saw her, trying not to imply that she looked terrible.

"Aw Sammy, you are sweet to worry about me. I probably *am* working too hard now, but the idea is that at some stage, I'll be able to quit my day job like Trudy, you know, if the business takes off. It's an investment of my time."

"OK," I said, not wanting to discourage her from her dream.

"This is OK with you, isn't it?" she said worriedly. "I mean, you will tell me if you need me at home?"

"No, no, I'm fine! I'm enjoying the independence, honestly. You know me – I like my alone time. In fact, Frog and I will make our own dinner tonight; we've gotten really into it."

"Really?" she said hopefully.

"Yes! You must stop worrying so much, Mum. Do you want us to make you some food too?"

"Oh, Sammy, you're the best daughter in the world! I'm fine though, thanks, I'll just get myself a snack later."

So, Frog and I made dinner together, sticking to our deal. We almost got caught when Mum came into the kitchen to get a glass of wine (she didn't quite make the full month, but we both knew better than to say anything). Luckily, she was too tired to notice Frog's plate of sausage and mash and my plate of peas and broccoli, but we decided it was best to eat in our rooms instead of the kitchen in case of the highly likely event that she came back in for a top-up. I ate the whole crown of broccoli, plus the peas, because that was to be my only sustenance until morning, and I was *starving.*

That was last night. On weekend mornings, I plan to have spinach and eggs for breakfast, but there's no time for that before school. Also, I need to ask Mum to buy spinach and eggs. So, this morning I had a spoonful of peanut butter and washed it down with a glass of milk. I don't think that's quite what they had in mind when they designed this diet, but it is low sugar... I think. For today's lunch, I had my tuna salad with kidney beans instead of sweet corn, and about half an hour later, when we were heading to our lockers before afternoon registration, my stomach started to ache. Not like a painful ache, but a gassy ache. Basically, I really, really needed to fart.

The locker room was at full capacity – literally every year seven was in there getting their books and bags for afternoon lessons, so I thought, what's the worst that can happen? If I fart and someone smells it, they'll never be able to trace it back to me, the place is far too crowded. So, I let it out. I'm telling you now, you have never smelled anything like it. It was like rotten eggs and boiled cabbage – so potent, so foul, and the worst part is, the farts just kept coming. The smell filled the room with abominable speed, everyone could already smell it, I knew because I was hearing comments like 'phew, what's that smell?' So, there was no point holding in the rest; it was already out there. All I could do was to let it out and pray that nobody pointed the finger at me. The smell was outrageous, but my gut felt so relieved! And then someone shouted.

"STINK BOMB!"

And everyone went into a frenzy of panic and excitement. People started running and screaming as if it were a real bomb. A teacher came out of one of the surrounding classrooms, smelled the unavoidable stench of my gas, and came to the same conclusion.

After several minutes of trying to regain calm and get everyone's attention, he said, "Right everyone, some very childish person has let off another one of those foul stink bombs. We will evacuate the area and take registration at the fire safety point in the playground. I will inform Mrs Barnaby next door and she will lead the way while I let the rest of the staff know."

Mrs Barnaby is my form tutor. She's usually very patient and forgiving, but she looked most displeased to be uprooted from her desk and her cup of tea to be dragged out into the January frost in the playground. Then again, she looked positively assaulted by the reek outside her classroom; clearly, she could see (or smell) why these measures were being taken. I didn't even feel bad. I *wanted* to feel bad, but all I felt was that I was getting away with murder. I ought to write to Eric Derek thanking him for saving me from the biggest embarrassment of my life, but from what I've seen of him, he'd probably track me down and embarrass me a million times over by sharing my story with his followers.

I hung back amidst the stampede of year sevens, staying deep within the heart of the crowd in case I needed to fart again. If you've got ten people within a one-foot radius of your body, no one can pinpoint which one of you farted, can they? People would probably assume it was another stink bomb and the culprits were just trying to offload their stash before they got searched. I farted again. It was the perfect crime.

Thank you, Eric Derek, you obnoxious man-baby.

I briefly caught up with Danny and Carla before we had to line up in our separate classes. We all said how pointless and ridiculous all these stink bombs are and tried to guess who had thrown it. We all agreed Johnny Acapulci was the most likely suspect – he's the sort of loudmouth class clown everyone knows the name of by the end of their first day at school. I could never tell the truth; this one is going to my grave.

As it wasn't a fire drill and there was no urgent need to check everyone was safe and accounted for, none of us took the evacuation seriously, and it took the teachers quite a while to get us all organised and calm again. In the end, we shaved off a good ten minutes of our afternoon lessons, and when I went to get my coat at the end of the day, the putrid smell of my insides had all but vanished from the year seven locker area.

I wonder if I'm the first person to ever have their farts mistaken for a stink bomb. Still, I got away with it, and that's the main thing.

Friday 31st January 2020

This morning at school, we had a special year seven assembly about practical jokes and especially stink bombs. Mr Wilcox, our head teacher, said they were not only repulsive but extremely disruptive, and that the school would be taking a 'zero tolerance policy' (whatever that means). He urged the culprit to come forward and assured us that if anything like this happens again, there will be consequences for the whole of year seven. I still could not believe this was all because of me. There were over two hundred people in that assembly hall, and they were all there because of me.

But it wasn't over. At the end of assembly, to my horror, Mr Wilcox said that as an extra precaution he and our form tutors would be searching ALL our lockers. Every single one. I couldn't believe it. I farted us all into this mess, but there was no way I was getting us out of it. Imagine if I confessed now! It would haunt me for the rest of my school days and beyond. So, I went along with it, opening my locker when it was my turn, revealing nothing but my lunch and a few books. Some others were less fortunate, though, and for them I did feel bad.

Several handheld games consoles were confiscated until the end of the day, plus a few Eric Derek items that were yet to be deployed. I even felt a little bad for Beth Amory who, as it turns out, keeps a set of hair straighteners in her locker so that she can use them in the tech rooms at lunch. One kid had an old egg mayo sandwich in his locker which was rancid, and I'm afraid his popularity is going to suffer as a result. Overall, the impact of this has been huge. Frogsplash can keep his greasy foods if he wants, but there's no way I'm eating just vegetables for dinner again. From now on, it's a balanced diet on weekdays and whatever I fancy at the weekend. Any diet that makes your farts *that* toxic CANNOT be healthy.

Saturday 1st February 2020

DREAD AND DISBELIEF AS DAFT DAD DUNCAN DRURY DOESN'T DROP DISASTROUSLY DIRE NEWS, LEAVES DAUGHTER DESTITUTE, DUMBSTRUCK AND IN DEEPEST DESPAIR!

Local father, Duncan Drury, has left his only daughter in a state of shock by failing to warn her ahead of a life-changing decision made in her absence. The young girl is currently unavailable for comment. She is beginning a long recovery process and is said to be in a stable condition.

It's a Dad weekend and in typical Dad form, it didn't occur to him until after we'd arrived to inform us of quite a major change to his living situation which is going to affect our weekends there. Let me introduce you to Richard. Richard is forty years old, almost completely bald, and remarkably snotty for a man of his years who shows no other signs of having a cold. As of last weekend, Richard is a single man, his wife having chucked him out on Saturday. He spent two nights sleeping on his parents' sofa, and since then he's been staying at Dad's. In my room. That's where he lives now. I only spend one night in every two weeks at Dad's, but I do wish he'd have warned me about this all the same.

So, from now on I'm sharing a room with Frogsplash, which is not cool. I considered suggesting that we do alternate weekends seeing as it's a bit crowded now, but then every Dad weekend would be as cringe as the one where we went to see *American High School*. I need Frogsplash; he's my buffer. I suppose it won't be too bad – he always stays up late watching TV with Dad, so I can come up to our room (I'm here now) and still get my alone time before bed. He's a heavy sleeper, too, and can easily sleep until noon, so I'll be able to read and write in the mornings without him getting in my way.

So, what's the problem, you may ask? Well let's just say that Richard is a little too… raw, now. He seemed OK when we first arrived, just a bit tired and awkward. But as the afternoon set in, he started on the beers and started to get a bit too chatty, telling us a few too many of the unpleasant details surrounding his recent break-up. As much as I hate being forced into *activities* and *doing stuff,* especially in winter, I really feel that, on this occasion, Dad should have organised something that would get us out of the flat for the day.

There's only one TV in Dad's flat; it's in the front room and Richard seems to have taken up permanent residence in front of it. At around dinner time, a dating show came on the TV, and it was around that sort of time that Richard switched from beer to whisky. Initially, he started making bitter jeers at the contestants on the show, telling them that love is a myth, it'll never last, and not to

187

bother throwing the best years of your life away just to have it all thrown back in your face by some cold-hearted woman who promised to spend the rest of her life with you.

Then his mood changed somewhat. He started crying; sobbing like a hurt child, and Dad *still* didn't appear to find any of this inappropriate. Richard took his phone from his pocket and began scrolling through his camera roll, showing me and Froggo every damn photo of his wife, him and his wife (including one of them on the beach, Richard's hairy beer belly on full display – ugh), plus pictures of their two daughters and even a few of their beloved family cat Clawdius (I know it's spelled Clawdius because he told us three times). He really was an absolute mess, but Dad and Frogsplash seemed to find it all rather amusing, this tragic excuse for a man bearing his soul and bawling his eyes out in front of an estranged friend and his bewildered children.

"She said to me, she said, 'when you lost all your hair, you lost all my respect' and you know what, I don't blame her. I didn't cope well; I lost my hair, I lost her respect, I lost my dignity, and now I've lost her. I spent our holiday money on hair regrowth pills on the internet, and none of them worked. I'm not ashamed to admit that I cried when the bottle was empty and not a single hair had grown back. Can you believe that? A grown man crying!"

Yes, I can believe that, Richard, you've been crying for the past half hour.

"No, I wasn't the perfect husband..." he went on. By this point, Dad and Frogsplash were watching the sports highlights of the day, so Richard had only me to direct his regrets and woes towards.

Lucky, lucky me. Still, it could be worse. I could be Richard.

"I never forgot our anniversary. I never lied to her. But I could've been more attentive. I could've spent more time with the girls and less time down the pub. But it's not too late to change! I can see the mistakes of the past clearly now! If she takes me back, I'll never take her for granted again! Maybe she doesn't think I can change. Or maybe she *does* think I can change and this was all a big trick to get me to see what a fool I've been! Of course! She doesn't *really* want a divorce! This is all part of her plan! She *wants* our marriage to work! It's not over! I can change! I need to tell her! I should call her!"

"Um…" this seemed like a bad idea, but who am I to give relationship advice to someone thirty years my senior?

"I'm going to call her! What's the worst that can happen? She can't chuck me out again!"

"Err… Dad?" I said.

"Yes, Sam?" he said, eyes still on the TV.

"Err… Richard is going to call his wife right now… do you think that's a good idea?"

"Oh, Rich," Dad said, suddenly alert. "You called Fran yesterday, remember? It didn't go well. She said she needs space. That means *leave her alone!*"

"I just want to hear her voice, that's all!"

I thought you wanted to tell her you could change? Get your story straight, Rich!

"Listen, Rich," Dad said in his most reasonable voice, "Being single is a blessing. I know it's tough now, but that's because you haven't *adjusted* yet. It took me a while, too, but trust me, once you get back on your feet, you'll be much happier than you were before."

Happier than when you were living with me and Froggo? Cheers, Dad.

"No, Duncan, it's not the same; I still love her! I love her so much!"

Oh, Rich.

Richard sounded like he was going to start crying again. Frogsplash had his phone in his hand, and the way his thumb was hovering over the main button looked a lot like he was preparing to record a video of the impending sob-fest.

"Well, if you still love her, give her what she wants. Give her space."

How very mature of you Dad.

"And go out to parties with younger women and post it all on social media – that'll make her jealous!"

Oh, Dad.

When the conversation got *even more* personal (don't ask me; I'll never repeat it) I decided to come up to bed. I hope Richard does get back with his wife. He's not the most fun flatmate ever.

Thursday 13ᵗʰ February 2020

Danny, Carla and I spent our lunch break as we usually do, listening to music and chatting in our soundproofed bubble in the music department. When it was nearing the end of lunchtime, we went to the year seven locker area and into the adjacent toilets, where we were surprised to hear someone crying in the end cubicle.

"Hello?" I said. "Are you OK?" Which was kind of a stupid question, but it was the first thing that came to mind.

"Yeah, I'm fine," came a broken voice.

"No, you're not," Carla said. "Come on, come out. Tell us what's wrong."

"No, I'm fine, really…"

"We're not leaving until you come out," Carla said, sternly but not impatiently.

After a moment's hesitation, we heard the metal lock slide open, and I think we were all taken aback when we saw Beth Amory emerge, looking somewhat more dishevelled than usual. Since her hair straighteners have been confiscated, she's been wearing her thick, glossy, brown hair in natural waves which, if anything, makes her look even more beautiful. Her eyes were green as ever, but they were puffy from crying, and smears of mascara stained the golden skin underneath.

"What happened?" Carla asked earnestly.

"Jake dumped me," she said, not looking up at our faces. "Just now at lunchtime in front of all his friends. It was so humiliating! I never even saw it coming!"

"Oh no, what a horrible thing to do!" said Danny. "You deserve so much better than someone who would treat you like that."

"You really do deserve better than him," I said. "He and his friends are horrible people. One time they threw oranges at me on the bus just because I was reading a book!"

"Really?" asked Beth. "That's awful! You know… they all laughed when I started to cry."

"Boys are the worst," said Carla. "Especially at our age. You're much better off having fun with your girlfriends."

"What girlfriends?" Beth sobbed. "I don't have any anymore! While I was spending time with Jake, Charlotte decided she should be head of the group and then she edged me out completely. I never saw myself as head of the group – I just talked and they listened! Apparently, that's not the way she saw it. She made me out to be mad and self-obsessed!"

"Charlotte?" I said. "You mean Charlotte Henderson? She's almost as bad as Jake! You deserve better than her too."

"Why are you being so nice to me?" she said. "I was so mean to you…"

"Oh… were you? I don't remember…" I said. I'm not a very good liar.

"Yes, you do! I said something about you not being on a diet. I felt awful about it for ages afterwards. I kept

192

trying to pluck up the nerve to apologise to you, but the time went by and then it seemed stupid and pointless. Sorry, that's a terrible excuse. OK, here goes: I'm sorry for what I said."

"That's OK," I said, very surprised and warmed to hear it.

"Why did you say it then?" Carla asked, getting defensive of me, as she does.

"Honestly, it's so stupid," Beth said. "I was just jealous of your lunch and the fact that you can eat what you want. I remember exactly what was on your plate; I can still remember the smell – I wanted it so bad! My mum always has me on a diet – for the modelling. She was a model before she had me and my brother. I like photo shoots, but sometimes I just want chips!"

"That's terrible," said Danny. "You're far too young to be on a diet!"

"That's what Jake said! I really thought he cared about me."

"Did he say why he broke up with you?" Danny asked.

"That was the worst part!" said Beth. "He said he got bored of me weeks ago but couldn't be bothered to dump me. The only reason he did it today was so he wouldn't have to buy me anything for Valentine's Day… *and* he said he fancies Charlotte more than me now!"

"That's just unnecessarily cruel!" said Carla.

"You know why he said that," I said. "Because he and Charlotte are a match made in hell. I mean, it's probably not even true, he probably just said it to be mean but that's *exactly* the sort of thing Charlotte would do too."

"You want me to get revenge for you?" Carla said. "My sisters know a thing or two about getting back at boys…"

"Carla, no! She gets like this," I said to Beth. "She was ready to pick a fight with Charlotte for me once!"

That made Beth smile a bit. Then the bell rang for afternoon registration.

"Oh no, I can't go out there – I'm a mess!" Beth said.

"Wait, I have baby wipes in my bag," said Danny. We all looked at her curiously.

"What?" she said defensively. "My little brothers are disgusting, and they always get their sticky hands on my stuff."

She handed the packet to Beth, who began wiping the mascara smears off her cheeks.

"You know, you really are better off without him," Danny said.

"And you're definitely better off without Charlotte, too," I said.

"See, this is why I think we need another women's movement," said Danny. "We should be supporting each other, not banishing each other from friendship groups. We need to unite against boys like Jake. If those girls had ever been your true friends, they'd have told you from the start that he wasn't good enough for you!"

"Thank you… sorry, I don't know your name."

"I'm Danny."

"She's our budding activist," I said. "I'm Sam and this is Carla."

"Thank you, all of you. You're really nice people."

"So are you," said Danny.

"Do I look OK?"

"You look perfect," said Carla. "Just like you always do."

So, I was wrong about Beth Amory. She said one mean thing to me and was it even that mean? And she apologised. I feel bad for her, her mum pushing her into modelling like that. And I feel bad for her, having had to spend time with Jake Atkinson. What an idiot. She will get happier without him in her life, and he'll probably get sadder without her.

You know, in *American High School,* and in pretty much every other teen movie or TV show I've seen, they always portray the pretty, popular girls as the mean ones. That's unfair. It's like they're trying to make everyone else feel better by saying 'Hey, they're not so great – they're all cold-hearted bullies!' Well it's not true, and I feel bad that I fell for it. I know you should never make assumptions based on the way people look, and yet those ideas that you learn from the culture and the media around you stay in your mind until something happens that changes them. Talking to Beth today was the thing that needed to happen. But how many other people have I misread?

Friday 14th February 2020

Ugh, Valentine's Day. It's a made-up day. I mean, when you think about it, all days are made up, even if they're just Tuesdays or inset days, but some have been made up for a valid reason, whereas some have not. At Duke John Jameson, you can buy a rose for two pounds and have it delivered to whoever you want in the school, complete with your own personalised message printed in fake cursive in the tag. I don't usually go in for all that stuff, but I must admit those roses were nice. They were real red roses with the thorns removed and with a sort of plastic cap sealed onto the end of the stem which had water in it to keep it fresh. I liked that part. It's clever and neat.

Carla and I talked about getting one for Danny, because she's such a hopeless romantic and all, but in the end, we decided it would only disappoint her once she found out it was from us. She wants the romance, not empty gestures.

"I'm not saying I have to get married to be happy," she said when the subject came up at lunch. "I just want someone who'll love and support me, and be my partner and my friend, not my *other half*."

"What's the difference?" I asked.

"Well it's just words, really," she said. "Except that words are never just words. They are always loaded with context and meaning. The *other half* implies that you're not a whole person without them. And I know I'm a whole person. I don't need someone else to help me *exist*. I would just like a companion, eventually, you know, not urgently."

The thing about Danny is she's not a hopeless romantic. She's a romantic.

"That's nice," said Carla. You should put that in your wedding vows!"

"I don't know if I want to get married," I said. "It just seems like a huge risk to take. How do you know you're going to love the same person forever?"

"Unless it's Mr Achilles, of course," Danny joked.

"Oh ha, ha, ha!" I said. "Haven't either of you ever had a crush?"

"I fancied a boy in primary school," said Danny. "His name was Daniel, but we all called him Dan."

"So… Dan and Danny?" I laughed.

"Well yeah, it would have been if we ever got together!"

"What about you, Carla? You've gone awfully quiet on the subject."

"Well…" she said nervously.

"It's not like you to be shy," I said. I wouldn't normally push, but she always does it to us, and I remembered how she pushed Beth into coming out of the cubicle and talking to us yesterday. "You can tell us, you know."

"I do have a bit of a crush actually," she said at last.

"Come on then, who is it? We won't laugh, I promise!" I said.

"Well, um… it's a girl, actually. You know Grace in the year above?"

"Oh, um, no, which one is she?" I said, trying not to sound too surprised.

"She has curly red hair. She works in the library sometimes."

"Oh, I know her! She seems nice. Anyone who works in the library is all right in my books!"

I didn't even intend that as a pun. Now it looks like I'm trying to make a joke because I don't know how to handle this conversation. I was doing OK before – but now I don't know how to handle this conversation!

"Oh, very clever," said Carla. "It's OK; you don't have to pretend not to be surprised."

"Sorry," I said. "I wasn't expecting it but it's OK, you know."

"Yeah, it's really not a big deal. I'm really glad you told us though," said Danny.

"Thanks," said Carla.

"So, why don't we ever hang out in the library?" I asked. "If I knew Mr Achilles worked in the library, you couldn't tear me away!"

"She's only in there sometimes," said Carla. "And I thought it would be kind of creepy if I just kept going there on the off chance that I'd see her… not that I haven't thought about it! Plus, she'd probably notice me staring after a while."

"Too true," I said. "I'm always worried Mr Achilles will catch me going all soppy-eyed on him during his lessons – can you imagine!"

"Ugh, I never had to worry about that with Dan," said Danny. "In fact, I *wanted* him to pick up my signals, but he was an idiot – totally oblivious!"

"I'm sure you'll get over it," said Carla. "I mean, what even *is* a boyfriend in primary school, occasional hand-holding and sharing lollipops?"

"Yeah, I probably dodged a bullet there," Danny said. "He always had a cold!"

That was probably one of my favourite conversations I've ever had. I don't know though – that one I had the other weekend with Richard was pretty good (just kidding!). I don't think I've ever known what true friendship is, but now I feel surer than ever that this is the real thing. It didn't shock me that Carla fancies Grace, I just wasn't expecting it – does that make sense? Like it didn't freak me out or anything, it's just that the idea never occurred to me. She said she knows her family won't mind if she starts dating girls when she's older, but she doesn't feel the need to tell them anything yet, which sounds sensible to me – I wouldn't tell my parents anything about boyfriends unless I absolutely had to!

Speaking of parents and all things cringe, there was a red envelope on the doormat when I got home from school today and it was addressed to me. It was a Valentine's card with a fuzzy bear on the front sent from 'your secret admirer', but it was so painfully obvious that it was from Dad. For one thing, the only people on this planet who know my home address are blood relatives, plus he'd made no attempt to disguise his horrible grown-up handwriting. I don't know if it's ironic, but it's certainly unfortunate that the one occasion he does remember to send me a card on time is the only one I don't want him to and the only one for which he can take no credit.

Friday 21st February 2020

I love my room. A few years ago, it was all sickly pink like bubble gum and marshmallows, so I asked Mum and Dad if they would redecorate it for me. I didn't know it, but Dad was deep into his affair at the time, and I guess at that stage he must have known he was going to leave us, because he took on the project of my room like nothing he'd ever done before. Maybe he was using it to distract himself from his own guilt, or maybe it was an excuse not to spend time with Mum. Maybe his frequent trips to the hardware shop were combined with visits to the other woman – *Sophie,* I think she was called. But I like to think it was his parting gift to me – a sort of apology without words.

At first, I wanted a jungle theme but when I saw how enthusiastic Dad was about the whole thing, I got worried that he was going to attempt to paint tigers and parrots on my walls, so I changed it to a genie-in-a-bottle theme, which seemed like a far more grown-up idea anyway. He let me choose turquoise and purple patterned wallpaper, which he spent ages putting up because he had to get the patterns lined up just right with each sheet. I remember hearing him cursing impatiently over the sound of the radio he was listening to while he worked. I felt guilty at the time as he was working tirelessly, and all for me! He hung sheer, billowing sheets of fabric up on the ceiling in all shades of green, blue, pink, purple and gold. He put a gold-framed mirror up on the wall and decorated my desk and bedside table with beautiful lamps, ombre glass vases and candles.

The final touch, and my absolute favourite, was the huge magic carpet he bought online. It's genuinely stunning, with ornate patterns covering every inch. Of course, it's not actually magic, but it's totally authentic and I adore it. I always make sure no one steps on it in shoes, and I try to keep people off it (and out of my room!) in general. Add to that my big, comfy bed with cushions and sheets to match the walls, and Dad had created my perfect bedroom, my sanctuary; my girl-cave. It was less than two weeks later that all the magic and brightness faded before my eyes.

So, have you ever noticed in school that there are some kids who, when you pay close attention, you realise don't have a very happy family life? Often, they're the ones who don't seem very happy themselves, or perhaps they're very bold, a bravado made up of 'thick skin'. Well I noticed them. I felt really, badly sorry for them. Their parents were always fighting, and the instability was plain, even to me, a distant observer with a child's perception (I was a child, after all. Not anymore, though).

I was not one of them, not by half. My family did activities together, we supported each other, we had inside jokes and we knew how to make each other smile no matter what. We went on bad holidays and still had fun – it was kind of our thing. We were just as a family ought to be, not a fairy tale but perfectly functional and even more wonderful for all our flaws and mishaps.

The day Dad walked out – it must have been a Saturday – Mum was out shopping, Froggo was playing video games in his room and I was playing something in mine… isn't it strange that I can't remember? I think it was a make-believe game I played on my own, but did I still do that childish sort of thing when I was nine? Anyway, I went downstairs, and Dad was ironing all his shirts, which immediately felt strange because ironing shirts is a Sunday evening activity, not a Saturday lunchtime thing in any normal circumstances. But come on, what was I supposed to infer from a bit of ironing? Nothing else seemed suspicious…

A short while afterwards I heard his footsteps on the gravel which covers our driveway. I've always been tuned in to that gravel. My bedroom overlooks the front of the house so, understandably curious, I looked out, and I saw my dad putting a big suitcase into the boot of his car. Do you think, perhaps, I grew concerned... or at the very least more curious? If so, you are wrong. It seems so stupid now, but when I saw that I thought 'ah – he must be going on a business trip, that explains the ironing!' despite the fact that he'd never to my knowledge been on a business trip before, despite the fact that neither he nor Mum had mentioned any upcoming disturbances to our routine, and despite the fact that the suitcase I saw him load into the car was big enough for a two week stay, at least. I'm not being sarcastic here, I was honestly, one hundred per cent oblivious. Until he came to say goodbye.

He came up, knocked on my door, and when I said 'come in' the look on his face gave it all away. Just kidding! Even then I had absolutely no idea.

"Sam, I need to talk to you," he said. "Sit down for a minute."

That's when I knew. Dad was never that serious. I perched on the edge of my bed, the silky purple duvet covers still brand new and luxurious, smooth and cold under my fingers. I remember the little silver mirrors. The duvet cover had this embroidered strip near the head of the bed with swirling patterns and these little round mirrors inset into the fabric. They reflected the sunlight from the window and made patterns of white spots on the sheets of coloured fabric on my ceiling. I still have the same duvet cover, but a lot of the little mirrors have come out in the wash and I don't use it so much anymore.

"Sam, I'm not going to live here anymore," he got straight to the point. "I'm leaving your mum because I don't love her anymore. I still love you and your brother, and you'll still get to see me all the time. This is not your fault, and it's not your mum's fault either; it's my fault."

I started to cry, uncontrollably, the tears were streaming down my face and my throat was all choked up, so I couldn't speak at all.

"Don't cry; please don't cry," he said, but he must have known that I wasn't going to stop. "I'm going to live nearby, so you can come and see me whenever you like. Things are going to change, but I promise I'll do everything I can to make it as easy and as pain-free as possible. What will never, ever change is that I am your dad and I love you."

I didn't say I loved him too; I just cried and cried and cried. He hugged me for a while, but he had to go. He had two more stops to make. I heard him go into Froggo's room, where he must have delivered the same speech, but I don't think Frogsplash cried at all, at least not in front of anyone. Then he went downstairs and waited for Mum to get back from the shops. I heard her car tyres crunching on the gravel, and I wondered if she had any idea what was coming. I didn't think she did, because she had seemed so happy before she left.

So, I was the first to know, and Mum was the last. That didn't seem right to me. It felt like I was keeping a secret from Mum, because I had this knowledge – I knew this huge thing that was going to change our lives forever, and she was blissfully unaware of it, even if only for a few minutes. It felt as though I was betraying her, but what could I do to stop it? I stayed in my room until she came up to get me and Frog, but Frog wouldn't come down. At the time, I thought that was because Frog just didn't care, but now I realise it was just his way of dealing with it. She'd already called her mum and dad, her brother, her sister and a few of her friends and they all dropped everything and came over, and we all sat in the living room – they talked, and I just listened.

The living room was where it all got dragged out, combed through and pored over, over and over and over, but my room was still my personal space, and it still is my home, away from the impact of other people's words. Except Dad's, of course, but that's all ancient history now. If you could see my room, you'd understand why I rarely want to leave it; I'm happy here on my own. So why didn't I just say that? Why did I have to lie?

It was half term this week and I was hoping for a quiet one. Well you know what they say – be careful what you wish for. Danny usually goes to her street dance class after school on Mondays and this week they had a special half term deal where you could bring up to two friends along for a free session. Obviously, it's just a way for them to try and recruit new members, but Danny thought it would be fun anyway, so she invited me and Carla. Well you can imagine how much fun *I* thought it would be. Dancing, me? Remember what happened the last time I danced in public? I got photographically humiliated by my arch nemesis Charlotte Henderson.

I'm still recovering from the shame, but the truth is I don't think I'll ever get over it. It was what you call a character-defining moment. Is that a thing? Or is it character-building? Whatever that was, it didn't build my character. More like shatter it into a million splintered shards. Carla and Danny have helped to rebuild me, but I may just have blown that.

So obviously the notion of *me* doing proper, choreographed dancing in front of a group of *trained dancers* was out of the question, and I felt this rush of fear and anxiety at the mere thought of it. I panicked and went back to that old mind-set I used to use when Summer tried to get me to commit to spending time with her. At that moment in time, I just couldn't think of anything worse in the entire world than me having to go to that dance class and being exposed, whether I danced badly or failed to dance at all. Remember the 'basic' trust exercise I failed in my first P.E. lesson? I could picture it all in my mind's eye and I felt like I was drowning in that place – like I was already there in that dance hall surrounded by fit, slim, talented dancers all staring and laughing at me and my two left feet and thighs thick as tree trunks but wobbly like jelly.

My body is holding me back. It is holding me back from doing those things that other girls do… or is it my brain? Is it my brain?

I need this journal to keep me sane.

Either way, it was all closing in on me, and I had only a split second to make my decision and make my escape. It was the only way I could see out of there, like I was stuck at the bottom of an empty jar and someone was closing the

205

lid on me – *Danny* was closing the lid on me. I had no time to think, so I said the thing I always used to say.

If you make a lie too elaborate people will start to question it, so keep it simple. Don't flinch, Sam, don't sweat, don't let them see how your heart is racing, just save yourself from drowning. Do it! Do it now!

"I can't. I'll be at my dad's."

And breathe.

If they'd have questioned further, I'd have made something up about how my dad had taken time off work. Put as much truth into your lies as you can – that's another trick I've learnt. I could have told them about Richard and used him somehow. I'd have said he's bringing Dad down or that Dad took time off to help him get back on his feet and out of his flat. But they didn't ask, and I also know that if you offer detail that was never sought it makes you look more suspicious. I sound like a master of deceit, I know, and that's bad. I don't lie to be bad, I just lie because sometimes I have to say no, and I don't know how. I'm conscious of this now and I know it's something I must change. But before you cast me off as a bad person, please let me try to explain.

I don't know if you remember me talking about the summer holidays before I started at Duke John Jameson. Well that was when Summer was really bothering me. You might even say she was harassing me, but I wouldn't call it that because I know that she'd have stopped if she'd *known* that I just didn't want to be friends anymore. She just couldn't take the hint, and I just couldn't be that cruel. We'd been friends for a long time, and to tell someone that you just don't like their personality – well that's harsh.

Anyway, we were about to go to separate schools, it just made sense to keep her at bay until we drifted apart naturally.

So, I just kept saying 'No, I can't come tomorrow' and she kept saying, 'What about the next day? What about the day after that?' until I ran out of excuses and I was trapped. She got me in such a panic; I mean it *really* stressed me out. I didn't know what to do. And now... I don't know, but it all came flooding back to me, even though I know Danny is nothing like Summer. I just crumbled. My brain went into meltdown.

Is it my brain?

So, I said I was at Dad's and that was me off the hook. It seemed like a valid excuse; those two get to see their dads every day – I don't. So, I felt OK about it. Usually when I go to Dad's on a Saturday, I get there for about midday and stay until after dinner the next day. So, not wanting to complicate the lie, I stuck to the same structure and told them I was going to Dad's midday Monday and returning home Tuesday evening. All good. Nice and smooth.

I felt relieved after that, and much more relaxed. Cancelled plans really are the best of all plans. But, as I'm sure you can tell from my tone, this story does not have a happy ending. I spent Monday catching up on homework and a few TV shows, taking a break at lunchtime to try and cobble together a meal from the dregs in the fridge. When Mum got back from work, she noticed that the cupboards were bare and realised that she couldn't leave me and Frog to starve, so she cancelled her plans with Trudy and the make-up group (see – cancelled plans to the rescue!) so that she could do the grocery shopping.

She asked me and Frogsplash if we wanted to come. Frog said he was going to Hayden's house and would have dinner there, but I'm still trying to eat a healthy diet, so I decided I'd go with Mum to make sure she bought all the fruit and vegetables that I like (and to dissuade her from impulse buying tempting treats that I know I'll snack on if they're in the house). So, we got in the car and headed off to the supermarket. We were browsing the antipasti section in the usual way that Mum and I like to browse, which is to deliberate over adding new items to our regular shop throwing pros and cons backwards and forwards until we've reached a decision.

"Are olives healthy?" Mum said, holding a jar of large green olives stuffed with feta cheese.

"Well of course they are," I said. "They're a fruit, aren't they? And olive oil is good for your skin I think."

"Olives aren't a fruit!" she said.

"They grow on trees, don't they? That makes them a fruit."

"Well, I suppose, but you don't eat them fresh like you would an apple. You can't just pluck one from a tree and eat it; they go through all these processes where they drench them in salt and oil – that's not good for you."

"True," I said. "And I guess stuffing them with cheese isn't too healthy either."

"Especially these ones in the jars," she said. "They're far from fresh, and they've been sitting in this brine for God knows how long, which means even more salt."

"We could get some fresh ones from the deli," I said.

"But they're so *expensive* there," mum said.

"True," I agreed. "And they're not *fresh*, I suppose…"

"They do taste a lot nicer though," Mum said. "OK, let's go and see what they've got."

And it was at that moment, when we finally popped out of our olive mini-verse, that I looked around and saw Carla and Danny, still in their dance clothes, staring right at me, scowling, next to a shopping trolley carrying two small boys. They must have seen the way my face dropped, the way I froze on the spot: it was so obvious that they'd caught me out.

"Sorry about that, girls," a woman came rushing in and started pushing the trolley away, she must have been Danny's mum. "The twins keep sneaking chocolate mousses into the trolley, and if I don't put them back in the chilled aisle they'll go off. I told you boys, we're just getting dinner!" The twins giggled as they were carted away in the opposite direction, followed by Carla and Danny, who did not say a word to me. I grew very quiet after that and lost all interest in mindless conversations about non-perishable foodstuffs. I just wanted to go home, get my phone, and try to dig myself out of the hole I'd thrown myself in.

"I'm sorry I lied. I just couldn't bear the thought of dancing in front of people," was the feeble text I sent to our group chat. I received no reply.

That was four days ago, and I've still not heard from either of them. It's been a miserable half term. Time and time again I've thought about sending another text, but I doubt they'd respond, and all it would achieve is making me feel like even more of a fool. Of course, I will talk to them on Monday, but I'm dreading it.

Monday 24th February 2020

RECONCILIATION REPORT: PANIC TURNS TO PEACE AS PALS PUT PETTY PROBLEMS PERMANENTLY IN THE PAST!

A group of friends located at the centre of the entire universe and widely known to be the definitive example of true friendship has recently undergone turbulent times. The iconic trio, often referred to as the 'Three Wise Women' are responsible for keeping the world in balance, and so it is with great relief that we report an end to their internal dispute.

I was overwrought with nerves all morning. I've had a week to think about what I was going to say and boy, did I overthink it. I'd blown it up in my head into huge, unmanageable proportions, and I'm sure if it had been anyone else, I'd have cut my losses and never spoken to them again, but there's no way I'm losing Danny and Carla like that. No way. I could have lied to them again, come up with some lame excuse about my dad cancelling or whatever, but it was lying that got me into this mess, and lying to get myself out of things is the thing I need to work on. My friends don't deserve it. They deserve the truth.

They deserve a better me. Anyway, why lie when the truth does the same job? Well, because the truth is long, and it makes me feel very vulnerable to admit how badly I can be affected by social situations.

Carla and Danny are much chattier than me, and much more confident. They find it a lot easier to get on with other people, even people they have nothing in common with. They don't get intimidated like I do. Like at Carla's house – it didn't even occur to Danny that I might fear Carla's sister Rosie, so she volunteered me into giving her a makeover and I was *petrified.* I suppose I was scared that they wouldn't understand, and so it seemed easier to lie. But they've told me things that must have been scary to admit, and it didn't change the way I felt about them at all.

Time to be brave, Samantha Drury.

When I walked into the music room at lunchtime, they were both already there. My heart started pounding when I saw them, and my legs felt like jelly as I walked closer, but I couldn't back away. They hadn't put any music on yet, and their conversation stopped dead when I entered, so I was welcomed by cold silence. I felt so ashamed, like a child who's come off the naughty step after a huge tantrum. It was hard to believe they were only two people; it felt like there was a whole audience there to witness my public execution. They stared at me, unsmiling and stony-eyed, but when I sat down and started talking, they softened.

I explained to them how it made me feel when someone pressures me into doing something, and that I was worried that if I'd just said I didn't want to do it, they would start pressuring me and pushing me into a corner like Summer used to do. I told them all about Summer and I explained to them that even though I know they're nothing like her, I panicked because I had to think on the spot, so I didn't think it through properly.

I reminded them of the photo of me dancing on the front page of *The Daily Duke* and how humiliated and upset I'd felt about it. And then I said that even though I hoped this would help them understand, it's no excuse for lying and I won't do it again; I'm working on being more open and I never want to do anything to risk our friendship.

They were very understanding, and they even apologised for not giving me the opportunity to explain sooner. They said they would never, ever pressure me into doing anything, and that they will always accept no as an answer. Danny said what I described sounded like it could be a panic attack, and that maybe I should talk to the school counsellor. I told them of the ridiculous meeting I'd had with him at the start of the school year, but that I was quite keen to skip P.E., so perhaps I'd reconsider.

Now that things are back to normal and I no longer have this heavy weight on my shoulders, I am free to ponder. No, not ponder. *Ponder* implies a light-spirited, casually inquisitive river of thoughts flowing freely with the natural current. What I do is analyse. Perhaps it's over-analysis that causes my anxiety, but I know what caused me to lie to my friends. It was the opposite of analysis; it was being asked a question and not having the time to think it over before I answered. So, I ended up responding irrationally. I need my thinking time. Lots and lots of it.

I was so unhappy last week. Part of that was shame and frustration with my own behaviour, but the other part was loneliness. And that's what I find interesting, because before Monday I was perfectly happy with the prospect of spending the entire week alone and now, I realise that feeling lonely has nothing to do with being physically isolated. It wasn't that my friends weren't with me there in my room, it was that they weren't with me in spirit, because I knew they didn't want to talk to me. Loneliness is in the mind. It's a feeling, not a physical state. Fascinating.

I think about all the time I spent with Summer after I'd outgrown our friendship. I felt very lonely then. I felt so much lonelier than when I was alone, I think because I knew something was missing that should have been there. She didn't share the space in my mind with me, and I had no interest in entering hers. But she still wanted the friendship, she wanted to connect with me, but she couldn't, and I wondered if the thing that was missing was something in me. Maybe I'd lost a part of my soul. Maybe I would never be able to connect with anybody. It was a scary thought, and one which I didn't want to face, so I didn't test it. I didn't try connecting because I was scared.

It's not just that though, is it? Yes, I feared rejection, but I also really, genuinely enjoyed my own company, and I still do. I want you to know that. It's important to me that you know that because I don't think people always believe me when I say that I'm happy by myself. They think I'm putting on a brave face and I get the impression they feel sorry for me. Maybe that's part of the reason I don't always connect with people: because when I do try and tell them how I feel they don't believe me. What's the point in confiding in someone when they won't even believe you when you've been brave enough to be honest with them? And then I think, is it so weird? Am I so odd that what's normal to me is simply unbelievable to others? If that's the case then I am an oddball, and there's no point trying to connect with people if you're an oddball – by definition, you are un-relatable.

Danny and Carla aren't exactly oddballs, but for some reason or other they didn't find any proper friends until us three got together. They're more like misfits. Danny is the most personable of the three of us. She gets on with loads of people and stops to chat to them whenever she sees them. Before we got close she was, as she puts it, a social nomad – flitting from group to group, perfectly happy to spend time with any of them but never settling in one place. She loves a catch-up and the occasional gossip, but she has higher things on her agenda. She prefers to talk about ideas rather than people or events. She likes meeting lots of people because she likes hearing alternative perspectives. She never judges and as much as she likes talking, she's very good at listening.

And then there's Carla. Carla is cool, but not in that fake, 'popular' sort of way like in *American High School,* the opposite of that. She loves music, she *plays* music, she's laid back and she doesn't care what people think. I guess she's quietly confident. She hates injustice and she's highly protective of her friends, but she never goes looking for trouble. She's less interested in impressing people than either me or Danny, and perhaps it's because of that that she's the most at ease with herself. I never see her flustered. I'm in awe of her, but for some reason she doesn't intimidate me. She can sometimes be brooding, and other times be funny. I think she's very soulful.

They're both very, very intelligent, even by Duke John Jameson standards. I sometimes wonder where I fit in with these two, but I know that's one thing I shouldn't analyse.

Sunday 1st March 2020

THE BUTTERFLY EFFECT: A SPRINGTIME PHENOMENON

Adults everywhere are undergoing a bizarre and previously unobserved metamorphosis, emerging from their wintry cocoons looking brighter, feeling lighter, and aiming higher. But are some more flighty than others? Who will achieve new heights and who will fly too close to the sun?

I suppose Mum's long overdue for one of her phases, and as they go, this one doesn't seem too ridiculous. At some point last week, she had an epiphany.

"Guys, I've had an epiphany," she said to me and Frogsplash when we sat down for dinner on Wednesday. "Remember what I said at the start of the year about being more independent?"

"I'm not doing more chores, Mum – you can't make me!" Frogsplash said with more than a hint of panic in his voice.

"I meant about *me* being more independent," she said. "I realised I've been going about it all wrong. How can I be a truly independent businesswoman by latching onto Trudy and her business? Don't get me wrong, I get on great with Trudy and I like the make-up scene, but it's not *my thing,* and to be honest with you, I'm feeling like a bit of a spare part at most of our evenings. I mean, she doesn't have a day job anymore, so she can spend all day preparing pitches and watching make-up tutorials ready for the evening sales, and I just come across like a daft assistant who doesn't know her blusher from her bronzer!

"So, the other night I was sat in the utility area sipping my glass of wine, tending to the home brew and thinking… what *is* my thing? And then it hit me – wine! I love to drink it; I love to make it; I'm *passionate* about wine! And then it all started falling into place when I remembered something Graham told me…"

"Who's Graham?" Frogsplash asked, again sounding a little concerned.

"Oh, you know Graham – your mate Billy's dad!"

"*That* loser! He's a total low-life, Mum; he spends his whole life in the pub! What's he got to do with any of this anyway?"

"Well, if you'll let me finish! First, he's not a loser. Secondly, he spends his whole life in the pub because he is a pub landlord…"

"Ha! You idiot, Frogsplash!" I said, smirking.

"And since he divorced his wife," mum went on. "He lives in the flat above the pub. So, you see, it makes perfect sense once you know all the details. Anyway, I've contacted him about selling my wine in his pub as a local, English product. He says English wines are really popular now, and that he'd love to try it out."

"That's great, Mum," I said.

"Thank you, Samantha. In the meantime, I've decided to go back to just doing Thursday make-up club, but

Trudy's letting me take the lead on those, and I'm going to serve my wine to the ladies and see if I can sell a few bottles to them too."

"Don't you need a license for that?" asked Froggo.

"I'll be all right just selling to my friends – no one's going to sue me!" she said optimistically.

"You could get arrested," Frog said.

"No, I couldn't!" Mum replied cheerily, but Frog gave me a look which spoke a thousand words, and here is what I have surmised:

I think he, and possibly his friends, were considering selling Mum's home brew to other kids in their school. Maybe they even did sell some. But somewhere along the line, something got them into wondering what would happen if they got caught, so they looked it up and probably became semi-experts in the field of licensing laws. It might only be illegal to sell to kids, but Frog's face seemed concerned enough. Of course, he couldn't tell Mum that he knew this much, because then she'd ask questions.

"Maybe ask Graham about it," I said. "He should know."

"Can't do any harm, I suppose!" said Mum.

"How do you even know him, anyway?" Frog asked.

"We got chatting at your party, remember? He gave me his number in case of any emergencies, like you lot getting drunk again!"

"You realise that's extremely likely if you start brewing on a bigger scale… you won't even notice!" Frog said.

"I certainly will! I'll get top of the range security on all the equipment! Anyway, it's early days yet, but Graham seems to be excited about it, and so am I!"

Maybe that was *all* Mum was excited about, and maybe Graham too, but I remember seeing them together at the party and I remember my conversation with Jessica. I suppose it doesn't matter if it's the new business pursuit or a budding relationship with Graham, if she's happy.

And if she doesn't get arrested.

It's already getting warmer and sunnier outside, which is very early by English standards. It probably won't last. What it'll do is trick the flowers and the wildlife into coming out early, then it'll frost over again and kill anything too young to survive the cold. It seems to happen every year now like a mini ice age for the poor little daffodils and ducklings. But for now, spring is in the air, and with the seasons come change.

We went to Dad's again this weekend. He picked us up as usual (which means twenty minutes late) and drove us to his flat. "I've got a bit of a surprise for you two this weekend," he told us in the car. "Well actually, I can't take the credit. It was all Richard's doing really, but I think you'll like it."

That didn't bode well. As we approached Dad's front door, we could hear music blasting from inside the flat.

"Is that Free Parking?" I said, surprised.

"That's right!" said Dad. "Richard's really into them now… they're pretty good, aren't they? I like that one… what's it called? *Rolled Gold.*"

"Rose Gold!" Froggo said, annoyed. He liked Free Parking even before I did. Richard had just started playing

Fishbowl Beach and as we got closer, we could hear him singing along badly, out of tune and lyrically disastrous.

I bet they think we'll be impressed by this. Why can't adults leave youth culture to the youth?

When Dad opened the door and led us to the living room, we got quite a shock. Richard had taken the motorised shredder out of the tiny computer room Dad calls his home office and had placed it on the small dining table we rarely eat at because it's only big enough for two. Richard, who had somehow acquired quite a deep tan since we'd last seen him, was singing and dancing whilst shredding a huge stack of photographs one by one. He looked very cheerful indeed, the puffiness was gone from his face, he wore a hat to conceal his baldness, and on closer inspection he had also acquired an eyebrow piercing. He nodded to acknowledge our arrival, but carried on singing:

"You thought your mind was an ocean so vast
You thought your soul was too deep to reach.
But your thoughts are sand in an hourglass
And your heart's a plastic fishbowl beach.

You thought your horizons were beautiful, golden and broad
You thought you had a paradise inside yourself.
You said you were the ocean and me the surfboard
But you're an empty fishbowl on a dusty shelf.

I am an island but you're not the sea
You're just a siren who tried to trick me

Our sun has set; I am out of your reach
You can live in regret on your fishbowl beach.

You washed up like a castaway on my shore
Acting the exotic mermaid princess.
But you're no precious pearl on the ocean floor
You're a washed-up liar in a torn-up beach dress.

Like a summer breeze you played it cool
Like a fishbowl cocktail with ice
But when the ice melts you're left with a pool
Of salty water that don't taste too nice.

I am an island but you're not the sea
You're just a siren who tried to trick me
Our sun has set; I am out of your reach
You can live in regret on your fishbowl beach."

Fishbowl Beach, as you may have gathered, is one of Free Parking's more bitter songs. It's also Richard's favourite. After he'd played it three more times, he turned the music off and sat down on the sofa with me and Frog, both of us on our phones pretending not to notice Richard's dramatic personality change.

"So, did your dad tell you?" he said excitedly.

"He said something about a surprise," I said, trying not to come across too nervous.

"I got us tickets! Free Parking tickets!"

I hope he means for the car park.

"The concert's tonight! Isn't that amazing?"

"Are you serious?" said Froggo. "Those cost a bomb! You mean we're going tonight?"

"Yes!" Richard said. "All four of us!"

I saw Froggo's face drop. He's been wanting to see Free Parking live for years. I bet he never thought it would be with his little sister, his dad and some lunatic called Richard.

"It's a funny story really," Richard went on. "I bought the tickets for me and my family to win them back... but apparently none of them wanted to come with me."

Yeah, that's a funny story.

"Well, what do you say?" Dad prompted us.

"Oh... thanks!" Frogsplash and I said. Richard spent the rest of the afternoon talking about Free Parking and trying to get more gratitude from me and Frog by saying things like, "Oh yeah, these are the best seats in the house... cost me an absolute fortune... of course, I could have just sold them online..."

I suppose I was grateful – it would certainly be something to tell Danny and Carla! But when Richard offered to make us both lunch, I realised something, he's using us as substitutes for his children. This is scary. I do not need Richard as a step-dad.

Imagine if Mum marries Graham and Richard starts co-parenting with Dad: Suddenly we'll have three father figures! Talk about dysfunctional!

After lunch (Frog and I made our own but thanked Richard for the offer), Richard went back to shredding photographs of his soon-to-be-ex-wife. The thing was, he was shredding *every* photo of her, even ones that had his daughters in them. Now I'm no expert at break-ups, but couldn't he just cut her out of the pictures and keep the rest? He was shredding all their memories. And tonight, he would be creating new memories with me and Frogsplash. *Agh!*

"I'm just popping to the shops to get a few beers," Dad announced suddenly. "You two will be all right here with Richard for a bit, won't you?"

No Dad, no! Please don't leave us alone with this maniac! He's going to kidnap us!

I tried to communicate my panic to Dad with a desperate, pleading glare as he was putting his jacket on, but all he said was, "I won't be long – see you in a bit!"

While he was gone, Richard started asking us how school was going and whether we had any homework to do over the weekend or any important exams coming up. I tried to keep it vague while Frogsplash tried to veer the conversation towards the football match that was on the TV. Fortunately, Richard got bored of listening to us talk and started to show us photos on his phone again. Only this time they weren't of his family or their pets, they were all of sports cars, and he said he was trying to decide which one to buy.

"Yeah, it's either a car or a hair transplant," he said when he'd finished scrolling through them all. He may have been smiling, but I'm telling you now he was in a far worse state than the last time we saw him.

Incredibly, Dad returned before we'd been abducted, and what's more is he had a *good* surprise for us – a TV for our room!

"There's this documentary on this afternoon that I really want to watch," Dad said. "But I know how boring you two will find it, so I got you this, so you can watch what you like in your room."

"Yes, Dad! Thank you! Thank you!" It truly was Christmas come early. Dad has never watched a documentary in his life, so I know he was doing it to spare us an afternoon with Richard.

I am so glad you are my dad, Duncan Drury. You are NOT totally oblivious; you are the hero of the hour, and best of all... YOU ARE NOT RICHARD!

Imagine having Richard for a dad.

Dad put on his boring documentary, which I know he must have hated, while Frogsplash and I spent the remainder of the afternoon in our shared bedroom. I didn't mind that Frog put the football on, I was just grateful for an excuse to hide for a few hours, and after a break from the intensity of Richard's presence, I was starting to feel genuinely excited for the concert.

We left at five and got the train to the station nearest the venue. On the way, we picked up two pizzas and we ate them in the queue. Most of the people there were Froggo's age or a few years older, so we kind of stood out with me being so young and Dad and Richard so old, but no one seemed to care so I didn't. People were singing Free Parking songs while they waited, and we soon got into the spirit of things and joined in. There was a real buzz in the air; a real and glowing sense of anticipation, and before long I forgot who I was with. I was with the crowd, not with Dad or Richard or Frogsplash.

When we got in, the feeling was amplified by a thousand, it felt *electric.* Suddenly I felt so happy to be there, so lucky and so *alive.* It was like I was part of this huge event, like some shared experience with all these other, like-minded people who just wanted to have a good time, and we knew – we *knew* that it was going to happen, that we were all going to witness this unforgettable, incredible thing, and we could all feel it coming, brewing in the atmosphere like a purple electric storm...

Then there was this huge eruption of cheers and screams and I knew it meant they were coming onstage – I could see movement and hear guitars tuning but I couldn't see the band because there were dozens, maybe hundreds of much taller people in front of me and for a moment I thought I was missing out on the defining moment of my personal journey through music but then I heard the voice of an angel telling me everything was going to be all right and all was not lost – not by a long shot.

"Good evening, London! We're Tartan Paint and we're warming up for Free Parking tonight! Are you ready?"

Phew. I think I read something about Tartan Paint in one of Carla's dad's magazines, but I didn't need to see them, not really. Still, I craned my neck trying to see the stage, because I couldn't spend the entire evening like that.

"Do you want to see?" Dad shouted over the music when he saw me struggle. "Climb on my shoulders!"

"Not yet!" I shouted back, slightly worried that my weight would be too much for him if he had to support it all night. "Later!" I said, and he understood what I meant.

When Tartan Paint had finished their third and final song, Dad helped me onto his shoulders and at last, I could see everything. I could see over all the teenagers and I felt invincible being up so high with all of them down below. Some of them started chanting "Free Parking! Free Parking! Free Parking!" and I was so excited, I joined in. Some of them turned around to see who was chanting from so high above them, and when they saw how young I was, I thought they'd turn away, annoyed at me crashing their night, but they all smiled, waved and cheered like they were impressed with me or something – it was *awesome!*

But the best was yet to come. When the band finally came out everyone screamed, and I found myself screaming louder and higher than I've ever done in my entire life! They opened with *Crumpet Dump* to get the crowd going, not that we needed it, and I sang along to every word, and I swear I didn't care one tiny bit if my face was red and my arms were flailing like at the Isle of Wight disco, because I'd never meant it more. There was so much *spirit,* so much *passion* in that room I could hardly believe it was real. At one stage I could have sworn that Darcie, the bassist, looked right at me and smiled, but now when I think back on it, I must have been imagining things – that's way too unreal!

When Dad got too tired to have me on his shoulders, Richard offered to take over and you know what, I was grateful, not just for the shoulder boost but for the whole night. Yeah, Richard is a bit full-on, but he's going through some stuff now, and he could have sold the tickets like he said… he could've put the money towards those hair transplants! Anyway, it was one of the best nights of my life, and I don't regret for a minute who I spent it with. Even Frogsplash seemed really caught-up in the thrill and the magic of it all, his face was glowing with sweat and joy whenever I looked down on him, and I'm pretty sure I saw him and Richard with their arms round each other's shoulders during *Fishbowl Beach!*

Monday 2nd March 2020

The girls could not believe it when I told them about the concert! I did my very best to describe it, but there are some things you just can't put into words. I said I wished they could have been there on the night, which is true, and we promised each other that the next time Free Parking are touring, we'll all go together.

Sadly, though, that wasn't the main event of the day.

It was during art this afternoon. I still haven't caught up on sleep after staying up late for the concert on Saturday night; it doesn't seem to matter how late I go to bed, I always wake up before eight a.m. Anyway, I drank two diet colas at lunch because the caffeine in them perks me up a bit, but in Art, all I could hear was the rain gushing out of the broken guttering outside the window, and suddenly I was bursting for a wee. As you know, my Art teacher Mack takes a very relaxed approach to timetabling, so unlike most teachers, he doesn't care if you miss a few minutes of his lesson to go to the toilet.

As I approached the ladies', I thought I caught a whiff of cigarette smoke, but then decided that it must have just been lingering in my nose from the stale smell of Mack's smoking jacket as he was leaning over me to 'correct' my painting. Some people get annoyed with him for completely taking over their projects for them, telling them what to do or how to make it look better. They get even more annoyed when, even after they've taken his advice, he still doesn't think they've done a good enough job of it, grabs the paintbrush out of their hand and paints over their work with his own, much better interpretation of the subject. Personally, I appreciate Mack's passion, and whenever he honours my work with his own brushstrokes it's always a massive improvement. Don't argue with the experts, I say.

It was only after I'd entered the girls' toilets that I realised my initial instinct had been correct. I should not have gone in, but it was too late now because they'd seen me. At first, they just ignored me and carried on smoking and saying horrible things about some poor girl in their year that they'd obviously been tormenting. It was the blazer gang from year eleven, and I hadn't seen them up close since I'd managed to outrun them the day I met Carla.

"Hey, you know who that is?" I heard one of them say while I was in the cubicle. I froze. Even though my bladder was full I couldn't pee. "That's blazer girl; the little year seven, remember?"

Oh God, please don't let me die on the toilet.

"Hey, blazer girl!" said Megan, the one with the half-shaved head. "What are you doing in there?"

And then something awful happened. She went into the cubicle next to me, put the lid down on the toilet, stood on top of it and leaned over the side so she could see me sat there on the toilet with my knickers down. I felt so *vulnerable;* and so embarrassed. There was no way I could go with her watching.

"Hey, blazer girl, I don't hear peeing," she said, still watching over me. "You must be done. Here, let me help you," and then she yanked the chain from the top, so the toilet flushed while I was still sat on it. The toilet water erupted underneath me, soaking my entire bum and some of my skirt. The other girls, Ali, Fiona and Yasmin (I don't know which one is which) came to watch, too, one of them with Megan and the other two in the cubicle the other side of me. Four sets of eyes all on me while I struggled to my feet, trying to hide my bum at the same time as drying it hurriedly. They were all laughing hysterically, staring down at me cackling like evil overlords watching their subjects burn.

As soon as my bum was dry enough not to soak through my knickers and my skirt, I bolted out of the cubicle. They all scrambled down from on top of the toilets and tried to run after me to block my exit, but there were too many of them getting in each other's way and, as before, I was too fast. I ran to the next nearest toilets where I tried to calm myself down, prayed that they wouldn't follow me, and eventually relaxed enough to go for a wee. Any other teacher would have demanded an explanation for why my toilet break took almost fifteen minutes, but Mack took no notice, and a good thing too, because I know not to tell on girls like that.

Tuesday 3rd March 2020

I told Danny and Carla about what happened yesterday and they both hugged me and did all they could to make me feel better about it.

"I wish I could avenge you!" Carla said with all the fury of a raging bull.

"Don't you dare!" I said. "Or it'll be your head in the flushing toilet next!"

"The only good thing is," she said. "They'll be leaving in a few months, and I don't care how well they do in their GCSEs, there's no way they're coming back here for sixth form!"

"Oh God, I hope you're right," I said. "I can't go on living in fear for two more years!"

"Trust me; people like that always get what's coming to them," Danny said. "They think they can get away with it now, but they're going to get a nasty shock when they have to go out in the real world."

"I wish I could be there to see that!" I said gleefully.

Little did we know that our dealings with mean girls were not yet over for the day. At least this time we were in it together, and this time we were being picked on by someone our own size. The sun was back out again today, and after yesterday's heavy rain, we decided to make the most of it by going for a stroll outside after eating lunch, being careful to avoid the smoky woods. We walked past a large group of boys playing football, caking the bottoms of their school trousers in sloppy brown mud, and I thought of their poor mothers having to do their laundry for them later this evening. We were just at the top of the main field when we saw some familiar but not-too-friendly faces sunbathing in the middle of our path.

The rest of the field was too wet and boggy to walk through, so it was either walk on or turn back the way we came. We couldn't really turn back. Ahead of us were

Charlotte Henderson and her clinger-on, Andrea Michael, with their skirts bunched up as high as they could go without showing their knickers and their shirts tied up above their midriffs, trying to catch the sun in the 11°C heat. I was somewhat disappointed to see that Beth Amory had re-joined the group; after our chat and after all Charlotte had done to her, I thought she might have done better for herself. It didn't take long, though, to figure out that Charlotte was the leader of the gang now.

"Hey look, it's Danny, Sam and Carl!" she said. "Shouldn't you boys be playing football or trying to grow moustaches?"

"Oh, what, because we have boys' names?" Danny said. "Oh yeah – that's *so* clever, *Charlie!* The thing is, even if we did try to grow moustaches, we'd never be able to get one as thick as yours!"

And then, just as Charlotte opened her mouth to retaliate, Carla ran away superfast back in the direction we'd come from. Charlotte started laughing.

"Oh no, poor Carl's run off crying! We must have hit a nerve! Not surprising really; she's the manliest one by far," Charlotte said, still laughing.

But it was surprising to me, and to Danny. It was not like Carla at all to run away from confrontation. For a moment, we both stood there like lemons, not knowing what to do. We wanted to run after Carla and make sure she was OK, but we didn't want to run away from Charlotte and have her think that she'd defeated all three of us.

"You really think it's funny, don't you?" I said to her. "You must have something wrong with you, to enjoy being such an ugly person."

"Ha! *You* are calling *me* ugly!" she laughed, and just then, we heard feet shuffling on the grass behind us. It was Carla, and she'd got the football from the group of boys we'd seen playing a few minutes back down the path. She was dribbling it closer, and Danny and I realised what she was going to do. We ran towards her, getting behind her just in time for her to give the ball a huge, belting kick so it landed at full pelt in the boggy mud right next to the path where Charlotte, Andrea and Beth were sunbathing.

I must hand it to Carla; her strength was phenomenal, and her accuracy was astounding! The ball sunk gloriously into the wet ground, splattering thick, brown mud all over the three girls, their uniforms and their bare midriffs, with more than a bit going in their hair. By this point the boys who'd been playing football had come running over, wanting to know what the hell Carla thought she was doing nicking their ball like that, but when they saw the results, they burst out laughing, while the three girls got to their feet, horrified, trying hopelessly to wipe off the mud.

"You were so right, Charlotte," said Carla. "This *is* a great place to play football!" she picked up the ball and walked over to the group of boys. She handed it back to the one she'd tackled it from and he high-fived her. They all wanted to high-five her after that, such was the joy and entertainment she'd provided, not to mention her impressive football skills.

"My uncle plays semi-pro," she told us later. "My sisters and I spent every summer around his place whenever my parents had to work. Even Rosie's got some skills, believe it or not!"

It was the greatest victory in football history. But don't tell Dad or Froggo I said that.

Saturday 7th March 2020

Today at lunchtime, Mum went to Graham's pub, The Mill on the Hill, so that he could sample her wine. She was very nervous, but who's to say whether that was because of the wine or because of Graham himself. She took extra time and care in choosing her outfit and fixing her hair and make-up, because, she said, she wanted to make a good impression. She'd bought these fancy glass bottles with these tricky metal stoppers that I can't work out; she filled them with her wine and chilled them before taking them with her. I noticed that she walked there instead of driving, and I wondered if she was planning to drink a lot of it herself.

I must admit I feel proud of my mum when I see her do things like this. She's not afraid to put herself out there. That's not quite true. She *is* afraid, she gets nervous, but she always follows through with it. I was nervous for her today. Obviously, I've never tried her wine, and even if I had done, I wouldn't have a clue whether it was any good or not. She makes it from these tiny green grapes that grow in our garden. She's not especially green-fingered, but it was already well established when we moved in and she tried to maintain it because she thought it was a nice 'feature'. The grapes taste awful when you eat them fresh, but that doesn't necessarily mean the wine's bad, does it?

Frogsplash has been a bit quiet about the whole business. He's clearly suspicious of Mum's relationship with Billy's dad. I don't see what the problem is; if they move in together, then he'll get to live with one of his best mates!

Mum got back a few hours later, and I won't bore you with too many details, but Graham liked the wine and he wants to sell it in his pub! It's not as simple as that, obviously there are health codes and stuff, but Graham wants Mum to make the wine in his pub kitchen, and they're going to sell it as their 'exclusive English wine'. It costs so little to make that they won't have to charge much for it, and that'll make it incredibly popular. Mum said she can't expect to be able to quit the day job any time soon, but this will be fun for her and she'll see some profit from it, so she's happy.

She's so happy, in fact, that she's throwing a party next Saturday to celebrate, and she wants me to invite all my friends *and* their mums. Now I'm the one who's nervous! Danny and Carla have never been to my house before, but I guess it's about time.

Sunday 15th March 2020

The party was… eventful. I have spent the best part of today trying to piece together everything that happened, so forgive me if my retelling is a bit haphazard. Mum felt especially grateful to Trudy for introducing her to the make-up circle, which inspired her to start up her own business, so she invited Trudy before anyone else, and allowed her to bring her make-up testers to promote the business in the process. So, Trudy arrived early with her current boyfriend, Alex, and of course, Jessica. Trudy started laying out all her make-up supplies and tools, but Alex seemed almost desperate to do anything to please Trudy, so when Mum offered her a drink, she accepted it and sat down, leaving Alex to do the rest.

"He's like this whenever he comes around," Jessica said to me in hushed tones. "He waits on Mum hand and foot – he's like a trained puppy!"

"I hope you don't mind," Trudy said to Mum. "But I invited my friend, Francesca, she could do with a decent night out. She's bringing her two with her, one's Jessica's age and I think the other one's the same age as your Sam."

"Oh, perfect," said Mum. "The more, the merrier!"

Graham was next to arrive and of course, he brought Billy along with him. He also brought his much older son, Arnie, who Mum obviously recognised from the pub. Arnie, I have learnt, is Billy's half-brother from Graham's first wife. He works as manager for the family pub and seems equally enthusiastic about Mum's wine, which I take to be a good sign. Before, I wasn't sure if Graham only wanted Mum's wine because he fancies her, but if Arnie likes it too, then it must be half decent.

Danny's parents couldn't come, what with the twins still being quite young, so Danny came with the entire Figueroa family, with the exclusion of the oldest daughter Louisa, who had to work on her Sociology coursework. At some point, Hayden and Joshua arrived, but of course they 'forgot' to invite their parents. Add a few of Mum's co-workers and the party was in full swing.

I showed Danny and Carla my bedroom and they both loved it.

"You're so lucky," Danny said. "My mum won't let me decorate my room any other colour. She wants every room to be plain white with 'traditional' furniture so it's all in-keeping with the house. It's so boring!"

"Hey, at least you don't have to share with Rosie!" said Carla. "I can't wait for when Louisa goes to university, so I can have her room."

Before we went back downstairs, I told them about Graham and how I think he and Mum might be getting together, so we should keep an eye on them to see if we can see any signs that might give it away. They seemed very excited at having a little side-mission for the evening.

When we re-joined the party, we found Rosie getting a makeover from Jessica, and they seemed to be getting on very well. Rosie was telling Jessica all about her relationship troubles with her boyfriend, and Jessica had plenty of advice for her. Jessica seems very worldly when it comes to the art of dating, I think she's picked up a lot from her mum over the years.

"Whatever you do, don't text him now," she was saying to Rosie. "I know it's tempting and you want to give him a piece of your mind, but trust me, he knows what he's done, and he's going to try and make you feel desperate enough to forgive him. Don't let him. *You* need to make *him* feel desperate. It's Saturday night, that's the perfect opportunity to ignore him, because then he'll think you're out having such a great time that you're not even thinking about him."

"You're so right," said Rosie. "You know what I'm going to do? I'm going to put my phone in my dad's car, so I can't even look at it."

"Excellent decision," said Jessica. "With any luck, you'll have him worshipping the ground you walk on. If not – get rid of him! My mum is an expert; watch and learn!"

She nodded over in the direction of Trudy and stopped doing Rosie's eyeliner so that she could observe. Trudy was sat on the sofa chatting away to one of Mum's work friends who sometimes comes to make-up Thursdays, and Alex was standing next to her, looking at her adoringly as he refilled her wine glass.

We never did find out exactly what Rosie's boyfriend had done to deserve the silent treatment, but it can't have been eating her up too badly because when we got back down, she was up dancing with Jessica, who had obviously won her over with her sage advice and spectacular makeover.

We went to find Mum and Graham to see if we could spot any signs of romance, but instead we found them engaged in separate conversations with Carla's parents. Carla's dad, James, who works in advertising, was talking to Mum about the branding of her wine. I found out afterwards that she's been thinking of going back to her maiden name, Darling, for quite some time, but she couldn't be bothered with all the paperwork and getting new bank cards and stuff. But she wants it to be called 'Cassie Darling's Proper English Wine' which sounds a bit posh to me, but maybe that's a good thing when it comes to wine.

Graham, meanwhile, was very interested to learn that Carla's mum, Maria, is a carpenter. Carla says she mainly makes furniture, like fancy dining tables and stuff, but that she's picked up a lot of other skills along the way. Apparently, Graham wants some work doing in the pub which his ex-wife didn't approve of, but now that he's single, he can do what he likes with it.

Hmm… single. So, he's NOT Mum's boyfriend?

So, Carla's mum got a job fixing up the dining area in the pub, and Mum got some advice on how to get her wine noticed. A great day for independent women! That is, until Francesca showed up. When she arrived, she seemed very nervous, which I suppose is understandable when you turn up late to a party where you don't know anyone. But I think there was more to it than that. I *think* this may have been her first proper night out since she split up from her husband. How can I possibly know that, you may ask? Well let's just say I'd seen her face before, only this time it was a little less *shredded.*

Yes, Fran. As in Richard's soon-to-be-ex-wife, Fran. The daughters were there too, the ones who were mad enough to miss out on the opportunity to see Free Parking live. I felt a little bad for taking their places at the concert, not that they knew about it. After a short while in their presence, though, I soon got over the pangs of guilt.

"Ew, Mummy, why on *Earth* did you bring us here?" the older one said as I led them to the kitchen to get a drink. The younger one shoved her jacket into my arms without saying a word or even making eye contact. "Is this *it*?" She said when she saw the selection of crisps and sausage rolls on the table. "It's all carbs, Mummy!"

"I'm sorry, dear, I didn't know," Francesca replied, with an equally disgusted, snobbish look on her face. "Look, I can see some hummus and carrot batons at the back, that'll have to do for now, sweetie."

"Fine; I'll try it," she said like she'd just been told to swallow needles. "But I'll be able to tell if it's not organic!"

I did not like Fran or her daughters one bit. As annoying and oblivious as Richard can be, he is nowhere near as bad as them. I couldn't really imagine them ever having a good time together, and I honestly have no idea why he'd want to stay married to *her!* What was equally bewildering was how she and Trudy had ever become friends. Trudy is warm, fun-loving, open-minded and happy to chat to anyone (apart from her boyfriend, Alex, as far as I could tell!). So, I went back into the living room and asked Jessica about it.

"Oh God, not *her*!" she said. "Mum met her in the gym about a year ago and decided to take her under her wing. She's an unbearable snob, but she's an absolute mess when it comes to men, and Mum thought she needed help. When they met, she was having an affair with this younger bloke who then went on to cheat on her with someone even younger! If you ask me, she had what's coming to her; she was the one cheating on her husband!"

Poor Richard. Poor, oblivious Richard.

"Mum likes to think she's a relationship coach or something, but she's just as bad really; I don't think she'll ever settle down. At least she's happy, though, not like Fran. Oh, and as for Fran's daughters – do not even go there. It's like trying to make friends with a block of ice."

For some reason that really got me thinking. I loved the way Jessica put it, *it's like trying to make friends with a block of ice.* I used to think that's how other people felt when they tried to talk to me, because I'm so quiet at first meetings, but Jessica obviously doesn't see me that way. I often worry that when I don't say very much, people misread me as cold, but a lot of that is probably just in my head. Most people are smart enough to tell the difference between shyness and aloofness. I'm sure there will be some people I come across in life who won't want to give me the chance to come out of my shell, people who think I'm boring because I appear to have nothing to say, or people who think I'm a snob because I don't make small talk with them straight away, but the majority will be able to tell that I just don't find it that easy on the first go, or even the second and third. I can't go through life expecting people to not like me, even though inevitably some of them won't.

Easier said than done, Samantha.

Back in the room (and out of my head), I could see a classic Frogsplash moment brewing, and as ridiculous as these play-wrestling fights are, I must admit I was quite excited for Danny and Carla to witness it for themselves. I've been trying to explain to them how Frogsplash got his nickname, and whilst I'm sure they believed that these fights happen, I don't think they understood just how much of a show they can really be. I was also pleased to see that Fran and her two minions had joined the living room, each of them nibbling tentatively on a raw carrot stick. I couldn't wait to see *their* reactions to the impending display of teenage testosterone!

It was Billy who started the scuffle. He charged at Frogsplash with his head down, kind of like a bull, only less graceful. But Hayden was quick to react and grabbed him from behind in a heavy hug which seemed to squeeze the air out of him. Meanwhile Joshua and Frogsplash had time to prepare their attacks, and soon everyone around them was watching. When they were younger, Mum used to try and stop them, but as they got into their teen years, she decided it was better than them fighting for real out on the streets where she can't see them, so she lets them carry on with it until someone gets hurt.

Naturally, Fran has never had to worry about such things, and I have a feeling she may have a different view. "Good grief! Is this some sort of joke?" She said loudly, her two goggle-eyed daughters gawping at the wild animals rutting menacingly on our beige carpet. Trudy laughed and topped up Fran's glass of wine, which I later found out was a particularly strong batch of mum's home brew… or should I say, *Cassie Darling's Proper English Wine.*

They were very goggle-eyed. Their faces were thin and strained with no colour to them at all, and even though they were the same age as me and Jessica, they had dark circles under their eyes and their mouths were pulled tight, almost as if they were *trying* to make frown lines appear. They didn't look happy. It's hard to tell what Richard is normally like; he's been so volatile, but if he's friends with Dad, and if his mood at the Free Parking concert was anything to go by, he's a fun-loving, young-at-heart sort of guy. His daughters looked more like the sort who would pop your balloon if they thought you were enjoying it too much.

Trudy tried to distract Fran using her expert salesmanship. Actually *Saleswomanship*. She started talking about Mum's wine, telling her about the business idea, saying how amazing it was that Mum brewed it herself.

"Well that's all well and good," Fran said, her lips loosening somewhat. "But you can't just make wine and expect money to fall into your lap – that would be like me writing a book and expecting it to just crop up on the shelves! How is she going to *sell it*?"

"I can answer that," said Arnie, who had obviously been eavesdropping whilst chewing on his cheddar and onion pastry twist (I think Alana brought them – they certainly weren't baked in our kitchen!) Arnie began explaining to Fran all about his Dad's pub, and she seemed almost instantly warmer. Arnie had tanned skin, thick eyebrows, a neatly trimmed beard and long hair which he wore up in a bun. He wore a smart, tight-fitting shirt and skinny jeans. He was very tall, like his dad, and must have been in his mid-twenties. He did have a few flakes of pastry in his beard, but he carried it well. Despite his obvious charms, it was still a surprise to see how much Fran seemed to change once she'd started talking to him. She looked elegant and natural.

Back to the fight, things were heating up. Jessica had seen it once before and was keen for a second viewing, so she and Rosie joined me, Carla and Danny to watch from the side line. It's not that any of it is impressive – quite the opposite, in fact. It's so ridiculous and childish, but Froggo and his mates are almost the size of fully-grown men, so it's incredibly comical, and I'm not sure they're even aware of it. Frogsplash backed off from the other three, and that could mean only one thing. Usually, if he can, he'll launch himself off from the sofa, but there were too many people seated, so he leapt from the side and Frog splashed all three of them with expert arm and leg coverage. Us girls all cheered at what we thought was the crescendo of the spectacle, but the fight continued.

Joshua and Hayden stood up, brushed themselves off and found the can of beer they'd been sharing (Mum had rationed them a few) but Billy and Frogsplash seemed to be locked together on the floor like deer locking antlers, and the comical element suddenly vanished.

"It's not up to you!" I heard Frog say through pained gasps.

"You have no right to get involved in my family!" said Billy.

"I don't want your family! In fact, I want them to stay well away from my mum, she's a million times better than your eighty-year-old, two-divorce dad!"

Oh no. This is real.

"He is NOT eighty and he is married to my mum!"

"Not for long!"

"They're going to get back together!"

"Good! He's not good enough for our family!"

"Why does your mum keep sniffing around then?"

"She is not SNIFFING…"

"BILLY!"

"FROGSPLASH!"

Mum and Graham had, until that moment, been in the kitchen, blissfully unaware of what was going on in the living room, but something must have alerted them to the sudden change in atmosphere, because they both came rushing in and Graham was clearly horrified by what he saw.

"Arnie – why didn't you stop your brother?" he demanded.

The entire room was watching, apart from Arnie and Fran, who had been too busy gazing drunkenly into each other's eyes whilst discussing crudités and the rise and fall of the cheese board. It was the most boring conversation since records began according to Alana, who told me about it later.

After they'd broken up the fight, Mum and Graham looked kind of embarrassed, I guess because it was kind of obvious what the boys had been fighting about, so they'd basically exposed the relationship in the most public and dramatic way possible. Mum and Graham took them upstairs to calm them down, and after a few minutes she called me and Arnie upstairs too.

"So, I guess there's no point hiding it anymore," Mum said. "It's not that we wanted to keep it a secret from you, it's just that we didn't want to put too much pressure on the relationship at such an early stage."

"Well, that backfired magnificently!" said Arnie, who was more than a little drunk by that point, and somehow still had pastry in his beard.

"Well, yes," said Graham. "We understand it's going to be difficult to adjust to the idea, but nothing else is going to change, at least not until you guys are ready."

I don't mind Mum having a boyfriend, and Graham seems nice. As long as he doesn't suddenly feel the need to 'get to know me' or 'spend time with me' or anything like that, I'm fine with him being around. Billy and Frogsplash seemed more accepting of the idea now that it was out in the open, and Arnie didn't seem bothered at all, but I guess that makes sense because Graham divorced *his* mum about twenty years ago.

We re-joined the party and I told Danny and Carla what had happened while Mum and Graham tried to act like nothing had happened at all. It was a bit awkward for a while, but as people got more and more drunk, it seemed to matter less and less. We spent the rest of the evening watching Arnie and Fran flirting with each other. Fran was *really* drunk and seemed like a completely different person from when she'd arrived, but her daughters were still stiff and disdainful, and it was obvious that they found their mum's behaviour very distasteful indeed.

Mum and Graham gathered us kids in the kitchen just before ten p.m. and told us that they were planning to raise a toast to their new business partnership, and that they might as well also tell everyone about their relationship, seeing as the cat was out of the bag anyway. They wanted us to turn off the music and try and keep everyone quiet for a few moments while they made a little speech. So, we went back into the living room, turned off the music and told our friends what was about to happen. Just at that moment, though, something quite unexpected happened.

Trudy's devoted boyfriend Alex stood up, cleared his throat and called for silence.

"Can I have everyone's attention please," he said loudly. I was pretty sure this wasn't part of the plan, but I was interested to see where it was going. Mum and Graham entered with a giant bottle of champagne, but when they walked into a completely silent room, they realised something was going on.

"I may have only spent two months with this gorgeous, incredible lady," Alex went on. "But they have been the best two months of my life, and I can't imagine ever going back to the way things were before. Trudy, you are an amazing woman, you are the love of my life, and I don't ever want to be apart from you again…"

He got down on one knee and pulled a ring from his pocket.

"Trudy Palmer, will you be my wife?"

I looked around the room in search of Jessica; I wanted to see her reaction. I saw Danny, who looked all hazy-eyed and dreamy, and Carla, who was sort of smirking in amusement, and then I found Jessica, who was burying her head in her hands.

"Oh, Alex," Trudy said. Literally everyone was staring in silence. "I had no idea you felt that way! This was only ever meant to be a casual fling. I don't want to marry you. In fact, I think we should break up."

WOW. OUCH.

At that moment we were all frozen in time. We all wanted the silence to be broken, but none of us were brave enough to do it. It was painful. Not as painful as the look on Alex's face, but still bad. I thought maybe if I turned the music back up that would help break the silence and fix the mood a little bit. But when I did it was this upbeat, cheery song called *'You and Me Always'* which really, *really* emphasised the cold and abrupt shut-down that Trudy had just delivered to Alex. Still no one said a word.

Mum did what she thought was best. It was the only thing she could do to try and get the party back on track. She made her announcement about the business, then Graham made the announcement about their relationship, and they popped the huge bottle of champagne and everyone cheered, trying to forget that the unpleasantness of a few moments earlier had ever happened. I felt sorry for Alex, especially now that everyone was celebrating this new union while he'd just got dumped, but the weirdest thing was, he *stayed.* Why didn't he leave? Was he trying to prove a point? No one dared speak to him afterwards, he was like a ghost haunting the party, floating around aimlessly, trying to communicate with the living but realising that they were looking straight through him. Adult life is so messed up.

Monday 16th March 2020

HISTORICAL NEWS: DUKE JOHN JAMESON DUPES DRUNKARD INTO DEBT, DEPRESSION, DESPERATION AND DEATH!

It's been three hundred years since the great honourable Duke first discovered the use for con-artistry in the education system, making him the founding father of crippling scams and compulsive lying that we all still respect and adore today. Hail to the Duke, our role model and inspiration!

We were all excited to see each other again today so that we could relive all the drama from Saturday. It was certainly a rollercoaster, and one to remember, which is why I'm so glad Carla and Danny were there, we now have stories to tell, ones that bind us together, and that's kind of special. Plus, the stories are funny! Carla said her parents loved the party and they hadn't seen that much excitement in years, and even Rosie, who had been dreading the evening, said she had a great time and is apparently staying in touch with Jessica. So, a resounding success! Well, not for poor Alex.

But time goes on, as always, and this week we are celebrating that fact with the three hundredth anniversary of our school. Mr Bellows is head of History, head of upper school, and the proud leader of the Duke John Jameson fan club, which is a real thing. He is a man of tradition, a fact which I found out today through his very traditional (tedious) ninety-minute, year seven only assembly on the history of the school. We skipped Maths and half of Geography for his special assembly, and I can tell you now I'd rather be learning about tectonic plates or Pythagoras' Theorem than sit in an audience with Mr Bellows any day. I understand three hundred years is a big deal, but I've never known anyone to be so truly enthusiastic about a school. He genuinely *loves* the place! People say he was married once but she left him because he was too in love with Duke John Jameson (whether they mean the person or the institution, I'm not entirely sure).

He must be in his sixties, maybe older, and he was a student at the school when he was a boy. He had to go elsewhere to study at university, of course, and in his assembly, he briefly referred to those three years as 'a dull, unrewarding necessity'. As soon as he graduated, he returned to the school as a teacher, and he's never worked anywhere else. He sounds kind of obsessed if you ask me. I bet he's got a shrine to the school somewhere in his house. He's certainly got a lot of old photos – he showed us about a thousand of them in a slideshow. I wonder what he does in summer holidays. Cries himself to sleep each night, probably. It's great that he's so passionate but I can't help but wonder what might go through his mind when he's old, like on death's door. Won't he wish he'd spread his wings a bit more? Will he regret spending his entire life in the same place, doing the same thing?

The only good bit about the assembly was the story of Duke John Jameson and how he founded the school. I'd never heard it until today, and it was certainly eye-opening.

John Jameson was not a Duke, but he pretended to be one during his university years so that he could attend high class parties. He was not from a wealthy family but had charmed a rich and desperately lonely older lady as a boy, and she had funded his education for him. He was so convincing in the role and quickly acquired so many upper-class friends that no one questioned his Dukedom thereafter, and he continued the pretence for the rest of his life. He was an exceptionally good liar.

OK, so we've got liar and con-artist – check!

He carried on living this indulgent, luxurious lifestyle quite happily for many years, until he came across a wealthy, young woman named Carolina, who he very much admired. But Carolina was a philanthropist who didn't believe in the sort of selfish, hedonistic life that John was living, so he would have to fool her, just as he had done many others in the past.

Now there's tricking a woman into a relationship to add to his achievements.

He finally plucked up the courage to talk to her one day and endeavoured to get to know her. He found out that she loved literature and academia as well as her charitable pursuits, which gave him all the information he needed to formulate the perfect lie.

Oh, hold up – so he didn't know anything about her? He just liked the look of her! They didn't have anything in common! So, he was shallow and unromantic as well.

He told Carolina that he had founded a school for academic children whose parents could not afford an education for them. He said that it was his life's work and his only dream to ensure that gifted children were given the same opportunities as rich children.

So, what, the poor children who weren't especially bright should just crawl off and die somewhere?

So impressed was Carolina that she demanded to see John's school for herself, believing it to be a revolution in the education system.

To be fair, it was revolutionary for the time.

So, John had a rather large problem on his hands; the size of an entire school, to be exact. But John was a man of many talents and finding the means to build a school was apparently a walk in the park for such a clever (scheming) gentleman. There was a brewery owner in the neighbouring village by the name of Alexander Bell who was an infamous drunk and reckless gambler. What happened between him and John Jameson remains something of a mystery. Some say he lost a bet to John fair and square, others say John cheated on a wager, while others say there was no gambling at all and John used only his clever words to trick the old drunk into giving up a large amount of his land and wealth.

John was also a manipulative, exploitative man, by the way.

However, it was done, John got what he needed to build the school. How he kept up the lie for that long without Carolina finding out is another mystery. The next problem he faced was the issue of staff. He could not afford to pay teachers proper wages, but as you may have figured out by now, John was not one to let the small matter of money get in the way. He worked tirelessly to find the most immoral teachers and professionals from all the nearby villages. He had friends in high places, don't forget, and he used them to get dirt on all of them. Some were having affairs, others were thieves, there were even some rumours of murder, but this was all the better for John. He forced them to work at his school, or else he'd tell the church, their spouses and the entire village of their crimes.

So that's blackmail and possibly slavery... and leaving potentially dangerous people in charge of his pupils!

Meanwhile, the poor brewery owner was bitterly regretting whatever circumstances it was that led him to lose a large chunk of his wealth, and he soon gambled and drank away the remainder of it. He died falling from the roof of a church, whether through drunkenness or suicide we do not know. This wonderful news was so pleasing to the lady Carolina (who loathed drunkenness and gambling) that she agreed to marry John Jameson.

So, she wasn't THAT charitable then, was she?

They lived happily ever after, and John's school was a great success and one of the building blocks for free schooling in Britain, so I suppose that's why people still hail him as a hero.

My main questions are to do with Carolina. I think she knew exactly what was going on. First, how does she not notice the construction of the school nor question why it's taking so long for John to allow her to visit it? Perhaps she lived quite far away and maybe they only got to see each other every few months back in those days. But that still doesn't explain everything. If she knew nothing about John's deal with Alexander Bell, which came *after* he'd said he founded the school, then how can Bell's death be the thing that prompted her to marry John? I'm sure a lot of it has been changed over the years, but for whose benefit? It doesn't really paint any of them in a good light.

Mr Bellows went on to say that Duke John Jameson (the person) epitomises the core values of Duke John Jameson (the school) to this very day, because he was not a wealthy or privileged man, but he was clever, and that's what granted him his success.

That, and a complete absence of morality, but, you know, whatever…

Mr Bellows then reminded us of this Friday's anniversary celebration. There's going to be *another* super long assembly (ugh) only this time it's a full school assembly and we will have guest speakers, some of whom are ex-students who've gone on to be successful. There will be a concert by the school's orchestra, a speech from the head and finally, we will all sing the school song. We rehearsed the school song at the end of Mr Bellows' assembly today, but it's long and I can't remember it all, so you'll have to wait until I get a copy of the song sheet. Anyway, I wouldn't want to spoil it for you just yet – it's a real treat.

Friday 20th March 2020

Most of the assembly was boring, but the guest speakers were good. One of them had only left the school five years ago and she was already running her own restaurant which recently won a prestigious award. One was a stand-up comedian and she was funny, but also, I think the most inspiring. She said it took her a long time and a lot of dead-end jobs and desperation before she found something she loved doing, and even then, she went through a lot of failure, rejection and feelings of hopelessness. She said the hardest part was when some of her own friends and family told her she'd never make it, but there were always the ones who believed in her, and she never stopped believing in herself, which is what got her there in the end.

The last one was less entertaining but just as informative. He was a graphic designer and he showed us some of the logos and adverts he'd helped design. He said that if you want a career you should start working towards it now in any way you can. Even at our age, we can always be learning and acquiring skills and experience which we can later put down on our applications to college, university and jobs. He said you should take advantage of everything the school has to offer, such as clubs, and you should ask teachers for advice whenever you need it.

I bet they loved that part.

It did get me thinking about the school newspaper. I want to be a journalist, and I shouldn't let Charlotte Henderson get in the way of that. She is the person I hate most in the world, and because we're in the same year, we'd have to work together on the paper if I joined. Maybe I can edge her out. Summer is coming – won't she want to be out sunbathing with her cronies rather than sat indoors at a computer? That's something to think about, but I've no idea how I'd go about it.

We ended the afternoon with a hearty rendition of the school song. At Monday's rehearsal, we sang along to Mr Bellows on the piano, but today we had the proper backing music, which made it a million times better. It was very old-timey; it sounded medieval to me, but it can't be *that* old. There was some sort of wind instrument, like a flute or a panpipe maybe, and I guess the string instrument must have been a lute. It fit well with the form and structure of the song, which is like a ballad. You'll have to imagine the music, but I saved the lyrics especially for you:

Behold the legend of the Duke – BEHOLD!
We carry his great name with pride!
For he was a man both virtuous and bold
May his spirit be our conscience and guide!

With great responsibility his great honour came
But in his wisdom, he knew what to do
He took the title of Duke, fixed it to his name
And from thence his bravery grew.

The Duke took on fine and gracious pursuits
But nothing could be truer or finer
Than the lady he hoped would bear him his fruits
The charitable and kindly Carolina.

The lady so pure struck a chord in his heart
So, he told her his version of truth [WINK]

That he shared in her passion for books and for art
And had founded a school for poor youth.

His love for the girl grew deep and strong
And in him a great notion stirred
That he must build this school before too long
And so, make good his word.

But how to acquire the land and the bricks
To achieve such a selfless feat?
There were up his sleeve a great many tricks
For he was a wise master of deceit.

He met with a brewer and shook his hand
But the man was a weak, drunken fool
For he gambled away every inch of his land
So that Duke John could build his school!

The work was not done, though the bricks were all laid
For a school needs masters as well
John knew not how they all would get paid
But he had to act fast and not dwell.

Duke John used knowledge for his only tool
He sought teachers who had something to hide
He forced them to work for free at his school
Or he'd tell the church how they'd lied!

Meanwhile the brewer grew deeper in debt
John had taken his life and his pride

He grew mad with drink and bitter regret,
Jumped from the church roof and died.

The silly old man, let us laugh at his shame!
So drunk that he took his own life!
But so, honoured now was the Jameson name
That Carolina agreed to be his wife.

Our history is written, we thank the Duke for his part
Our future is now ours to carve
He was strong in his spirit and true in his heart
Now thanks to him we shall not starve!

Behold the legend of the Duke – BEHOLD!
We carry his great name with pride!
For he was a man both virtuous and bold
May his spirit be our conscience and guide!

It's the greatest song I've ever heard. It might even be better than Free Parking.

Sunday 22nd March 2020

We had a much more ordinary weekend at Dad's this time. Richard's daughters had agreed to see him, but don't worry, he didn't bring them over! Not the blocks of ice! If they thought they were too good for Mum's house, I can only imagine how they'd react to Dad's little flat! So, it was just me, Frogsplash and Dad for most of the day. He asked us what's new and so we hesitantly told him about Mum and Graham. He seemed happy for her and asked us

257

a few questions about him, just to make sure he sounded like a decent enough guy, and that was about it. Then we told him about the party and how dreadful Richard's ex-wife and daughters were – he seemed to find that very funny!

<u>Wednesday 1st April 2020</u>

It's been a pretty horrible week and I can't believe it's not over yet. In fact, I think the worst is still to come. It's public speaking week at school, and I *hate* public speaking. Is there anything worse than getting up on your own in front of a silent classroom of your peers who are obviously going to be bored listening to your boring speech on a boring subject, and who all have their eyes on you for several minutes and you can't even tell them to stop staring, and you can't hide behind anything or look away! I mean, does anyone *enjoy* public speaking? It's nothing like being in a school play. For starters, a play is fun and entertaining, but also, it's pretend, you're not being yourself and that makes all the difference in the world.

Of course, public speaking isn't applicable to subjects like Maths, P.E. or Art, so that's a relief. We had to do a little speech in German yesterday but that was nothing because we barely know any German yet, so we were all pretty much limited to saying the same basic phrases, so no one could really judge anyone else. The biggies are English and History, and English was today. We've had a few weeks to prepare our speeches, and we're allowed to use visual aids to make them more exciting. They had to be between three and five minutes long, but apart from that there was no brief, the speech could be on any subject you wanted. That's too much choice. Not only does that make it difficult to think of something, it also makes it so that people can judge you on the *subject* you've chosen as well as your delivery.

Obviously, I was panicking. I had no idea what to do my speech on, and I don't exactly have any friends in my English class, so I couldn't ask everyone else what they were doing. I just didn't want it to be boring. Sometimes I think I can still hear whispers of the name *Samantha Dreary* and I'm worried it might stick. So, I took to the internet and looked up 'great speeches throughout history'. The first few were from political leaders, mostly during wartime and other massive crises. While these were truly brilliant speeches, and probably better than any others I came across, I didn't think I could really apply that same idea to this rather mundane school assignment.

The other common theme I noticed was that a lot of them were addressing social injustices, particularly oppression, and all of them were motivated by a need for change. That was the thing that brought them all together, an *urgent* need for change. Revolution, even! There were many that interested me, and many more that felt really moving just reading about them, but the only one I thought that I could justifiably talk about was feminism. So, after a bit more research, I chose to do my speech on the oppression of women throughout history.

I found out some powerful stuff. A lot of women protested their oppression in the early women's rights movement... they had almost no power at all back then, and they weren't even allowed to vote! What is the point of having an election if not everyone has the right to vote? I just can't believe that people ever thought that was OK! I wonder if Danny knows about this. A lot of them got arrested and sent to prison just for protesting. They felt so strongly about what they believed in that they went on hunger strike while they were in prison to make their point using the only power they had left. They were willing to starve themselves to death for what they believed in. It's kind of crazy when you think about how many women and girls starve themselves nowadays just to look pretty! But the prison officers couldn't allow them to die, so they force-fed them through their nostrils, which was extremely painful and inhumane.

There was this one woman, Emily Davison, who was force-fed forty-nine times! She must have been incredibly strong and exceptionally devoted, because she died during a protest by throwing herself in front of the king's horse. When the First World War began, all politics were shut down, so the protests had to stop. During the war, women contributed so heavily to the workforce while the men were away fighting that afterwards, at last, politicians recognised that they were actual human beings, and gave them the vote.

It's nasty the way women are treated in some countries even now, and if they try to object to these rules, the punishments can be truly horrific, like I can't even imagine how that would feel. There are also a lot of ways women are still treated unfairly here in the UK, and so many of them are things that I'd never even realised were wrong until now. They're just things I've blindly accepted as 'the way it is' when actually, it doesn't have to be that way at all. I learnt a lot researching this project, and I found myself growing more and more passionate about it, so I decided to keep it hard-hitting, like a true journalist, by not shying away from any of the ugly facts and harsh realities. It was going to be ground-breaking.

So today was the day. A few minutes past one p.m. and Mrs McAlpine began picking people to do their speeches at random, so that none of us would feel the pressure that came from knowing that we were next. I see the logic, but it didn't work for me. The longer I had to wait, the worse the nerves got. I wouldn't have liked to have gone first, but second or third would have been OK, just one other person to break the ice, then you go and have your turn and get it out of the way – that's the way to do it! I tried to concentrate on the speeches I was hearing rather than my own upcoming presentation, but that only made things worse.

The first person to talk was Emily Reid, who did a pleasant PowerPoint Presentation on cats, telling us all about the variations in different breeds, with loads of adorable photos and video clips to keep us entertained, including some of her own cats which she'd taken at home. It was very cute, but a bit babyish. It went down well, though.

The second was Liam Rutter, who told us all about the ups and downs of his favourite football team Leicester City. It was less cute. I didn't feel that he made the effort to appeal to a wider audience. It was like he assumed we were all already massive fans, not just of football, but of

Leicester City in particular. He was too close to his subject and not close enough to us.

The third was Angela O'Shea, who told us all about her favourite band, The Dreamers. Her favourite member is Dillon James Scott, who seems to be everyone's favourite member, but I'm not sure why. Maybe it's his hair, or maybe it's the fact that he has three first names… whatever it is, it can't be his 'talent'. Angela also had a lot of photos and not a lot of substance. I'm not judging, honestly, I was just getting nervous. More than nervous… *alarmed.* My speech seemed quite *different* from the rest.

The next one was Rashid Khan, and he did a presentation on his holiday to France last summer. It was mostly a slideshow with lots of photos; lots of nice, happy memories.

Sean Rodrigues did a very exciting talk on his dance troupe which included lots of video clips but also a lot of things I never knew about Sean which I really found interesting. He even ended on a surprise breakdance pose which got most people cheering and Mrs McAlpine slightly worried about health and safety. It was slightly more edgy that the rest, but still nothing like mine.

Mine wasn't about a personal hobby or interest. Mine wasn't cheerful. Mine didn't have a lot of colourful pictures or heart-warming sub-plots like Emily finding her cat Bobo after it had been missing for two months. I didn't have a Bobo. I did have an Emily, but I was starting to get very concerned that Emily Reid wasn't quite ready to hear about Emily Davison.

"Samantha Drury!" Mrs McAlpine called me up. I couldn't exactly change my speech then. I was extremely nervous, and the sound of my notes flapping in my hand because I was shaking so much seemed to fill the classroom. I had to control it. I couldn't control it.

Think of Emily Davison; this would never have scared her.

I thought it was a bit harsh when someone groaned after I told them what my speech was going to be about. Mrs McAlpine shushed them loudly, which only drew more attention to it and distracted me even more. I was conscious of how many times I said 'um' and how infrequently I looked up at my audience. Mrs McAlpine had really emphasised the importance of eye contact, so I forced myself to look directly at them, but it felt like I was *staring into their souls* rather than just holding my audience. They all looked really bored.

It was right around the time I showed them all the very realistic drawing of a force-feeding that the mood started to change. They all looked either bewildered or horrified. I wanted to stop, but I couldn't just say 'the end' and go and sit down. So, I carried on describing the various atrocities that women have suffered in their fight for equality throughout history and across the world. I won't share all the gruesome details with you, because if I've learnt anything from today, it's that not everyone wants to hear them. Especially not a room full of twelve-year-olds who spend most of their time thinking about fluffy kittens.

It felt like I'd been up there for a good twenty minutes, but it can't have been because I rehearsed it several times at home and it never ran over five. When I walked back to my desk, a few people looked at me with utter disgust, as though I was the one responsible for all the oppression I'd

263

just told them about… don't shoot the messenger! I sat back down in my seat feeling like I'd just crashed a five-year-old's birthday party and told all the kids about the holocaust. At the end of the lesson, Mrs McAlpine gave us all our marks and I got nine out of ten, which is excellent considering my nerves. No one got a ten, anyway. I was pleased with my grade, but I'm not sure if it was worth completely alienating myself from everyone else in my class.

Who am I kidding? Of course it was!

Friday 3rd April 2020

Today was the day of the history presentations, which we've been preparing for weeks. To make it easier on us, Mr Achilles assigned us group presentations instead of solo speeches. It does make it less nerve-wracking when you stand up in front of the class, but there's a price to pay for that and it's not worth it. Working in a group is terrible. Even at the best of times, it is the absolute worst. And this was not the best of times. Let me introduce you to the dream team:

Samantha Drury: socially awkward, fear of public speaking, crippling crush on the teacher which makes her mind go completely blank whenever she looks at him, hates working with other people.

Beth Amory: self-obsessed, hates appearing as though she's 'trying too hard' – especially when it comes to school projects, said she hated Charlotte Henderson but has since become best friends with her again, tries to make herself feel better by putting others down, tells bizarre and hugely exaggerated lies to get attention.

Rob Battley: verbally bullies Samantha Drury on the bus (and once with oranges), extremely lazy, hates school, hates being told what to do, wants to fail and bring everyone else down with him, thinks everyone else is going to make him look stupid, is, genuinely stupid.

Ross Rillington: the most pompous boy in the universe, thinks his ideas are better than anyone else's, doesn't want to let you do any of the work because he doesn't believe you're capable, but then tells you off for being 'lazy' because you haven't done any of the work, hideously arrogant, Samantha Drury's second most hated person after Charlotte Henderson.

It's the most disastrous combination of people to be put together since Mum and Dad at the Christmas play. Ross was being unfair towards me. He obviously recognised that the other two didn't even want to do well, so he was breathing down my neck trying to get me to pick up the slack. He could tell that I was desperate to get a good grade. Maybe he could even tell that I was desperately in love with Mr Achilles. I don't know how he'd know that, but he certainly *behaved* as though he knew everything.

We were given the choice to do our presentation on anything we've studied in History this year. We spent far too long deciding which subject to choose because Ross wanted it to be something obscure that we barely touched upon in class, just so we could do loads of extra research and show off our superior knowledge. Knowledge is overrated. Knowledge of facts and dates comes cheap now that we have the internet at our disposal. We need substance and wit to deliver the presentation effectively. Ross didn't want to know; he's a textbook grade-chaser, in it for the merits, not the education.

This was two weeks ago, and I knew that if we didn't get it done in class, we'd have to meet up at break. Ugh. We weren't getting anywhere, and the clock was ticking, so I called a vote and my choice, Richard III, won. But the battle was far from over. We started from the beginning, as you do, and discussed how Richard got to the throne.

"Well, he had his nephews locked in the tower of London, didn't he?" I said.

"No – we learned about this!" Ross said, "The Tower of London was a royal palace at the time; *not* a prison! And no one really knows what Richard did with them."

"I was locked up once," Beth said out of the blue.

"What?" Ross said impatiently, and in this instance, I was on his side.

"I was locked up in a hostage situation," she continued. Suddenly, I was reminded of my first ever encounter with Beth, way back when I was still eating lunch in the canteen, and she'd told that story about Victoria Beckham stealing her dress design. I didn't believe that then and I wasn't about to believe her hostage story now. Ross and I tried to ignore her, but Rob Battley egged her on. It's possible he even believed her.

"I was on holiday in New York with my parents. We went to the bank and suddenly these gangsters came swarming in with balaclavas on their faces and they were holding guns, *big machine guns* and…

"Shut up, Beth, we all know you're lying," said Ross. I quite liked that. People don't usually tell Beth to shut up.

"I'm not lying!" Beth said. "It was the scariest moment of my life! I'm lucky I even survived; they shot *six* people."

"Whatever," I said. "We have to get on with this project."

"Yes, and *you* need to get your facts straight!" Ross said to me. Ugh. Whose side was he even on?

"Oh my God, you utter LOSERS! Who even cares?" said Rob helpfully.

"Some of us do care, actually, and you're dragging us down," I said to him.

"Shut up, Riding Hood, you drag yourself down whenever you open your mouth."

I didn't know what he meant by that, and I didn't want to either.

"At least you *can* open your mouth," Beth said. "You have no idea what it's like having your jaw wired shut."

Oh, here we go…

"My mum had it done to me a few years ago to make me lose weight. It was horrible, but I'm glad she did it. I might get it done again soon, actually."

"There is no medical professional in the world that would do that to a child, and I'd be very surprised if your mother did that to you either – that would be child abuse," Ross said.

Beth's compulsive lying is getting out of hand. She must know that no one believes her. I think she must be craving attention since Charlotte usurped her as leader of their group. But what kind of attention can that get you? It can't be very satisfying. You can't expect to make any friends that way either. It's irritating… no, worse than that – it's *insulting* having to listen to such blatant fabrications and being expected to believe it! How stupid does she think we all are? But something about it makes me feel sorry for her, not angry. I can't explain it, because I don't really understand why she does it, but I feel like it's coming from some place sad.

It's funny, because when I first saw her and heard her talking to those girls and commanding their attention in such a way, she seemed so powerful and I was awestruck at the confidence she appeared to have. Then when we saw her crying in the toilets, I saw she was vulnerable and much more down-to-earth and friendly than I'd first thought. Now I see her in this context, I realise that the only thing I know for sure about her is that I know nothing. I want to like her because I think she's complicated and I think she's an introvert like me, deep down. She's not comfortable in her own skin but she makes it so hard sometimes. She wears many masks, and much like the balaclava-clad bank robbers of New York, you can't trust someone who never shows their face.

Our presentation was a fractured affair, with Ross acting like a BBC news correspondent, reporting the facts without bias, but also without any sense of humour or personality. Rob read out his lines in a dull monotone as though each word was boring him into a brain-dead stupor. Beth carried hers off flawlessly. I know, because I've been working with her for the last two weeks, that she had no idea what it was she was saying, but you'd never know that just from watching. She delivered it all with style and a smile. She is the queen of style and smile. Then there was me, eager to please but stuttering and spluttering, trying to play it cool, trying to do the style and smile and give it a bit of character, but coming across like a glitchy robot baring its motherboard in lieu of a soul. But the content was there, and the rest got sucked into the void of our inattentive audience. I tried not to look at Mr Achilles.

One of the things about public speaking is, I've noticed, that unlike other nerve-wracking but necessary things in life, you don't get that huge euphoria of relief when it's over. Maybe it's just me, but when I've finished giving a speech, the nerves don't leave my body, they stay in me and pickle. I replay the speech over and over in my head, hearing every vocal tick, every stutter and 'um', wondering if I sound too posh when I don't drop my 't's (wor-tuh or wor-uh? Or wat*er,* emphasis on the *er?)*

But worse, much worse than that, is the visual replay, because, that, I can only imagine. I don't remember much of the faces in the audience because I was too busy concentrating and, anyway, I hardly dared to look at them. So instead, I imagine what *I* looked like to *them.* Flustered, definitely; and scruffy; always. I was probably shifting around on my feet, scraping my hair back over my scalp with my clawed hand in that nervous way I do. I looked so weak, so desperate for their approval, they could smell my neediness, I was practically begging with my eyes. Pathetic.

I wrote a little rhyme to remind me that people don't care anywhere near as much as I think they do, and that they're all far too wrapped up in how they look to notice any of my shortcomings.

Whatever you did, whatever you said
How it looks to you now is all in your head.
Nobody is watching your every move
They're watching their own hoping you will approve.

I came up with that in my head while my nerves were pickling. Unfortunately, something happened very soon after that completely contradicted it. I was watching someone closely, and it did affect my perception of them as a person.

About twenty minutes before the end of the lesson, we'd all finished our group presentations and Mr Achilles hadn't got anything else scheduled to fill the time. So, as a 'treat' for our hard work on our projects, he switched on the interactive whiteboard, opened the internet browser and clicked on 'online video'. I couldn't believe it when I saw what letters he was typing in:

E... r... i... c... D... e... r... e... k

Mr Achilles likes Eric Derek! No, of course he doesn't. He's just being a crowd-pleaser, appealing to the masses. For shame!

Since I last saw Eric Derek's videos, they haven't changed much. It's all the same tired old pranks. There's one where he's sat on a public bench reading a newspaper. He waits until some random person comes to sit next to him, usually an old lady or an upper-class businessman. Then he folds up the newspaper and you see that his pants and trousers are pulled down to his knees and that he's sat on a fake toilet seat built into the bench. He pulls the fake flush, but it doesn't work, so he just shrugs, pulls up his trousers and walks away, leaving a very realistic looking poo in the bench-toilet. It always ends with the unsuspecting member of the public looking down into the toilet bowl in disgust. He must have done it hundreds of times; I'm surprised there's anyone left in the world that's not yet wise to his tricks. They're probably all actors anyway.

I watched Mr Achilles' face, thinking that surely a smart, witty man like him will realise his mistake putting rubbish like that on the screen for us to watch. But no, he was laughing. Not just laughing but guffawing and hee-hawing like a donkey. It was hideous! Suddenly, he seemed to have this huge mouth and he was hysterically cry-laughing. I'm not sure what was worse – the laughter itself or the fact that he was laughing at something so stupid! – I couldn't bear to look at him anymore, but my only other option was to watch Eric Derek and his antics. It was so appallingly bad, I accidentally said aloud, "What an infantile moron; I can't believe he makes a living out of this."

Ross, who was still sitting next to me, must have heard me muttering in disbelief, because he responded, "Couldn't agree more. I don't know who's worse, the man himself or the thousands of followers who legitimise and fund his daft behaviour." He's such a snob.

Sunday 5th April 2020

Dad was working from home all weekend but for some reason he still thought we'd rather be at his than in our nice, *separate* bedrooms at home. Sometimes I wonder if he's too scared to tell Mum that he's too busy to have us or if he just simply doesn't think things through. Anyway, he's got this huge client he's got to plan a summer event for and he was on the phone and in his office trying to hire gazebos and order hundreds of bottles of champagne and find the best prawn cocktails or whatever... I can't help but wonder how much money he's in charge of when he's sorting out stuff like this – how did *my dad* end up with so much responsibility?

Richard was experiencing another low point because it would have been he and Fran's fifteen-year anniversary. He was sat in the front room, watching rom-coms, crying a lot and doing that thing where he shouts at the actors on the screen telling them to get real and warning them that they're going to die alone. Dad conducted most of his work from his office but every now and then he'd walk through hurriedly to get some paperwork from his briefcase and notice Richard moping about on the sofa. It was the first time Dad looked irritated by him. I wonder if he knew Richard was planning to stay this long. He still talks about getting a sports car, but he's never mentioned finding himself a flat.

Richard kept talking to me and Frogsplash, so it felt rude to leave him on his own, especially when he was in that state. We stayed and watched the end of the film with him, then made our excuses and went to our room. I didn't mind Frogsplash putting sport on the TV – even *I'd* rather watch football than love films!

Wednesday 8th April 2020

It's the last week of school before two weeks of Easter holidays and in Monday's assembly, they made a few announcements. There will be two events at the end of the school year and anyone who would like to take part should show their interest by putting their name on the sign-up sheet before the end of the week. Obviously, I counted myself out after I heard the bit about showing interest. Remember rule eight of Samantha's top ten tips? Don't show any interest in anything!

The first event is the end of term talent show, which doesn't apply to me anyway because I don't have any talent, but Danny and Carla seem interested and, of course, I will support them every step of the way. The second is the end of term school play, which is apparently a big deal because it includes actors from years seven to thirteen and it's always a Shakespeare play. I honestly hadn't even considered auditioning – remember rule six? No limelight! But Danny and Carla keep saying I should do it because I was so good in *A Festive Carol,* and today, Mrs Willis herself tracked me down while I was putting my books in my locker before lunch.

"Samantha Drury, I've been looking for you all week!" she said. "I just wanted to ask if you'd thought about auditioning for the play?"

"Um, no… not really," I said, but I knew that wouldn't be the end of it.

"I really think you ought to," she said. "You were such a star in the Christmas production! And let me just say… off the record… we don't often give speaking parts to first-years because Shakespeare can be a bit tricky, but for you I would *definitely* make an exception!"

"Wow!" said Danny, whose locker is close to mine. "You have to do it!"

"I don't know…"

"OK, how about this…" said Mrs Willis. "Just put your name on the list for now, that's all you have to do. Think about it over the holidays and if you don't want to do it, then you don't have to audition, OK?"

"Oh… OK then!" I said at last, and before I could change my mind, Danny and Carla marched me down to the drama department where I wrote my name on the sheet. It's no big deal really; I don't have to do it, do I?

It's not like they're going to drag me to the audition as well.

Saturday 11th April 2020

BREAKING NEWS: AN EVENT HAS OCCURRED!

In a certain place and at a certain time, something happened. After thorough investigation and analysis, we can confirm that it is very important and exciting news. This journalist knows all about it, but she is keeping it a secret!

It's the beginning of the Easter holidays and Mum's been reminding us all week that she'd be going out on a day trip with Graham today. He's taking her to some vineyard to do wine-tasting. Apparently, you're supposed to spit the wine out after you taste it, but I bet they'll come home drunk anyway. Graham was going to leave Billy here with Frogsplash, so it only made sense that Joshua and Hayden came over too.

"What, so I have to share the house with *them* all weekend?" I said. I didn't care at all about Frog's friends – this was purely tactical.

"You can invite your friends over too," Mum said. She'd fallen right into my trap. I wasn't sure if she'd let me have them over with no adult supervision, but if I made a fuss about Frogsplash having his mates over and reminded her that even though I'm younger, I'm far more mature, then I knew it would work. As it turns out, I didn't even need to make a fuss, but it's better to be safe than sorry when you're pushing boundaries with parents, if you fail to prepare, then prepare to fail!

"But no more than three friends each," she said. That was fine by me – I only wanted two.

Graham arrived at ten a.m. this morning, but he came alone.

"Where's Billy?" I heard Mum ask. "He's not still holding a grudge, is he? Look – if things are moving too fast for him…"

"Everything moves too fast for that boy," said Graham "It takes him three hours to get out of bed! I tried to wake him an hour ago, but he mumbled something about cycling here himself when he's ready to get up."

That was a relief. If Billy had turned up on time, I'd have been left alone with him until Frogsplash woke up – which would be midday at the earliest… awkward! Although, of all Froggo's friends, Billy is probably the easiest to get along with. We have nothing at all in common, but he's one of those people who will get along with everyone – a bit like Danny, only he's a football and rugby lad rather than a socially conscious feminist who loves fairy-tales. He's worked as a 'glass collector' at his dad's pub since whenever he was old enough, and apparently, he serves drinks as well even though he's not really supposed to. He chats to all the customers, and that's where he gets that easy-going sociability thing that I will never, *ever* have. He's a bit cheeky, a bit of a wind-up, but he's respectful too.

Joshua is probably the most mature of the group, but that's not saying much at all. He's the only one who has a girlfriend, and even though they mock him about it constantly, he never rises to it. He's more into music than sport, and he fancies himself as a music producer. He likes to sample old songs and stuff, which is kind of cool – he'd probably get on with Carla's dad!

Hayden is the video gamer and, in that sense, he's just as immature as the others. He's the one who's probably most like me but again, that's not saying much at all. He's the shyest, most self-conscious one, and he probably even reads books. He likes sci-fi stuff and comics, I know that. I bet he'd like to have a girlfriend, but he has no idea how to talk to the ladies.

Danny and Carla arrived at midday and we went up to my room to hang out. We put some music on and talked about our upcoming auditions. Carla is obviously going to play guitar, and she said she thinks she might sing as well, but she's not sure. I've never heard her sing, and even though I bet she's good, I still think that's a brave thing to do. There's something so personal about singing and to do it in front of an audience takes a lot of courage. I didn't say that though, as I didn't want to put her off!

Danny isn't even sure if she wants to audition, but if she did, it would be dance. She said she didn't think she was good enough, especially not on her own, but Carla kept saying how amazing she was. I felt bad because I've never seen Danny dance, and that's because I lied and said I couldn't go with them to that dance class. I tried to be as encouraging as I could, but I didn't want to come across as being false. If I told her now that I thought she was a great dancer it wouldn't be genuine, and then if she ever asked my opinion again, how could she possibly believe my answer? I lied once and I'm not going to do it again.

At some point, we heard Frogsplash's friends dragging their feet across the gravel on the driveway, and we heard Froggo let them in, so we knew he was awake at last. We talked a bit about my audition and I realised I might have to prepare for this one. I hadn't thought about it much since signing the sheet on Wednesday, but I quite like the idea of doing Shakespeare. I know I won't get a big part, not when there are sixth formers auditioning, but that suits me just fine. We had a look on the school website and they haven't announced which play it's going to be yet but there are five samples of scripts and we can choose any one of them to do for our audition. The old language looks very daunting, and you do really need to know what you're saying in your audition, but Danny and Carla have promised they'll help me.

It was only when we heard Frog, Billy, Joshua and Hayden raiding the fridge that we realised it was well into lunchtime. Mum had left us a classic snack bits selection, which is always easy and always popular, but by the time we got to the kitchen there wasn't all that much left for us three. The cucumber and carrot sticks appeared untouched, and there were at least some crisps and dips remaining, but the main bulk had vanished, packaging and all, so we were pretty sure the lazy teenagers had just taken the whole lot upstairs to be consumed out of sight and out of reach.

Not on my watch, fellas!

Danny and Carla insisted it didn't matter, but I knew how many chicken drumsticks and cocktail sausages were in that fridge this morning, and I wasn't about to let them hog the whole lot, especially not when it would leave my friends to go without. It was just plain inconsiderate.

I stood outside his door with Danny and Carla on either side of me and I knocked hard. I was surprised at the speed of the response; usually Frogsplash seems oblivious to anyone trying to communicate with him for at least the first minute. He poked his head round the door.

"SHHHHHH!" he said. "No need to make a racket!" That was weird, too. Usually he doesn't care about noise.

"Why not?" I said. "Is someone sleeping in there?"

"Someone *was* sleeping in here," I heard Billy say.

"Oh, sorry Billy, I didn't realise you still took afternoon naps!" I laughed.

"No, not me!" he said. "Go on Frog, let them in – they can keep a secret!"

Frogsplash rolled his eyes but he pulled the door inwards anyway and we cautiously stepped inside. We looked around, trying to figure out what was out of the ordinary. Neither Danny nor Carla had been in Froggo's room before, so they had a lot more to take in (mostly empty cereal bowls and drinks cans) but I followed the eye line of all four boys and I saw, curled up in a cardboard box in the corner, a lovely, shaggy-coated, caramel-coloured dog resting, but now awake thanks to me banging on the door.

"Oh, my God!" I said, getting down on the floor next to the box so I could pet it, with Danny and Carla close to follow. "Who is this?"

"He doesn't have a collar or a tag, so I've been calling him Max," Billy said.

"You mean he's a stray?"

"I think so. I found him in the cellar of my dad's pub two days ago and he seemed like he hadn't been fed in ages."

"Why didn't you tell your dad?"

"Because look…" Billy picked up a tennis ball and waved it around in front of Max. "Come on boy, fetch!" he threw the ball, but Max just lay there. "I think he's sick, or maybe just really old. If I tell my dad, he'll take him straight to the vet and they'll put him down."

"Maybe he just doesn't know fetch," Carla said.

"Maybe," said Billy. "But he doesn't want to go for a walk either. He's been lying in that box for two whole days, only getting up to go to the toilet. He doesn't seem to want to do anything."

"Maybe we should take him in the garden," I said. "Even if it's just for a toilet break."

Frogsplash, who probably didn't want a dog peeing in his room, agreed with this idea, and so we all followed behind as Billy carried Max down the stairs. Max was a small to medium sized dog, bigger than those tiny handbag dogs but smaller than a collie, but it still must have been quite a struggle for Billy to have carried him all the way over here in his cardboard box.

He didn't do much in the garden either. He did a little wee and sniffed around a little bit but then he went back inside and headed straight towards his box.

"But if he's sick then he needs to see a vet," I said as we followed Max back up. "They might be able to make him better. He might be suffering, and what kind of life is it if he doesn't want to walk or play or eat…"

"Oh, he eats," said Frogsplash.

"Look," said Hayden, and he grabbed a cocktail sausage from the packet on Frog's desk and threw it to Max. Max caught it in his mouth and ate it gratefully.

"Didn't *any* of you notice anything while we were in the garden?" Danny said. We all looked at her blankly. "Maybe none of you know dogs very well... boy dogs lift one leg up to pee, but girl dogs squat like Max here. I think Max is short for *Maxine!*"

"No way!" said Billy.

"And I think there's a reason she's so attached to this box... I think she's nesting. My mum was the same when she was due with the twins..."

"Oh, my God! We're having puppies!" said Billy, who was now as excited as a *real* expectant father. Then we all got excited and started jumping up and down and clapping, overjoyed at the thought of tiny, fluffy little Maxes running around and playing.

"So, what should we do?" Billy asked Danny, who seemed to be the expert on all things pregnancy related.

"Well, if she's been in that box for two days now, I'd say she's getting ready to give birth pretty soon. I think she should stay here until the babies are born."

"Oh, what?" Billy said, annoyed.

"It's OK, you can stay over," Frogsplash assured him.

"What about Mum?" I said.

"We'll do our best to keep it a secret from her as long as we can," said Frogsplash. "She's never let us have a dog so I'm not sure how she'll feel about a whole litter of puppies in her house..."

"Can you imagine how cute they're going to be though?" said Danny. "There's no way she'll be able to stay mad at you when she sees them!"

"What about when they start peeing on the carpet?" said Joshua, who I'd noticed was keeping a good distance from Max.

"What's up with you? Do you not like dogs or something?" I asked him.

"He just doesn't want fur on his best pink shirt!" said Hayden.

"It's *mauve*," Joshua defended himself. Unlike the other three, Joshua takes a certain amount of pride in his appearance.

"He's got a point though," said Carla. "You can't keep them all here once they start growing up... they're going to need homes."

"Not Max, he... I mean *she's* staying with me," Billy said.

"You think your dad will let you?" asked Frogsplash.

"I don't know... I was never allowed one before, but I think that was more down to my mum..."

"I hate to be the one to say this," Carla broke in. "But have you considered the possibility that Max might already have an owner?"

"She's right," said Joshua. "A dog doesn't just turn up out of nowhere."

Everyone looked a little glum at that prospect, and Carla started backtracking.

"I mean, chances are she was abandoned because her previous owner couldn't afford to take care of the puppies

– that happens a lot, doesn't it? But I'm just saying… don't get your hopes up, in case you have to give her back."

"That is a fair point," I said. "Imagine if Max *was* your dog and then she disappeared because some other family took her. You don't know, she could have a family with a six-year-old boy who adores her more than anything else in the entire world! Or a little old lady whose husband is dead and whose children never visit and her only remaining companion is this lovely fluffy dog…"

"All right, *all right,* point taken!" said Billy. "But the longer she stays here the more we'll get attached to her. We should make posters to try and find her owners. If no one comes forward, then we'll know she needs a home."

And so, even though we all wanted Max to stay (except for Joshua), we all sat around Froggo's PC and helped make a poster.

FOUND
Small, long-haired, light brown dog, heavily pregnant!
No collar or tag.
Found in the Mill on the Hill pub on 9th April 2020
Please call: 08811 233 899

Billy took a photo of Max on his phone and uploaded it onto the file. We printed forty copies, put each one in a clear plastic sleeve (which we 'borrowed' from Mum's desk) and went out to post them up around the neighbourhood. We put ten posters up near our house and split the rest between Billy, Joshua, Hayden, Danny and Carla so they could put some up nearer their own homes.

They all wanted to sleep over, but they didn't have permission and anyway, we didn't want to raise suspicion. So, they all left just before dinner, apart from Billy, who was sleeping over. They promised they'd put the posters up tomorrow and we promised they could come back on Monday to see how Max is doing.

Sunday 12th April 2020

I wish I could stay in Frogsplash's room all day and keep my eye on Max but even hangover Mum might be alert enough to notice how out of ordinary that would be. He's promised to text me if she shows any signs of imminent puppy-birth.

Yes, Sam, that's a very promising promise. Of course, the fifteen-year-old boy who goes by the name of 'Frogsplash' knows exactly what labour looks like!

The others have all put up their posters, but we've had no calls yet. I don't think Max has an owner, or if she does, they don't want her anymore. I understand puppies are hard work, but how could you turn away a lovely, pregnant fluff-ball like that?

Monday 13th April 2020

Frogsplash doesn't usually get up until around eleven a.m. during school holidays, so I knew something must have happened when he sent me a text at nine a.m.

He said only two words, "They're here!"

Mum had already left for work, so we didn't have to be sneaky, I ran straight to his room and tapped gently on the door (as excited as I was, I didn't want to walk in on him in his pants). He let me in and there they were, these gorgeous, golden sausage rolls all lined up by Max's belly, nestled in her fur in a big, furry bundle. I crouched down slowly, quietly, so as not to alarm any of them, and I just sat and smiled at them for ages. They were the most amazing, beautiful, helpless little portions of puppy in the entire world.

"When did it happen?" I asked Frog.

"I don't know... I must have woken up when Mum slammed the front door shut when she left for work... I think I drifted back off for a minute, but then I rolled over and I saw them. They must have been born during the night."

"You mean a dog gave birth right next to your bed and you didn't even wake up?" I laughed.

"Clearly giving birth isn't that much of a big deal... I don't know why human women make such a big fuss about it." He said. I think Mum would have slapped him if she'd been there to hear that.

"So how many are there?" I asked, choosing to ignore his previous comment.

"It's hard to tell; they're all bundled up so tightly I keep miscounting."

Eventually we managed to count five. Five puppies! They have the tiniest little faces with the cutest little noses and their eyes are all still closed, and their paws are the size of buttons and I love them all! I want to give them names, but we probably shouldn't because we can't keep them all. We both sent texts to our friends inviting them over to meet them and by midday, they had all joined us, even Joshua. We spent most of the day just sitting and staring at them. Poor Max probably wanted a bit of peace, so we sat downstairs to eat our lunch, then Billy took her to the garden for a toilet break. While she was there, the puppies just wriggled around rolling over each other, keeping each other warm. Occasionally one would separate from the group and that's when we got a good look at their faces. They are so, so lovely.

We decided there was no point keeping it a secret from Mum any longer, and we also thought that if we told her as soon as she got in, before our friends went home for dinner, then she might not shout at us because it's rude to shout in front of guests. It's been a while since Frog and I have worked together to ease Mum into the right mood to accept or forgive something we've done. It's not often we team up to do anything mischievous these days, as we generally have very different ideas of what counts as fun. But this was not about fun, this was about puppies.

As per our usual technique, I went first. This is because Mum expects me to at least say hi to her when she gets in from work, so it doesn't strike her as particularly odd when I start talking to her the moment she gets in the door. If Frogsplash emerged from his room to greet her, she'd know straight away that something was off key.

"Hi Mum," I said. "I hope you don't mind but I've got my friends over – don't worry, they're not staying for dinner, I just thought I'd let you know."

"Oh no, I don't mind at all! It's a rare treat when *you* have friends over!"

Hey! What's that supposed to mean?

"So, how was your day, anyway?" I asked her.

"Oh, same old… I won't bore you with it."

Then Frogsplash came downstairs.

"Just getting some drinks for me and the guys," he said casually. "You want anything, Mum?"

"Oh yeah, I'll have a glass of wine please," Mum said. Perfect.

"Speaking of wine," Frog said when he came back into the living room. "How was your day at the vineyard? I've barely spoken to you since Saturday!"

If you ask me, Frogsplash was laying it on a bit thick. He was talking to Mum like he was an old friend from her book club and they'd just bumped into each other in Sainsbury's, but Mum was so keen to talk about her day trip I don't think she noticed.

"You know what, it was absolutely *lovely* – and very educational. Graham's a nice man, you know, I'm so glad you two are all right with me and him. You are still all right with it, aren't you?"

I felt bad then. There we were manipulating her, *pretending* to care about her life, when all we really wanted was to get away with lying to her.

"Of course, we are, Mum!" Frogsplash said reassuringly. But I wasn't reassured. The conversation was getting out of my control.

"Billy's upstairs!" I said suddenly. It felt like our only chance.

"Oh yes of course, you've got friends over; don't let me keep you," Mum said.

"Billy brought something around the other day…" Frogsplash said, and Mum suddenly tuned in to his tone.

"Is everything OK? You didn't have another fight, did you?"

"No, not at all," said Frogsplash, still sounding very book club-ish. "In fact, it's brought us a lot closer together."

I see what you're doing brother… very good.

"What has? What's going on?"

We waited for her to take another sip of wine.

"He didn't tell me he was going to bring it over," Froggo continued. "He just turned up on Saturday with this big box…"

Put it all on Billy… nice!

"By that point, it was too late to move her," I added. "Billy didn't know… he thought she was sick, but it turns out…"

"She was pregnant," Frogsplash finished.

This, here, is the artful bit. You lead the person to believe that something much worse has happened than the reality of it, so they'll be pleasantly relieved when the true outcome is revealed.

"PREGNANT? WHO'S PREGNANT?" Mum panicked. At that stag,e she must have been thinking that either Frog or Billy had got a girl pregnant. It was tough, but it would all be over soon.

"A dog, Mum," Frogsplash said at last. "She's in my room."

"Only she's not pregnant anymore," I said. "Come and see."

We led her upstairs quietly, gently pushed open Frog's door and let Mum see all our friends in a circle around the cardboard box. We'd tucked a blanket underneath Max and laid down a few sheets of newspaper under the puppies. Mum's face melted when she saw them.

"They're… they're precious! They're unbelievable! Why didn't you tell me sooner?"

"They were only born last night," said Froggo. "I only knew this morning when I woke up – you'd already left for work."

"You should have sent a text! I'd have come home! And you've been looking after her on your own?"

We explained everything to her, about how Billy had found her and thought she was ill, and how he hadn't told Graham because he didn't want her to be put down. We told her about the 'found' posters and that we still hadn't had any calls. She called Graham soon after and told him everything but made him promise not to be mad at Billy because he'd done a kind thing. The others had to go home soon after, but Billy stayed, and Graham came by after work. He was a bit peeved about being kept in the dark, especially when he found out that Max had been hiding out in *his* pub, but he melted when he saw them too.

Sunday 26th April 2020

It's been a wonderful two weeks. Our friends have been over most days, as well as some of their parents and siblings *and* some of Mum's friends. Everybody wants to see the puppies. Even Joshua can't stop cuddling them! They're still with Max most of the time, but she's happy to go out for short walks now. We still haven't had anyone come forward to claim her. The puppies have opened their eyes and they're even cuter now that they're a bit podgy and can stand up on their own. The vet came around to check them over yesterday and said we'd done a wonderful job of supporting Max and looking after them all. She scanned Max for an electronic tag, but she didn't have one.

The puppies will be ready to find new homes from the age of eight weeks. I don't want them to leave! Billy is gradually persuading Graham to let him keep Max, and Frogsplash and I are working on Mum to let us keep one of the pups… fingers crossed!

Monday 27th April 2020

Back to school today and the start of a new term. You may remember at the start of last term we had a new subject for P.E. Well today was no different, except that we also had a new teacher. Miss Milne was still there, for 'support', but our main teacher for this term is going to be Ms Lafayette.

"I'll still be here if you need me," Miss Milne said. "I'm trained in first aid, so I can take care of any injuries. I'm also responsible for checking attendance and for assessing your performance and giving you your final grade, so don't think you'll be getting off lightly with Ms Lafayette!"

"So, what's Ms Lafayette here for?" asked Vicky.

"Well," Miss Milne said. "I'm more *sports* oriented…"

Yes! I hate sports! I haven't got a coordinated bone in my body!

"Ms Lafayette is better equipped to be your dance teacher."

Oh, dear God, no! Oh, Samantha of fifteen seconds ago – what a sweet, naïve thing you were! Oh, fifteen seconds ago – simpler times!

"Thank you, Miss Milne! That's right, I'm classically trained, not *treadmill* trained!" Ms Lafayette said with what I could have sworn was a hint of scorn in her voice. "But we're going to be doing something a little bit more modern here today. We're going to start with a *creative flow session*, so if you could all please sit down on the floor so we can begin."

We all sat down apart from Miss Milne, who already looked bored.

"Some people say dance is expression through movement," Ms Lafayette began. "But *I* say dance is movement through expression!" she paused for a moment, as though she'd just said something truly profound. "Every dance tells a story, and every good dance teaches us something important. The very best dances tell us something we urgently need to know, they represent a cause… they make us *believe* in something."

This didn't seem like something we should believe in. I'm pretty sure our dance isn't going to be a ground-breaking documentary exposing the shocking truths of the world. I'm pretty sure it's going to be a dance… and an underwhelming one at that. I looked over at Miss Milne during this attempt at an inspirational speech, and even she was struggling not to roll her eyes.

"So, now the ball's in your court," Ms Lafayette continued.

Nice, make it sound sporty – that'll do the trick!

"We need to come together as a *team* and work out what *our* dance is together… we have to find our dance story and TELL IT TO THE WORLD!"

Ugh.

"What story can we tell, guys? Come on guys, talk to me! What's relevant to you guys right now?"

Go on, say 'guys' a few more times, that'll help us relate to you!

"What needs to be said? There must be something urgent that we need to express… what is the story that you desperately need to tell? What are the issues of your generation?"

She made us sit in an 'ideas circle' which was just a regular circle, then she produced a beach ball from somewhere and called it 'the inspiration bubble'. She could at least have found a see-through one rather than a hot pink one with 'I heart Marbella' printed on it. We had to throw the ball… sorry, *inspiration bubble,* to each other, and whoever caught it had to suggest an issue of our generation.

We had climate change, university costs, internet privacy, online security, online photo-sharing (once we got to internet-based issues, we kind of got stuck in a rut), cyber bullying, fake news, FOMO, unrealistic expectations of body image caused by photo editing… the list carried on down this rather pitiful route until Ms Lafayette put a stop to it and decided to pick one of our suggestions at random. So, just to prolong the affair even further, she wrote each idea down on a bit of paper, folded them all up and put them all in the 'unbiased selection bowl' (it was her empty lunchbox) and had one of us pick one out.

The lucky winner was (drumroll please…) online security. Not to be confused with internet safety (not talking to strangers online, etc.), online security is about having passwords that aren't easy to guess and not saving your bank details on your devices. We're going to do a dance about that this term. It'll be just like Swan Lake, only more… passwordy.

By the time all of that was over, we only had fifteen minutes left of the lesson, but they were the worst by a long shot. We had to dance around the room whilst thinking about online security. Seriously. Ms Lafayette said we had to keep thinking about online security and what it means to us, and 'let all of the ideas and thoughts surrounding online security flow through our bodies and externalise themselves as dance moves'. You know… like you usually do. She didn't even give us music to dance to – she said that would 'block communication between our minds and bodies'. I wish I could block communication from her mouth to my ears.

I told the girls about it at lunch and they found it hilarious, especially Danny, who takes *actual* dance lessons. She's been staying late with her dance teacher the past couple of weeks, so he can help her choreograph a routine for the talent show. She won't show it to us yet because she's too embarrassed, but if she's putting this much preparation into it, I'm sure it'll be great. Carla is still deciding which song to play for her talent show entry. It appears she spent most of her Easter holidays exploring her dad's record collection (which is extremely vast) and rather than narrowing down her choices she now has even more songs she wants to play. I've been so distracted by the puppies, I haven't given any thought at all to my audition for the play.

Monday 4th May 2020

Max is still staying in our house with the puppies which means that Billy is pretty much living with us too, and because Billy is pretty much living with us, Graham is a regular visitor too. So, I guess the house dynamic has changed quite a bit over the past few weeks. Graham has seen how much Billy loves Max, and he's probably quite relieved to see him and Frogsplash getting along so well after their fight at the party, so he's letting Billy keep Max once the puppies have been rehomed.

It is a bit weird suddenly having all these extra people in the house. If it hadn't been for Max and the puppies, there's no way Mum would have had Graham over all the time like this, but because Billy's always here anyway, it just makes sense that Graham comes by after work. He works odd shifts at the pub so he's not here *all the time,* but in a way that's worse because I never know when he's going to be here, so I must be mentally prepared for it at any given time. It's not his fault, or Mum's… nobody's *asked* me to be mentally prepared; they probably don't even realise that it affects me in any way. It doesn't need to affect me, it just does.

When it's just me, Mum and Frogsplash I know I can just go downstairs, get a glass of water and come back up to my room without having a conversation with anyone and that's totally normal. But when Graham's here I feel *obliged* to talk to him; if I walk into the kitchen and he's there I suddenly feel *aware* of my silence, even if he doesn't say anything to me. And if he does talk to me then I have to have a conversation, and that's weird too.

And there are other little things. The other day I was in the kitchen and I saw him sitting in the garden relaxing. Mum came in to get the washing out of the machine and took it outside to dry. Without even thinking about it he got up to help her hang it on the line, and at first, I thought that was nice because he's obviously aware that he's more than just a guest here and so he's doing his bit. But then I saw him pegging a pair of *my knickers* on the line and I could have died. Who is he? Who is this strange man touching my pink polka dot knickers! AGH!

Mum has been altering her behaviour for his benefit a little bit as well. Usually, she doesn't mind if we eat dinner separately, in our rooms or in front of the TV, if we're eating healthy(ish) and clean up after ourselves. But when Graham and Billy are here, we always eat dinner together at the table. It feels very peculiar, because it's like we're eating dinner as a real family, only it's not real at all; it's all fake because the very fact that we're eating at the table is a pretence. It's us, the Drurys, pretending to them, the Wilsons, that we are the sort of family who eats dinner at the table. If we were a real family, we wouldn't feel the need to pretend to be better than we are, at least not to each other.

On the plus side, Graham seems very nice. Like Billy, he's very easy to talk to and appears to get along well with everyone. I don't know exactly how old he is, but I'd say around ten years older than Mum, and Mum's nearly forty. He's into sports but in a casual sort of way, and I wonder if he only keeps up with it so he has something to talk about with his customers in the pub. He loves film and television and seems to know the name of every single actor and remember everything they've ever been in. He was very excited when I mentioned that I might audition for the school play. He said I should go for it.

Mrs Willis still hasn't announced which play we'll be doing yet, but everyone knows it's going to be Shakespeare, so I decided to audition as Lady Macbeth. I don't know much about any Shakespeare, but I skimmed through a little bit of Macbeth when we were playing the three witches in *A Festive Carol*. My audition is this Friday at lunchtime and I'm as ready as I'll ever be.

Saturday 9th May 2020

Yesterday's audition seemed to go well, although it's hard to be completely sure. Mrs Willis was delighted just to see me turn up, so for all I know my audition went terribly and she was just oblivious to my failings. It's a strange feeling, having to wait to see if I got a part. If I do get a part, then it'll mean a lot of extra work for me, learning lines and going to rehearsals, plus, of course, the utter, gut-wrenching terror of getting up on stage and performing in front of an audience. But if I don't get a part, I will be disappointed because I will have failed, and for some strange reason, I really enjoy acting, so it would be nice if I was good at it. I've never really been good at anything, apart from passing tests and finishing my homework, but no one gives you trophies or medals for that.

It was meant to be our weekend with Dad, but he's absolutely swamped with this big summer client and, to be honest, we were more than happy to stay here with the puppies. They're a lot more independent now, which is good for Max because she needs her walks. They're starting to get the same wavy fur as her, only the waves are all in miniature, and you can see their little pot bellies poking through the fluff – it's utterly adorable!

There are three boys and two girls, but we haven't named them because we mustn't get too attached. They are hard work, but I really, *really* don't want them to leave! We're still getting a lot of visitors who want to play with them. Joshua has taken a real liking to the runt of the litter – he didn't even mind when she peed on his new skinny jeans! They're playing all over the house and they have had a few 'accidents', that would normally stress Mum out but having Graham around seems to mellow her out a little bit. Either that or she's trying to hide her moody side from him for as long as possible!

Instead of going to Dad's, we video-called him on the tablet. We showed him Max and the puppies, and he couldn't get enough of them, just like everybody else.

"Hang on a sec," he said. "I've got something to show you, too…"

He held his tablet up to his face as he walked into the hallway and out of his flat. He went down the communal stairs and stepped out onto the street and into the daylight. We had no idea what he was up to or how far he was going to walk, but I for one was intrigued. He didn't say anything the entire time he was walking, so Frogsplash and I were left watching his smirking face at a funny angle moving with the motion of his stride wondering what on Earth he was about to show us. He must have gone a minute or two down the road before he stopped dead in front of a shiny, lime green, convertible sports car.

"I'll give you one guess who this belongs to!" he said at last, still stifling a giggle.

"Oh no… he didn't!" I said.

"Richard!" laughed Frogsplash.

"Well it sure as hell isn't mine!" Dad said.

He gave us the full three hundred and sixty degrees view of the automotive atrocity and we all had a good laugh about it.

"But wait, it gets better!" Dad said. "I haven't got a photo of it yet, but it shouldn't be a problem getting one, he gets *really* excited whenever there's an opportunity to show it off…"

"What is it?" we asked.

"No… no… I won't spoil the surprise. Just wait – you'll see!"

Normally I hate speaking to someone on the phone; it makes me anxious when I can't see their face but am still required to respond instantaneously. I don't mind a text conversation because there's no pressure to reply straight away, so you get time to slip into the depths of your own mind and *think*. I feel most comfortable when I've had time to think things through. If I can't have the gift of thinking or space/time, then I prefer to converse face-to-face rather than over the phone because the other person can't hide from you… or should I say, hide *their intentions* from you.

I'm not paranoid, OK? But they say that most communication is non-verbal, we communicate with gestures and facial expressions. But when you're on the phone, you miss all of that. I stutter and stammer on the phone… the words lose their way between my brain and my mouth and then, when they've failed me, I wonder if they had ever been there at all. I'm acutely aware that my voice and the words it forms are the *only* thing that the other person is concentrating on. I can't smile or stare or flare my nostrils to indicate some hidden meaning or buried emotion. In that way, it's even worse than public speaking! It must be direct, and that's a lot of pressure.

But the video call was fun. Partly because we could see each other's faces, and partly because Frogsplash was there to diffuse the tension (which was all in my head, but I live in my head, so for me it is omnipresent). If we'd been at Dad's flat in person, I doubt we would have spoken to him as much as we did on videophone. When you're communicating with someone in that way, you can't just get distracted by the TV or whatever, you must *talk*. And that's what we did, and it was great! Who says modern technology gets in the way of human interaction?

Either way, though, communication is one of the most complicated things in human existence. Is it just me who thinks that?

We got our surprise later in the evening and it was worth the wait. Dad sent us a photo image without a caption, but no words were needed. The photo showed the upper arm of a man. I could tell it was a man's arm from how hairy it was, only a large section of it had been crudely shaved off. The shaved section was the focus of the shot because it featured a fresh, vibrant tattoo. The tattoo was of a very familiar-looking lime green convertible sports car and written in a banner above it were the words 'life in the fast lane'. It was the worst, most brilliant tattoo in the entire world, and I can't wait to see it in the flesh.

Wednesday 13th May 2020

We are experiencing another heat wave. It's the second one this year if you include the slightly milder than

300

expected temperatures of this March. That's as extreme as things get in England, although usually it's the other way around and we get snow in May and floods in August. So, it probably is climate change, but so far, it's not exactly been problematic. Well… apart from the skirts.

A lot of the girls in my year have started rolling up their school skirts to show off their legs now that they've been freed from the wintry imprisonment of tights. It's just a trend, I know, but now I feel like my skirt is stupidly long just because it reaches my knees. I can't roll my skirt up because my thighs don't look like their thighs, so they need to stay covered up. Why is it that the only part of the body that's exposed while wearing school uniform is the legs? I'm going to be faced with this same problem for at least four more years!

It's nice that we can sit outside to eat our packed lunches though. Our music room is probably going to be occupied for the rest of the term with school play auditions and then rehearsals, so if we couldn't go outside during lunchbreak, we'd have to eat in the dreaded canteen! We've had a couple of near run-ins with Megan, the year eleven and her retinue, and we've had to be careful to avoid Charlotte Henderson and her crew, but apart from that it's been quite pleasant. Just think how much nicer school would be without all the terrible people!

Friday 15th May 2020

Auditions for the play ended yesterday and today in assembly, Mrs Willis announced that we're going to be doing *A Midsummer Night's Dream.* I say 'we', but I don't know if I'm even going to be in it yet; the casting is going to be announced in next Friday's assembly, so I've got another week of anxiously waiting until I find out. I mustn't get my hopes up, Carla's sister, Louisa, said that year sevens hardly ever get cast in the whole school play and those that do rarely say more than one or two lines. But on the other hand, Mrs Willis sought me out especially because she wanted me to audition, and for some reason, she seems very fond of me. I mustn't let that get to my head!

Carla and Danny don't have to fret so much about the talent show because there are no auditions, they just wrote their names down on a list with a short description of what they plan to do for their performance. Danny saw that Charlotte Henderson, Beth Amory and Andrea Michael had put their names down and wrote that they would be doing a 'group dance' and that got her worried because that makes them her competition. It's not like there are any prizes or anything, but people will talk about it and obviously those girls are higher up the social ladder than us, so they'll probably get more support from other people. Also, don't forget, Charlotte is still on the school paper, and it would be very unlike her to say something nice when instead she could make herself look good by putting others down.

Carla has chosen her talent show song, but she's decided to keep it a secret from us so today at lunchtime, she went to the music room alone to rehearse. It's probably a good thing she's keeping it a secret; if we were sat with her while she rehearsed every day, then we'd probably get sick of hearing it! I know she's going to be brilliant and I want the full impact of that when I see her on stage – I can't wait! Danny is practising her routine after school, so it was just me and her eating lunch out on the field today. We caught a glimpse of Charlotte, Beth and Andrea practising their dance routine while we were out there. We didn't want to stare so we only caught bits of it, but it seemed very basic to me, and kind of... adult. It was like a music video where the dancers are just there to be sexy, rather than showing real skill or technique. I'm not saying it was *bad,* it just didn't seem right for a school talent show.

Monday 18th May 2020

EPIDEMIC: FEARS GROW AS HUGE VIRUS SPREADS UNCONTROLLABLY, INFECTING SCHOOLS AND CAUSING MAYHEM!

A new and highly contagious strain of a virus has been spreading through youth communities at an alarming rate. Medics are calling the virus 'dance fever' and are advising the use of anti-virus technology to help combat the vicious infection. As a preventative measure, they also recommend putting up firewalls at all student gateways which should block entry for this extremely potent and destructive threat to security.

Yes, it was dance class today, and Ms Lafayette has really done her research on online security. When she first began teaching us, she seemed to want us to take the lead and come up with our own ideas. I think she realised her mistake when 'our own ideas' ended up with us doing a dance about online security. I think if I was her, I'd have admitted that it was a terrible idea putting us lot in the driver's seat, but she's either too proud to admit she was wrong or she *really* enjoys a challenge.

Since then I think she's been itching to take back control of the class, and today she did just that when she arrived with her own dance plan which we will be putting into action as a group. I say 'dance plan' rather than 'choreography' because she hasn't shown us any dance *moves,* she just sort of roughly described what she wants it to look like. I'm beginning to wonder if she's ever actually taught a class before.

"OK, listen up girls!" she said when we were all sat quietly in the 'listening circle', which was very similar to the 'ideas circle' which was such a huge, unbridled success last time. "We're going to start off with six girls dancing together steadily, rhythmically and completely coordinated with each other; you're going to be our smoothly running, healthy, fully operational computer, OK? Then there will be a bold, dominating entrance from five new dancers, who will be welcomed by the kind, trusting rhythmic dancers in the original line-up. These will be our Trojan virus. They will gradually work their way in between the others, getting in the way of their smoothly coordinated dance and setting off a completely new and erratic rhythm which causes mass havoc and distress."

Nothing can be more distressing than the prospect of this dance. Anything but this! Give me a Trojan virus any day, but not this!

"The original six dancers will be brought to a complete standstill until five new dancers, all holding hands, enter the floor and stand between them and the Trojan virus. These five will be our Firewall. They will fight the virus and then introduce one dancer, who will be our password, and three more, who will be our security questions. They will stand between each of the five members of the firewall and all hold hands, coming into a circle which locks around the original six dancers, keeping them safe from the virus outside."

I found out today that I'm going to play the part of a security question. Finally, I have a purpose in this life.

Friday 22nd May 2020

I have this huge gumball of nausea at the pit of my stomach and my heart feels like it's grown wings and is fluttering somewhere in my throat. I haven't been able to focus on anything because I can't stop thinking about it, trying to decide how I should feel and what I should do. Even the puppies weren't enough to distract me, even when I got home hours after I found out. Am I really going to do it? I don't think I can. It's too big.

I'm Puck. Mrs Willis cast me as Puck. All the other characters are being played by year nines and over – most of them are sixth formers! Puck links the entire play together; Puck is the entertainer… I can't be Puck! It's not *the* main part but I think it's a lead role. It's hard to tell; I haven't read the whole play. I don't even know the play I'm meant to be acting in! Rehearsals start on Monday. What am I going to do?

You are going to shine, Samantha Drury.

Ha! Yeah right. You're going to make a massive fool of yourself and ruin the play for everyone else.

Why did you audition if you didn't want to perform?

My friends encouraged me!

They encouraged you – they didn't force you!

...and Mrs Willis told me I should do it, and everyone said I'd only get a small part... I never thought it would turn out this way. Year sevens don't get lead roles!

So why did you then? You must be good if she gave you the part.

She thinks I'm good. But what if she's the only one?

Why do you always assume that you can't do things? Isn't it just as reasonable to assume that you can?

Because if I assume I can't do it, then I don't have to try.

Friday 29th May 2020

END OF DAYS: RIOTING, MASS HYSTERIA, BREAKDOWN OF SOCIAL NORMS AND COMPLETE ABANDONMENT OF STATUS QUO. STAY IN YOUR HOMES! DO NOT BREACH THE SAFETY BOUNDARIES! STAY VIGILANT!

As young people face their last day of life as they know it, total freedom from civilised society becomes their final endeavour. Citizens are warned to stay within the boundaries assigned by the authorities to stay safe and avoid getting caught in the crossfire between members of the Youth Armageddon League who will be staging action throughout the day.

Today was the last day of lessons for year eleven before they go on study leave, and apparently, it's traditional for them to go completely savage and attempt to destroy the entire school like chimpanzees in a department store. I must admit it did look like an awful lot of fun. None of it was permitted by the school, but because everyone in the entire year was doing it, there was very little the teachers could do to control it, which just goes to show the power that people have when they come together in large numbers. It makes one wonder what else could be achieved if we all united for a common cause. In the end, though, the authorities always find a way to take liberty back from the people.

"It's a rite of passage," Carla explained to us as we sat outside for morning break watching the year elevens, some with cans of silly string in their hands, others with cans of spray paint, and plenty with cans of beer. "Even if you're coming back for sixth form, you have to go wild on your last day of year eleven. If nothing else, it's the last time you'll ever have to wear school uniform, and that's *something* to celebrate! It doesn't seem to matter who you are or how well behaved you've been for the rest of the term, *everybody* lets loose on leaving day."

"What about Mr Bellows? I bet he bawled his eyes out on his last day!" I said.

"Well yeah, everyone except him, I guess!" Carla laughed.

"What about your sister?" Danny asked her. "What did her and her mates get up to last year?"

"Not as much as you'd think, actually. There was a bit of silly string and a lot of alcohol, but I don't think they did any graffiti like this lot! There was a water fight up on the fields, though, and then a group of boys managed to carry a table and seven chairs from the maths department and chuck them in the lake! After that, Mr Wilcox cracked down on it hard and said that if anyone was caught doing anything other than signing people's shirts, then they wouldn't be allowed to sit their GCSEs."

"Can they do that?" Danny asked, shocked.

"Who knows," said Carla. "But it's not worth the risk, is it?"

At lunch break, we took a stroll up to the fields to see what the year elevens were up to, but it didn't last long. Some of them had brought up a wireless speaker and they were playing the same song on repeat; it seemed to be their anthem, driving them on to do reckless things and completely let loose. It was a Free Parking song from one of their earlier, more rough-around-the-edges albums. Carla says that's when they were at their best, when they were true to punk, but their new stuff has proper melodies and a lot more comedy to it and that's more my cup of tea. Still, you can't argue that the song the year elevens chose was a great soundtrack for rebellion. It's called *School of Debt,* and this is how it goes:

> *"They say we should be content because we've got our youth*
> *But I'd rather take a swim in the fountain of truth.*
> *They kick us and beat us then tell us to smile*
> *And when we kick back, they're full of denial!*
> *From the day we're born they lie to our face*
> *Just to make us all part of their filthy rat race.*
> *They say revolution is the world's biggest threat*
> *And make us settle down in the school of debt.*
>
> *I enrolled in the school of debt*
> *Now I'm drowning in a pool of sweat!*
> *Wanted education, but what did I get?*
> *Desperation and crippling regret!*

We don't learn a thing; they just train us for work
Where we'll produce profit for some greedy jerk.
They make us pay more than we could ever afford
Just to pass our exams and spend our whole lives
bored!
You clock in the hours; the years drift by.
You wonder when it was that you let your dreams die.

The day you get paid is the closest you'll get
But you'll never repay a whole lifetime of debt.

I enrolled in the school of debt
Now I'm drowning in a pool of sweat!
Wanted education, but what did I get?
Desperation and crippling regret!

They were throwing water balloons at each other, nothing more than that, but the teachers had decided they'd had enough and came striding out of the school building only minutes after the lunch bell had rang.

"ENOUGH!" bellowed Mr Wilcox, a fleet of teachers behind him. "The fields and the lake are out of bounds for the rest of the day – everyone inside, NOW!"

The lower years, ourselves included, followed orders swiftly, but the year elevens were too deep into the spirit of things and they carried on as they were, undeterred by the severity of Mr Wilcox's tone. Danny, Carla and I were just on the threshold of the entrance to the main school building when we heard him shout, "All year elevens will return to the school building IMMEDIATELY. Anyone found outside will be banned from sitting their exams!"

And just like that, the fun was over. You'd have thought, given the nature of the song they were listening to, that at least some of them would have decided they didn't care at all about their GCSEs, but they had worked hard all their lives to get this far, and as bleak as their futures may or may not turn out to be, having zero qualifications was not going to improve anything for anyone.

Wow. I am the least punk person ever. Forgive me, Carla.

Even the toughest, roughest year elevens quickly fell in line after word had spread of Mr Wilcox's threat. We had not yet eaten our lunches, and Mrs Willis appears to have taken up residence in our favourite music room while she prepares for the play, so we had little choice but to join the masses and dine in the canteen. I've never seen it as full as it was today, every single table was heaving, and almost all of them seated an awkward mix of different year groups and odd members of contrasting cliques who ordinarily would not dare to be seen in the same social spaces, but these were exceptional circumstances.

There was a real buzz in the air, particularly because the year elevens had all been herded into this one large, open space, and whilst the teachers had managed to contain them physically, they had done nothing to stifle their mood. They were talking and laughing raucously, many of them drinking from soda bottles that probably had something much stronger in them. I understand Mr Wilcox wanted to keep them from damaging school property, but this proximity of highly charged teens seemed just as dangerous. Now it was intoxicating the entire school.

Carla, Danny and I stood and watched in awe, unable to hear each other over the roar of voices around us. The fizzing, popping, electric atmosphere reminded me of the Free Parking gig, and it got me thinking about how powerful music can be in moving people to think and act and feel. We still hadn't eaten because we couldn't see anywhere to sit. The only free seats were on the long, wooden table at the back of the hall where the teachers always sit. Students almost never sit there because no one wants to be under the eye of the teachers while they're on lunch break, but like I said, these were exceptional circumstances.

At least ten, probably closer to fifteen year elevens were already sat at the teachers' table and they were behaving exactly as they pleased, not caring a wink about the proximity of the teachers, so we thought we'd be safe enough sitting there just this one time. If the teachers were going to call anyone up on their dining etiquette, it wasn't going to be us. It wasn't until after we'd taken our seats that I realised that opposite us and along four places were Megan Brown, the blazer queen, and her three royal subjects. I made eyes at Danny and Carla, but Carla made eyes back at me as if to say, 'don't you dare allow them to dictate our lives!' and Danny just shrugged because she doesn't know them by sight and it was too noisy to explain the whole thing to her right then and there.

I would have been more anxious, but we were surrounded by teachers and so many other people that I felt safe enough. The only times I've ever come close to falling victim to Megan and her cronies is when they've cornered me alone, and even then, I've always managed to escape relatively unscathed. The mood was light, and Megan seemed to be enjoying her last day, so I couldn't see any reason for her to pick me out of the crowd and torment me. I was protected by a thick layer of sound.

I was mildly preoccupied with the task of picking the sun-dried tomatoes out of my pasta salad (what even are they? Giant, acidic raisins, that's what) when a fast-moving object caught my eye. It was a girl, much taller and older than me, with long auburn hair and long legs in a short, pleated skirt and black stockings that weren't school uniform. She was walking swiftly and with purpose on the other side of the table from me, walking past the row of people seated opposite, and she had the fiercest, most determined look on her face, her lips painted pillar box red and pouting resolutely. She stopped suddenly, directly behind Megan the blazer bully, and she cleared her throat so loudly that she managed to command the attention of everyone at the long wooden table and most of the people beyond it.

Megan, who was deep in conversation with her three little sidekicks, was slow to react, possibly because of the suspicious-looking, highlighter-yellow liquid that was in her water bottle, and before she could turn around the red-lipped, red-haired wonder woman had cracked an egg on the crown of her head and it's thick, gooey contents and broken shards of shell were dripping slowly, oozing through her black hair on the one side and her shaved scalp on the other, sliding down her face in great, viscous blobs of justice. The nameless girl, who will forever be my hero, smiled peacefully and walked away. Everybody had seen it, and everybody was now watching Megan scramble to

314

her feet in utter shock and panic, trying to contain the gloopy drips and shrieking at the indignity of it all.

I don't know what Megan did to that girl, but I know that justice was served at lunchtime this day. Imagine Megan being in your year, being in your classes, on your school trips, at your school discos, always there in the shadows for five of the most socially awkward, sensitive years of your life. Of course, an egg to the head can never make up for such a prolonged ordeal, but it's not a bad crack at revenge!

Megan's reaction made it infinitely more satisfying to watch. I suppose it's hard to keep your cool when something that gross is sliding down your head and onto your face, but if she'd just kept it a bit more discreet, she would have saved herself a large chunk of the embarrassment. Instead, she was howling, not crying, but whining like a spoilt child who'd just dropped their ice cream cone, and everyone was watching and revelling in her misfortune. The way people rejoiced so openly in the event was a testament to her past cruelty to all of them. Even the teachers, who were sat so close to her, turned a blind eye to the misdemeanour of the mystery girl, and I'm sure I saw a barely-contained smirk from a few of those who had clearly had the misfortune of teaching eggy Meggy in the past.

Watching Megan trying to scrape the gloopy substance off her scalp and out of her hair was a wonderful moment of wish fulfilment. It got me wondering who I would like to get back at on my last day. I could only think of Charlotte Henderson, but to be fair to her, she's nothing

315

at all like Megan, and she has four years left to see the error of her ways.

<u>Wednesday 3rd June 2020</u>

Something kind of weird happened today, but I think it's going to be OK. You know when something embarrassing happens to someone else and you're just *so* relieved that it was them and not you? Well this is kind of like that, except it wasn't embarrassing… it was just one of those things that, had it happened to me, I'd have replayed in my head a billion times wondering if it was OK or if I'd totally weirded everything out and made things super awkward. But it didn't happen to me; I just happened to be there.

It must have been about four p.m., because I was already home from school, but it was nowhere near the time when Mum usually gets home. The house was quiet, Frogsplash's keys weren't on the hook and his giant, muddy trainers weren't on the doormat waiting to trip me up like they usually are, so I guessed I was home alone. I like to know when there's someone else in the house and when there's not. You must know how my brain works by now – I have a set state of mind depending on what degree of solitude I'm currently in.

There's completely alone, which is when I'm most relaxed. Then there's when Mum, Dad or Frogsplash are around, which is when I'm on guard but conscious that I won't have to modify my behaviour at all and will merely have to speak when spoken to. Then there's when I'm with my close friends, where I'm comfortable but aware that I will need to be more responsive and tuned in to the people around me and will benefit from trying to be funny, or supportive, or give good advice. Then there's being around other people, like at school or a party, where I must be fully switched on and prepared for anything, whether it's awkward small talk or full-on confrontation. There are other variations, such as being at home but having unfamiliar guests, like distant relatives... or Richard. Or being around other people but not having to talk, like sitting on the bus.

But why am I telling you all this? This is all perfectly normal thinking, isn't it? So, you must know all this already. It's just human nature... right?

So, I was at home alone and in fully relaxed, guard-down mode, which was the perfect opportunity to practise reading my lines for the play. I don't like doing it when other people are home because they might think I've gone mad and started talking to myself. You must project your voice when you're performing on stage, and I like to rehearse as I would perform, so I do it loudly! I haven't got around to mentioning my role in the play to my family just yet, but if they do hear me and realise that I've not gone mad and am in fact just rehearsing, then I'll have to tell them and then they'll want to know *everything* about it. The most important reason, though, is that there's no point rehearsing at home if I'm conscious of my family hearing me, because it won't be a real rehearsal if I'm thinking about them. How can I be in character, how can I believe that I *am* Puck, if I'm thinking about Samantha Drury's mother and brother?

After about twenty minutes, I went downstairs to get a drink from the kitchen. I was just diluting my orange

317

squash when I heard an unusual noise coming from the utility room located to the rear of the kitchen. It was kind of muffled and at first, I couldn't make it out, so I carried on listening, not daring to go and investigate but not content to just leave it be. The utility room is right at the back of the house, and if an intruder were to enter via the back garden that's where they'd start from. You always think the worst when you're taken by surprise like that, don't you? But as I stood there, perfectly still and as silent as I could be, no one emerged with a crowbar and a looting sack, and the sound became clearer.

It was a non-threatening sound that put me back at ease; it was whimpering, and I realised that one of the puppies must have got trapped in there and was crying to get out. They're getting all over the house now and it's almost impossible to keep track of them all. I wondered how long it had been stuck and how many times it had gone to the toilet while it was in there, probably on top of a pile of freshly washed and dried towels or my crisp, white school shirts. I braced myself for the smell and went to free the tiny beast, but instead of a sobbing puppy, I found Billy, sitting on the floor, crying and cuddling Max.

"Oh… sorry…" I said, and for some reason I hovered there on the threshold of the tiny room. It was incredibly awkward. I wanted to dissolve.

"Oh God… I thought… I forgot you'd be home. You're usually hiding in your room so I just…"

"Yeah I was. I just came down to get a drink. You're here on your own?"

318

"Yeah. I came back here after school with Froggo, Josh and Hayden. They went to the park for a kick about, but I didn't fancy it, so I said I'd stay here with Max."

"Is everything OK?" I asked tentatively.

"Yeah," he gave a deep sigh. "It's my mum's birthday today."

"Oh," I said. I hardly know anything about Billy's mum, but I know she and Graham haven't been separated for that long.

"Every year we'd go for a long weekend away in Cornwall," he continued. "Last year was her fortieth so we went for a whole week and my aunt and cousins came along too… it rained the entire time!"

"Typical!" I said. "When was the last time you saw her?"

"The day she left," he said sadly.

"Oh God… I had no idea! You mean...?"

"She just packed her bags and never looked back," he said.

"Jeez, Billy, that's horrible! How could anyone do that? I mean…" I stopped myself before I said anything offensive. "Sorry, she's your mum, I shouldn't have said that."

"No, no, you're right. I ask that same question every day. How could she do that?"

"Has she ever tried to get in touch?" I asked.

"No. Not once. It's been ten months. She told Dad she wanted a new life. She didn't even say goodbye to me. That was it… They say life begins at forty; I guess for her that really was true."

319

"That's no excuse though, is it? You can't just erase forty years of your life, because it's not just *your* life, is it? It affects everyone around you. It's the same for all of us."

We both stopped talking for a moment and reflected on what I'd just said. At some point while we were talking, I'd stepped into the utility room and sat on the floor next to Billy without even thinking about it. I stroked Max's head while she was still cradled in Billy's arms.

"I never saw it coming, you know," Billy said. "One day she was just my normal mum, and the next she was gone."

"It was the same with my dad. My parents never argued; I thought they were the perfect couple. Then it was all over. But what your mum did, how she dealt with it afterwards, I can't imagine what that feels like…"

I watched him squeezing Max, holding her close to his chest and nuzzling up against her crimped caramel fur. Max, bless her, was completely content with being clutched like a child's comfort blanket.

"Do you miss her?" I asked.

"Kind of," said Billy. "I miss the old her. I miss who she was when she was there. But who she is now, in my head, that's a completely different person. The old mum would never have done that to me. What's sad, the thing that bothers me most, is that the mum I had when I was growing up is gone forever. Even if that woman came back into my life today with the same name and the same face and the same passport, she wouldn't be my mum. She can never undo these past ten months."

"What would you do if she did come back?"

320

"I'd have some questions, that's for sure. I'd give her a chance to explain, but I wouldn't forgive her. I'll never let her be my mum again."

"I can understand that. Do you ever talk to Frogsplash about this kind of stuff?"

"Yeah, right!" he laughed.

"Yeah, sorry – stupid question!" I said.

"Speaking of which, they'll be back soon... I'd better get out of here and try to look normal!"

"You – normal? Good luck with that!" I joked.

"Ha. Ha. Not even remotely funny. But thanks, Sam, it was good to talk to you."

And that was that. I'm glad he talked to me. It wouldn't be so bad if he ended up being my step brother.

Later, we all ate dinner together and Billy was back on form, joking around and winding everyone up.

"So, Sam, who's your new boyfriend?" he asked me.

"What?" I said, feeling my cheeks turning a healthy shade of crimson. "I don't have a boyfriend!"

"Well I heard you talking to someone in your room earlier. Either you've got a boy stashed away up there or you're getting far too friendly with the puppies!"

He must have walked past my room when he was looking for Max. I was projecting my voice; he would have heard my Shakespearean English, so he must have known what I was doing. He was winding me up because he knew the rest of the family was waiting to hear about the play. I've been trying to avoid telling them because I know they'll make a fuss. Oh well, it had to come out eventually.

"I was learning my lines, if you must know. Cheers for that Billy!" I said playfully.

"So, you're in the play?" Mum asked excitedly.

"What part did you get?" Graham asked with equal enthusiasm.

"I'm playing Puck… it's not a big deal…"

"I don't believe you," said Billy. "If it was no big deal, why did you not tell us sooner?"

Then he got out his phone and started tapping away.

"Err – no devices at the dinner table, thank you!" Graham said. He's so old-fashioned sometimes.

"I'm just looking it up!" Billy said. "Hang on! *Though there is no single lead role in A Midsummer Night's Dream, Puck is often considered the most entertaining and enjoyable character in the play. Puck is a clever, mischievous sprite with powerful supernatural powers whose antics propel the main storylines in the play…* sounds like a pretty big deal to me!"

"That's fantastic!" said Mum. "Sam, why didn't you tell us?"

"I was going to, it's just… I don't want you to make a big deal out of it. To be perfectly honest, I think my drama teacher is a bit nuts. I think she cast me as a gimmick, to see what would happen if you put a year seven in with a bunch of trained, upper school drama students. I'm like the butt of her experiment… it's probably going to be a disaster."

"Oh, don't be so modest!" said Graham. "I can't wait to see you on stage!"

Oh great. Now the cat's out of the bag AND Graham's invited himself to the play!

I really wasn't being modest. It probably is going to be a disaster.

Saturday 13th June 2020

THE DOG DAYS ARE OVER: MAX THE MYSTERY MUTT IS MOVING OUT AND HER PRECIOUS PUPS ARE PARTING PAWS TOWARDS PERMANENT PLACES TO PLAY!

Friends and family of the Drury household have been left howling at the news of the doggy departure, which is set to take place this afternoon. Members of the household and those close to them have expressed their deepest sadness at this turn of events. A spokesperson for the humans involved say they will be pining for the pooches once they're gone; let's hope the canines are more prepared for the changes up ahead.

It's the day we've all been dreading. It's goodbye forever day, apart from Max, who's going to live with Billy and Graham so hopefully we'll get to see her from time to time. I'm not sure how things are going to develop between our two families without Max holding us together. She has been a real blessing but going from six dogs to none is probably the most depressing thing ever. All the energy and playfulness that's been bouncing around our home for the past eight weeks is going to

323

disappear. And we won't get all these visitors, all the friends and family who have been so excited to come to our house just for half an hour or so because they can't resist the fun house of fluffy puppies! It was like a constant party – a holiday from all the regular dullness, but now it's all over. It's going to feel like a playground in a town where all the children have died.

And this year's award for the most melancholic dramatization goes to… Samantha Drury!

Mum didn't want any money for the puppies; she just wanted to find them all a loving home, so she advertised them online and found a nice family for each one. She asked them all the right questions, like whether they had any small children or any other pets – not that that's necessarily a bad thing, she just wanted to see how they'd answer to see if they'd fully considered the implications of introducing a puppy into the family home – they may be adorable, but they can be exhausting! She asked how often they'd be able to walk the dog, if they went on regular holidays and whether they'd done their research on how to care for them. She did a very thorough job, especially when you remember that she didn't sign up for any of this!

She arranged for them all to come today so that it would all be over with in one go to make it less painful for me, Frog and Max, like ripping off a plaster quickly because it allegedly makes it painless. That never worked for me when I was little and it's not going to work today. Billy stayed over last night, and he's been here ever since. He's been extra protective of Max, giving her loads of attention and cuddles even though she's the one he gets to keep. I think Max is a real comfort to Billy, what with all the stuff that happened with his mum. I wonder if it's bothering him thinking about how she's going to be separated from her babies after today and how she'll never get to see them again. I bet he's been thinking about it a lot. Dogs probably don't really miss their families once they're old enough to look after themselves, but I suppose we can't really know that for sure.

Danny, Carla, Joshua and Hayden have all become really attached to the puppies as well, so Mum suggested we invite them all over to say goodbye, and to make it a marginally less miserable experience for us too. So, they all arrived at approximately midday today, giving us one final hour to play with the five balls of fur.

Joshua, who only two months ago had not wanted to go anywhere near Max for fear of getting fur on his clothes, was now walking around the house with Tiny, the gorgeous runt of the litter, sat in the front pocket of his designer, combat-style jacket, her perfect little front paws perched over the edge and her inquisitive little face peeking out over the big wide world. He was keeping her close to his heart because he loved her, but also for her own good, because her brothers and sisters had a naughty habit of picking on her. They were all playing together, chasing a selection of neon-bright, miniature tennis balls that Hayden had ordered the day they were born.

Danny was close to tears when one of them jumped on her lap, climbed on her chest and started licking her face. I didn't tell her it was only because she had biscuit crumbs around her mouth from when Mum had passed round the tin of stale Family Selection we had in the cupboard leftover from Christmas. I may have gone heavy on the snacks post-December, but I don't much like sweet things, and I can't stand the sawdust dryness of old biscuits! Hayden kept trying to comfort Danny, and I wonder if it was because he's just a gentle soul or because he really fancies her.

Carla brought her oldest sister Louisa with her because she hadn't had a chance to see them before, what with all her revision for AS exams. She was overwhelmed when she saw them all, and she fell completely in love with the little rogue we call Scratchy, because of the way he gets so excited to chase his brothers and sisters or the little neon tennis balls that he can't seem to keep control of his little slippery legs and gets stuck running on the spot like in old cartoons where the legs are spinning in a super-speedy circle, his tiny pinpoint claws scratching and making marks on the laminate flooring in the kitchen and hallway. The amount of times they've soiled the living room carpet and used the hallway as a skating rink, I'm surprised we have any floor left at all! Mum has been very forgiving, but she did seem kind of excited for one p.m., when they'd all be out of her hair at last.

At ten to one, I heard the familiar sound of footsteps crunching on the gravel in the front driveway followed by the doorbell, which got the puppies all excited, some of them yelping, Scratchy skidding on the laminate trying to keep up with them. We all held our breath, bracing ourselves to bid farewell to whichever puppy got chosen first, but it was only Graham popping by to help, and possibly to ensure none of us tried to obstruct the adoption process. Ten minutes later the doorbell rang again, and this time it wasn't a drill.

"Sammy, could you get it please? I'm just putting the kettle on," Mum called from the kitchen.

Could turn them away… tell them they got the wrong address…

But when I opened the door, it was just Joshua's mum.

"Oh, hi Mrs…" I couldn't remember her name. I've only met her once or twice before; Joshua gets super embarrassed at the mention of her.

"Call me Sharon," she told me in a warm, friendly sort of way.

"Sorry – Sharon," I said. I led her through to the living room where everyone else was sitting with the puppies.

"Mum! What are you doing here?" Joshua's face was bright red. She was clearly cramping his style, existing right there in front of all of us like the shameful composition of human certainty that she was!

"Oh – these must be the little darlings!" she said, ignoring her son and sitting down with the puppies. "Aren't they precious!" she cooed, and Joshua cringed hugely.

"Oh hi, Sharon," Mum entered the room pleasantly. "Tea or coffee?"

The doorbell rang again.

"I'll get it!" Graham yelled from the hallway.

"Hi, Graham! We met at the party, remember?"

Carla and Louisa's ears pricked up.

"Is that…" Louisa began.

"Dad?" Carla finished.

"… and Mum!" Maria, Carla's mum, poked her head into the living room cheerfully, followed by Carla's dad, James.

"What's going on?" said Carla, but there was no time to explain. Graham hadn't even shut the door before more guests arrived, first Hayden's parents, then Danny's mum with the two-year-old terror twins who had just woken up grumpy from a nap in the car. Mum came in with a tray of drinks, being careful not to trip over any puppies or toddlers on the way. On the tray was a plate of the leftover Christmas biscuits that Danny had been enjoying earlier, a teapot I hadn't seen in years and a cafetière filled with fresh filter coffee she must have bought specially for the occasion, because normally we only have instant.

So, this was all planned. I think I see what's happening here...

"OK... well..." mum hesitated. "Surprise!"

"What?" said Frogsplash.

Oh brother... how slow are you?

"These people right here... these are the people your mum chose to adopt the puppies!" Graham explained.

"Seriously?" said Joshua.

"Us as well?" asked Danny.

"Yes!" said Danny's mum. "As long as you promise to look after her!"

"Aaaaaah!" Danny squealed.

"So, I can keep Tiny?" Joshua said ecstatically, no longer embarrassed by the presence of his mother.

"One for each family," Mum said. "One for Joshua, one for Hayden, one for Danny, one for Carla and one for us!"

I couldn't believe it! What an amazing surprise!

Wait... did Mum just refer to us as a family? As in... us, Graham and Billy?

328

We've got a puppy! We're keeping him!

Carla chose Scratchy, Joshua chose Tiny and Danny chose the second girl, who she named Tinker. There were two boys left, and I was just so over the moon, I really didn't mind which one we got. In the end we felt that the only right thing to do was to let Mum choose, seeing as she'd arranged this entire thing herself, not to mention allowed the puppies to stay in her house for two months. I knew which one she'd choose because he's been her favourite since we were first able to tell them apart. We've been calling him Trousers because his fur is darker on his back legs and his bum, so it looks like he's wearing a little pair of fuzzy trousers. It makes Mum laugh every time she sees him padding along down the hall or about the house – and now he can bring laughter to all of us forever! I'm so happy!

Hayden got the last little guy who he named The Doctor, or Doc for short. Everyone stayed for at least an hour after The Choosing. Danny's brothers were starting to fuss and become too much of a handful, so her mum said her goodbyes and left with Danny, the twin tinkers and Tinker. Gradually everybody else went home apart from Graham and Billy, who stayed very close to Max in case she needed comforting as she watched her babies leave. At the end of it all, she seemed fine, and the rest of us were left making a fuss of Trousers and arguing over who got to share their bed with him at night. Going from six dogs to one (two if you include Max) is a completely different thing than none.

Thursday 17th June 2020

Mum's been at the charity shop on her lunch break today. It used to be a bad habit of hers a few years ago, like a kind of obsession, maybe even a compulsion. I'm not saying it's bad to buy stuff from the charity shop. Obviously, it's good for the environment to buy things second-hand and it's even better when the profit goes to charity instead of some huge, faceless corporation. But some people, my well-meaning mother included, get so excited by a bargain that they can't see how useless the thing really is.

Take today for example, today she came home with a CD rack decorated with piano keys down the sides. Let me explain, CDs are – or were – these flat, circular plates that looked like compact mirrors only nowhere near compact enough. There was a hole in the middle of each one, like a bagel that you couldn't eat and wasn't even nice to look at. I don't know what the hole was for, but the shiny surface of the disc had data saved on it, kind of like a memory stick, except it was a lot more rubbish for a lot of valid reasons:

- You could only store music on it.
- You usually didn't get to choose the exact set of songs that was on it.
- Once the songs were on it you couldn't delete them, add more to the list, edit the list.
- It only held about twenty songs.
- It couldn't possibly fit in your pocket.

Also, the CD only *stored* the music. If you wanted to hear it you needed a CD player, which was hefty and very pricey for something that only performed one function. You had to buy CDs in the shops, as in physically *go to* the shop, take them off the shelf and pay at the checkout like you're buying a bottle of milk or a latte. And the shop didn't even have *all* the CDs! If they didn't have it, you'd just have to find another shop – and they probably wouldn't have it there either!

The worst part, though, is that if they got damaged or lost then you just had to buy the whole thing again. Like, even though you'd already paid for it once you had to pay again – it wasn't like clothes that you can take to the dry cleaners or when you wipe your phone and you must transfer all your data from your laptop – you *literally* had to buy it again! What a scam!

Oh, and did I mention that they got damaged *easily*? They got scratched if you left them out of the case for even a minute; you had to hold them by the edges, which were razor thin, because you couldn't get fingerprints on them. People used to get CD cuts, like paper cuts, all the time. Once they were scratched the CD player couldn't read them. Even Carla's dad's records are more resilient than that and they're way older! At least with records you're transported to a different time. With CDs you get transported to a time which quite frankly ought to be scrapped from the history books.

Anyway, a CD rack is like a toast rack for CDs. It has these thin slots, about a centimetre each, which you put your CDs in. I'm sure they were useful once, but if anything, they're probably even more obsolete than the CDs themselves. A CD works without a CD rack, but a CD rack doesn't work without CDs. When Mum walked in with it, I had no idea what it was for.

"What is *that*?" I asked.

"It's a CD rack!" she said proudly.

"Oh. I thought maybe you bought it for Graham's pub. It looks like the perfect place to dry off beer mats after drunken spillages."

"It's lovely, isn't it? You see the piano keys? Because, you know, music… CDs…"

"Yeah, but… why? All your CDs are in a box somewhere in the loft."

"It'll be nice to have them all down here on display!" she said, and she really meant it.

"Why? They're not decorative. Why would anyone want to look at them?"

"I'll have you know album covers are a beautiful and really cool, dying art form!"

If it's cool, then why is it dying?

"It'll be fun to get them all back down and have a listen!"

"You can listen to them right now on the laptop."

"It's not the same!"

"No, it's better. Songs can't get scratched on the laptop."

"Oh, you wouldn't understand; you're a different generation!"

"Is this because Graham doesn't know how to use the laptop media player?"

"Graham's great with computers! He sent me an email the other day!"

I rolled my eyes and left it at that. There's no point arguing over a CD rack. Hopefully Trousers will mistake it for a lamppost and pee on it.

Speaking of Trousers, the other stupid thing Mum bought today was a book on dog training. Maybe not that stupid, considering we've got a puppy, but this is exactly the sort of thing the internet is for! The best thing about the internet, at least when it comes to research, is that you can always get a second opinion if the first one you find seems suspiciously ill-informed, or in this case, mental. This book Mum's got, entitled *How to Communicate with Your Dog* was written thirty years ago by a lady who appears to have a very loose grip on reality and who severely overestimates the cognitive capacity of the canine brain.

Now I'm no expert, but this woman, this 'author' by the name of Marianne Duval, believes that everything her dogs do is a direct attempt to tell her something, and that it is her mission and life's work to decipher every bark, scratch, yelp, wee, poo, run, slobber, puppy-dog eye, head tilt, paw placement, tail wag and butt sniff each of her six dogs does. I honestly can't believe this thing got published. Sadly, I *can* believe that my mum bought it, and I'm not particularly surprised that she's now treating it as THE dog owner's bible. Here is an excerpt I found when I flicked through it earlier:

"Today I awoke to find Jonty, the younger of the two Jack Russells, sat on the floor at the foot of my bed, his gaze fixed on my face in acute adoration. 'Marianne' he said to me with his eyes, 'I dreamt you were sailing a large ship, and I was floating in a row boat beside you, drifting further and further away from you with the swelling of the sea'. I knew Jonty had separation anxiety, but until this morning, I'd had no idea how bad it was. You must be careful to let your dog know that you will never abandon them but that they cannot be wholly dependent on you. So, to counteract his water-based anxieties he expressed in his dream, I took him into the bath with me and shampooed him just as tenderly as I would my own infant child. I rinsed him off and lifted him out of the tub, but I did not towel dry him, for he must learn to shake himself off. He must not expect me to mother him."

It went on:

"When I got downstairs Archie and Amy, the pit-bull twins, were sat on the dog sofa, looking grumpy. 'We're cross with you,' Archie said. He likes to speak on his sister's behalf; he's a proud and protective big brother. They were cross because they hadn't been invited into the bath with me and Jonty. 'When you and your sister learn to stop peeing in the bath water, you are welcome to join me in the tub again,' I said to him sternly, and he dropped his head in acceptance. You must be firm sometimes.

"Darcey the retriever was sat in the kitchen scratching behind his ears with his back leg. This is his way of playing hard to get. He pretends not to notice when I've gotten out of bed and pretends to focus on something else, like scratching or chasing a fly. Well two can play at that game, Darcey!

"Bella the collie was by the front door waiting for the post and whacking her tail on the hardwood floor. 'This is all for you!' she told me with a flick of her tail. 'I'm protecting you from the mailman,' she said with another thump. 'I'm the most loyal one,' she didn't say, but I read between the lines. Bella is desperate to be the favourite. She needs approval. This is all a popularity contest to her.

With dogs you must listen to what they're *not* saying – they won't tell you everything explicitly. They like to play mind games, so be sure to question the things they tell you as they may just be manipulating you for their own personal gain."

I looked over at Trousers, who had fallen asleep in between two sofa cushions and was almost swallowed up between them with his tongue hanging out of his mouth. What a shrewd game he's playing.

Monday 22st June 2020

Rehearsals for the end of year play have been… well, I'm not telling you how the *actual* rehearsals are going, that would be bad luck, but spending time with the older kids has been great. I feel more comfortable, at least in this environment. It's like a special sort of community where everyone helps and supports each other instead of all the competition and mockery you get in normal school life. They're all especially keen to look out for me because I'm the youngest, but they're not afraid to give me advice on how I can improve my performance. A lot of them are year elevens doing their drama GCSE and they're going to be assessed on the night of the performance – talk about piling on the pressure!

The sixth formers are probably my favourites though. Tiana, who plays Titania, and Otis, who plays Oberon, have taught me about all the old superstitions people had, and still do have, when they're treading the boards (that's professional actors' speak for performing on stage). First, you should *never* say out loud the name of the play I auditioned with, you must call it *The Scottish Play* (I'm talking about Macbeth – I guess it's OK to write it down) it is a pretty creepy play, and people back then probably believed in all sorts! You should also never say good luck to someone before they're about to perform, you have to say 'break a leg' for some weird reason. Anyway, I'm not going to tell you or anyone else anything more – I don't want to jinx it!

Saturday 27th June 2020

AN INVESTIGATION INTO THE UNKNOWN: WHO IS THE SHROUDED FIGURE?

Members of the public have reported numerous sightings (one is a number) of the so-called 'shrouded figure', who has sparked intrigue in the community due to her masked identity and the bizarre company she inexplicably keeps. Some say she has been voluntarily spending her time with irritating morons with ridiculous wrestling nicknames. Others doubt her very existence. Either way, she is something of an enigma.

At last the equipment pre-approved by the food hygiene association has been installed so that Mum can start making her wine in Graham's pub kitchen. While the business is in its infancy, Mum is still working her regular job, so she's busy at the pub most evenings getting it all up and running as quickly as possible. It's set to be a huge success, or at least that's what Graham reckons, because they can advertise it as 'genuine English wine made on-site exclusively for the Mill on the Hill' – apparently the customers will love that.

But that's not the big news. Well, it's not the juicy gossip anyway. While Mum and Graham have been busy at the pub, Billy's been there too, helping with basic bar duties while Graham gets Mum settled in. So, I was surprised yesterday when I heard Frogsplash talking to somebody in his room. We had Max at the house, and of course Trousers as well, but I knew they were both downstairs in the living room, and Froggo doesn't usually talk to the dogs out loud anyway. No, I knew he had someone in his room, and I was sure it was a girl. Normally I'm not that nosy, but this was kind of a big deal. *My* brother, who behaves like a seven-year-old *all the time,* has managed to get a girl to like him! She must be crazy! Or even dumber than he is.

Maybe I was wrong. Maybe he was just talking on the phone. He doesn't usually use his phone for calls. None of it added up. I had to investigate. I am a serious journalist. An *investigative journalist.* That's why I eavesdropped on my brother. His room is next to mine, so all I had to do was press my ear against the wall, listen and wait. Frogsplash was telling a story, quite a long one in fact. If he did have a girl in there, he must have been boring the poor thing to death. The story he was telling sounded incredibly exaggerated. I couldn't catch every word, but I heard him when he raised his voice and said, "The BIGGEST bull you've ever seen!" At some stage I heard the words "had to run six miles at least!" and "never would have made it out alive without me!" and then I heard her. "Wow – that's incredible!" she said. I couldn't believe she was buying his story… I could barely believe she was real!

I couldn't stand listening to any more of Froggo's ridiculous brag-fest, so I left them to it. When I heard his door open, I considered slipping out of my room pretending I needed the loo just so I could see her face, but I decided to save the poor girl the embarrassment. Instead I crept softly towards my window and peered out over the ledge. I didn't want her to look up and see me standing there like an ominous creep, so I squatted on the floor like an inconspicuous creep, because that's what good journalists do. If any passer-by had happened to look up at my window just then they would have seen a young girl cut off at the top of the nose so that only the eyes were in view, like an alligator watching its prey just above the surface of the water.

I heard her step onto the gravel of our front drive before I saw her. I love that gravel. I don't think I'm overstating it at all when I say that that gravel has made me who I am today. She was a tall, slim figure, undoubtedly female from the length of her legs and the pleated, charcoal grey skirt that barely covered them. But she wore a hood and she did not look back, so I couldn't see her face. She was literally shrouded in mystery.

Monday 29th June 2020

Today Ms Lafayette decided that we had finally perfected our online security dance, and speaking as an extremely well-coordinated security question, I'd have to agree. So that was that. You can't improve on perfection, so I guess it was time to move on and (dare I say it?) get back to some proper P.E.

WRONG!

Our dance is *so* good, and let's not forget how informative it is to members of our generation who need reminding of the importance of online security *specifically through the medium of dance* (is there any better way to communicate such subject matter?) So naturally Ms Lafayette decided that we simply *had to* perform it in front of the entire year group at the next vacant assembly. If this doesn't kill me, nothing will. At least I only have a small part; it's not like I'm a Trojan virus. Anyway, it's all worth it to see the look on Miss Milne (the proper P.E. teacher)'s face during this whole debacle. I can tell she thinks it's a complete waste of time and nothing like what we should be learning.

How am I so calm about this? Well, it *is* going to be funny, and I do like entertaining people.

Sunday 5th July 2020

MEDICAL ADVANCEMENT WITH MULTIPLE TRANSPLANTMENT!

Doctors are going head-over-heels for this eye-opening new surgery. Heads are spinning and hearts are pounding at news of an astonishing new procedure that has left some people weak at the knees. Our readers will be chilled to the bone by these blood-curdling accounts from recent patients, some of whom have outrage pulsing through their veins, calling the surgeons 'spineless toe-rags' while others have much less of a burden on their hands. Let's hope they all land firmly on their feet after their extreme transplants.

We went to Dad's this weekend and it appears Richard has undergone yet another personality transplant. First, he was abjectly depressed, then he went all surrogate dad on us, then there was the textbook midlife crisis (the 'life in the fast lane' tattoo is glorious, by the way) and now he's being serious and acting kind of paranoid. Apparently, he saw his daughters last weekend and the older one, Gertie, was acting weird.

"I don't know what's up with her," Richard said, though none of us had asked. "It's like she's had a complete personality transplant!"

I wonder where she gets it from…

"She barely said a word to me. She was distracted… and so rude!"

Sounds like she hasn't changed at all since I met her.

"I miss the days when she was just my sweet little girl. I'm kind of regretting shredding all of those family photos, if I'm honest."

Yeah – who'd have guessed that would turn out to be a bad parenting move?

"She's constantly on her phone and it's like she wants to be somewhere else entirely! I wonder if her mum's been feeding her ideas, telling her tales about me… something's going on… there's somebody, some other influence getting involved… getting inside her head…"

Sounds like a normal teenager to me!

I looked over at Frogsplash, who I assumed would be distracted, on his phone, and acting like he wanted to be somewhere else entirely, but he looked oddly alert and uncharacteristically focussed. He was tuned in to the conversation… he looked like he had something to hide; like he was in some way invested in whatever it was we were talking about.

"Well it must be her mother," Richard continued. "Because I *know* she doesn't have a boyfriend. I *insisted* she went to an all girls' school for that very reason!"

Oh poor, naïve Richard – you think she couldn't meet boys elsewhere? On the internet; in the supermarket; on holiday; at a party…

Not that I imagine Gertie *does* have a boyfriend. She's so moody and uptight I can't imagine *anyone* would be charmed by her!

Then again, I never would have imagined Frogsplash could get a girlfriend, but he did. He's so immature and scruffy, how could anyone be charmed by him?

Wait a minute… Frogsplash's mystery girlfriend… the guilty look on his face when Richard was talking about Gertie… They met at the party, didn't they? But… no, surely not… Could it be? Really, brother? Gertie, the stuck-up, organic food princess? And really, Gertie? My greasy, brace-face brother?

"She's far too young to have a boyfriend… she's *fourteen!* If I find out she's dating someone… I'll kill him! I'll punch his lights out! I'll break every one of his fingers to make sure his greasy hands never touch my daughter again! My first born! She's too young!"

Oh Froggo… you're in big trouble, brother!

This is epic. I wonder if I can use it to my advantage.

Monday 6th July 2020

I can't believe it's nearly the end of the year! The talent show is next week, the play is the week after that and then it's the summer! I'm thinking about inviting Dad to see the play. Don't think I've forgotten how disastrous it was last time when he and Mum came to the Christmas play, but surely, they wouldn't make the same mistake twice? And this time I'd insist that they're seated separately. Dad has every right to be there, and this is a big deal for me. I've never been one to stand out from the crowd and Mum and Dad have probably resigned themselves to the fact that their daughter is a shy little wallflower, so to show them that I'm capable of entertaining a huge crowd would be incredible.

But there's another problem – Graham is coming. How will that make Dad feel? Of course, it's going to be awkward, but if Graham's here to stay I suppose we'd all better get used to it, Dad included. You never know, in twenty years' time, they might both be walking me down the aisle. That's a weird thought! Do I even want to get married? Maybe… as long as it's not to Mr Achilles… cringe! But it's not just about 'getting used to it' because to tell you the truth, I really want Graham to be there – and Billy, too.

For one thing, Graham's the only member of the family who knows the play (he's seen several versions of it on the small screen, most recently a modernised adaptation starring what's-his-face from *Casualty* and 'that woman who played the murderer's mother in that crime drama'). He also really wants to come, which is a big gesture I think, because it means he's interested in me and my achievements. But the main reason I want both him and Billy there is because I am a quiet, awkward person most of the time and it must be hard for them (who are the total opposite) to come into our home and try to fit in when I'm there being all insular and probably being inadvertently hostile just simply because I don't have a clue how to be myself around them.

They've spent quite a lot of time at our house but we're still not that close. You know when you're close enough to somebody that you can wind them up and it's not even rude? Like with me and Frogsplash, that's just our normal way of interacting. I'm getting there with Billy, because wind-ups are like his second language, but I don't really know how to communicate with Graham. If they come to the play, then they'll get to know me a lot better. Which is weird because I won't be me; I'll be Puck. But if they can see that side of me that can *be Puck,* then I think they'll get to know me on a whole new level.

Mum, Dad and Frog have known me since I was born so they know all my levels, and Danny and Carla don't make me feel awkward, so I can be myself around them, but this modern family arrangement is all kinds of complicated.

I can't wait for show time because none of this will matter on the night. I will be Puck and none of these problems will exist. I will be the creator of problems – or at least mischief! Ha-ha!

Wednesday 8th July 2020

As it's getting closer to the big day, our rehearsals have gotten longer and more frequent, meaning we need to skip lessons instead of taking time out of our lunch breaks (yes!) I was already missing out on P.E., which is a devastating shame because, apparently, Miss Milne is having to fill in for me as the third security question in the dance (how I'd love to see that!) Now I'm missing D&T and Textiles as well. I don't really care about the lessons, but its great having my lunch breaks with Danny and Carla again. The weather has been gorgeous and everyone's getting into the spirit of summer. It just makes you feel free, doesn't it?

This week some of the older years decided to start water fights on the fields by the lake and it's caught on quick. It started on Monday with squirting water bottles, but the next day everyone had the same idea and had brought in water pistols and lots of water balloons. It's been fun; basically, the rule is if you're on the field, you're in the fight. If you don't want to get wet, get off the field! At first, we had to borrow water balloons, but today we came fully prepared. Danny borrowed two pistols that her brothers got as free gifts from a magazine, Carla bought some balloons on her way to school and I sneaked in Froggo's huge jet soaker, which wasn't easy, but it was totally worth it.

It was an absolute water fest, an aquatic free-for-all, and it didn't seem to matter who you were, what year you were in or who you'd normally hang around with, everyone was taking part, and everyone was playing as equals. Everyone apart from Charlotte, Beth and Andrea, that is. They were up on the fields by the lake, but they weren't armed or dangerous... they weren't even on their feet. They were sunbathing again, with their shirts rolled up and their skirts just covering their knickers. A group of boys from our year went up to them and saw that they were lacking in supplies.

"Hey, you want some balloons? We've got loads!" said a boy called Nathan who sits in front of me in maths class. I thought it was very decent of him to offer up free ammunition instead of just attacking.

"You're joking, right?" Charlotte looked up at him, shielding her eyes from the sun. "You think people like *us* want to play silly, childish games with people like *you?*

That's not how it works," she scoffed, and we listened closer. "Listen very carefully, OK? We are up *here* on the ladder… look at us… look at the way we look. Now look at *you*… look at the way you look and the sort of things you do for fun. *You* are at the bottom of the ladder. You will always be at the bottom of the ladder. Do not presume to talk to us…"

None of us could believe it. Even for Charlotte, this was a new level of meanness and arrogance. We were stood behind her and the other two, about two metres behind their feet. They were still sunbathing, lying on their fronts so they couldn't see us. We could see the backs of their heads propped up on their hands as they continued to face Nathan and his friends head-on. There was only one thing for it. I pumped up the jet soaker. Carla filled up a balloon. Danny had a pistol in each hand like a cowboy in one of those old Western films. Charlotte was going to get it.

She was still ranting at poor Nathan, and it seemed she was getting to him. By this point, she was saying much more personal things, basically stripping away at every detail of his appearance and what she assumed his personality to be like, though of course she's never taken the time to get to know him. She was humiliating him in front of his friends, and then she started on them too. It was brutal, and they just stood there, listening to it. I know that feeling, when somebody is saying something so hurtful that you know if you open your mouth to respond, you'll let out a cry because that's all your body will allow you to do.

347

Or maybe they couldn't think of the words to say. Maybe they were so astonished at the brazenness of this completely unprovoked attack that they couldn't form the words. They didn't want to walk away, either. They didn't want to show weakness, I understood. Why didn't her friends stop her? She had gone too far; far too far. Maybe they were scared to stand up to her too. But while all this was going on, we had time to prepare. She couldn't see us. We could be heroes. On the count of three, we went charging in, all of us aiming our weapons at Charlotte. We came in from behind; she never saw us coming.

BAM! Carla threw the balloon, I pulled the trigger on the jet soaker, aiming right at the back of her head and Danny pointed the pistols at her bum, throwing out the occasional shot at Beth and Andrea just for good measure. Charlotte screamed and jumped straight to her feet, yelling at us that we're losers and that she's going to get us back for this, but her outrage did nothing to deter us, so she had no choice but to run. Seeing her soaking and fleeing in disgrace after what she'd just been saying about being so much better than those boys was so incredibly satisfying. That was my year eleven, egg-on-the-head moment.

Friday 10th July 2020

BUSTING THE MYTH FOR OUR FRIENDS WHO BUTT-SNIFF: CANINE OBEDIENCE TRAINING – WE'VE BEEN DOING IT ALL WRONG!

Thanks to certified dog expert, Marianne Duval, we now know that to live in harmony with man's best friend, we must allow them to communicate their needs to us rather than trying to communicate our demands to them. We must cater to every one of those needs and sacrifice as much of our human lifestyle as we possibly can to provide them with every comfort and make them feel special, superior and in control.

Mum's done all she can do with the wine making process, so she's been at home in the evenings trying to train Trousers. According to Marianne Duval, you must treat your puppy as you would a much-loved elderly relative.

"Treat them with the respect they deserve," she says. "Remember that they don't have as much control over their bodily functions as you do. They like consistency and walks in the park. They can't digest rich foods. They love blankets. They grow nervous when some stranger knocks

349

on the door. They may fall asleep on the sofa, and they may snore or drool whilst doing so. A lot of them have a distinct odour, but you must not blame them for this. They will have a favourite spot in which to relax, and you must not let anyone else, even guests, sit in this place. You will have to repeat yourself several times before they understand you…"

It seemed kind of insulting to old people to compare them to dogs. I wonder how many human friends Marianne Duval has. Nevertheless, Mum was taking her completely seriously. Not a pinch of salt in sight. She drew up a doggy rota, she walks Trousers on Fridays, Saturdays and Sundays; I walk him on Mondays and Wednesdays and Frogsplash walks him on Tuesdays and Thursdays. I was tempted to point out that dogs do not have any comprehension of the days of the week, so this set-up would probably seem random and very inconsistent to Trousers, but then it occurred to me that I don't believe a single word in Marianne's book, so it really didn't matter at all.

Trousers has his blanket in the corner of the living room which is sacrosanct and must not be defiled by us smelly humans, but seeing as I have no immediate plans to sleep on the dog's bed, I'm OK with that too. Before we got a dog, I had no idea how little discipline is involved in dog training. I love Trousers to pieces, but I don't think he's going to grow up to be the brightest dog, at least not at this rate. I think Marianne should rename her book *How to Fit Your Life around Your Dog's Needs*. But to be honest, I doubt she's still alive. Her dogs probably ate her years ago.

Today I got a little reminder of what it's like to perform in front of an audience, because today we had to dance to the tune of online security. Of course, I told Danny and Carla about it in advance, and they couldn't wait to see how ridiculous it was in the flesh. I knew they'd find it utterly hilarious and because of that, I was almost looking forward to it. Some of the other girls were nervous, and I could understand that. If I didn't have my two best friends out there in the crowd, I'd have been just the same.

When we got out there and saw everyone sat in their rows of plastic seats, I felt a turn in my stomach, but I scanned the audience until I found Carla and Danny, who were sat next to each other in the middle of the audience. They both smiled cheeky smiles at me, the sort of smile you exchange with someone when you've got an inside joke together. It was all fun and games after that. No one in the audience was bold enough to laugh out loud, not when Ms Lafayette presented it so seriously, but I saw some sniggers and lots of smirks while I was up there dancing my heart out as one of the most expressive security questions ever to perform in front of a live audience. It was all over very quickly, and Ms Lafayette looked very proud. You've got to hand it to her, that woman follows through on her misjudged ideas to the bitter end.

Friday 17th July 2020

SCHOOL TALENT SHOW KICKS OFF!
GOOD LUCK TO ALL CONTESTANTS!
OR SHOULD I SAY – BREAK A LEG?

All the best and brightest performers from Duke John Jameson School will showcase a variety of skills and entertainment live before your very eyes! One day only! Today is the day! Prepare to be amazed! Their talents will astound you! Nothing can possibly go wrong!

Well, it was a mixed bag, but perhaps that's half the fun. It started off with an incredible gymnastics display from a boy in year ten who had an unbelievably muscular body for someone of his age but a terribly spotty face and kind of dull, unfeeling eyes. Not that his facial appearance mattered, because his performance was beautiful. He looked ever so serious during the routine, and at the end he bowed modestly but didn't acknowledge anyone in the crowd or break into a smile, despite a raucous applause.

He was one of those talented people you see that are hard to like because it's difficult to see them as *human.* He was so perfect at what he did and so well composed that he seemed a bit like a robot. He was very, *very* good, but there was nothing there to relate to. On TV talent shows, they always have a back story, don't they? Usually it's something heart-wrenching, but no matter what, it humanises the person. It shouldn't matter, not in the context of a talent show, but it does.

The next act could not have been more different. It was another year ten boy, who I know to be the brother of Hassan Ahmed. Hassan was one of the gang who threw oranges at me on the bus, but to be perfectly honest, I can't remember how involved he even was in that whole thing. Anyway, this guy on stage was not Hassan, but his brother. It's easy to assume that when people are related, they're similar, but I wouldn't want someone judging me on Froggo's behaviour, so I tried not to let the bus antics that Hassan was loosely linked to cloud my judgment of his older sibling. We are all our own people, aren't we?

He was very relaxed and confident; he came across like he was everybody's best friend and every joke was an inside joke between us there in that room and 'them', the unspecified others. He was a natural on stage and I was sure that this could not possibly have been his first time performing. He did a very funny stand-up session that had everyone laughing and everyone totally, one hundred percent, on his side, like we were all comrades – that's a kind of skill I get really blown away by because I don't know how you get it! It was obviously his own original work because most of it was specific to our school and its teachers. He was only a tiny bit rude, but he was so smooth, I don't think anyone noticed or cared. When he finished, he had a group of his mates cheering and chanting his name, along with applause from an audience more affectionate than astounded at his act.

Next, was a year eight duo: a boy and girl doing a below-average magic act, if I'm being honest. I felt sorry for them really; they looked so nervous, but that's what ruined the act in the end. Before they'd even got any kind of momentum or rapport going with the audience, things began to falter. They started making mistakes. Probably their hands were shaking or sweating or something, because they completely messed up the card trick and it seemed they could not recover from that. It was a bit of an embarrassment really, and the audience were not impressed.

Or maybe they were. They certainly seemed to enjoy it. It was as though they had been waiting for someone weak. Cruel hunters always prey on the weak. There were some boos, a lot of silence, but nothing of comfort. The crowd had turned; they were no longer supportive – they were hungry. Some people were taking malicious joy in this public failure and humiliation. Basically, they had gone from sweet to rotten, and this was not good news. In fact, I was very, very worried, because I knew Carla was up next.

I could only imagine what she must have been feeling watching that disaster unfold from that purgatory otherwise known as the side-stage area, with which I have become more and more familiar with the ever-more frequent rehearsals I have recently been taking. But the side-stage holds no tension, no fears nor apprehension, unless the main stage is switched on and there is an audience present. It has been a long time since I've known that fear.

Good luck, best friend! Or should I say, break a leg!

I wouldn't have blamed her if she'd decided to back out, but I knew she wouldn't – not Carla. Have I told you about my friend Carla? She is the bravest; she is the best. The two magicians walked off in disgrace, which had been very harsh, but that is what you subject yourself to with things of this nature. That's why I was so scared for Carla. There was total silence. Everyone held their breath (or was it just me?).

She walked on, cool as ever in her jeans and t-shirt with her acoustic guitar slung across her back. She sat down on the rubbery blue safety mat that was still in the centre of the stage from the gymnastics display that had kicked off this whole rollercoaster. In her own time and at her own pace (unlike the jittery magicians), she slowly crossed her legs and rested her guitar on her left knee. It looked huge on her lap like that, and she looked so small there on her own, the youngest person to get up on that stage so far, half swallowed up by the puffy blue mat beneath her, cool as a thousand chilled cucumbers. She was utterly serene. The silence held strong, but it didn't silence Carla.

When she began to deftly, softly strum the guitar, I knew why she had seemed so peaceful. Her mind was set in the song, a bit like when I get into character I guess, only much braver, because she had to be herself. It was a beautiful, mellow song; gentle but slightly sad. Beautiful doesn't describe it. It made me think of a time and a place that has never existed – at least not in any way I have ever known.

All these words I've read before in stories I've loved… I thought I understood them. I followed the stories well enough, and I enjoyed them even more, but the things they were describing I only *thought* I knew. I guessed what they meant, even though I knew the definition, that's just not the same thing. I know that now. Nobody spoke those words to me today, but today I felt the *impact* of them. At last, they meant something that I could feel. *Ethereal. Melancholic. Celestial. Poignant.* Now they had a sense to them. That sense was sound, and the sound was Carla's song.

She sang perfectly in that sweet, sad tone that seemed to ring through the air and cast a spell on all who heard it. I felt like it was what I might hear just after I die. I could see water rippling like pretty dancers, glistening silver and careless over pearly pebbles, glinting shades of lilac in a cold winter sun. It is summer now, I know, but the summer sun is playful and fleeting, and it always comes back to the cold, hard light of winter. The river ran through a thick forest, golden, green and sighing with age, but I knew it would never die.

She told us later that it was called *Going to California,* and it was by Led Zeppelin. I remember listening to one of their records with Carla's dad at their house, but that had been rock music – nothing at all like the sensitive, soulful melody I heard her sing today. When she was finished, she looked drained but content, like she had given her life's breath to that performance. She got a huge round of applause – the biggest one yet, I'm sure. I felt very sorry for the act that had to follow that. At least I did, until I found out who it was.

Charlotte Henderson, Beth Amory and Andrea Michael strutted onto the stage like they owned it, like we were all there to see them and only them, as though everything else had just been building up to this moment. It struck me then that they must truly believe that everybody worships them. I've known for some time now that Beth is deluded because she tells such outrageous lies, but the biggest lie of all is the one that all three of them tell themselves all the time: that they are the only ones who matter.

They were wearing these stupid little outfits: shiny, tiny tube tops and tube skirts to match, with big, pink furry boots. The contrast between Carla's performance and theirs was going to be phenomenal. The song that they put on was the latest one by Dylan James Scott, who has left that band he was in and started collaborating with various DJs to produce dance tracks instead of soppy love songs. They danced more or less in unison, but it was far from inspiring, especially as a follow-up to Carla.

It was their own choreographed routine: twirls, hip shakes, that sort of thing. But it got increasingly raunchy, and I caught a glimpse of their knickers at one point. It was around the time they started slapping their own bums that a rather shocked and slightly embarrassed-looking teacher made the decision to step in and stop the performance.

I bet you wish you'd held auditions now!

She climbed up the four steps to the stage and huddled the girls in close to her, so she could talk to them without the rest of us hearing, but it was obvious that she was stopping them because their dance was inappropriate. The music stopped abruptly and the three of them were led off stage in shame. I must admit, it was satisfying! I'm not sure how I feel about the other two, but Charlotte needed

357

taking down a peg or two – probably more like ten, actually!

There was some commotion in the audience as people started to wonder and whisper that the whole show had been called off and that we'd have to go back to whatever lessons we were missing, but then Danny wandered onto the stage a little anxiously, no doubt thrown off course by the sudden departure of her predecessors. But she had nothing to worry about, I knew, because she was about to do a very different dance routine to the horror show we'd just witnessed.

Good luck, best friend! Or should I say, break a leg!

She was incredible. Truly amazing, and *truly* nothing like Charlotte and the gang! What they did can't possibly be described as dance when you put it next to Danny. I had no idea how amazing she was! She did a double back flip! She was so technical and so *strong!* I don't know the names of half the moves she did, but they were amazing. It was like ballet and street dance and gymnastics all rolled into one! The crowd was astonished; they were cheering and clapping even before she'd finished. She went in for another back flip, double, no, triple! But the stage wasn't big enough for a triple flip. She's never practised on the school stage before. They didn't hold auditions…

They should have held auditions!

She flipped right off the stage and landed somewhere down the left side at the bottom of the stairs. She screamed. Everyone gasped, many of us ran over to help, including me, Carla and the teachers. She was huddled in pain and her foot was bent in a direction which was far from natural. The school medic was called, then Danny's parents, then an ambulance. Then she was gone. Everyone was left in shock. The remainder of the talent show was postponed, but by the time all the fuss had died down, it was near enough time to go home.

I've never seen anyone get hurt that badly before, let alone one of my best friends. Mum once put her finger in a food mixer when she thought it was switched off, but luckily it was just a deep cut and she didn't lose any of her digits. Dad drove her to the hospital, but he couldn't leave us alone, so Frogsplash and I had to go with them. We sat waiting in Accident and Emergency for absolutely ages. Eventually Mum got a few stitches and that was that.

I don't know how long Danny had to wait but I know she's OK now. She sent a message to me and Carla; she's broken her ankle and it's in a cast, but she's going to be just fine, thank God!

Saturday 18th July 2020

We got to visit Danny at her house today. She seemed fine, apart from the fact that she was *dying* from embarrassment after falling off the stage in front of the whole school.

"Don't be daft!" I said. "You were amazing! I never knew you could dance like that!"

"Maybe," she said. "But I think people are going to remember the dramatic fall off the stage rather than whatever I did *on* the stage!"

"Maybe so," said Carla. "But what happened to you was a complete accident and you *more than* made up for it with your talent… What happened with Charlotte and the tube top twins was way, *way* more embarrassing!"

"Speaking of twins…"

Danny's younger brothers came charging in with felt tip pens in their hands.

"No! Not again! You already signed it!"

Danny's cast had been scribbled on quite excessively by her brothers, Finn and Jim, who were not yet old enough to sign their names, but that had not stopped them from having a good old go at it, there was barely any space left for Carla and me to sign!

We stayed all day to keep her company because she was bored and kind of frustrated with not being able to dance or do anything else active. By the way, her house is *huge!* We played with Tinker the puppy, who seemed to be getting along just fine in her mansion, and we helped Danny practise walking on her crutches ready for school on Monday (Carla and I had a go on them too, just for fun!).

I met Danny's dad, Alistair, for the first time today too. He was very nice, but very… proper. Not *posh* exactly, but straight-laced. He seemed like the sort of guy who would never leave the house in an un-ironed shirt or go on a car journey without mapping it out on the sat-nav in advance. Basically, he's nothing like my dad. He asked us lots of questions about our 'studies' (like we're in university, not year seven!) and he wanted to hear our opinions on all the teachers. It seemed like he was trying to find out if they were good enough at their subjects and their ability to teach and control the class.

I got the impression that he was probably smarter and far more educated than all our teachers, not that he was showing off or anything, you could just tell. He was very impressed that Carla was on grade five of guitar. He said he tried to get Danny to learn piano when she was younger but that she'd never been able to sit still for long enough, so she went to ballet instead. He sat down at the piano (they have a grand piano in their back room!) and sat Finn and Jim on either side of him. He tried to get them to tinkle a few keys at either end of the instrument, but they were climbing down from the stool as soon as they'd got up there.

"They're just the same," said Mr Dankworth with a gentle smile. "Can't sit still for two seconds! As long as they channel it into something productive, I'll be more than happy… although I'd prefer if they didn't choose something too dangerous – they're even more accident-prone than their sister!"

Danny's white cheeks went rosy-pink as she could feel the conversation turning to her, and was no doubt worrying that her dad was about to reveal some embarrassing tales of a younger Danny doing something stupid – parents love to do that, don't they?

"Sam's got a part in the end-of-year school play," she said, wisely diverting the conversation.

"Oh fantastic!" he said. "I'm a huge fan of the theatre! Of course, I rarely get the chance to go these days, what with the twins and everything. Is it a play I might have heard of?"

Of course, he'd heard of *A Midsummer Night's Dream,* so we talked about that for a while until he excused himself to go and make a start on the dinner, which we were invited to stay for. We went to hang out in Danny's room after that; she struggled to climb the winding stairs in her crutches, but she insisted.

"It's the only haven from the twins; they're not allowed in my room. I'm sure you guys think they're cute but wait until they put ketchup in your hair at six in the morning – I woke up and thought my brain was bleeding! Anyway, I need to practise stairs."

Her room was huge and full of lilac and lavender. She had a vast bookshelf which I greatly envied, and a selection of dance trophies on her dresser which I admired. I hope her ankle heals quickly as Danny not being able to dance is like me not being able to write!

"I'm mortified," she said. "I've never misjudged something so badly before! I was so confident with the routine I didn't even question going ahead with it, it was all planned out and nothing was going to go wrong! And now, on Monday, everyone's going to be like 'there she goes; there's the girl who threw herself off the stage!' And even if they didn't recognise my face it'll be pretty bloody obvious once they clock the cast and crutches!"

"It'll be fine!" I assured her. "Nobody was laughing at you yesterday and they won't be on Monday either. You were *hurt;* people were worried about you, that's all."

"Exactly," said Carla. "And for all they knew, you could have been really, seriously injured. If somebody finds that funny, then there's something very wrong with them."

"Do you think it will be front page news?" Danny asked. She was referring to *The Daily Duke* she's not deluded.

"Hmm… depends…" I said.

"On what?" she asked worriedly.

"On Charlotte *bloody* Henderson – that's what!" I said, and I felt the tone of irritation rise through my throat and into my voice and the words it spoke. "She'll have to write about the talent show, of course, but from what angle? She might want to play down her own part in it, bearing in mind how utterly humiliating it was! But then she might go the other way and try to brush off that humiliation by making it out to be an unfair dismissal. She could say that they were unjustly robbed of the opportunity to perform, that way she could paint her own picture and say that they hadn't done anything embarrassing at all. What it all comes down to, I guess, is whether or not she's ready to face the limelight."

Danny sighed resignedly, but I was pretty sure I knew which way it would go.

<u>Monday 20th July 2020</u>

It's the last week of term and I'm getting serious butterflies. HUGE butterflies – when you see those giant, fat caterpillars and you think 'what the hell do *they* grow into?' well, these are them, GIANT BUTTERFLIES! And they're in my stomach. The play is on Friday and rehearsals are intensifying. Tomorrow, Wednesday and Thursday, we'll be doing dress rehearsals after school as well. I'm too busy to be excited. At break and lunch today, a lot of people came up to us to ask Danny how she was and to sign her cast.

I forget sometimes how much more sociable she is than me and Carla, she has chosen us as her best friends, but she has no trouble getting along with lots and lots of other people besides us. I feel very privileged to be one of the chosen two, but it's so different from the way I function that I get quite befuddled and I feel sort of alien when I'm confronted with it so immediately. She has all these peripheral friends from all her classes, and she attracted quite a crowd of them today! They all seemed very nice, but it was a bit much for me.

I can't think properly with that many people around because I don't know how to be myself in that situation. I'm focussing so much on being the version of me that's most acceptable to all these different people. It's stressful. Carla prefers to be in our little trio and she has a sensible level of mistrust for outsiders, but she's always calm around new people and she will always be herself, not like me.

A lot of our classes have started to relax now that it's the end of term and the teachers have run out of teaching material. It would be fun if I was like Danny and I had friends in my classes, but I'm not and I don't, so instead I'm being thrown awkwardly into random groups of friends who don't really want me on their team for the pop quiz or whatever but don't have any choice because we were told to split into teams of four and there's only three of them so they get dumped with me like a spare part they have to pay extra for even though they know it's useless and UGH, I hate it! I am always the odd one out because I am ODD!

Wednesday 22nd July 2020

We sang the school song in this morning's special, whole school, end of term assembly. You remember the song about Duke John Jameson? I still can't believe my entire education is based on the life of a scoundrel like that. I would be laughing, but I can't. I can't laugh. How can you laugh when you can't *breathe?*

It's getting too much. I want to escape. I want to just run and run and run away but I'm trapped. There is pressure from all around, like it's pressing in on me and I'm just having to keep squishing myself in because nobody else will give it a rest or give up. They keep pressing on and I keep letting them. I'm drawing myself inwards to accommodate them. I'm withdrawing and they're overstepping. It's all about space, and space is all in the mind. My mind is my space and they're treading all over it.

It's getting too much. I need a break from all the people in my life. It's like sleep deprivation. I must be alert all the time; constantly engaging with the outside world. I'm giving all my energy away and I'm not getting any time to recharge. It's exhausting. It's unnatural. I *can't* be the only one who feels this way. Why is it so hard and so draining just to go through all the motions of being a *normal* person? Fitting in to normal scenes is such a strain on who I really am – it's a devastating struggle. I must be worse than abnormal, I must be defective.

Friday 24th July 2020

That's it – it's all over! The play, the school year – it's all done and dusted! I can't tell you how I'm feeling, because

I don't know yet. It all just happened and then it stopped. I feel overwhelmed. How did I just do that? I just did that! It's not real. It can't be real. This feels so utterly surreal. Is this what life is like for people who take risks all the time? Like it's constantly passing you by because you can't believe what just happened? Or maybe I'm just not used to this adrenaline. I can't cope, but in a totally good way. It's like the opposite of how I couldn't cope before.

The play went amazingly well. It was everything we'd all hoped it would be, and all our hopes were laid firmly in the hands of our audience. They all laughed in the right places, I saw them all smiling, I didn't make a single mistake and I enjoyed every single second of it. Mum and Dad and Graham were all very proud and there were no arguments or anything like that. Billy came too, and I was especially pleased about that because I really wanted him to see that I can be funny and entertaining like how he is all the time.

Carla and Danny came too, and I was so happy to have them, especially Danny, who had to hobble her way there on her crutches. Having people to support me in the audience is important because it reminds me why I love acting, because I want to entertain people; I want to make them smile, because life can be disappointing, life can be difficult. I think of Billy and how his mum abandoned him. If I can make him smile and laugh, then I must be worth something. Having friends and family there makes me feel proud. I've worked hard in rehearsals for such a long time, but they didn't see any of that; they didn't know what I was capable of before tonight.

That's why I was so disappointed with Frogsplash. He didn't come, and I know why. He saw his girlfriend. He's keeping her secret, so tonight would have been the perfect opportunity to invite her over while everyone else was out of the house. Normally I wouldn't have minded that he'd chosen her over me. If it had been something else, anything else, even my birthday, I wouldn't have minded, but this was a huge deal for me and it might never happen again. For all I know, this was the last chance I'll ever get to show my brother that I'm more than just his annoying little sister who never does anything fun, who reads books and does all her homework on time and thinks that wrestling and Eric Derek's pranks are stupid. I wanted him, more than anyone, to see that I'm not Samantha Dreary.

But *I* know I'm not Samantha Dreary. Look how far I've come! Remember what I was like in September? Now I'm here feeling so proud I could burst because I was one of the lead roles in the whole school play and I nailed it. If this were the Oscars and I had to do a speech, I know who I'd thank. Danny and Carla have encouraged me in the most amazing, gentle way. They've shown me what it is to have a friend. Friends build you up without pushing you over the edge. Friends are the ladder, but they never force you to climb up. Instead they make you *want* to climb, they comfort you when you fall, and if you do fall, they're right there to be your ladder again, every time. You can't stay down for long when you have friends.

Standing on that stage and taking my final bows tonight was the greatest moment of my life. That feeling is electric. I want to do it again and again and again.

Monday 27th July 2020

THE SILENCE OF THE FROG: MARVEL AT THE MUTED MUTANT FROG-BOY AS HE MISSES SISTER'S MEMORABLE MOMENT WITHOUT MENTION!

The absentee amphibian was not in attendance at his younger sister's school play. He failed to witness her outstanding Shakespearean performance, which critics are hailing as the greatest portrayal of Puck this century has ever seen. To add insult to injury, he has not uttered any word of apology or remorse. The girl was keen to be acknowledged by her older sibling, but he's not worth the trouble! Throw the Frog in the cauldron and let it bubble!

So Frogsplash hasn't said anything about missing my play, and he hasn't congratulated me on it either. He's obviously avoiding the subject because he knows he let me down. Mum seems blissfully unaware. I suppose she thinks that it doesn't bother me. I don't usually get bothered about things, but this was different. Now he's being a coward about it, and now I'm mad at him. He's my real brother. Not that I don't appreciate Billy being there… in fact, this makes me appreciate it even more, because Billy didn't have to come but he still did.

Frogsplash has been there all my life. He's supposed to be there for me and he let me down. When Mum and Dad split up, he wasn't always there… he hid in his room because he was too sad to come out. That was different. This time he was just being selfish. If he had been there, it would have been a perfect night. And now he's just acting like nothing happened. Maybe he's not acting; maybe he hasn't said anything because he doesn't even realise he did something wrong. Maybe he doesn't feel guilty at all. It probably wasn't a big deal to him, but this wasn't about him.

I must try not to dwell on it. It's the summer holidays and it's my birthday in one week. I should be happy.

Friday 31st July 2020

I still haven't spoken to Frogsplash, although that's mostly because we haven't crossed paths. He's always out, I don't know if he's with friends or with Gertie, but he's not at home, apart from in the evenings when he and Billy play videogames in his room. Graham and Billy practically live here now. They stay over most nights and they keep clothes and toothbrushes here. I'm getting more used to it. I thought having more people in the house would mean I'd never get any time or space to myself, but it's not like that at all. Mum saves all her boring conversations about work for Graham, Frogsplash is too busy annoying Billy to annoy me, so I get peace and quiet! Jackpot!

Mum and Graham seem happy, not just with each other but in general. Mum's English wine is growing ever more successful at the pub and that's amazing. It's not about the money, it's the fact that she's done this all by herself and people love it. She can literally see people enjoying the thing that she's made, and that must be a real sense of achievement. She's achieved absolutely nothing in her efforts to train Trousers, so I guess this balances that out a bit!

I had a great time at Carla's today with her and Danny. Carla's parents were both off work because they're going to Puerto Rico on Monday and they need to prepare. Normally when my mum packs for a holiday, she gets all stressed and panicky and has about a million lists and goes to the shop twelve times a day because she forgot the refill for the mosquito repellent or earplugs for the plane. It's such an ordeal it's barely worth the holiday. But Carla's parents were totally chill and in very good spirits. Maria was very excited to see her family, and I think James was just happy that she was happy. She was singing and dancing around the house (much to Carla's embarrassment) while we listened to music with James. He played us the original version of *Going to California* by Led Zeppelin. It was beautiful, but Carla's version was way better.

"I'm really going to miss you guys!" said Danny, who's leaving for Italy on Monday.

"Me too!" I said.

"And I can't believe we're both missing your birthday!" Carla added.

"As long as you're there for my party tomorrow!" I said.

"Wouldn't miss it for the world!" said Carla.

"Oh, by the way, Mum said you can bring the puppies if you want," I said.

"Ooh yay – doggy family reunion!" Danny cheered.

"You do know that's going to be chaos, right?" said Carla.

"Yeah!" I laughed. "Mum thinks she's a dog whisperer now – it's going to be hilarious!"

Saturday 1st August 2020

What a day! It was wonderful, from start to finish. It kicked off with a knock on the door at nine a.m. I was awake, but I wasn't properly up, I was lying in my bed, reading. I assumed it was Mum asking me how many hot dog buns to take out of the freezer or checking for the tenth time that none of my friends are vegetarian. But I was wrong. It was Frogsplash, which was weird for so many reasons. Firstly, he never gets up before eleven a.m. unless he must. Secondly, he never knocks on my door, and thirdly, he's been avoiding me since the play. I was wearing my butterfly print pyjamas, he was wearing his faded World Wrestling Federation pyjamas, and both of us had major bedhead. He was holding a gift-wrapped box that looked quite heavy.

"I know it's not your actual birthday yet," he said, avoiding any direct eye contact. "But you know me; I never give your present on time!"

He was not wrong. Every year on my birthday he tells me he's ordered me something online and that it's 'in the post'. Usually he makes up some rubbish like, "I don't know what happened to it; I ordered it months ago! I'm going to send an email to their complaints department! Terrible customer service!" And then when it finally does arrive, he gives it to me still in postal packaging, half of the time it's got the receipt in the box saying how much it cost and the date he ordered it (not 'months ago!') But this year, it was early, and he had wrapped it (I could tell he had done it himself, and by the looks of it, Trousers had helped too!).

I invited him in. Already I had completely forgiven him because of all the effort he had so obviously made. This is how we communicate, me and my brother, we don't do apologies or hugs, we do non-verbal gestures and light-hearted wind-ups (and sometimes mean-spirited wind-ups as well). I sat down on the edge of my unmade bed and ripped open the wrapping paper excitedly while Frogsplash stood nervously and watched. Usually I get all awkward about opening presents in front of people but in this instance, I was so grateful that he'd tried so hard that I couldn't possibly look disappointed. Anyway, I wasn't. When only half the paper was off, I could already tell what it was, although I couldn't quite believe it. When I'd completely unwrapped it, I turned it on its' side to read:

The Complete Works of William Shakespeare

What an amazing, thoughtful gift! I thanked him profusely, trying not to freak him out with an awkward display of overt affection, then I told him he could go back to bed now if he wanted. He didn't need telling twice; he sloped off back to his room and I sat in mine. I was blown away. I wanted to read them all, but I didn't want to touch them with my filthy human paws. You know when you get a brand-new book and it's perfectly crisp and the spine has never been bent? It's such a precious thing, you just want to treasure and protect it. Of course, the real treasure is what's inside the books on the pages, and a book would have no value at all if you never opened it, so I let myself read the first few pages of *A Midsummer Night's Dream.*

The book was beautiful, inside and out. It's the best present my brother has ever given me. It was only later, after I'd got dressed and I was gathering up the torn wrapping paper to put in the recycling bin that I realised there had been a card taped to it. I hadn't thought to look for one – Frogsplash *never* does cards. He thinks they're pointless, usually. So, I was very intrigued to open it.

'You'll be needing these!' is all he'd written in his teenage boy scrawl. It was perfect.

After I'd washed and dressed, I got a video call from Dad. His big client is this weekend so he's busy, but once it's over, he'll have a lot more time to spare. I'm going to see him next weekend, which works out well because none of my friends are going to be here then anyway. When I got downstairs, Mum and Graham were both in the kitchen chopping salads and filling ice trays and stuff like that. Mum said she had a few 'surprises' to set up, so I got out of their way and took Trousers to the park. It was a beautiful summer's day. I could hear an aeroplane howling through the sky in the far distance; it's such a peaceful sound.

I threw the ball for Trousers for a bit until he caught a glimpse of a squirrel and then that was it, he was in full hunting mode. I sat down on a bench and watched his ridiculous little face pretending to be all serious like a true hunting dog. He's not much bigger than a squirrel himself, and I don't think he even wants to catch them; it's just a fun game for him. He lowers his body close to the ground and stalks forward towards the squirrel slowly, stealth mode. But the squirrel is a good ten metres away and its half way up a tree, so he has no chance at all. His eyes are locked on his target and nothing can distract him, but he's just a fluffy little puppy so he looks like a toddler playing at being a grown up.

Eventually, the squirrel ran all the way up the tree and out of sight, and I was able to get Trousers' attention again. We strolled back towards the exit in no rush. It was a nice, quiet and best of all, *solitary,* way to prepare myself for what I was sure would be a day full of noise, mayhem and lots of people all in one place. When we got back to the house, the front door was covered in balloons with the number 'twelve' on them. Trousers, who had grown tired and was now in my arms, barked at the balloons as though they were an unwanted intruder in his home. When they refused to run away from his vicious bark, he bit one of them and it popped, then he started barking even more furiously, clawing to get out of my arms, scratching them to pieces in the process.

"Really Mum, balloons?" I said when we finally made it inside. "I'm turning twelve, not six, and they drove Trousers nuts!"

"Hey, no complaining on your birthday; you're not a teenager yet!" she said cheerfully. "Anyway, they're for the guests, to let them know which house it is."

"They've all been here before!" I said, but I wasn't really annoyed at all. I offered to help with the final preparations, but Mum was having none of it.

"No, no, don't be silly, it's your birthday! We'll take care of it; you go and get ready."

What's that supposed to mean? I AM ready!

I went up to my room and got changed, not that there was anything wrong with my first outfit, but it did have quite a lot of dog fur on it from when I'd carried Trousers. It wasn't long before the guests started to arrive. Mum had invited Frogsplash's friends to 'make up the numbers' (in other words, I don't have enough friends of my own). So, it was a proper canine family reunion. Of course, we had Max and Trousers, then there was Scratchy, Tinker, Doc and Tiny – it was mayhem, but it was so much fun!

Graham was manning the barbecue, which must have required a lot of patience because the dogs kept sneaking up and stealing sausages from the plate next to the grill. Seeing little Tiny running off with a whole sausage in her mouth was probably the funniest thing I've ever seen! We had a lot of music (mostly Free Parking), a piñata, rainbow jelly and so, so much more food. At some point, seemingly out of nowhere, Gertie appeared and then spent the remainder of the afternoon quietly at Froggo's side. She barely said a word, but she seemed less snooty than when I first met her. Mum and I exchanged a glance which meant 'ooh, what's going on there then?' but we didn't draw any attention to it because we knew that Froggo bringing his first girlfriend home was a big step.

The adults got drunk on Mum's wine, and the teenagers sneaked some too, but no one got sick or broke anything, so I didn't mind at all. For me it was the perfect birthday, no dramas, no surprises, just good friends and lots of food. When everyone asked me what I wanted for my birthday I said, "Your favourite book" because I love to have books and I dream of having a huge bookcase full of my collection. There were some wonderful choices; even the graphic novel from Hayden looks interesting, and I've not read any of them before. The whole day was perfect.

Monday 3rd August 2020

MILD CHILD TO WILD CHILD? FINAL YEAR OF CHILDHOOD NOT TO BE WASTED, INSISTS BORING TWELVE-YEAR-OLD WITH NO SENSE OF ADVENTURE

As a last-minute holiday is announced, one young girl makes a last-ditch attempt to build lasting memories for her last year of childhood, but how long will it last, and is life moving too fast?

Well, I'm officially twelve! I suppose this is my last year of childhood, technically speaking. Next year, I'll become a teenager and then I'll be stuck like that until I'm an adult. When you put it like that, it sounds like a curse… maybe it is. It's a very strange thought. Suddenly my life is going so fast. Am I wasting it by being such an insular, indoorsy bookworm? This is my last year of childhood, but I don't act much like a child. I'm just not a free spirit. I get too anxious to be carefree, I'm more care*ful,* but does that make me boring? I worry so much that I'm boring. Does *that* make me boring?

Mum and Graham surprised us today with a last-minute holiday booking – we leave in one week! It's nothing exotic, just a little cottage by the sea in Cornwall, but that suits me just fine! I love the sea. The sea is so powerful and beautiful. It can carry people to distant shores, it can kill people, and it inhabits millions of Earth's weirdest species, some of them still undiscovered. It's so mysterious it's like magic! Why do people spend so much time exploring outer space when there's so much more to discover under the sea? I don't know how much there is to see on our British beaches, but I'm happy rock-pooling and eating proper Cornish ice cream (it's the best).

Frogsplash has been a bit mopey since the announcement, probably because he'd rather spend the week with Gertie, but I'm sure he'll enjoy it once we're there. Either way, I'm not going to let him get me down. He can be the dreary one for once! I'm going to have fun. I'm going to *do things,* even if I hate them!

Sunday 9th August 2020

We've been at Dad's this weekend for the first time in ages. When we arrived yesterday afternoon, I was struck by a huge, hideous abomination of a painting in the hallway. It portrayed a devil-like woman who bore an uncanny resemblance to Richard's ex-wife, two angelic young girls, presumably his daughters, and a man with a pained expression on his face and a saintly glow about him, who looked a little bit like Jesus, only he was completely bald.

"Oh Jesus!" said Frogsplash when he saw it. "What the hell is *that?*"

"Ah yes, you missed Richard's 'art' phase," Dad said. "He wanted this one up here to greet our guests. I think he's completely forgotten that *he* is a guest here too."

"No sign of him moving out, then?" Frog asked hopefully.

"Nope!" said Dad. He led us through to the living room, and I think we all felt our faces go red when we saw the enormous painting next to the small dining table. The painting was of Dad's living room, exactly as it is in real life, the only difference being that on the sofa was a completely naked woman sprawled out in a way that exposed... well, *everything*.

"Jesus," said Frogsplash again.

This man is the father of your girlfriend, my brother. They are genetically similar. You may end up marrying into this family. Let THAT sink in! Ha-ha!

"So where is Picasso right now?" I asked as we tried to make ourselves comfortable on the sofa. It wasn't easy; I couldn't help but wonder if Richard had used a model and painted from real life.

Am I sitting where the naked lady sat?

"He's out on a ten-mile jog," said Dad casually. "He's really into fitness now."

There's a surprise.

We sat and chatted for a bit with the TV on in the background. Dad gave me my belated birthday present, which was a Free Parking t shirt and a beautiful, luxury writing set. I was really pleased with both, obviously Dad knows I'm into Free Parking, so he took a safe bet on that, but the writing set was a lovely surprise. I didn't think he knew how much I love to write. There's no way he could have found this diary… is there?

Dad told us some funny stories about the awful, demanding clients he's had to deal with at work. One of them called up after their event to complain about him to the manager because the drinks he'd provided for the guests had attracted too many bees! When he told them that he *was* the manager and *not* a beekeeper, they went all quiet and then hung up! It was only at dinner time that Dad started to act a bit weird. He kept checking his phone and he seemed totally distracted suddenly. I wasn't going to say anything, but Frogsplash took his chance.

"Well if *you're* going to use your phone at the dinner table, so am I!" he said and got his out of his pocket.

"Oh, sorry guys… it's just… it's this new dating app… this woman sent me a message, so I sent one back, and now she's not replying even though I can clearly see that she's online!"

"You're on a dating app?" we laughed.

"Yes, yes, I know, your father trying to keep up in the modern world! It's just… I don't have time to meet anyone the old-fashioned way, not with my work schedule, and seeing your mum with her new fella the other day made me realise that there was something missing in my life" I *definitely* caught his eyes wandering over to the naked lady in the painting at that point. "You two will understand soon enough."

"I think Frogsplash already understands," I said. "He's got a girlfriend!"

"Sam!" Froggo said.

379

"Oh, come on, it's not a secret any longer, you brought her to my party!"

"Well, congratulations!" said Dad. "Who's the lucky lady?"

"That's the best bit!" I said excitedly.

"What do you mean?" Dad asked.

"Her name's Gertie," Frogsplash confessed. "She's Richard's oldest daughter."

Dad burst out laughing at this incredible revelation. "Brilliant!" he said. "This is hilarious!"

"You can't tell him!" Frogsplash said.

"I won't, I won't, don't worry! Well, since you're the expert suddenly, maybe you can help me figure out where I'm going wrong with this whole dating thing…"

He showed us both his dating profile and honestly, it was a train wreck. He hadn't even uploaded a photo!

"Dad, what do you think these women are going to think when they get a message from a bloke with no photo?" I asked.

"Well come on now, looks aren't everything… I didn't want them to judge me on my face; I wanted them to get to know my personality first!"

"Well that's all well and good," I said with an air of authority. "But they're going to think you're a complete weirdo, maybe even a fake profile. At the very least, they're going to assume you're hideously ugly! And what's this here? You put that you're divorced because you had an affair! Why on Earth did you write that?!"

"Because it said in the guidelines that you should mention if you're divorced and if you have kids because a lot of people will be searching for someone who's had similar experiences to their own."

"And you thought it was a good idea to mention that you cheated on Mum?" Froggo said. "Come on, Dad, even I know that's a stupid idea!"

"Well, now that you mention it, most messages I've received have been rather negative... kind of hateful, actually..."

"Look, you don't have to be so... *honest,*" said Frogsplash.

"But don't lie either!" I added.

"She's right," said Froggo. "A relationship based on lies is never going to work."

When did he become a life coach?

"You just need to highlight the good qualities and play down the bad ones. And you *need* a photo! It needs to be a recent one, and it needs to make you look good, but not like a show-off."

"Here, I'll take one," said Frogsplash, and he took Dad's phone and snapped a few quick shots. "No, no serious faces, you have to smile!" he said encouragingly, then he handed the phone to me for my assessment.

"Not bad," I said. "It's just a shame there's a painting of a giant naked lady in the background."

"Ah yes," said Dad. "That probably wouldn't go down too well, would it?"

"Let's do the photo tomorrow, outside in natural light, that's what it says here on the app. For now, let's focus on the bio you've written..."

This is how Dad introduced himself.

"Hi. My name is Duncan Drury and I'm forty-one years old. I live in a flat with my mate, Richard. I am an events and catering manager, so you can be sure I'll always cater to your every need!"

Cringe.

"I have two children, a boy and a girl. I divorced their mother three years ago after I confessed to my infidelity. Don't worry, the ex-wife is in a relationship now, so she won't go all crazy on you!"

Best not mention that part to Mum!

"I like football and chilling out. I guess I'm just your average sort of bloke."

Would YOU date that guy?

"This is terrible, Dad!" I said. "Somehow it manages to be both bland and obnoxious at the same time!"

"What's wrong with it? I say it like it is!"

"OK, well, first, you don't need to include your name or age in the text; it comes up in bold under your profile picture... or should I say, the blank space where your profile picture *should* be. Don't waste people's time with things they don't need to read – this is supposed to be attention-grabbing. So, we'll cut that first bit out, which means your opening sentence is, 'I live in a flat with my mate Richard.' That's your first impression. They don't need to know that you live in a flat – that doesn't tell them anything personal about you; it's not unique. And they definitely don't need to know about Richard!"

"Although if you do invite a woman over here at any stage ,you should give them fair warning," Frogsplash cut in. "And take down the paintings."

"Right," I continued. "That brings us to the catering joke. It's not good, Dad. It's just not good. We've already discussed the mention of the affair, but why on Earth did you think that referring to a potentially crazy ex-wife would be funny?"

Dad looked a bit embarrassed then. I think he forgot he'd put that part in when he showed us the profile. That *is* our mother, after all.

"Honestly, Dad, this is a dating profile. You are an adult professional. If you're half as bad in person as you are in this profile, I'm going to have to tag along to all your dates, hide in a secret booth and tell you what to say through a tiny earpiece!

"And finally, your closing statement. Probably the worst two sentences I've ever read. You may get lucky and find a woman who loves football as much as you do, but you're narrowing down your appeal by only mentioning that one thing. Think of some things that women your age are likely to enjoy. Even if they're things you only vaguely enjoy… or things you can just about tolerate. And finally, this bit here where you literally describe yourself as average. Do I even need to explain that one to you?"

He paused for a moment before saying, "I suppose you're right… quite right, in fact. I just didn't realise you were going to be quite so brutal!"

I could have stopped, I could have apologised, I could have taken it all back, but I was in full swing, and something deep down inside me was compelling me to keep going. On some level this had been building up for a long time.

"I'm being brutal because this is what you need to hear! If I thought this dreadful online profile was an accurate reflection of your personality, then I wouldn't be criticising it! The fact is, you're a much better person than you're making yourself out to be here. You just need to take it seriously and put some *effort* into it!"

Just as the student becomes the master, the child becomes the parent.

Dad *did* need to hear it, I realised that. Mum used to give him these talks from time to time, but she's not here to do that anymore. At work, Dad is a complete professional and people respect and fear him. Even if his co-workers knew what a mess his personal life was, they'd never have the guts to tell him to his face. Richard is far too wrapped up in his own ever-changing pursuits, and the rest of Dad's friends are casual pub buddies who would never bother with this level of involvement. Frogsplash might have said something if he'd realised Dad needed to hear it, but the two of them are jokers, partners in crime, they can't do the serious stuff with each other. I don't know if it was right for me to talk to Dad in that way. The older I get, the more I realise that none of us are ever sure that the decisions we make are the right ones.

Just then, as if to rescue us from this bizarre role-shift, Richard returned from his run. Apparently, he had been suffering from severely stiff legs, and had stopped off at the pub for a beer to 'relax his muscles'. Of course, he had also worked up an appetite after all that running, so he treated himself to a curry and a few more pints. He also apparently did not feel the need to shower or change after the day's activities. A ten-mile run in AUGUST followed by a spicy meal and a lot of alcohol apparently was not enough to warrant a wash.

"It feels amazing, you know, all the endorphins," Richard began. "I'm in the best shape of my life!"

Yeah sure, if your favourite shape is that of a potato.

"It's such an amazing feeling, you should try it!" he said to no one in particular.

I know that this is what people do when they get fit, or even just do a little bit more exercise than they usually do, and I understand it must give you a positive feeling, but don't they understand that no one has ever, *ever* wanted to hear about somebody else's accelerating fitness? Dad eventually managed to swerve the conversation towards a more mutually agreeable topic. We talked about the silly comedy film that was playing on the TV in the background, but it was hard to concentrate even on that rather inane subject because Richard had quite clearly picked up a new and highly distracting habit.

He kept flexing his muscles mid-conversation. Not just tensing them slightly but lifting his arms up and squeezing them as hard as possible like he was in the middle of some strong man competition. He never said anything to accompany this behaviour, he just carried on with the conversation as normal. It grew significantly more awkward when he rose from his seat and began alternating between lunges and squats right there in front of us, all the while holding conversation and eye contact. Don't forget he had eaten a curry and drunk a load of beer, and all this physical motion was causing him to let out these horrific acid burps in between hiccups. He was drunk and a little off balance, and at one point he made an ungraceful slip to

385

one side which revealed a bit too much of the contents of his shorts.

Frogsplash's face was a picture.

"You've got to keep moving! You've got to keep moving!" Richard chanted as he squatted. "You've got to keep moving! No excuses!" He slipped and lost his balance again. "I just need to rest my quads," he said, and he went to get a beer from the fridge and sat back down again.

We didn't see Richard this morning. Whether he was out on another run or sleeping off his hangover, I don't know. We're heading back home a little earlier than usual today; we've got a holiday to pack for!

Monday 10th August 2020

We're here! It was a long, boring and, at times, quite stressful four-hour drive, but finally, we're here. We're staying in this lovely old cottage which is all cluttered with jigsaw puzzles and mismatched crockery, so it feels like a home from home rather than a hotel. There's a sense of adventure staying in a new place where everything's different and you don't know your way around. I like exploring the house, checking which cupboard the plates are in, seeing if the sink has one tap or two, admiring the artwork on the walls, listening for creaky floorboards, feeling the weight of the doors and the pressure of the water from the shower.

In the morning, I like listening to how quiet it is outside and feeling whether the kitchen tiles are warm or cold under my bare feet. And then, when the family is all up, I love exploring the town. I would do that bit on my own, but I'm too young to wander around in a strange place, and I would wander too far if they let me. We'll walk around the village, checking out the local shops, making sure we know where to pick up milk and tea bags and eyeing up the best restaurants for dinner later. There's always a curious old shop with curious old things in it that I'll want but have no use for, so instead I'll just peer through the crooked shop window and ponder over how they were made and why.

The locals will say hello to us as they pass, just like they never do back home, and there'll be pubs with low lighting and even lower ceilings that adults must duck their heads to get into. I hope there will be steep hills and cobbled stones, and perhaps a museum no bigger than a house, one which displays old relics of Paganism or witchcraft or some other local tradition. There'll be quaint little tearooms filled with more local people, and I'll wonder if we're the only people who are here on holiday. We'll pass cottages with perfect front gardens full of wishing wells, gnomes and things decorated with seashells.

We'll see a phone box still in use or a post box so old that there are a hundred layers of red paint flaking off it. We will see every breed of dog we can think of, and this time we will have our own dogs, who will sniff them or bark at them, depending on how threatened or excited they get. We will exhaust ourselves with walking and then decide that we are hungry. We will walk even more in search of the best place to eat. When at last we find it, the food will take an hour to come because there is only one cook and he makes everything fresh. By the time it arrives, we will be so hungry and so grateful that it will be the best meal we've ever tasted. I'm looking forward to tomorrow.

SHAKING NEWS: YOUNG GIRL BRAVES THE ICY BRITISH SEA IN A CHILLING MOVE WHICH SHAKES ONE TO THE VERY CORE

In a courageous display of determination, a pre-teen defied the odds on a Cornish beach when today, she took on the might of Neptune himself. Her family could do nothing but watch on helplessly as the small girl stepped ever closer until she was finally swallowed up by the great wide blue.

It wasn't the warmest of days today, there was a strong breeze and we woke up to clouds, but the sun pushed through and by the time Frogsplash and Billy were up and ready, it was shining bright and we headed out, chalky-faced with sun cream, for a long walk with the dogs. The morning was as I predicted yesterday, and I enjoyed it just as much as I'd hoped. After a café lunch ,we headed down to the beach, taking it in turns to carry the dogs, who were exhausted.

Mum and Graham read books and sunbathed while the rest of us messed around in the gritty English sand, burying each other and building sand sculptures which Trousers happily destroyed. Both he and Max had clearly recovered from the morning's walk, so we started throwing balls into the sea for them to run after. They started galloping excitedly, clearly loving the water, so we decided to join them. We stripped down to our swimsuits and already felt a chill. We walked forth together until the water lapped at our ankles. That's when Frogsplash and Billy got cold feet.

"It's bloody freezing!" said Billy.

"It is *actually* freezing," Frogsplash agreed. "No one in their right mind would swim in this!"

"Oh, come on!" I said. "We're on holiday! When do we ever get the chance to swim with the dogs?"

We all walked in a little deeper, holding our breath and bracing ourselves for every swell of the water. Then Billy pushed Frogsplash so that he fell forward onto his hands and knees, and the cold shocked him so badly, he jumped up dramatically like a frightened cat, making a big old fuss, then he turned and ran back to Mum and Graham acting like he'd just been plunged into an ice bucket. Billy thought it was hilarious seeing Frogsplash being such a wimp, but he was so busy laughing he didn't notice a big wave coming up, so he wasn't prepared for the shock. It splashed us up to our knees, and then it was his turn to go running back and my turn to laugh!

It was just me, Max and Trousers, and I was the only one without a woolly fur coat, but I couldn't back out, not now; it would be so satisfying seeing the boys whimpering on dry land while I waded in the beautiful blue ocean. Blue, just like my toes, my hands and my lips. I think I was blue all over. My skin was covered in Goosebumps, but I kept walking forward, thinking warm thoughts. Hot chocolate. Open fires. Chicken and mushroom pie with rich, steaming gravy.

It'll be great once you get used to it. Go for it! Jump in!

I didn't jump in. I tried to convince myself to do it, but my body was fighting back; it was *refusing* to do as I willed it! I was waist deep by then, and the cold was so sharp, it was squeezing the air right out of me. My body was spending all its energy on trying to keep warm. I decided I had to swim. It was either turn back or jump in; I couldn't keep standing there letting my blood slowly freeze! Three... Two... One...

PLUNGE!

I went right under; and it felt like ice all around my head, like brain freeze from the outside in. I opened my eyes, even though I knew the salt would sting because I wanted to see the blue underworld. It was hazy and blank, but it was still a magical new world, completely different from my own surface world. I could see the tiny legs of the two dogs paddling near the shore, but I wanted to go deeper. I bobbed back up and swam out, rising and falling with the waves, but as soon as I could no longer reach the bottom with my toes I turned back to play with the dogs. I can't have stayed in there more than ten minutes, but I was proud of myself, and the family were impressed too!

Later, after we'd washed and re-dressed (and I'd just about regained human body temperature), we went for dinner in an Italian restaurant right on the sea front. In previous years, we would have gone for something more traditional, but the only traditional British food I can think of is the classic pub dinner, and Billy and Graham have seen enough of those to last one lifetime! Still, I'm not sure if I could ever get sick of proper Yorkshire puddings and gravy… YUM!

Friday 14th August 2020

Yesterday, we discovered body boarding and we can't get enough! Even wimps like my two brothers can do it because you can hire a wetsuit. It's basically surfing without any of the skill or risk, because you just lie down on the board and ride the waves that way. The sea gets choppy here in England (way more than Greece, where we went last year) so you get some decent waves. When the sea is calmer, we're allowed to board with the dogs, which is AWESOME.

Max won't board with anyone other than Billy because she's a bit more nervous, but Trousers is so excited to get involved, he'll go with anyone. The sea must seem so vast through his little eyes! He's still quite small so I tuck him under my chest and prop myself up on my forearms so he's semi-protected from the spray and I can grab him quickly if he slips. We may not have the weather of Italy or Puerto Rico, but I get to body board with my puppy! I love him so much and being able to share these experiences with him is incredible. He's seeing so many things for the first time and he's endlessly intrigued by it all. That must be such a happy existence! Graham reckons he's about the same age as me in dog years. I wish there wasn't such a thing as dog years. I wish we could always be the same age and grow up together.

It rained today, but we had a great, long muddy walk, which made a nice change after a week of crispy, sea-salted hair and sand in our shoes and pants. We were all particularly exhausted last night after all this fresh air and exercise we're not used to, so we went up to bed quite early. Billy and Frogsplash are sharing a room, as are Mum and Graham, of course, so I was quite happily left alone in the only single room in the cottage. It was, to my surprise, therefore, that I received a text message from Billy while I was reading in bed.

"You are SO lucky you get your own room! Frogsplash is on videophone with his GF and it's making me want to puke!"

I laughed out loud involuntarily and replied, "Ew, gross! What are they saying?"

Billy sent: "A bunch of made up soppy stuff! He keeps saying how miserable he is without her. I didn't see him crying while we were body boarding and eating giant ice creams together!"

"Ha-ha what a loser! Maybe you should gate-crash the conversation?" I replied.

"OK. I'll start with some background noise…"

I listened through the wall and, true to his word, Billy made a long, disgusting fart noise.

"What did she say?"

"She's pretending not to hear it. She's too caught up in her own drama. She says her dad's reading all these psychology books suddenly, and she reckons he's going to figure out she's got a boyfriend. Who cares!"

"Ha! That does sound like Richard."

"Richard?"

"You don't know?"

All this time I'd just assumed that Frogsplash had told him about Richard being Gertie's father, but I guess he was too embarrassed to admit that his girlfriend was related to a man like that! I, on the other hand, took great pleasure in telling Billy all about Richard and he, in turn, was grateful for a distraction from Frogsplash and Gertie's revolting love fest.

Monday 17th August 2020

I'm in the car on the way home. It's been a great week but I'm looking forward to sleeping in my own bed tonight, and I can't wait to see Danny and Carla tomorrow! They're probably going to be all tanned and full of exciting stories about their two weeks abroad, but I won't mind at all. They've already landed back in the UK and we've arranged to go to Danny's house tomorrow afternoon. Danny's mum, Amelia Dankworth, is a stay-at-home mum because apparently it would cost more to put the twins in nursery than she would earn in any normal job – how ridiculous is that! So, she's always at home and able to keep an eye on us. I'm glad we're going there, hers is the biggest and nicest house by far! Not that I don't like Carla's house, when her parents are there it has a wonderful, fun vibe to it, but during the week it'll just be her sisters, and the middle one still terrifies me!

Tuesday 18th August 2020

Great news! After a wonderful day catching up at Danny's house, Mum came to pick me up and Carla's mum arrived soon after. Danny's mum was so excited to have adult company after being stuck in the house keeping permanent watch on the twins that she invited them in for a drink. Mum is never one to say no to a glass of wine, and Carla's mum is never one to say no to a social invitation, so in they came. They sat out on the terrace in the garden chatting away for ages, and they obviously got on well.

At some point, their conversation turned to our plans for the rest of the summer, and as both my mum and Maria must work, and as Danny is near enough housebound in her cast, Amelia suggested we make a regular thing of hanging out at the Dankworth residence during the week. They all thought it was a great idea, and of course they offered to pay Amelia for her trouble, and she insisted that it was no trouble at all. Her only request was that they stay for a drink and a chat to keep her company in the evenings. So that's my plans sorted for the rest of the summer! It's going to fly by.

Tuesday 24th August 2020

The girls didn't believe it when I told them, so to make a change to the routine I invited them over here to see for themselves. It happened over the weekend, and I can still barely believe it myself! Mum is at work, but Graham has the day off while Arnie and Billy take care of the pub. The girls have only met Frogsplash a handful of times, but they got the measure of him, and they will have seen his casual, laid-back style. He appears not to care about his appearance, often wearing the same faded t shirt three days in a row (whether he or the T-shirt get washed in between the days, I do not know) and always putting comfort over style. But all that has changed.

I think he's been spending a lot of the summer with Gertie, because Billy has been working a lot, presumably because he feels like a third wheel around the house. Frogsplash must have assumed that I'd be out at Danny's today. He and Gertie were watching TV in the living room and Graham was doing some gardening out the back when the doorbell rang, and I came thundering down the stairs to greet Danny and Carla. I welcomed them in and led them to the living room to join Frogsplash and Gertie, who were a lot less welcoming.

Danny and Carla could barely suppress their laughter. Frogsplash was sat stiffly on the sofa wearing a short-sleeved button-up shirt with an oversized collar and a mauve floral pattern with some very short, very tight lavender-coloured shorts and some perfectly white, neatly laced canvas plimsolls. His hair had been freshly cut in a smart hairstyle with a straight side-parting. He looked like he'd just stepped out of a catalogue for posh young gentlemen! This girl sure is a bad influence on my brother! We sat in awkward silence for an uncomfortably long time with Frogsplash occasionally staring daggers at me.

You've had the house and the TV to yourself all summer, brother! It's my turn.

Eventually he cracked, and he and Gertie went up to his room to watch stuff on his laptop instead. As soon as we heard his door click safely shut, we all burst out laughing.

"What the hell happened there?" Carla cackled.

"I don't know but I bet he hates it!" I said.

"Does he dress like that even when she's not around?" asked Danny.

"He's got no choice," I said. "She made him chuck all his old clothes away!"

We all exploded into fits of laughter once again and we went on to enjoy a peaceful afternoon uninterrupted by brothers, young or old.

Friday 27th August 2020

It's been wonderful. It's been our girls' club, and it's been just the same for our mums, in the evenings, at least. I love that they get along so well. They're so different from each other, and so are we. Danny's mum is super laid-back and friendly, the sort of person who asks how you are and always wants to hear the long version of the answer. Carla's mum is practical and confident, she always has good advice and knows how to make the best of any situation. And my mum is… well, she's my mum! I suppose she's funny, and she has a lot of stories to tell. She's the entertainer.

She is also the provider of wine, seeing as she makes it herself. It's her way of thanking Amelia for looking after me all summer (not that I need 'looking after' but you know what I mean). Maria brings the snacks, usually home-made, and they can go for hours before they realise that we need to get back home. Not that we mind, of course, but it can be annoying when we have to walk home because they've had too much wine to drive!

We have gotten to know each other even better, too. We're completely in sync. We talk about the future and what we hope it will be like. We talk about going to each other's weddings. (Danny has her entire wedding planned already, with sketches of the dress and everything!) We talk about people at school and laugh about things that have happened. They know when I'm having a quiet day and don't feel much like talking, and they know that it doesn't mean there's anything wrong or that I'm not enjoying myself, or that I want them to stop talking too. They know that sometimes I just prefer to listen.

As it was Friday today, our mums had an extra-long session drinking wine and laughing and talking as they usually do. Danny's dad brought home some takeaway food for us all, so we didn't even have to go home for dinner. At half seven, Danny's mum had to excuse herself to help him put the twins to bed, which left my mum and Maria alone and, with the addition of wine, this proved to be a deadly combination! Amidst the sound of the twins screaming in protest at being so unfairly tucked up in bed by their loving parents, the two remaining mums apparently got talking about Danny's mum and all that she'd done for us over the summer.

Although she seems genuine when she says it's no bother at all, it really has been a wonderful arrangement and we have her to thank for it. So, Maria Figueroa and Cassie Drury (or Cassie Darling – I don't even know!) very bravely, stupidly, drunkenly decided that they would thank Amelia Dankworth by taking the terrible two-year-old twins off her hands for a full day. They have no idea what they're in for! After what sounded like a very stressful bedtime, Amelia and Alistair were extremely grateful.

And so, it has been arranged that me, Danny, Carla, Carla's parents, my mum and Graham are taking the twins to the zoo all day tomorrow. Afterwards, we will come back here to Danny's house, give the twins their dinner, put them to bed and stay until Amelia and Alistair return from a romantic dinner-for-two at a fancy restaurant. It's going to be exhausting.

Sunday 29th August 2020

PLANET OF THE APES! PRIMATE EXPERIMENT GOES HORRIBLY WRONG AS TWO INFANT CHIMPANZEES ARE LET LOOSE IN A LOCAL ZOO!

The two were unwisely unleashed after fuelling themselves with mashed up bananas and peanut butter. It became a huge strain on the authorities to control the two wild animals, who caused mayhem and destruction wherever they went. Several bystanders have been left traumatised by the incident and are being urged to seek professional help as a matter of public safety. Those who encountered the creatures may need to be put in isolation for several days. We are pleased to report that the problematic pair, who are quite remarkable in their abilities to both communicate verbally and express themselves physically, are now safely back in their enclosures.

It was exhausting. Fun, but exhausting. Even with four responsible adults and us three on hand to help, the twins were a handful to say the least. Of course, they are very attached to their mum, who is with them all day every day, so getting them in the car to drive away from the house was hard enough. They were throwing a double tantrum, screaming at the top of their lungs and making it very near impossible to strap them into their car seats because they kept straightening out their bodies into stiff little planks which simply refused to bend into the seating position.

"They'll calm down once you get going," Amelia said. "The moment they realise I'm gone, they always stop crying." I'm sure she believed that, but how can she possibly know for sure? After a noisy car journey in which one of the twins had produced a squashed and melted chocolate bar from his pocket and managed to smear it all over himself and the surrounding area, we arrived. On Alistair's recommendation, we kept the boys firmly strapped into the double buggy until we'd passed the ticket barriers so that we could at least be sure that wherever they wandered they couldn't possibly escape the grounds of the zoo.

"I don't know what all the fuss is about," my Mum said. "I never had any trouble keeping track of my two."

Even if that is true, Frog and I were no match for these two. I was quiet, inactive and obedient even then, and Frogsplash was dopey and could easily be distracted with toys or bribed with the promise of sweets. Also, of course, we were never the same age, and we never worked together to double-cross our parents. The twins are high energy and just when you think you know where they both are, you realise that you've only been tracking one of them. They look the same, they are dressed the same, but they move so fast that you'd be forgiven for thinking you'd seen both rather than just the same one in two places.

Keeping an eye on twins is like a million-pound game-show challenge.

Carla's parents seemed happily oblivious to the stress of it all and let the twins run free while we sat down in front of the penguins for a drink and a snack. They were good at keeping track of the twins' whereabouts, initially at least, but they found out the hard way that knowing where they are and keeping them out of trouble were two very different things. We heard a high-pitched yelp as one of them ran into a small girl, causing her to knock her own ice cream onto her chest, then he himself fell over, grazed his knee and began to cry. The other one found this highly amusing and stood in front of his brother pointing and laughing, which made the other one even more upset.

Danny's mum probably thinks it's cute to dress them in identical outfits, and she probably has no idea of the trouble it can cause because the mother of twins can always tell them apart. But we couldn't. One of them had wandered into another family's group photo, successfully passed himself off as one of the grandchildren and acquired a box of cheesy breadsticks. Of course, we didn't find him until the other twin realised he was missing and tuned into his twin telepathy thing to locate him. He went stomping off and we all followed him in a panic.

He toddled over to join his brother, who was feeding cheesy breadsticks through the wired fence which separated him from a huge, boulder-like gorilla sat cross-legged and peaceful on the periphery of his man-made, 'natural' enclosure. The adults were shocked and horrified at the proximity of the gorilla. It was quite a sight to behold, but I found it quite extraordinary. The two boys, so small and innocent, were not in the least bit afraid and were happily sharing their food with this enormous beast that any adult human would find intimidating.

I'm not suggesting that zoos should encourage visitors to feed their animals by hand, but the twins clearly weren't in any danger. In fact – it was the calmest and quietest I'd seen them all day – perhaps *ever*. They were stunned by the gorilla, enthralled by its powerful size and wise eyes. It seemed incredibly gentle and intelligent. Whenever it wanted another breadstick, it would point at the packet and then at itself, and the twins seemed to understand this much more clearly than all the many hundreds of words the seven of us had been desperately yelling and pleading at them all day.

It was beautiful, but it was inadvisable. Mum was particularly conscious of Danny and the fact that she might tell her parents how out of control things had gotten, but none of the day's events seemed particularly out of the ordinary to Danny, and as long as the twins both came back in one piece, all was well. After the gorilla incident, they stayed firmly strapped into the buggy, save for a few traumatic toilet breaks about which I will not go into detail. They complained a bit, laughed a bit, and did a lot of screaming which could have been through joy or frustration, but we were all too tired to care by then.

I can't honestly say that I remember seeing any animals yesterday, apart from the gorilla. We might as well have taken the twins for a walk around the car park! The problems did not end when we got back to the Dankworth house. The problem with strapping kids in like psychiatric patients is that they don't wear themselves out during the day. We let them run riot for an hour or so, then Danny, Carla and I played hide and seek or as the twins call it, hide and *sink,* with them while the adults got their dinner ready. When it was our turn to hide, we all hung out in Danny's room, which is out of bounds for the twins, so they didn't think to look there and spent ages searching the rest of the house. I got the impression Danny does that quite a lot, and I don't blame her!

They didn't eat any of their dinner, but they liked playing with it well enough, and within five minutes none of it was left on their plates. Carla's parents, who appeared to have endless patience with Finn and Jim, volunteered to put them to bed while the rest of us cleaned up the mess they'd made. When at last all the work was done, and peace had been restored, we all sat silently in front of the TV like zombies. Mum and Graham insisted that Carla and her family went home, seeing as they'd braved the bedtime routine, so it was down to just me, Danny, Mum and Graham.

Danny and I snuggled under a blanket on the sofa and we must have drifted off together, because suddenly I heard keys in the door and laughter in the hallway. Danny's parents were home at last. Mum and Graham nudged me out of my cosy seat and we said a very, *very* quiet goodbye. I was bleary-eyed and still half-asleep, but I remember seeing Danny's mum all dressed up and glamorous, and I remember thinking that she looked stunning. It was only a short drive home, then I shuffled up the stairs, changed into my pyjamas without even thinking about it, and passed out in my heavenly soft bed.

I must humbly confess that I had no idea how hard it was looking after tiny humans. I won't do it again in a hurry, but it's amazing having our three families come together like that. I hope we all stay this way. Sometimes, when things are at their best, I can't help but worry and obsess over how it could all go wrong one day. Carla, Danny and I could fall out, or our parents could, or maybe one of us must move away or there's some horrible break-up or someone gets sick... it'll probably be none of those things; it'll be something I never saw coming. I don't know that something bad is going to happen, but I do know that nothing ever stays the same.

Why can't you just be happy, Samantha Drury? Things are great right now, and the only thing that's stopping you from enjoying it is YOU. You can't just live in the moment, can you?

Wednesday 1st September 2020

It's the last week of the holidays. Danny's house feels like home, and her family feels like my family. Danny and Carla feel like more than family to me now, because good friends *are* more than family. You choose them, and they choose you. You weren't born with them, but you never walk away from them. This summer could not have been more different from the last one. If you'd have told me then what things would be like now, I would never have believed you! That's one of the most remarkable things about life, I suppose, you never know where it's going to lead you.

I don't want next summer to be any different from this one, because this one was perfect. But change is a constant, and change is necessary, so I suppose all I can hope is that I'll be as happy then as I am today. Change is what got me here, and that means that change can take you to better places. Bring on the change; and bring on year eight!

Saturday 4th September 2020

I can't believe we go back to school in two days! It's been unreal. We're at Dad's this weekend, and you should have seen his face when he picked us up and saw what Frogsplash was wearing! It's the first time he's seen the makeover prescribed and administered by Doctor Gertie, and it's the first time he's ever seen his son trying to be fashionable. It was funny enough for me when I first saw it, but Dad thinks that fashion trends are all completely ridiculous and loves laughing at young people's so-called 'style'.

"I'm not surprised," he said in the car once the initial wave of hysteria had subsided. "You have to change with the times… especially if you're in Richard's family! If my calculations are correct, you'll be due for your mid-life crisis next week!"

Frogsplash rolled his eyes while Dad and I revelled in the glorious moment. He's the parent you can always rely on to laugh with you when someone else does something stupid.

"But seriously," Dad said later. "You're *still* going out with Richard's daughter?"

"She's nothing like him! You can't blame a child for their parent's shortcomings," Frogsplash said, holding a glare at Dad as he spoke.

"Never mind that," I said before things got too personal. "They're in a *happy relationship.* How are things going with you and the dating app?" I asked Dad.

"Better," he said. "I've got a date next weekend actually."

"And you waited until now to tell us?" I said excitedly. "Come on then, who is she?"

"No, no, no… I'm not telling you anything. You'll pick apart her dating profile just like you did with mine! And then all your vicious remarks will be at the back of my mind when I meet her in person."

"Fair enough," I said. "That is what I'd do."

"I should thank you I suppose," Dad said. "I'm not sure I'd have even made it to this stage if it weren't for all your… constructive criticism!"

"Helpful advice, you mean!" I said. "But you shouldn't thank me just yet… this woman might end up ruining your life!"

"Cheers for that!" he said, laughing. "I'll try to keep that thought out of my mind while I'm having dinner with her next week!"

"PHWOAR, great session! GREAT SESSION!" Richard burst in through the front door during dinner. "That was an EPIC session at the ramps!" he stood in the middle of the room, leaning on his skateboard, fresh and un-scuffed, suggesting that this phase was in its mere infancy. I noticed he had a split lip and a limp which made him wince when he walked. The bump on his bald head was hard to ignore, too.

"Great session," he said again. "Oh hey, nice outfit, Frogsplash, loving the new look!" (I stifled a laugh). "Yeah, must have been at the ramps for nearly six hours today. I feel young, agile, ALIVE! I can't wait to get back out there!" he slumped heavily on the sofa. He looked like he'd just been in a minor car crash.

Later, when I was in bed and Richard had disappeared off somewhere (hopefully to a hospital), I heard Dad attempt a heart-to-heart conversation with Frogsplash. It can't have been easy, but bless him, he tried.

"You know, it's OK to change your tastes," he began. "Richard makes it look pretty stupid, but that's because I don't think he enjoys half the stuff he's pretending to. He's doing it for appearances – God knows why! But you should only ever change if that's what *you* want. You don't have to talk to me about anything – I don't expect you to. But you need to have a conversation with *yourself.* Who are you doing this for? If somebody says they like you then they shouldn't want to change anything about you…"

He trailed off after that. Perhaps Frogsplash had rolled his eyes or tried to look busy on his phone, or perhaps Dad had exceeded his maximum capacity for serious parenting, but that was the end of it, and I think he did a pretty good job. To be honest, I was so busy laughing at Frogsplash it never occurred to me that Gertie had been unfair to him. It just goes to show, sometimes Dad can be more mature than me!

Sunday 5th September 2020

Back to school tomorrow – I can't believe it! I wouldn't exactly say I'm looking forward to it, but at least Dad's taking us shopping for school supplies today and I LOVE STATIONERY! Pens are sublime, notebooks are things of beauty, and anything that organises paperwork projects is a gift from the gods. Naturally I pretend to Dad that I need more than I do for school, that way I get pens and books for writing at home.

They don't have to be fancy or heavily decorated, but the pages should be thick, and the cover should be hardback and spined (not spiral bound or [gulp] perforated). It should be lined, because it's for writing, and although I can write neatly, I tend to go crazy when the words are flowing faster than my hand can move, and then

I need ruled lines to keep me in check. I love all pens, but coloured ones are more fun, and ballpoint make for the best handwriting. I love seeing it all so beautifully displayed in the shops, too. Notebooks are my bread and pens are my butter!

Frogsplash is less keen to go shopping for school supplies. He's going into year eleven, and that's serious stuff. He's going to have GCSE exams at the end of the year, and they really matter. He doesn't usually care about important stuff like that, but I guess his teachers have hammered it in hard by now. He can't be placated with pretty pens and notebooks though. He doesn't love them like I do – he doesn't even own a pencil case! He just turns up to school with a leaky biro floating somewhere in the depths of his enormous backpack. It's barbaric!

That's why Frogsplash is still in bed and Dad and I are watching one of those live cooking shows. They're tasting wines even though its breakfast time. I wonder if Mum could get her wine on TV – that would really boost her sales, and her confidence. At last we hear a door open, but it's just Richard.

"I'm putting the kettle on, anyone fancy a brew?" he says cheerfully as he strides on through.

I'm so bored and impatient, I'm writing this in real time. Richard has just entered the kitchen. I feel like a proper journalist writing things down as they happen! The kettle is on. Richard is yawning loudly. He opens the fridge. No milk. He groans.

"Can I nick a bit of your milk, Duncan?"

"Yeah, go for it; it needs using up anyway," Dad says.

This is the most boring news report ever.

The people on TV are pretending they can taste peach and melon in their wine, even though it's made of grapes just like every other wine. They're talking about why it goes so well with the seafood they're eating. The food looks slimy. Richard is singing in the kitchen. He's not usually this perky on a Sunday morning. He didn't get drunk last night. Maybe he was too exhausted from the 'great session' of skateboarding. Maybe he was worried that alcohol combined with head trauma might kill him. Or maybe he really was high on adrenaline and this whole skateboarding thing really is for him… ha!

I can smell toast. Richard has decided to make breakfast while he drinks his tea. I love the smell of toast. It always makes me want to eat, even when I'm not hungry. Toast with proper butter is probably one of my favourite foods, but it must be done just right. Why do I feel like we've been here before? I can smell bacon. I think I can smell eggs and beans, but maybe that's my brain playing tricks on my nose.

The cooking show is still on. It cut away from the people live in the studio to let them finish the seafood dish while some lower-down staff member clears the workstation ready for the next recipe. Now it's showing some archive footage of an old TV chef back when he was young. He's travelling around rural Italy sampling dishes the locals cook and eat at home. He knows quite a bit of Italian. This is not his first visit. The food looks amazing, but when you think about it, this is more of a travel show than a cooking show.

There's no point in me trying to cook this recipe at home. Half the ingredients aren't available here in England, and the rest is low-quality produce which tastes nothing like it does in Italy because it doesn't grow well

411

here. He's not telling me how to cook; he's telling me to go to Italy. I wonder how these Italian people feel about this strange English man coming into their homes with all his cameras and using all their pots and pans. I bet he made a right mess.

Richard's making a right mess. I heard him drop something – the ketchup, maybe. It's OK; it's a plastic bottle. Do they even do ketchup in glass bottles anymore? Glass is easier to recycle, but it's also easier to smash. Crash. He's tossed the pans into the sink. He'll say he's going to wash them later, but that always means tomorrow. Tap. I hear the tap running. He's putting them in to soak, at least. Tap. I hear a tap at the front door. Knock. Someone is knocking on the front door.

"I'll get it!" Richard shouts cheerily. The kitchen is closest to the front door. He's left the tap running. I can't hear the voices clearly over the sound of gushing water, but I don't have to eavesdrop. He's coming in and he's leading someone through with him. Dad's face loses all its' colour when he sees her.

"Sophie?" he says faintly.

"She's here to see you," says Richard cheerfully. "She says you've met before."

I feel like I have met her before too. She seems familiar. She has a small child with her, a little girl a bit smaller than Danny's brothers.

"Hello Duncan," the woman…Sophie says. "I want you to meet Stephanie. She's your daughter."

I have a sister. Oh my God!